The Gunpowder Plot

and Other Stories

by

David Brown

Published by

MELROSE BOOKS

An Imprint of Melrose Press Limited
St Thomas Place, Ely
Cambridgeshire
CB7 4GG, UK
www.melrosebooks.com

FIRST EDITION

Cover design and Illustrations by Jeremy Kay

ISBN 978 1 907732 13 3

Printed and bound in Great Britain by:
CPI Group (UK) Ltd, Croydon, CR0 4YY

CONTENTS

CONTENTS (CONT.)

PREFACE

This volume contains twenty-five short stories which were written sporadically over a period of some 10–12 years.

They cover quite a wide variety of topics, but there are some common themes, such as dogs and canals, reflecting areas of the author's own interest and experience. They are for the most part light, humorous and ironic, with unexpected twists in the tail, but in some instances they lack a happy ending.

There is no high drama, and the stories contain no explicit sex, gratuitous foul language or overt violence, rendering them eminently suitable for adults. They owe their origin, albeit remotely, to actual events, living people and real locations, heavily laced with artistic licence.

The characters are not drawn in fine detail, as it is a fact that the author is not really concerned with them as people, confining himself to recounting their usually mundane conversations and sometimes bizarre actions. ("By their deeds ye shall know them.) The reader is free to attribute reasoning and motives, guilt or innocence, and to heap praise or blame, credit or calumny upon these persons as s/he thinks fit – an admirable example of audience participation!

1

NINE LIVES

We were less than delighted to receive the unsolicited gift from the other side of the world. The real difficulties arose when we tried to get rid of it.

When we arrived back from holiday there was the usual accumulation of mail on the doormat – a catalogue of totally resistible bargains, unsolicited offers of life assurance, 'Best Prices Paid for Old Gold, Silver and Jewellery', 'Vote for Capelhurst', three free newspapers and, finally, one or two items which were actually of some interest. It is a curious fact that when we are at home, the postman seems never to call at the house, but when we are away we are inundated with mail. This phenomenon is worthy of a clinical study, and when I can spare the time I will carry it out. On this occasion there was something else – an odd cylindrical parcel which barely fitted through the letterbox. It bore New Zealand postage stamps and, according to the customs declaration, it was a 'gift', value $3.50 (NZ, that is).

"It's from Cousin Dotty," I remarked to my wife.

"Her name is Dorothy."

"Well, judging from the cost of the as yet unwrapped 'gift', Dotty seems more appropriate," I retorted. "What is it anyway?" I demanded, as by this time the mysterious package was being opened.

It revealed itself to be a hideous toy cat, made of some shiny black plastic substance laid over what seemed to be natural shell. It was in a sitting posture with red eyes asquint, and it had real whiskers. Around its neck was a distinctly tatty chequered bow. My wife examined the object critically, and upon turning it upside down discovered the legend 'Lucky' embossed on the bottom.

"More like 'Mucky'," I said disparagingly. "Look at the state of that bow. I'm going to christen him 'Drongo'." I had heard this term once or twice in an antipodean context, and whilst I don't know what it means, I believe there to be some derogatory inference.

It was the start of the summer fête season and we were debating what of the bring-and-buy variety we should donate over at East Wilmington.

"I always take something for the bric-a-brac stall," said my wife, "but I simply cannot find anything this year."

“Take Drongo,” I suggested helpfully. “There’s no accounting for taste, and someone might actually like him.”

“Somebody does,” she replied, eyeing Drongo fondly. “And anyway, I can’t just get rid of Dorothy’s present.”

“I don’t see why not,” I persisted. “We have nowhere to put him and nothing else to give, so it seems like a very neat solution.”

In the end, common sense (by which I mean my opinion) prevailed and off Drongo went. He sat on the stall, leering at browsers with a price tag of £2.00 around his neck, which partially concealed the scruffy bow. By teatime he had gone and we went home Drongo-less to resume our normal lives.

Two weeks later we happened to drop in at the church bazaar at nearby Pitchfield, and there, to my wife’s horror and my private delight, prominently placed on the oddments stall was Drongo. His label now read £1.60. In the succeeding weeks he popped up at every fête in the district, at progressively lower asking prices. He did stage a brief rally on August bank holiday at Lower Knowlton when he was on offer at £1.25, but thereafter it was downhill all the way, culminating in a valuation of 50p in the last sale of the summer.

* * * * *

The next communication from New Zealand caused considerable alarm. “Dorothy’s coming to England for a few weeks and wants us to put her up for a while,” announced my wife.

“Fine,” I mumbled, my mind preoccupied with other matters.

“But what are we going to do?” she wailed.

“Do?” I said. “Do what we always do – put her in the spare bedroom.”

“But what about Drongo? She’ll expect to see him.”

Displaying my customary resource, I picked up the current issue of the free newspaper. “Ah, here it is,” I said with satisfaction.

“Here what is?”

"It's the Christmas Bazaar season, and on Saturday they're holding theirs over at Hazelhurst. He's sure to be there."

And he was. The price had risen once more to £1.75, but we felt it a small enough sum to pay for preserving family unity. He took pride of place in the centre of Dorothy's dressing table and kept his eyes, or more accurately one eye, on her during her stay, while the other wandered around the room.

* * * * *

"Well, I believe Dotty enjoyed her stay…" I started to remark to my wife as we were dismantling the spare bedroom. My voice tailed off. "It's Drongo!" I cried.

"What about him?"

"He's gone, he's finally gone."

* * * * *

"Did I hear the postman, dear?" my wife asked at breakfast.

"I'll go," I said. On reaching the hall I froze with horror. On the doormat was an odd cylindrical parcel which had just fitted through the letterbox. We didn't need to open it, nor read the customs declaration. Drongo had come home.

In her letter, Dotty explained:

> *I have a little confession to make. That black cat – the enclosed one – was a gift to me from an old school friend who now lives in Adelaide. I couldn't bear the sight of it, so I sent it to you, as I remembered how fond of animals you both are. Imagine my dismay when I got a letter from my friend saying she was coming to pay me a visit. I simply had to get him back. I know you will understand my predicament, my dears, and won't think any the worse of me. After all, blessed is the peacemaker.*

* * * * *

I put the wretched cat in the plastic refuse bag, tied the corners and placed the sack at the front gate. Next morning, alerted by the warning siren on the vehicle as the driver reversed it down the lane, I surreptitiously watched the final rites. The dustcart operative took the bag and swung it onto the rear of the lorry; as he did so I observed that the bag was split. A small black object fell onto the grass verge. The dustman picked it up, looked at it for an instant and then placed Drongo at the side window of the cab.

"Those wretched cats have been at the rubbish again," I told my wife as we met in the kitchen. "They're after the chicken bones."

"We didn't have chicken last week. They must have opened the bag for some other reason," she mused.

* * * * *

Some days later, I had gone into town to draw some money from the hole-in-the-wall cash dispenser. As I transacted my business, the dustcart pulled alongside. My eyes were irresistibly drawn to the driver's cab, and there, to my dread, I saw Drongo sitting in what was now clearly his customary place inside the window. Alongside him was a similar black cat, slightly smaller, with blue eyes, curled whiskers and a red velvet bow. Drongo had acquired a mate!

I dodged behind the war memorial and sneaked back down Sheep Lane towards the car park. I could feel the gaze of four baleful eyes boring into the back of my head. I turned up my coat collar. As I did so, the first squall of rain peppered the cobblestones.

2

GRAVE IMPORT

It was vital to convey the merchandise from the Continent into Britain, even if this entailed breaking the law, and elaborate arrangements were made to circumvent the regulations. But the law itself has the ability to spring its own surprise.

The fishing trawler nosed around the end of the outer harbour mole and entered the grey, oily-looking North Sea. Mercifully, it was calm, flat calm. Beyond the furthest part of the breakwater a forlorn marker buoy moved in the imperceptible swell, its green light revealing the legend 'OOSTENDE 46'. The lamps of the string of seaside resorts along the shore twinkled coldly, and a train on the coastal tramway headed towards the French border, its brightly lit windows giving the appearance of a slow-moving luminous snake.

The passenger on the trawler (to whom we shall refer simply as D in order to preserve anonymity and protect the guilty) felt no elation at having overcome the first hurdle in his mission. It had all gone so smoothly that there was a sense of anti-climax, of disappointment almost, now that the weeks of planning had been translated into action. It had happened exactly as the contact man, known to us as W, had predicted. The participants in our little drama had met in a small bar in the back streets of the town; the trawler captain had driven directly to the fishing wharf where they boarded the vessel. The harbour police knew the skipper well and he simply passed the gate with a nod and a perfunctory greeting. There were no difficulties with customs or immigration officials either – in fact, none were in evidence – and having negotiated the usual dockside clutter of railway lines, cranes, containers, chains and suchlike, the skipper parked his car in the lee of a warehouse. They walked across the plank onto the trawler. D was dressed in a woollen hat, anorak and sea boots and held the package tightly under his coat.

The other hazardous part of the enterprise would of course come at the journey's end. They had decided to bring the package ashore at a small decayed south coast port, since most smuggling activity (or so D persuaded himself) was concentrated on the more obvious eastern harbours with their close proximity to Europe. In any event, Customs and Excise, with their limited resources, couldn't be everywhere at once, and depended largely on intelligence and surveillance to detect clandestine activity. No one except those immediately involved had any knowledge of this trip, and the possibility of a leak was so remote as to be negligible. D himself, the contact man, the trawler captain and D's two accomplices in England, his partner

J and the owner of the motorboat, were the only people involved. No more than two of them had ever met at the same time; there had been no correspondence and no telephone calls. The skipper had accepted the passage money of ten bottles of whisky and a respectable sum in used banknotes, and that was the extent of his commitment, except of course for sailing his ship to the rendezvous. He was also the boat's owner, so could come and go with no reference to anyone else. The fishing vessels often stayed at sea for several days and ranged widely depending on the season, the weather, the prospects of a catch and the skipper's whim. They also habitually dropped anchor and communicated with other craft, so there would be nothing inherently suspicious in their behaviour on this trip. Furthermore, Customs had larger fish to fry and wouldn't be greatly interested in such a small package. All this had been D's reasoning when he and J had agreed to undertake the mission; the package was so vital to them that drastic actions were necessary, and the risks appeared not only small but also fully justified. D comforted himself with these thoughts and settled down to endure the journey. He would be at sea for twenty-four hours, as the drop had to take place during darkness. There was nothing to be done except to ensure that the package was secure and wait.

The motorboat was alongside the trawler for a mere couple of minutes. The sea was still subdued and the transfer took place just inside international waters, on the ocean side of the fishing boat. D scrambled over the net, which offered a convenient access to the smaller vessel, with the package inside a holdall, waved his thanks to the skipper and entered the cramped cabin. Not a word was exchanged. The relaxed mood of the last twenty-four hours was now replaced by tension and anxiety as the motorboat drew inexorably closer to the harbour entrance. The light was fading and the wind was getting up a little, producing short, choppy waves. The harbour entrance was narrow, and at this point carried considerable traffic – Continental and local ferries, naval vessels, pleasure craft of all descriptions, fishing boats. D's destination lay beyond all this at the highest tidal limit, which occurred at the end of several miles of tortuous channel. He fervently hoped that the boat's owner knew what he was doing and that no untoward incident would attract unwelcome attention. He need not have worried; absolutely nothing happened and no one evinced the least interest. Gradually, the harbour widened and became shallower. Protected from the influence of the open sea, the water was still and quiet, and soon the ferry terminals, naval bases and boatyards were left behind. Despite being close to large centres of population, the creek was surprisingly rural, with extensive mudflats and lines of trees growing right up to the water's edge.

The constant slap of rigging against masts betrayed the presence of pleasure craft, moored in long lines on both sides of the navigable channel. This itself was meandering and was marked with coloured lights, the significance of which, D hoped, were fully appreciated by his fellow conspirator. He clutched the precious package and began to relax – journey's end was in sight, figuratively if not literally, as it was quite dark. He had chosen this particular night because of the absence of any moon and was congratulating himself silently on the success of the whole scheme when he was abruptly brought back to reality with a bump: the boat was aground on a mudbank. D realised at once that, preoccupied with the phases of the moon, he had neglected to consider the state of the tide, which was crucial to the successful navigation of the upper reaches of the harbour. This was neither the time nor the place to remonstrate with the boat's owner and, in any case, D had chosen the date on which the attempt was to be made, so he was responsible for his own fate. There was nothing to be done except drop anchor and wait. They were barely a mile from the landing place – so near and yet so far! J would be waiting with the car, waiting and wondering. Mobile telephones had been ruled out; they had agreed that she would simply make herself as inconspicuous as possible and wait for him to arrive. They sat marooned on the malodorous mud in the dark, dank night.

After an interminable period, a comforting movement of the boat indicated that the water had returned and covered the mudbanks. The boatman started his engine and moved gingerly up the channel. Their progress was measured and stealthy, as the boat engine was inboard and water-cooled and she could hardly be heard at a distance of twenty yards. They arrived at their destination as dawn was breaking, revealing the outlines of buildings along the wharves. This had once been quite a busy little port, with two cranes constantly employed unloading seaborne coal and dredged sand and ballast. D could also just make out the shape of the former flour mill on the far bank. They nosed into the one-time boat builder's yard, once busy with the sound of riveters' hammers amidst the piles of seasoning elm timber. There was a small slipway with rails embedded in the concrete for carrying the launching cradle. Grasping the by now somewhat crumpled package, D leapt onto the concrete apron, walked swiftly through the deserted lane to the appointed place under the railway arch, got into the waiting car and disappeared. Once again, no conversation was called for.

Tired out by his experience on the mudflats, and soothed by the effects of a stiff drink, D gratefully crept into bed and soon fell asleep. He awoke with the autumn sun striking through his bedroom window, arose and looked out at the familiar scene. What he saw filled him simultaneously with horror and disbelief. Approaching the house was J, with a small and very lively silver poodle on the end of a long lead. The package was on very public display. He pulled on his trousers and a sweater, fumbled for his shoes and fairly ran down the stairs. As he crossed the hall, making towards the front door, his attention was caught by a newspaper lying on the semi-circular table. Despite his urgency, D's attention was caught by the item on the front page. He stopped in his tracks and picked up the paper, which bore a date two days previous, and read:

QUARANTINE ABOLISHED

In a dramatic move yesterday, the Government announced the immediate abolition of the compulsory six-month quarantine period for domestic pets being imported into the UK. Although long expected, the timing of this decision has taken most observers by surprise. Provided the animal has undergone specified immunisation procedures, it will now only be necessary to fill in a form at the point of entry. It can now be revealed that Customs' monitoring of UK ports aimed at preventing unlicensed importation of animals has recently been scaled down.

3
HERITAGE

There are liable to be shocks in store when you return home after forty years' absence. You can hardly expect the place to look exactly as it did when you left. Robert still found something of value in the midst of inexorable progress.

The platform canopy, the ticket collector's kiosk and the booking hall all looked comfortingly familiar when Robert Frost left the station on his arrival at his hometown for the first time in forty years. The plume of steam was missing as the train pulled away and the coal merchants' sidings had become a car park, but at least Dillington still had a railway. He had long cherished a desire to take another, possibly last, look at the places where he had spent his youth, and now, unexpectedly, the opportunity had arisen. Robert had been invited to spend some time with his brother Freddie, who had never lived anywhere else. He even escaped conscription for National Service on some mysterious pretext, and had devoted his life to his business and political interests. The high point of the latter had been his election this year as Mayor of Dillington, an event in which he took inordinate pride.

Any apprehensions about his welcome that Robert might have entertained were soon dispelled, as the two men resumed their easy fraternal relationship just as though the intervening years had never occurred. Next morning, Freddie was, as usual, extremely busy and suggested that his brother might like to accompany him to the Town Hall where he had an important meeting.

"It concerns the proposed motorway feeder link road," he explained. "I, or should I say my fellow councillors, strongly favour the Red Route. It's the cheapest and most direct option, as it mainly takes the course of the old canal. What this town badly needs is better road communications, as the streets are narrow and congested, and local industry is hampered accordingly. I have some influence with County and I reckon that if my proposals are adopted we'll see considerable benefits. If I play my cards right, I can see an MBE for services to local commerce."

"Is the old canal derelict then?" asked his brother.

"Well, there is one of those so-called preservation groups who've done a little bit, but it has no serious purpose, and anyway, they're just cranks who have their feet placed firmly in the eighteenth century. What we need here is progress; a modern, dynamic community."

* * * * *

It was a fine late autumn day and as they left the Town Hall after the meeting, Robert suggested that they walk home along the canal towpath.

"We might have a pint at the Coal Exchange for old time's sake," he urged.

"If there still is a Coal Exchange," replied Freddie. "I haven't been down there for donkey's years, and I seem to remember a planning application…"

They descended the worn stone steps onto the towpath. Sure enough, the canal was still there, a bit overgrown with weeds, perhaps, the water shallow and brackish, and the willow and alder trees lining the banks were much larger than Robert remembered. After a few yards, the noise of incessant road traffic vanished, being replaced by the harsh cry of a moorhen scuttling among the reeds at their approach and the soft rustle of the light wind in the aspen branches. Rounding a bend, they suddenly came upon the pub and entered the low doorway leading directly from the towpath. They were the only customers in the bar and sat on the old wooden settles which flanked the open fire. The only sound was the measured ticking of the grandfather clock and a barely discernible crackle as a log settled on the bed of wood ash in the great fireplace.

"Thank goodness for such places," offered Robert.

"It's just an anachronism," replied his brother, "not really a viable business proposition these days."

It was a curious irony, mused Robert, that I've spent my life roaming the world and yet I am so conservative, whilst Freddie, who has never left Dillington, wants to sweep it all away. Still, I'm glad he hasn't succeeded, as I have fond memories of the Coal Exchange, where as boys we learnt to drink beer, play darts and dominoes and take our places in adult society. They still serve a jolly good pint, too.

* * * * *

Dillington, like many other towns, had succumbed to the 'twin town' virus. Being a progressive place under Freddie's leadership, it was not sufficient to establish a link with a similarly sized town in Normandy or Holland; they had embraced glasnost with enthusiasm and had adopted the timber-producing city of Archangel as their partner. If this necessitated official trips to Northern Russia at taxpayers' expense, they could be justified in terms of enhanced trading prospects, not to mention improved status. Freddie had prevailed upon his opposite number up there in the woods to provide a huge Christmas tree to be installed in the market square at Dillington, inspired by the arrangement existing between Norway and London. Needless to say, the tree was to be taller than that erected in the capital, and would provide useful and high visible proof of the value of the twin town exercise.

* * * * *

Freddie came home from the meeting in a state of most uncharacteristic near panic. It seemed that the Christmas tree, having survived the journey from Russia unscathed, was now marooned on the edge of town, on account of the fact that it was much too large to be transported through the narrow and crooked streets which led to the square. Helicopters had been ruled out on some unspecified technical grounds.

"What about the canal?" suggested Robert. "I seem to remember huge baulks of timber going down to the wharf on barges when we were boys, and the canal runs under the bypass right into the town centre."

"Too shallow for motor vessels," said Freddie. "It's all silted up."

"Why not use flat-bottomed boats with very little draught and tow them with horses?"

"Horses!" cried Freddie.

"Why not? I once read that a horse can pull two tons on the road, eight tons on rails and fifty tons on water, or something like that."

"But no one operates on the canal."

"What about those preservation people?"

"They won't help – they'd be delighted to embarrass me since I want to use their precious canal as a road," wailed the distraught Mayor.

"Who's involved?" asked his brother.

"Peter Williams is the chairman."

"Peter Williams? Used to play football with him at school. I'll have a word," said Robert.

* * * * *

Robert glanced at the postmark on the letter: 'Dillington' it said proudly, 'Twin town Archangel'. He recognised his brother's handwriting at once.

"Well, old boy," the letter read, "I am pleased to report that my Christmas tree was a roaring success and I look like being nominated unopposed for a second term as Mayor. Good news on the link road front – the Government has coughed up the money and gone for the Blue Route, which they preferred anyway, on geological grounds. It seems that the canal will stay where it is. In fact, I have accepted the offer to become President of the Preservation Society and have got some exciting ideas for the restoration of the old timber dock. Meanwhile, we have established our new HQ in the Coal Exchange. I must have a word with County about erecting one of those brown signs on the motorway link – DILLINGTON TIMBER WHARF ARTS CENTRE. If I play my cards right, I can see an MBE for services to local heritage."

4

IMMEDIATE ACTION

Private Stringer was a reluctant soldier and on the face of it not the stuff of which heroes are made. The exigencies of war sometimes produce unexpected consequences, and there is many a true word spoken in jest.

Ask any soldier what his least favourite parade is and the chances are he will plump for the Remembrance Day ceremonies. This does not imply any lack of patriotism on his part – quite the contrary, in fact. The raison d'être for this parade is well acknowledged and respected and men are proud to wear the poppy on their cap; it is just the dreadful weather which always seems to accompany the annual proceedings. It is invariably cold, damp, misty and dreary, conditions guaranteed to negate the shine on best boots and inflict terminal damage to the pleats in a greatcoat. Add to this the fact that all manner of fringe bodies such as Old Comrades and Girl Guides tend to take part, prolonging the march-past and reducing it to a shambles. It was perhaps surprising, therefore, that the atmosphere in barrack room 23 at Muhlhausen Barracks on the North German plain during the preparations for the parade in 1950 were quite cheery. Most of the members of No. 6 platoon of B Company were conscripts; they had enlisted together and now the end of their eighteen months' National Service was in sight. This was reflected in the prevailing good humour. The exception was one Private William Stringer, whose lack of enthusiasm for any form of soldiering was universally known. He was not rebellious and there was no vice in him; ineptitude and sloth in equal measure had dogged him throughout his service and he was in consequence the butt simultaneously of his comrades' humour and official disapproval, bordering at times on despair. "You'll be the death of me, Stringer," was the oft-heard sally aimed at him by Company Sergeant Major Robert Stone.

Remembrance Parade was no exception.

"Done your boots, Stringy?" asked one of his fellows.

"Not likely," he retorted from his prone position on his bed. "I worked for hours on them before the Queen's Birthday Parade and haven't worn them since. They're good enough for me."

Unfortunately, this assessment was not shared by the Commanding Officer at his inspection of the Battalion prior to the march to the Garrison Church. Stringer's name found its way into the RSM's black book and he subsequently appeared before his Company Commander. Major Christopher Hayward was a genial soul who felt some sympathy for the wretch, whose misdeeds were regularly the subject of military jurisdiction.

"Let's see, you're due for demob soon, aren't you, Stringer?" asked the Major resignedly.

"Yes, sir, I have six weeks to do."

"Well, I hope you realise the gravity of offences like this. It brings the company into disrepute and attracts unfavourable attention from the CO; I have to take a serious view of this. I shall award you the maximum punishment within my powers – let this be a lesson, and just try to get through the remainder of your time without any more nonsense. Seven days' CB. March out, Sergeant Major." The CSM added some further strictures, ending with the customary, "You'll be the death of me yet, Stringer – report to the Provost Sergeant and get your name on the defaulters' list."

Stringer looked gloomier than ever at lunchtime and in response to a comradely, "How did you get on?" from his friend Bedford, replied, "Seven days' CB. This really puts the kibosh on the weekend – I'd arranged to go away. I don't know what to do – I really can't stay here."

"Pretty stupid idea, mate," said Bedford. "If you miss jankers' parade you'll really be for the high jump. With weeks to do it isn't worth it."

* * * * *

At that time, various philanthropic organisations operated leave centres for service personnel. These were typically situated in areas such as large towns, offering amenities lacking in other locations, and members of the armed forces could enjoy a few days away from their accustomed routine. Stringer's friends had, with great difficulty, persuaded him to accompany them on a weekend stay at one such establishment, so that he might see at least a little more of a foreign country before his army service expired, instead of lying listlessly on his barrack room bed in his spare time. With customary obduracy, having agreed to go, he was not prepared to forgo the trip despite being confined to barracks for a petty misdemeanour.

Stringer was arraigned before the Company Commander on Monday morning. As ill luck would have it, Major Hayward was away on a course, and the case was heard by the second-in-command, a young and ambitious captain who distinctly lacked the milk of human kindness which characterised Hayward.

"Your record is appalling," he snapped. "You have deliberately absented yourself whilst confined to barracks, so I have no option but to remand you in close arrest for the CO."

Later that morning, a chastened Stringer was paraded in front of the Colonel. Retribution was swift and savage. "I find you guilty of absence without leave and you will accordingly forfeit pay for the period you were missing. Your record is abysmal, and although this is the first time you have appeared before me, I award you fourteen days' detention."

Stringer, stunned, was whisked off to the guardroom to begin his period of incarceration. The CO, meanwhile, was addressing his adjutant: "Send a memo to company commanders, Toby, under my signature. Too much leniency is being shown to habitual offenders. I don't know what's going on in B Company, but I'm determined to stamp it out."

Great excitement prevailed when the list of soldiers forming the next release date was published. Most of 6 Platoon were to leave en masse. Stringer's name, however, did not appear and he duly presented himself at the company office to enquire the reason for this omission. CSM Stone was patient but firm.

"Non-reckonable service, of course. You lost three days for being AWOL and fourteen days when you were in the nick. So you owe the King seventeen days' service – your release has therefore been deferred until 1st January."

"But I was only absent two days and twenty minutes," wailed the hapless Stringer.

"Makes no difference. Six hours on the first day counts as one day. Any fraction of subsequent days counts as a full day. Should have run up the road when you came back to barracks and you'd have a day less to do."

The animated little group assembled at the guardroom to await the TCV that was to convey them to the railway station on the first stage of the journey that would take them to the Hook of Holland, over the North Sea to Harwich, thence to the Depot to be discharged. Despite their obvious relief and pleasure that it was all over and that they could go home and pick up the threads of their lives, few were without mixed feelings. Some were even a little sorry to be leaving. Many had acquired useful skills during their service, and without exception they had matured. Some had picked up more than a smattering of German, or made friendships that would endure for years; life would never be quite the same. All shook Stringer's hand and bade him farewell with genuine affection.

"Hang on, mate, you'll be gone after Christmas."

"Look after yourself, Stringy."

"Keep out of Stone's way."

The news stunned everyone in the unit, but none more so than William Stringer. With immediate effect, the period of National Service was extended from eighteen months to two years. All those still serving on 1st January were affected by this ruling. He had literally missed the boat by twenty minutes. If this intelligence was dispiriting, the next was positively alarming. After initial successes, the war in Korea had turned sour and allied forces were in retreat; the British contingent was to be reinforced immediately and Stringer's battalion had been chosen for this role. All soldiers with more than six months' residual service were to go. There was no embarkation leave and the whole unit was confined to barracks. This time there was no escape.

B Company HQ was established in a bunker on a bleak and bitterly cold hilltop. The OC and 2IC had been summoned to an urgent conference at Bn HQ. The only two occupants of the bunker were CSM Stone and Private Stringer. The situation was bad – there had been enemy activity on both flanks and the other companies in the unit had sustained casualties. The bunker was defended by a light machine gun and Stringer's task was to operate this weapon. It was mounted on a tripod, locked at night so that it fired on fixed lines down a track which was the only access to the bunker. The night was dark and all was quiet.

"Are all those magazines filled, Stringer?" asked the CSM.

"No," replied Stringer.

"You know perfectly well they should be – get on with it at once. I'm going out to the barbed wire to have a look round. Hold the fort and listen out for the radio."

Stone made his way gingerly out of the bunker, along the track and down below the crest of the hill. Suddenly, Stringer burned with resentment. "What am I doing in this hell-hole?" he asked himself. "All my mates are home, safe and well and back with their families. I'm cold, tired, scared and thousands of miles from where I belong, and all because some idiot thought my stupid boots had a bit of dust on them."

His torpor and lethargy left him as the gross injustice of his situation was brought home. He tore open the ammunition box and filled all the available magazines, cramming the rounds in against the tension of the springs with uncharacteristic venom. He loaded the gun and cocked the mechanism. At the same instant, on the hillside below the bunker, a score of Chinese soldiers stood up from their concealed positions and began blowing bugles and firing weapons in the direction of the bunker. A flare illuminated the scene and against its garish unnatural light, Stringer saw the form of CSM Stone running back along the rough path towards the shelter. He closed his eyes and pulled the trigger, letting go only when the magazine was empty. Somehow, he recalled his training: "Gun firing all right – gun stops – empty mag – first Immediate Action – cock gun, mag off, new mag on, carry on firing." As if in a trance, he fired magazine after magazine until the box was empty and the gun barrel glowed red.

* * * * *

The official communiqués were reproduced in the local newspaper: "It is with great regret that the War Office announces the death in action of Company Sergeant

Major Robert Stone, aged thirty-six, of the Greenshire Regiment, who has been killed in Korea. He was shot while manning an observation post. Following a general tactical withdrawal, it has not been possible to recover his body."

And then…

"The War Office announces the award of the Military Medal for gallantry to Private William Stringer, aged twenty, also of the Greenshire Regiment. He was present in the bunker with CSM Stone when the Sergeant Major was killed. Notwithstanding this, and despite his youth and inexperience, he single-handedly repelled a determined Chinese attack upon his position by firing his light machine gun to such effect that the enemy was forced to withdraw. His actions delayed the enemy advance sufficiently to enable a planned redeployment to take place. Private Stringer is the first conscripted soldier in his regiment to receive a gallantry award since the end of the 1939-45 War."

Epilogue

"Do you know where the dog is?" called June from the kitchen.

"In the garden, Mummy," replied her young son.

"Be a good boy and find her lead for me. Put on your coat and we'll all go out for a walk."

"Where to?"

"We'll go round and see Great Grandfather William." This last-named lived locally and the boy was named after him.

"Can I see William's medals again?" asked the child. As a very young boy he had been unable to comprehend his relationship with someone called a great grandfather, or even to articulate his title, so he had settled for William, and this had stuck.

"I expect so," replied June.

Shortly afterwards, seated at Great Grandfather's knee, he plied him with questions. "How did you get these?"

"I was in the army."

"Were you in the army a long time?"

"Longer than I expected. I went to war."

"Where?"

"In a place called Korea."

"Was it a nice place, William?"

"No, it was a nasty place. Very cold."

"And what about this one on the end?" asked the boy, indicating a medal with a purple and green ribbon.

"Malaya. Our regiment had a tough time of it in Korea so we left there and went to Malaya."

"Was it a better place than Korea?"

"No, worse. Very hot, always raining and lots of great big trees."

"Like a jungle?" queried the child.

"Like a jungle."

"Were there any tigers?"

"One or two."

"Did you kill any tigers?"

"No."

"Did you ever kill any people?"

"I think it's time for us to go home," interposed June. "Poppy wants her dinner, and Great Grandfather William has had enough of your questions for one day. He looks very tired."

5
A LITTLE ON ACCOUNT

The ambitious new member of the golf club aspired to the office of treasurer. He was now playing against powerful vested interests, and such are the hazards of the Royal and Ancient game that his adventurous shot landed him in a bunker.

"Just give me fifty quid, will you, Carter?" said the member brusquely, throwing his cheque across the golf club bar.

"I'm sorry, Mr Briggs," replied the steward deferentially, "we're no longer permitted to cash cheques."

"Why not?" enquired Briggs, more acerbic than ever.

"I'm under the strictest orders from the treasurer, sir. Major Forrest is a real stickler for rules, and since that unfortunate business before Christmas..."

"Time this club gave some decent service," snapped the frustrated Briggs, crumpling up the cheque and walking out.

Major George Forrest had occupied the post of treasurer of the Pitchfield Golf Club for thirty-four years, and his name was a byword for old-fashioned courtesy allied to scrupulous military efficiency. It was rumoured that he kept the books in his copperplate hand using a genuine fountain pen with real ink; certainly the club's finances were in a very sound state, and a mere cursory periodic audit from a sub-committee of the membership was all that was considered necessary to verify the details appearing on the annual balance sheet.

"The next item on the agenda is the election of officers for the next twelve months," intoned the chairman. "The only post for which we have more than one candidate is that of treasurer, so I suggest that we deal with that at the outset."

Gasps of surprise from the assembled members greeted this announcement. The idea of any opposition to the automatic annual re-election of Major Forrest as custodian of the club funds was unthinkable.

"You'll be aware that the retiring incumbent has expressed his willingness to continue in office for another year. Do I have a proposer from the floor?" A dozen hands shot up. "Thank you, yes, Colonel Sturminster-Newton; and a seconder?" The hands remained aloft. "Dr Pullinger. Thank you, ladies and gentlemen. We also have another nomination this year, in respect of Mr Donald Briggs. His name has been proposed in writing to the Management Committee prior to the meeting in accordance with our Rule of Procedure 64. Proposed by Mr Andrew Bradley and seconded by Mrs Elizabeth Bradley."

A buzz ran round the crowded room. Donald Briggs was something lucrative in the City and Elizabeth Bradley was his sister. He was a relative newcomer to the district and had been a member for only a couple of years.

"Major Forrest has been our treasurer for many years past, and I'm sure that all members will wish to join with me in paying a tribute to his dedication to the club's affairs over such a prolonged period," continued the chairman as soon as the hubbub had subsided. "In these unusual circumstances, perhaps each nominee will say a few words in support of his candidature to enable us to make a more informed choice. Is Mr Briggs present?"

Mr Briggs was present. He was seated in a prominent position in the front row, and upon hearing the chairman's pronouncement, he stood, donned a pair of half-spectacles, shuffled a bundle of papers he had brought to the meeting and began.

"Thank you, Chairman. I heartily endorse your remarks concerning the previous treasurer and would add my personal thanks for the manner in which he has held the fort. But, Mr Chairman and members, we live in progressive times and I like to believe that we are a forward-looking club. If elected, I shall bring this society's affairs into the twenty-first century by computerising the accounting system. I have made some preliminary enquiries and it just so happens that I can obtain a software package that will fit the bill admirably."

"But we don't have a computer of our own to run it," protested a voice from the floor.

"That exactly illustrates my point," continued Briggs, warming to his theme. "Naturally, my proposals include the acquisition of the latest hardware to support the system. I have produced a provisional costing for the total installation, and am pleased to inform this meeting that for a sum of only £15,500, including initial data capture, we can have the new system running in six months."

"Who is the supplier?" demanded an unidentified voice from behind a potted plant.

"Starship Enterprises, as a matter of fact," replied Briggs, slightly nettled by his unseen questioner.

"Aren't they an associate company of your own?" persisted the anonymous member.

"As it happens, we do have business links. That, ladies and gentlemen, is reflected in the generous discount which I have been able to obtain for the club. But for that, the system would cost in excess of £20,000."

"Are there any more points?" asked the chairman.

"Just a couple of minor things," said Major Forrest from his place on the rostrum, participating in the discussion for the first time. "I believe members, and in particular the committee, are interested in the performance of the proposed system and the advantages it can offer. How comprehensive are the facilities?"

"It can do anything you like," retorted Briggs airily.

"Good," replied Forrest genially. "Perhaps you could give the membership some details on specific points, since your proposal will involve the Club in considerable expenditure. For instance – how does it handle property depreciation?" Forrest smiled seraphically and sat down.

Briggs began to bluster. "I have every confidence in the ability of my proposed system, but naturally I'm not au fait with every minor technical detail."

"You'll need to be if you're the treasurer, Briggs," said the pot plant. "How much has it cost to run the books this year, George?"

Forrest rose again. "Thirty-seven pence," he announced. "I accidentally broke my ink bottle and had to invest in a replacement. Luckily, I found one at the church bazaar."

General confusion ensued, silenced only by the ferocious demeanour of the chairman.

Briggs was not quite ready to concede defeat. "This package has most comprehensive on-line user Help options, and can resolve any accountancy queries by reference to a database of specimen scenarios," he squeaked.

Forrest picked up a heavy tome bound in blue leather which was lying on the committee table. "Never be without this," he said. "*Principles and Practice of Double Entry Bookkeeping*, Ephraim Arbuthnott, 1867. Times may change; double entry does not. In fact, the Moors introduced it into Spain in the eighth century. There is no case not covered by Arbuthnott."

Shouts of laughter and approval greeted this intelligence. The result of the ballot for the post of treasurer of the Pitchfield Golf Club was a foregone conclusion.

The evening was not an unmitigated disaster for Mr Briggs, however. He succeeded in getting himself elected nem. con. to the audit sub-committee, a post, it must be said, regarded generally as a bore and characterised more by pressed men than volunteers.

"Can you pop over to the Club this afternoon? The auditors want to do a cash check – can't for the life of me think why," boomed the chairman's voice on Major Forrest's telephone.

"Aye, aye, sir," replied the obliging treasurer. The ledger showed a cash balance of zero, and this was verified by the empty brass-bound box which contained a single halfpenny coin.

"Well, it's much easier on these occasions just to pay all cash into the bank – then there's nothing to count," remarked Forrest. "Oh, the halfpenny! It somehow got overlooked when the coins ceased to be legal tender. I daresay it will increase in value one day." Not to be outdone, Briggs (for it was he who had instigated the surprise audit) asked to see the paying-in book. After perusal of this and comparison with the ledger, he marched triumphantly into the chairman's office.

"Seems to be an irregularity here, Admiral Iremonger. This paying-in book; on 10th September, twelve cheques were paid into the account, including one for £100 exactly. There is no receipt in the ledger of £100 exactly – someone has been cashing cheques through the Club account. Your rules specifically preclude this I seem to recall. Seems to me that what this club needs is some new blood on the committee." Admiral Iremonger (referred to universally, although never in his presence, as 'Ironsides') was a man of excellent qualities, but an appreciation of the finer points of accountancy was not among them.

"What's all this about, Forrest?" he enquired of the Major, who had quietly followed Briggs into the chairman's office.

"Really quite simple," replied Forrest. "Reggie Sturminster-Newton brought me a cheque for £100 to pay for his annual subscription. He had apparently overlooked the fact that the rate was recently raised to £112.50. Reggie didn't have his cheque book with him, so he gave me the odd money in cash; so the receipt came in two parts."

He handed the admiral a green leather-bound book. "Here's the record of members' subscriptions to confirm what I have told you."

'Ironsides' looked closely at the green book for several minutes. An uneasy silence fell on the assembled company, finally broken by the chairman.

"I see that your own subscription is overdue by more than six months, Briggs. Our rules are quite definite in such cases – your membership has automatically lapsed, and you will need to reapply. What's the current waiting period, Forrest?"

The treasurer, as urbane as ever but with the merest suspicion of a twinkle in his eye, replied, "About four years, Admiral."

6
MISTAKEN IDENTITY

Desperate measures were required to secure Dennis's release from incarceration. Although they succeeded, his erstwhile captors did not respond in the expected way.

It was the French air traffic controllers who started it. You know, those gentlemen who are prone to stage periodic strikes, particularly at holiday times, the effect of which is to play havoc with the airline schedules. Our flight was diverted halfway round Europe and as a result we landed in England at 6 p.m., when what we should have done was arrive at 11 a.m., in time to get Dennis out of the cage. Since that had to be done before five o'clock, he was condemned to spend another night behind bars. I should explain that Dennis is our long-haired dachshund, and that whenever we go abroad on holiday he goes to stay in the Bide-A-Wee Luxury Kennels. Because of this fact, he is less enthusiastic about foreign holidays than we are.

Eventually, we got out of the airport, collected the car and set off for home. The tedium of such journeys is mitigated by the car radio. The last news item made me sit bolt upright and nearly decapitate myself with the seatbelt: "Following the diagnosis of suspected rabies on an animal kept in a kennels in Pitchfield, the Ministry of Agriculture has declared a protected zone covering an area of ten miles around the affected premises. The movement of all animals liable to contract the infection to and from all farms, kennels and similar premises is banned until further notice. The prohibition is effective from midnight tonight, Tuesday, and includes domestic pets such as dogs and cats. Full details have been given to local police authorities to whom enquiries should be made in the first instance."

"But that includes our Dennis!" exclaimed my wife. "The kennels are well within ten miles of Pitchfield, aren't they?"

"Yes," I replied grimly, "it's only about four miles as the crow flies – if crows are still allowed to fly there."

"Don't be facetious," said my wife, "this is serious. They might keep him in for months, or start slaughtering animals next – you know how keen they are in cases such as this. They shoot everything that moves."

"Don't I know it," I replied.

* * * * *

We arrived home soon after 10 p.m. and I immediately telephoned the kennels. I was greeted by a recorded message on an answering machine. "How can they possibly not be there at a time like this?" I pondered. I put on my old anorak and got the car out of the garage.

"What are you doing?" queried my wife anxiously.

"Desperate situations call for desperate remedies," I replied. "I'm going round the kennels to get Dennis out before the deadline at midnight. Give them another ring, can you?"

* * * * *

I walked up the path to the house behind the kennels. On reaching the front door I was bathed in light – they had installed one of those lamps which is activated by any movement in the area. I rang the bell and waited impatiently. Nobody was in. I paced around the yard for a minute or two. It was 10.47 by my watch. Then I observed that the door into the wooden hut which housed the dogs was secured with quite a light chain. I also saw that beside the kennels was a garden shed, the door of which stood open. Illuminated by the floodlight, I saw the hacksaw hanging over the bench. "Very slack security," I mused. "Ought to have a word with them."

I'm not normally impulsive – quite the contrary in fact – and cannot now explain why I acted as I did. It was the work of a moment to cut the chain, open the door, enter the hut and examine the boards on the doors of the individual cages which bore the dogs' names in chalk. There was just enough light from the lamp on the house. I slid back the bolt of Dennis's door, grabbed the warm bundle of sleeping dog, wrapped the blanket from his basket around him, pulled the hut door to and legged it down the path.

The absolutely extraordinary thing was that this was accomplished in total silence. Dog owners will know that as soon as you get anywhere near a kennel, the most awful cacophony of barking and howling breaks out from the inmates, all of whom simply want to get out and are appealing to you to achieve this. I don't know what they put in the dogs' suppers, but it certainly ensures a sound sleep. Perhaps there were only a couple of dogs in there; maybe they were all old and deaf; possibly they too had heard the news on the radio…

Comforted with the thought that you cannot steal what already belongs to you, I made for home. I had pushed Dennis onto the rear seat and he stayed there, quietly joining in the conspiracy. Once home, I drove the car into the garage in total darkness, picked up the dog and slipped into the side door. We met in the kitchen.

"All right?" came an anxious enquiry.

"Fine – I managed to get the dog." My wife switched on the light. I don't know who was more surprised, my wife, myself or the King Charles spaniel happily licking my face. I had got the dog all right – the wrong dog.

* * * * *

"What happens now?" asked my wife, after we had both had a stiff drink.

"I've no idea – have to sleep on it," was all I could think of. I had exhausted all my initiative for one night.

We gave the little dog – by now christened Charlie – some supper, enjoined him to be quiet and went to bed.

On Wednesday morning after breakfast we held a council of war. It was decided that we should not do anything precipitate, but await events. My wife made several attempts during the day to get in touch with the kennels, but got no further than the engaged tone or the answering machine. The person least concerned was little Charlie, who spent the day rolling on the lawn, eating hearty meals and sleeping in the best armchair. The situation began to clarify after tea.

The local evening newspaper carried a report about the missing dog, and stated that a reward for his recovery was on offer. It also merited a short mention on the regional TV programme. Oddly enough, nothing was said about epidemics, but in our anxious condition we must have failed to observe this. We drew up our plan of action.

* * * * *

We drove off on Thursday morning to the local woods, a popular venue for dog walking. "Now, there are plenty of people walking dogs around here. Everyone has read the paper or seen the TV item and knows about Charlie. If we can just leave him he'll soon be rescued."

This was easier said than done. Despite our best efforts, we couldn't shake the dog off – the poor little chap must have walked miles. At long last he lingered and dropped out of sight behind a bush.

"Now!" I cried. "Let's split up – you go round by the stream and I'll cut over the hill. Meet you at the car."

We reached the agreed rendezvous at the same time – my wife by the stream, me by the hill and Charlie by the most direct route. Providence in the shape of two lads intervened.

"Is that your dog?"

"No."

"He looks just like the one we saw on the telly – the one someone nicked from them kennels."

"So he does. Isn't there a reward for his finder? Why don't you both take him to the police station? Wait a moment…" I rummaged in the boot for a piece of string. "Use this as a lead. Go straight there, won't you. He looks a bit tired and dirty."

* * * * *

When we got home about lunchtime, the telephone rang. It was Mrs Shoehorn (I can never remember her proper name), the proprietor of the kennels.

"Oh, hello, you're back home then. Have a nice holiday?"

"Fine," I said guardedly.

"I thought you were returning today. I couldn't quite make out the date in my book – must have written it without my glasses on. It could be the 16th or 18th. You didn't get any problems with those air traffic people?"

"Nothing serious," I replied, with masterly understatement. "I'll pop over and collect Dennis about two o'clock, if that's convenient. Has he been a good boy?"

"Oh, he's no trouble. We've had some adventures, though, while you were away. Someone came and took one of our little dogs, but he's been found loose this morning. Funnily enough, his name is Dennis, same as yours. Must have been one of those dreadful animal rights people. Then there was a rabies scare."

I tried to sound suitably surprised. "What! In this area?"

"Oh, no, thank goodness. Up in Litchfield, about two hundred miles away. And in any case, it was all a false alarm."

So that explained the lack of communication. She had recorded the date in her book wrongly and believed we were still in Italy. So as far as the victim of the outrage was concerned, we had a perfect alibi.

* * * * *

The trouble with holidays abroad is that they are strongly addictive. After two or three you simply cannot wait for the next one, and naturally the destinations tend to become more and more exotic and obscure. Lake Bala, Lake Balaton, Lake Baikal, Lake… As soon as the glossy coloured brochure arrives it is avidly seized and the pages scanned closely with the object of spotting somewhere nobody else has ever visited or, preferably, even heard of. For some reason, however, this year was different. We felt as though we had eaten a heavy Christmas lunch, then spent the afternoon with the chocolates, only to be confronted with a piece of rich and sticky cake for early tea. We picked delicately over the magazine without any feeling of enthusiasm.

"Why don't we drive up to Scotland, just for a change?" I volunteered.

We spoke simultaneously. "We can take Dennis with us."

7
DOGSBODY

"That dog is almost human," we often hear people say. This assertion may be much nearer to the truth than is generally realised.

'For him that is joined to all the living there is hope:
a living dog is better than a dead lion.'

Ecclesiastes, Ch 9 v 4 (Authorised Version)

'I'm going to come back on earth as a dog' is a sentiment which is occasionally heard. It is neither an expression of admiration for the dog's superior intelligence nor of envy at his superhuman physique, nor yet of any serious belief in the possibility of reincarnation. It is generally provoked by the image of a dog who has enjoyed an excellent dinner after a stimulating walk and is relaxing in the best chair or lying in a shady spot on the lawn. As I have remarked, no one really believes that they could come back to earth in canine form; whereas, in fact it is not only possible but quite straightforward if one has the right connections and follows the correct procedure. By the way, let me introduce myself: my name is Angus and I am, in my present manifestation, a West Highland terrier.

I haven't always been a dog, but lived a previous existence as a human, occasionally giving vent to the ambition quoted in my opening sentence, which in my own case was eventually realised. Please do not feel sorry for me, nor consider that my new life form implies any loss of status when compared with the previous one, despite the many pejorative references to dogs in human languages. What people fail to realise is that canines, or indeed any other animals, who were once higher primates retain all the faculties they possessed in their former existence. They can comprehend human speech ("I swear that dog understands every word I say") and can call upon all the memory and other skills acquired during their spell as Homo sapiens, or rather Homines sapientes, since we're in the plural here. They can also remember their Latin. And we have the advantage of being able to communicate to humans in their own tongue. It is obvious that this power is exercised only in the most extreme emergencies.

It goes without saying that these facilities are a very closely guarded secret, the disclosure of which would entail a most sudden and dramatic decline in the fortunes of such animals that fall into the category under discussion. Instead of living in the lap of luxury, we would be put to work programming computers or some such, in order to help defray our living costs. I'm sometimes quite alarmed at the activities of certain dogs appearing in television advertisements, for example, when the participants appear to be to be exhibiting quasi-human reasoning power and manual dexterity. If this goes on, someone in authority is sure to get suspicious and it could well put our privileged position in serious jeopardy. Some dogs have actually taken to barking in regional accents, while I confine myself strictly to Received Modified Cockney on security grounds.

On another topic, you may have observed from those dreadful television advertisements for dog food or perhaps from watching the coverage of Cruft's that humans often physically resemble their chosen breed of dog. The 'owner' (the quotation marks are mine) of a red setter, for instance, is very likely to be thin and rangy, with a nervous disposition and ginger hair. This is no mere coincidence, and cannot be explained away simply by continued close proximity, similar diet or use of the same shampoo. No, my friends, not only can one elect to be reincarnated as a dog; there is also the facility to manifest oneself as a specified person's dog. Some humans want to keep an eye on a favourite grandson, say, so they return as the family pet. The red setter associated with the man who shares his attributes was (is?) most probably his uncle.

I met a delightful fellow recently, in the guise of a cocker spaniel, and we had quite a long conversation. His name is Roger and we had a most interesting talk about this reincarnation phenomenon. One way in which I amuse myself is by collecting the post when it is delivered and giving it to my 'master' (a courtesy title this) at the breakfast table. He is so dilatory at dealing with his mail that it is all I can do to stop myself from opening the letters and preparing a suitable reply. I am sure you can appreciate my predicament.

"Do you bark at the mailman or snatch the letters from the box, or perhaps even pursue him down the garden path?" I enquired of Roger.

"Under no circumstances," replied the spaniel. "I was never one for practical jokes, and in my human existence I was a postman myself. In fact, I still retain honorary membership of the trade union and take a special interest in postage stamps."

Shortly after making Roger the spaniel's acquaintance I accompanied our family on a couple of weeks' holiday in the country, so I did not see my newfound friend for a while. When next we met he greeted me warmly and remarked that we had not seen each other recently, so I explained the reasons for my absence.

"I really must tell you of my experience with the rabbit," I said. "We were up on the Downs having a walk when I spotted this chap and ran over the grass to pass the time of day. My family thought I was chasing him and I didn't disillusion them. When we got behind the bushes, I stopped and introduced myself. He'd been a chartered accountant in his last life and was a very well-informed fellow. Well, to cut a long story short, I was so impressed by what I learnt that I have decided to return as a rabbit myself when the necessity arises. They have a lot of freedom, you know, Roger – no collars and nametags, no beastly inoculations and no notices all over the place prohibiting this, that and the other. As I understand it, there is a very good social life in those warrens, too. Since the cat died and metamorphosed into a camel it's been pretty lonely at home."

"Metamorphosed – a cat?" said Roger with a sly twinkle. "Don't you mean transmogrified? Anyway," he continued in a more serious vein, "I've decided that when I'm called to the Great Kennel in the Sky I shall return as a postman once more. I have kept in touch, as I told you, I enjoy the open air, and furthermore I understand that there is a new concession that in such cases one can claim at least some previous seniority."

8
STOPPED IN ITS TRACKS

The ghost train has certainly ceased to run its spectral journey, but who can claim the credit for laying it to rest? There are several candidates for this honour.

The Parson's Tale

I am the incumbent of St Peter's Church in Pitchfield, a venerable building whose many interesting features include a notable Jacobean carved pulpit, a mediaeval rood screen, some excellent stained glass, several unusual brasses and numerous monuments. If you are ever in the district I strongly recommend a visit. Among the many tablets in the church is a simple stone erected to the memory of five men who lost their lives in 1861 during the construction of the Oxbourn tunnel on the Dillington to Pitchfield railway, the eastern portal of which lies in this parish. Following an exceptionally heavy rainfall, the tunnel workings became unstable and part of the roof collapsed, burying five workers. Although their deaths are recorded in the church, they were not buried in the graveyard, since they were itinerants and their religious denominations could not be reliably ascertained; indeed, some were suspected of Roman Catholicism, and in the prevailing climate of opinion these unfortunates were interred in a common grave on spare ground lying just beyond the church precincts. Ever since, this has been known unofficially as Grave Green and it is still an open space, having never been developed.

There is a legend hereabouts that at regular intervals a strange apparition resembling a train makes an appearance in the tunnel, despite closure of the railway many years ago. So persistent have these stories been that susceptible persons have become alarmed, and with the Bishop's sanction I recently performed a service of exorcism at the tunnel site. Mercifully, the phenomenon has not reappeared, so it seems that my intercession was answered and the disturbed souls have finally achieved peace.

The Clerk's Tale

I am clerk to the Pitchfield Borough Council, a position whose origins are lost in the mists of time, since this ancient town was granted its first charter during the reign of Edward the Confessor. Pitchfield is a noted tourist attraction, as it has retained its mediaeval character remarkably well. Unfortunately, like all cities of a similar nature, it suffers from the most severe traffic congestion, the streets being narrow and constricted and the popularity of the town exacerbating the situation. My council has been addressing this problem with vigour and imagination, and we have devised a number of road improvements destined to alleviate these difficulties. One such scheme entails the realignment of St Peter's Street, incorporating part of the triangle of spare land adjacent to the church, forming a dual carriageway relief link road. I must admit that the proposal has not been greeted with universal local approbation, partly because of a legend that this land forms the burial place of some men who were killed during the cutting of the nearby railway tunnel. This latter, which has been disused since the Beeching reforms of the 1960s, is a source of controversy in various ways, not least of which is the wholly apocryphal story that a phantom train runs through it. Many people claim to have seen or heard it, but nothing has ever been substantiated. Another aspect of the problem lies in the activities of the local railway preservation society, who are making somewhat ineffectual efforts to reopen the railway along its whole length.

All this recently culminated in the holding of a referendum to obtain a reliable sample of local opinion, and it transpired that a considerable majority of the population was hostile to our enlightened proposals. In a true manifestation of democracy, entirely unconnected with the forthcoming local government elections, the council decided to abandon these plans and formulate acceptable alternatives. Curiously enough, since this decision was made known there have been no further reports of imaginary trains in the vicinity. It seems that the council, in their wisdom, have performed a public service in placating the ghost or whatever it was, if you believe in such things.

The Excavator's Tale

I work as a plant operative and usually drive one of those yellow tractor-mounted diggers which you will see on every construction site. Recently, my firm tendered for work involving the demolition of an old railway bridge in connection with the new Pitchfield ring road. We expected to get the go-ahead for work to commence on a Monday morning. Well, on the Friday I finished my previous job and the boss told me to take the digger up to the railway site so as to get a good early start on the Monday. When I got there it was just falling dusk, and I noticed the old tunnel a short distance up the track; something prompted me to have a look at it. I then remembered those stories about a train being seen, but these seemed pretty ridiculous at the time. The track had been removed and fair-sized saplings were growing from the ballast. The tunnel entrance had been closed off with breeze blocks to stop people going in, but a gap had been left at the top – something to do with bats, I dare say. I parked right next to the entrance and climbed up on the digger shovel to look over the wall. I couldn't see a thing, and since the tunnel was going to be resealed permanently, I decided to knock a couple of the blocks off. Well, those diggers are very powerful and I hardly touched the wall when most of it fell down. Couldn't have been built properly.

It was totally dark and had that stale, clammy smell associated with tunnels. Above my head the brickwork was stained black from the steam engines' exhaust, although the last one had passed more than twenty-five years ago. I was about to climb down when something attracted my attention. I distinctly heard the sound of a locomotive whistle and a faint rumbling sound. The noise grew louder until it became a persistent drumming. I could hear the rush of steam and dimly saw headlamps and the reflection of a fire on the tunnel sides. I nearly fell off the digger in my hurry to get away and scrambled into the cab. I started the engine and in my frantic haste failed to notice the edge of the shallow embankment, which started immediately at the tunnel entrance (the ground is very hilly). The digger lurched and fell on its side, as luck would have it throwing me clear. I was momentarily stunned by the impact and when I came to my senses it was quiet. Then I noticed that the tunnel mouth and the area around were covered in thick mist, almost like steam.

Well, the rest is history. We never did get the contract to cut through the railway – in fact nobody did, because the line was eventually reopened. The curious thing is that no trains have been seen or heard since. I reckon that when I opened the tunnel, I let the ghost out.

The Reeve's Tale

I am the chairman of the Pitchfield Railway Preservation Society. The objective of this organisation has been, since its inception, the reopening of the closed rail link between our town and Dillington, some twelve miles distant. This line, a very useful connection between two extant parts of the national rail network, was axed during the Beeching era and incorporates intermediate stations at Hopton, Brundle, Great Pixton and Thorsby, together with the Golf Club halt near Pitchfield itself. We have been negotiating the purchase of the trackbed, including the Oxbourn tunnel, and until recently were fairly confident of eventual success. However, some weeks ago, the blow fell – we were given an ultimatum: raise the sum of £150,000 in twenty-eight days, failing which the offer would close and the alignment revert to non-railway purposes.

Naturally, the Society's membership was completely devastated, since we are only a small group of modest means and had no prospect of raising so much money in such a short time. Demolition was due to start on Monday 28th October and an air of deep despondency reigned. Then came what can only be described as divine intervention. On the Friday preceding Doomsday I received the following letter from a firm of solicitors:

> *Dear Mr Reeve,*
> *We act as executors for the late Major Herbert George Axton, who died on 5th April last. I am pleased to inform you that after meeting expenses and minor bequests, the balance of Major Axton's estate has been left to your Society with the sole proviso that the money is applied to the cause of railway preservation. The sum involved is in excess of £347,000.*
> *Yours etc., etc.*

You can imagine the surprise and delight with which this news was received – our project had been thrown a lifeline at the eleventh hour and the fifty-ninth minute.

The sum concerned will defray the purchase of the entire trackbed and enable us to begin restoration immediately.

You have no doubt heard the stories about phantom trains supposedly running along the derelict railway. The amazing thing – perhaps in view of the cash bonanza, I should say the second amazing thing – is that since this news, no further reports of sightings or noises have been received. It seems that our benefactor has enabled the Society to lay the ghost to rest.

The Engine Driver's Tale

I am employed as a railway engine driver and am based at Barham locomotive depot. For quite some time I have been regularly engaged, among other things, with driving train number 62, which runs from Dillington to Pitchfield Junction with empty carriage stock on Fridays, departing 17.40 with arrival at 18.09. This train is not advertised in the public timetable, since its function is the conveyance of carriages to Pitchfield to form the 06.47 Saturdays-only departure to Foxborough. Some members of the travelling public in the know, however, do use this train and nobody in authority seems to mind. For this reason it has always been known as the 'Ghost Train'.

On Friday 25th October last I was on the regular run with my usual mate as fireman. The weather was fine and still, we were running a couple of minutes early and the trip was uneventful until we came out of the Oxbourn tunnel nearing Pitchfield. My mate thought he saw someone on the track near the tunnel portal, but owing to fading light and the steam which envelops everything when the train emerges, he couldn't be sure. I was on the other side of the cab looking out for the distant signal, so I saw nothing.

Funnily enough, I never drove that train again. In our engine shed there is a staff suggestion box, and some time previously I had submitted an idea for improving rolling stock utilisation which would involve the cancellation of the Ghost Train. I heard nothing for a while, and then my suggestion, with a few modifications so someone else could claim the credit, was adopted. I will always believe that it was me who stopped the Ghost Train running.

9

CALL A SPADE A SPADE

The young detective was assigned to a case of great significance to the local community. Possessing the advantages of local knowledge and an analytical mind, his proved to be a model investigation.

Fulton is one of those places where something is always going on. It is a large village with a strong sense of community, and is endowed with societies, groups, associations, clubs and leagues of every conceivable kind. In consequence, everyone knows everyone else very well and nobody has any secrets. Not that people are nosy or intrusive; quite the opposite in fact: respect for each other is fundamental. It is simply that people tend to tell others their business anyway. All of this made the incident which I am about to describe seem out of character and out of place, and as a result the case was a difficult one for a young detective constable investigating his first crime.

The annual Fulton show is one of the highlights of the calendar, and most people in the village are involved in one way or another, or indeed in several ways. There are many exhibition categories including fur, feather, cakes, handicraft and, of course, garden produce. Competition to grow the best, longest, heaviest or oddest-shaped vegetables is always particularly sharp, and this year was no exception. Men lavish extreme care on their onions, potatoes, leeks, carrots and parsnips for months on end in order to enhance their prospects of carrying off the coveted first prize rosette for their chosen category. Rivalry is extremely keen, but the contest is always conducted in a truly sporting spirit, as befits Friendly Fulton. Until this affair, that is.

The cultivators of the local allotments and gardens vie with each other annually to grow the largest pumpkin, the reward for which is recognised by the granting for one year of the Weaver Cup. This trophy is engraved with the winner's name on the very showground, and he is the proud possessor of it for the ensuing twelve months.

As the day of the show approaches, the activity associated with caring for the pumpkins and persuading them to gain the last ounce intensifies. Great secrecy and obscure rituals surround this process, every grower having his own treasured recipe for success.

* * * * *

I don't know why the station officer decided to assign me to the Great Pumpkin Case, as it became known in the annals of crime in the district. Normally, such a relatively trivial incident would have been dealt with by a uniformed officer, but circumstances were rather out of the ordinary. As I have explained, great store is set by the inhabitants of Fulton on success in the annual show; in addition, the villagers are proud of their reputation as a law-abiding community. People were in the habit of leaving their houses and cars unlocked as they pursued their daily business. Thus, every abrogation of law and order is taken very seriously. Another thing occurred to me: I was born in the village and knew everybody, and perhaps the Inspector thought that this would convey an advantage in attempting to solve the case. On the other hand, I was a very new boy and maybe he was testing me out…

* * * * *

I have learnt three things about evidence at scenes of crimes: firstly, it is of the greatest importance to discover it, and secondly, of even more importance, to recognise that it is evidence; that is to say that it has some bearing on the case being investigated, since this is not always glaringly obvious. And the third thing? Find it quickly, before it goes away. Some things are by nature ephemeral, and most things do not survive curious people with trampling feet.

So when I was detailed to investigate the affair, on the very morning of the show, I lost no time in getting down to the Mill Lane allotments with all possible speed.

On plot 17, rented by William Ditchburn, I discovered that a prize pumpkin which was being prepared for the show had been deliberately cut into two pieces with some kind of bladed instrument. I had the two pieces weighed together, which resulted in a value of 176 lbs. Clearly, this was a serious contender for the trophy, and if their combined weight was greater than that of the winning entry in the afternoon's show, I had established the motive for the demise of Mr Ditchburn's vegetable.

Next, I carried out the most meticulous search of the whole allotment area. After some two hours my persistence was rewarded when, lying hidden under some potato haulms in a patch at the far side of the garden, I discovered an agricultural implement. This consisted of a rectangular steel blade, eleven inches in height and eight inches wide. Attached to the top of the blade and integral with it was a hollow spine or quill, ten inches long, in which was a round handle made of ash wood. This was a further eighteen inches in length and was bifurcated at the top with a horizontal bar forming a handgrip. The wood and metal parts were secured by substantial rivets. The top edges of the blade on both sides of the handle were turned over to form a horizontal footrest about half an inch wide. It is commonly called a spade. It is employed as a digging tool in the following manner: the user holds the spade by the handle and drives it vertically down into the soil. With his weight on the right foot, he places his left foot on the flattened top of the blade and exerts downward pressure until the blade is fully buried. With the left hand lower down the handle as a fulcrum, he can raise the spade and remove a 'spit' of earth. The footrest on the spade becomes brightly polished from contact with the sole of the digger's boot, as does the blade itself from the abrasive effect of soil and stones. In the present case I clearly distinguished pieces of pumpkin flesh adhering to the blade, the width of which corresponded with the wounds to the gourd itself.

I examined the spade minutely, as I considered it to be vital evidence. Embossed on the metal shaft of the handle was a manufacturer's name, whilst punched above this were the letters FAGS. I debated as to the meaning of these: Forged something Graded Steel perhaps? At length I decided to consult the oracle.

Ted Weaver (he of the Weaver Pumpkin Cup) lived in a cottage nearby, so I immediately proceeded there and knocked on his door. As luck would have it he was at home. At the time he was eighty-four years of age and had lived for all of that time in Fulton. He knew everybody and everything that was worth knowing, and for many years had been associated with the allotment society. When advancing age obliged him to give up his plot, he presented the cup bearing his name for the annual competition. His evidence, as it turned out, was central to the investigation. Whilst the allotments now serve a largely recreational function (some are used to grow flowers, and there is even a pigeon loft on one plot), in times past the food produced there made a vital contribution to many domestic economies. This was especially true between the two World Wars. In those times, the Agricultural Society ran a scheme for supplying less fortunate men with essential tools for working their allotments, accepting payment of a few pence per week on a kind of hire-purchase basis. These tools were marked FAGS, symbolising Fulton Allotment Garden Society – hence the letters on the offending spade. Now, Ted Weaver was one-time secretary of the association (he was one-time secretary of everything) and was known affectionately as 'Squirrel', because he never threw anything away. It was a simple matter for him to consult the Society's old records and give me the names of men who had obtained spades under the erstwhile system. There were only four still living in Fulton, and only one in whom I was interested.

* * * * *

I arrested the culprit on suspicion of criminal damage and took him to the town police station, where he was kept in custody just long enough to prevent him from entering his pumpkin in the show. When confronted with the evidence he soon admitted liability.

Meanwhile, the show committee, in an inspired moment of wisdom, decided to allow the unfortunate pumpkin belonging to William Ditchburn to be included in the competition, reasoning that its division into two parts was the act of an outside agency, not attributable to any act or omission by the exhibitor. There was nothing in the rules at that time (although I believe that this has since been amended) to state that candidate pumpkins had to be in one piece. An extraordinary decision, but then Fulton is an extraordinary place. Ditchburn duly won the sought-after trophy.

The Inspector was so impressed by the rapid detection of this crime that he readily agreed to my recommendation that no charge should be preferred against the perpetrator of the outrage. This had a beneficial effect on the crime statistics for the parish, which currently stood at zero. So there was no crime; in point of fact there was no motive either, as the culprit's own pumpkin weighed in at 217 lbs and would have won the contest by a generous margin. His punishment was to lose the cup to his rival for twelve months.

Oh, yes, how did I know who had damaged the pumpkin? The top of the spade in question was worn shiny on the right-hand side of the blade; therefore, the owner must have been left-handed. I knew which spade owner was left-handed perfectly well – in those days, men in the village spent a lot of time in The Crown playing darts. I was one of them, and so was the left-handed pumpkin grower and dart thrower. We never knew why he discarded the spade on someone else's plot – perhaps he was disturbed when carrying out the foul deed, or reckoned without a thorough search of the allotments.

* * * * *

All of this took place thirty-five years ago. My career never looked back, but I will admit on the eve of retirement as Head of CID that I never again solved a crime in under six hours. Among the presents that I have received from my colleagues on ceasing work is a beautiful spade – I hope to spend more time in the garden.

10
THE GUNPOWDER PLOT

The Pitchfield Gunpowder Mill operated for a period of two hundred and fifty years on its original site, and remained in family ownership for all that time.

It owed its establishment to the availability of natural ingredients in the locality and enjoyed its prolonged existence untroubled by the outside world.

In recent times the business was hardly viable, and indeed its continuing function depended on a series of happy accidents (if that is the correct term to use concerning a gunpowder mill) involving a very unlikely benefactor – the national government, in the form of the urbane art-loving civil servant, James Ratcliff.

He is the real hero of the piece. Master of every situation, the course of his life is inextricably mixed with the history of the mill in modern times. His retirement at the end of a distinguished career was marked with the grant of a Life Peerage, but even then he still had a part to play.

1. In the Beginning, AD 1727

Gunpowder n.

An explosive mixture of potassium nitrate, charcoal and sulphur. Superseded as a propellant, it is still used for blasting and fireworks.

Spindle tree n.

Family: Celastraceae

Species: Euonymus europeaeus.

The spindle is indigenous throughout the British Isles, but cannot be said to be generally common. The hardness and toughness of spindle wood have long been esteemed in the fashioning of small articles where these qualities are essential, and its common name is a survival of the days when spinning was the occupation of most women. The spindles were in demand for winding the spun thread... The young shoots make a very fine charcoal favoured by artists, and formerly much in demand as a constituent of gunpowder (q.v.).

The establishment of Pitchfield Powder Mill was owing to the availability of ample supplies of spindle trees, which find in the district ideal soil and climatic conditions. Indeed, this plant has been cultivated in the Pitchfield area for precisely the purpose of supplying this vital ingredient. Add to this the extraordinary bounty of Nature in making accessible in the same vicinity both sulphur and potassium nitrate in commercial quantities (from a long-extinct volcano), and it is obvious why the industry came to be established in this location.

The advantages of the site were further enhanced by the discovery of workable seams of coal, near to the surface, thus providing a ready source of fuel for charcoal burning and the other processes associated with the manufacture of gunpowder. The company was established by the Foster family as long ago as 1727 and has remained in private hands, albeit with some official interventions, as will be described, ever since.

2. The Duration of the Emergency, AD 1939

One morning, early in 1939, the then managing director of the Pitchfield Powder Mill, Charles Foster, was enjoying his breakfast, which had been prepared by his wife Elizabeth, who coincidentally also filled the role of company secretary at the mill. As was his wont, he was glancing at the morning's mail, which had been delivered to his private house. The latter was situated adjacent to the mill, serving as manager's residence and company headquarters, a convenient arrangement which had existed as long as the mill itself.

Charles riffled through the associated letters and stopped on encountering an official-looking envelope marked 'Ministry of Munitions. Private and Confidential'.

"What now?" he muttered, opening the letter with his knife and thereby imparting a smear of fried egg to the back of the envelope. He scanned the contents and uttered an imprecation.

"Whatever is it, dear?" asked his wife solicitously.

"Listen to this," he said, and quoted from the letter:

> *In response to the deteriorating political and military situation in Europe, HM Government is implementing certain measures designed to enhance national security. These steps include the assumption of official control over the production of a range of vital materials including explosives. Please be informed, therefore, that in accordance with the emergency powers vested in the Secretary of State, the organisations listed in the Schedule to this letter are immediately placed under government managerial supervision.*

"That includes us," said Charles, and continued reading:

> *Full details will be sent to you in the near future. Meanwhile, enquiries should be directed to the Ministry of Munitions at the address shown.*

"What are we going to do?" asked Elizabeth.

"Better have a discreet word with the chap who signed this letter," replied Charles. "I'll give him a ring when the office opens."

* * * * *

"How did you get on with the Powers That Be?" asked Elizabeth at lunchtime.

"Usual official obfuscation. Couldn't get hold of the organ grinder so had to speak to the monkey. Wouldn't discuss it over the telephone – some nonsense about insecure lines – so I've arranged to go up to London on Thursday to beard him in his den. Probably the best thing to do in the circumstances."

"I'm sure you're right, dear," replied the company secretary. "What time is the train?"

"There's one at 8.27. Should be home by about half past six."

* * * * *

Charles entered the Whitehall office block. To his surprise, the inner recesses looked tatty and neglected in comparison with the grandiose exterior of the edifice. At a desk a receptionist took his name and consulted an appointments book on her table.

"I'm so sorry, Mr Foster, Mr Frobisher is not available today, so Mr Ratcliff, his deputy, will be dealing with you. Room 217 on the second floor. That way, up the stairs, please."

Charles mounted two flights of steps and with some difficulty found the desired door. "These places are worse than my coal mine," he reflected. A brass plate announced 'Room 217. Mr RJC Ratcliff. Assistant Secretary'. He knocked and entered, finding himself in an outer office containing a desk and a secretary. He explained his business briefly.

"Ah, yes, Mr Ratcliff is expecting you, sir." (In those days people in offices were polite). "Will you go in, please? He'll be along in just a moment."

Charles entered the inner sanctum, a palatial room in sharp contrast to the gloomy and indigent atmosphere of the other offices. A large polished mahogany desk with a swivel chair, at present unoccupied, was the focal point of the room. On one wall hung an enormous abstract painting, fully six feet by nine feet, and he could hardly fail to be intrigued by it. It consisted simply of a large expanse in a brownish-purple shade – I believe it is called 'smudge' – the sort of effect produced when you mix all the colours in a child's paintbox indiscriminately. Contrasting violently with this negative background was a bright yellow stripe running across the top left-hand corner of the canvas. On this band were what appeared to be three bicycle wheels. He could not resist an urge to cross the office carpet and read with disbelief the caption on the bottom of the frame: 'Alphonse Meurde, Pope Innocent XV, taking a swarm of bees. 1924'.

"I see you're admiring my picture," said a plummy voice. Charles turned, slightly embarrassed, to greet the newcomer. "I'm James Ratcliff. How do you do? Afraid my superior has been summoned to a most important conference. Do you like it?"

Charles, taken aback, merely said, "There isn't a Pope Innocent XV. The last one of that name was the thirteenth."

"Very observant of you, old boy. Are you interested in twentieth-century art?"

"Well, no, actually. I once had ideas about becoming a divinity student, but gunpowder claimed me."

"It has claimed quite a few, I should think," observed Ratcliff dryly, "but you're absolutely right about your popes. Meurde is the first, and so far the only, Crypto-Post-Futurist painter. This is an original and I must allow that it is my pride and joy. Would you like some coffee?"

"Thank you," said the bemused Mr Foster. He glanced at his watch. "I'm sure you're extremely busy and I don't want to take up too much of your valuable time..."

"Oh, yes, forgive me – I get just a little carried away when discussing my favourite subject. Now, let's see..." He glanced at a file on the polished table. "Ah, yes, munitions factory, isn't it?"

"Yes."

"Well, old boy, defence of the realm and all that. We live in difficult times, and we must all be prepared to make sacrifices. Mind you, not everyone is prepared to let the public interest override personal considerations. There have been some interesting cases over the years. Do you by any chance remember Rex versus the Bethlehem Percussion Company?"

"Can't say I do," replied Charles, totally nonplussed at his first experience of personal contact with Central Government.

"What I mean is," pursued Ratcliff, "the needs of the nation are paramount; your company will revert to private ownership just as soon as circumstances permit."

"That's what they told my father in 1915, but you've never given it back."

"You mean that you've remained under government control since 1915? Well, old man, this is, how shall I say, a most delicate situation. This sort of thing tends to generate adverse publicity. Why hasn't the matter been raised before?"

"Well, my father was a staunch loyalist and always impressed on me the need to support one's country. Besides, the government has been paying the staff wages in the interim period and this has proved very helpful. For our part, we were supposed to remit all profits, but you'll be well aware that we've been through a lean period."

"So you're not going to pursue this matter any further, old man?" asked Ratcliff.

"I just wondered if you might see your way clear to raising the men's wages. They've been frozen since 1920, and the value of money is being constantly eroded."

"That seems like an excellent compromise in the best spirit of co-operation. Leave it to me."

"There is just one final point, Mr Ratcliff. The powder mill operates a coal mine as a wholly owned subsidiary. It's essential that this arrangement continues in order to secure vital fuel supplies. Can I take it that the mine is included in these arrangements?"

"I don't envisage any problem there, Mr Foster. By the way, you will bear in mind that matters concerning munitions are secret, won't you? Thank you for calling, and for your constructive attitude. I must show you some more of my modern paintings some time."

"I look forward to that," said the departing Charles Foster. He escaped the building and made his way home as quickly as possible. It seemed that the Pitchfield Powder Mill had, at least for the time being, a secure future.

3. Post-War Credits, 1946

The peace dividend arrived at Powder Mill House in the form of two official letters. The first arrived from the Ministry of Munitions and concerned the gunpowder factory. In effect, the government was relinquishing control of the business consequent to the termination of hostilities.

Charles Foster studied it intently for some time.

"That looks official, dear," said the company secretary over the breakfast table, where the customary business meeting was being held. "Is it important?"

"Seems that we can have our business back – the nation has lost interest in explosives."

"Oh dear."

"It's not all bad news, though – listen to this," and he read a portion of the text verbatim:

> *HM Government is prepared to consider claims in respect of sequestered companies for expenses directly attributable to their having been taken into control for the duration of the recent war. Such claims must be received by 1st June next and should be classified under the following categories:*
>
> *a. return on capital employed at the rate of 4% per annum;*
>
> *b. costs of deferred maintenance, plus renewals of plant and machinery;*
>
> *c. depreciation of fixed assets, mineral reserves etc.*

"I reckon we can get something out of this, don't you? Should tide us over for a year or two."

"What happens then?" wondered Elizabeth pensively.

"Don't worry, dear, something will turn up. Something always does," replied her husband soothingly.

Something did turn up; in fact, something already had, in the shape of the second official letter. This emanated from the Ministry of Fuel and Power and concerned the gunpowder mill's coal mine. Charles quoted:

> *In the Matter of the Mines Act, 1945*
>
> *You will be aware that under the terms of recent legislation, HM Government intends to take into public ownership all open-cast, drift and deep coal mines, this to become effective from 1st*

January next. According to our records, you are the owner of the coal-producing facility situated at Cuckoo Pit, near Pitchfield, which premises fall into the category covered by the Act.

In order that the compensation falling due to you may be assessed, you are invited to complete the attached preliminary questionnaire, which should be returned to the above address by 1st August. If you have any difficulties in supplying the information called for or would like further assistance, please contact...

Charles broke off and laughed heartily. "It's him again!"

"Who?"

"Ratcliff – the one I met last time in 1939."

"Well, you did pretty well out of him then."

"Yes, I think another visit to the corridors of power is called for. By the way, it's time for us to redefine the relationship between the mill and the colliery."

* * * * *

Charles passed through the imposing main portal of the office building and was directed to Mr Ratcliff's lair.

"Room 442, fourth floor; I'm afraid the lift is out of action today."

After what seemed an interminable flight of shabby stairs, he found the appropriate corridor and located room 442. "Mr Ratcliff, Deputy Secretary," he read. "Ah, he's promoted himself. Hope he's in a receptive frame of mind," he mused.

Ratcliff was more bland and urbane than ever. "How do you do? Won't you take a seat?" he asked, motioning Charles into a plush armchair. "How can we help you?"

"It's the matter of the nationalisation of private coal mines," began Charles.

"Ah, yes, I have the particulars – Pitchfield. What precisely is the problem?"

"Well, you require details of share value. This has always been a private company with a nominal capital, and in my capacity as chairman, managing director and head of the family, I'm the sole shareholder. The shares are not quoted and there have been no dealings in them."

"How many shares are there?" asked Ratcliff.

"Well, one actually," said Charles diffidently.

"Perhaps we could assess the value of the concern by its trading results."

"In that case, the best indicator seems to me to be the production figures," suggested Charles. "I have some details here." He delved into his case.

"Fine. In fact we've used the TMS figure for this purpose in many other cases."

Charles paused, searched the innermost recesses of his mind, and then plunged in. "Well, our latest result comes out at 11.72."

"I say; that's quite an achievement. Puts you well up the league table." Ratcliff seemed so impressed by this intelligence that the rest of the discussion was cursory and the interview soon drew to its close. "Any other points, Mr Foster?"

"Well, there is the matter of the gunpowder mill. It's a wholly owned subsidiary of the mine and there are longstanding trading arrangements between the two. The mine depends on a reliable supply of explosives in order to function."

"Well, there are precedents. Other mines we've dealt with include such activities as coking plants and coal staithes as integral functions, so I don't envisage any particular difficulties. Mind you, it's not all been plain sailing. Not by any means. You may recall the famous test case – Rex versus the Brncwstrd[1] Anthracite Company?" Charles' silence prompted Ratcliff to continue. "It's our practice to send a small team down to visit the installation prior to finalisation. Someone will be in contact with you shortly."

There was a long hiatus. Ratcliff gave a discreet cough. Charles started. "Oh, I do beg your pardon!" he exclaimed. "I was quite engrossed by your picture."

The 'picture' in question was a large abstract painting hanging on the wall behind Ratcliff's desk and, in truth, Charles had been gazing at it in horrified

1 Pronounced 'brown kowsterd'.

fascination for some minutes. It beggared description; Charles later recalled that it depicted an amorphous black fog on a bilious green and purple ground. What seemed to be an alligator sitting on a teapot lent the only variety.

Ratcliff was delighted at Charles' words. "I'm so glad you like it," he enthused. "Theophilus Squibb, from his Atavistic Period. It's a portrait of Évêque Ghislain du Porc, the Huguenot—"

"The Martyr of Nîmes," interposed Charles.

"You know Squibb's work?" cried Ratcliff, overjoyed.

"Not really," Charles admitted, "but I remember the old bishop. I was once destined for the Church, but gunpowder intervened."

"Do you know," said Ratcliff thoughtfully, "I do believe we've met before somewhere."

4. Not What it Seams, 1946

Despite Ratcliff's threat to send somebody to cast an eye over the colliery and associated activities, for quite a while nobody actually arrived. Life in the industrial complex resumed its easy tenor and the Fosters allowed themselves to relax.

The next official communication arrived, in the form of an assessment of the compensation due in respect of nationalisation. Accustomed as they had grown to receiving largesse at the hands of the government of the day, the scale of the award took them totally by surprise. It amounted to the princely sum of £1,200,000.

"What are we going to do about this?" asked Elizabeth anxiously, after she had read the letter. "We can hardly just sit back this time."

"I agree," said Charles. "Whilst there's a great temptation to take their money and do nothing, I don't think that would be our best course. There would have to be some repercussions eventually. Nothing for it but to come clean, I suppose – we've done well in the past by a policy of co-operation. Seems like another interview with Ratcliff is called for. I'd better speak to him."

"Why not write?" suggested Elizabeth. "You can work out exactly what face to put on the case without the possible embarrassment of having to answer questions off the cuff."

"Good idea. My pretext will be that no one has been to see us yet. That way I'll be seen to be behaving correctly. Would you like to get a letter ready to the Ministry of Foul and Pure, please, dear?"

"I think you mean Fuel and Power, Charles."

So off went a guarded letter to the Ministry, which provoked a totally unexpected reply.

"Good morning, Mr Foster," said the cultured voice over the telephone. "James Ratcliff, Ministry of Fuel and Power. Thank you for your letter. Sorry we haven't been along to see you yet but we're kept pretty busy. For the present we've been concentrating on the less productive mines whose future is perhaps open to doubt. When we've looked at those, we'll be moving on to what I might call the mainstream facilities."

"I see," said Charles in disbelief at being in the 'mainstream'.

"As a matter of fact, we've just been dealing with your own case and I've recently approved the staff appointments."

"Staff?" murmured Charles weakly.

"Yes. I wonder if it would be convenient if I came along to see you on the eleventh of next month. Don't get out of the office too often and we find it instructive to see what happens at the coalface, if you'll excuse the pun."

Charles could not think of a suitable reply.

"That'll be fine," he stammered. "Perhaps you'd like some lunch?"

"That's most kind. Look forward to it. There'll be about five of us I should think. Goodbye for now!"

Two limousines rolled up at the powder mill at the appointed time. Ratcliff, sleeker than ever, alighted, followed by four other men. They wore large name badges, increasing rather than diminishing their air of anonymity, and rendering Ratcliff's very perfunctory introductions unnecessary. The latter, clearly in his element as leader of the expedition, was very effusive. "I say, what an absolutely beautiful house!"

"Yes, it is rather fine. Built in 1704 and never substantially altered." Charles looked at his watch. "It's almost lunchtime. Can I offer you a drink? And what about your drivers?"

"Yes please to the first, and not to worry about the second. They're happy to make their own arrangements – probably go to the pub in the village."

The party entered the house, passed through the cool and elegant interior and assembled in the lounge. Charles introduced Elizabeth, who circulated with a tray of sherry glasses.

"I'm afraid that lunch is a little informal, Mr Ratcliff," she explained. "We weren't sure how many of you there would be and whether you might have been delayed, so we're having a barbecue."

For once, Ratcliff looked slightly ill at ease. "Is that wise?" he asked. "After all, I couldn't help noticing the gunpowder mill next door. By the way, what a perfectly fascinating building."

"Oh, it's quite all right," interposed Charles, "we'll have it on this side of the house, down wind. We do an excellent barbecue, if I say so myself – it's the charcoal from the mill. Spindle wood, you know; nothing to beat it."

Fortified by several sherries and an excellent lunch, and perhaps also feeling relieved not to have been blown up, the party assembled in the lounge.

"Now," said Ratcliff, in his element, "let's get proceedings underway. The staff members designated will go and give the mine the once-over, whilst I would like to discuss the arrangements for the transfer of control, if you're agreeable."

"Fine," said Charles, who by this time was feeling that the whole thing was totally out of his hands, and had resigned himself to whatever Fate offered. "Let's go along to the office. I'll organise a pot of coffee."

Ratcliff unrolled a large sheet of paper, on which had been drawn a family tree. "This is the proposed management structure. The four gentlemen whom you have met will occupy these senior posts." He indicated boxes at the top of the tree. "John Redford, colliery manager."

"I see."

"Robert Alderton, sales manager."

"Sales manager? Why do you need a sales manager?"

"To liaise with the customers and promote sales."

"The mine only has one customer. The powder mill."

"You mean that the entire production of the colliery is burnt at the mill?"

"Not quite. We burn some in the static boiler which produces steam for the fireless locomotives on the railway, some is used at the sulphur and potash mine, and, of course, we need a little at the house."

"I see," said Ratcliff, visibly taken aback. He collected himself with admirable sang-froid, returning to the beautifully drawn and elaborate chart. "Here is Donald Truelove, purchasing manager elect."

"What will he do?"

"Why, oversee the supplies organisation."

"We only have one supplier."

"Who?"

"The powder mill. It supplies all the needs of the mines."

"So you sell products to each other?"

"Not exactly. The constituent parts of the business merely supply each other. No money changes hands. For many years past we've operated a system known as Perpetual Mutual Internal Credit. Saves a great deal of paperwork, not to mention bank charges."

"What about profit and loss?"

"We don't make any. You'll recall that the government paid the staff wages since 1915, although that recently ended, and apart from this, the various departments supported each other."

Ratcliff peered at his family tree. "So Henry Cook, the chief accountant in waiting, has no function?"

"No, he might as well have stayed in London."

"How many staff are there?"

"Including Elizabeth – she's company secretary – and myself, nine."

Ratcliff stared in disbelief. "But your production of coal…" He shuffled his papers. "Here we are – according to your return, it's 11.72 tonnes per man shift!"

"Tonnes per man shift?"

"Yes – TMS on the form. I have it here."

There was a long and awkward silence.

"It seems that we have a problem with terminology," said Charles eventually. "I took TMS to mean total monthly subterranean material."

* * * * *

The two limousines crunched on the gravel in the yard in front of the mill, disgorging their passengers. Ratcliff went to greet them, and an animated conversation ensued. Discretion being the better part of valour, Charles watched the proceedings through the office window but did not participate.

* * * * *

Ratcliff re-entered the house, and to Charles' relief and admiration had completely regained his aplomb.

"Thank you very much, Mr Foster. I'm obliged to you for all the trouble you've taken, and thank you, Mrs Foster; that was indeed the finest barbecue I have ever eaten. Spindle wood, I think you said? Must remember that. I simply love this beautiful house – what a lovely setting. And the old mill – quite fascinating. I've really enjoyed my day out of London. By the way," he said sotto voce to Charles, "I think we'll have to revise our plans. There is provision for the exclusion of certain mines from the general nationalisation programme – geological problems inhibiting development of the full potential; I think that will fit this case. I'm afraid that the level of compensation will have to be re-examined. However, let's look on the bright side. The government is anxious to be seen as even-handed, and perhaps a private mineral resource exploitive grant will be an acceptable alternative. I'll be in touch with you shortly. Love this house!"

He was gone, with the wave of an elegant gloved hand.

5. *On the Right Lines, 1947*

Shortly afterwards, Foster received the next in the series of official missives. The text was as follows:

> *In the Matter of the Transport Act 1946*
>
> *Under the provisions of recent legislation, HM Government hereby gives notice of the intention to take into public ownership the following transport undertaking:*
>
> *The Pitchfield and Littleworth Junction Railway.*
>
> *An inspector will visit your premises on the following date to carry out an initial assessment. Please have all relevant information available. In the event that this date is inconvenient please contact...*

"What is it this time, Charles?" asked Elizabeth over breakfast.

"Not satisfied with the powder mill and the mine, they want the railway now," replied Charles. "We're going to have another visitor. I must say that they're gluttons for punishment – you'd think they had learnt their lesson."

Given the history of official attempts to seize the Fosters' assets, it was wholly predictable that nobody turned up to Pitchfield on the appointed day. At 4 p.m. Charles returned to the house from his duties at the mill to have tea. Entering the office he encountered Elizabeth.

"Have a nice day, dear?" she asked.

"Very enjoyable."

"What have you been doing?"

"Engine driver. One of my favourite jobs. No one showed up then?"

"Not a sign. We didn't get the wrong day, did we?"

"Don't think so. Can I have a look at that last letter, please, dear?"

Charles perused it and looked at the calendar on the wall. "No, sure enough, it says 14th April. I suppose I'd better speak to someone in my role as conscientious citizen to find out what's going on. Let's see, who sent that letter?" He paused and then laughed loudly. "Not again! It's him, Elizabeth."

"Ratcliff?"

"Who else? And what's more, he's now Sir James. Better than ever! Seems like another visit to London is needed."

"Surely we can't get anything out of the railway?"

"We thought that about the mill and the mine, didn't we? I'd better speak to him about the matter."

* * * * *

Next morning, Charles telephoned Ratcliff, who greeted him fulsomely: delighted to see you; so sorry for the inconvenience; some communication failure; very busy department; sure this can be resolved; regards to Mrs Foster; will never forget the barbecue; spindle wood; beautiful house.

'Room 1217, Sir James Ratcliff, Under Secretary', the notice on the door declared. The office was larger and more airy, the desk more highly polished and the general ethos more palatial. In a very prominent position hung an enormous abstract painting in a black frame. Charles gathered a confused impression of brilliant orange, loosely reminiscent of a snakes and ladders board. He peered at it in incredulity.

"*Agnus Dei*, by TS Nagashakashuru," said a well-modulated voice. "Do you know his work?"

"I'm afraid not," admitted Charles.

"The leading exponent of chromospectroscopy. Extraordinary, don't you agree?"

"I certainly do."

The conversation turned to official matters. Ratcliff consulted a file and pressed a button on his desk, then spoke into a box. "Ask Mr Fanshawe to step in, will you, please?" There was an incomprehensible squawk from the box in reply, followed by a knock on the door. "Ah, Christopher, this is Mr Foster. File 2234/45. He's called in connection with the Pitchfield and Littleworth railway. Should have been visited. Seems it wasn't. What precisely is the problem?"

"Ah, yes, Sir James. Difficulties with the travel budget. It's temporarily overspent, so there was no hire car available."

"We have a very convenient train service," said Charles helpfully.

Fanshawe recoiled visibly at the mere suggestion that a railway inspector should actually travel by train, and appeared so taken aback as to be bereft of speech.

Foster saw his chance to take the initiative. "Have you ever been on a train, Mr Fanshawe?" he asked innocently.

The official struggled to regain his composure. "Naturally; very busy man; question of the optimum use of resources; most convenient way to travel; flexible."

Charles had to admire the way in which Ratcliff came to his subordinate's rescue. He intervened: "I went on one once. Got a smut in my eye. Nanny wouldn't let me travel that way again." General laughter ensued and the difficulties seemed to have been glossed over.

"Perhaps we can deal with the matter here and save everybody's time and money," suggested Charles.

"Splendid idea," announced Ratcliff. "Tell us about your railway. I have far-reaching plans to modernise the whole network."

"I don't think you can modernise this one."

"Why ever not? Electric traction, new rolling stock, revise the timetable, smart new livery, good corporate image … give the public what they deserve."

"The public have got nothing to do with it. The railway is entirely self-contained and is not connected to the national system."

"Why not connect it? Run some through trains."

"No, you can't," retorted Charles. "This is the only railway in the country, and probably in the world, with a gauge of 3 feet 7¾ inches."

"Convert it."

"Can't be done. It connects the Cuckoo Pit coalmine with the Pitchfield Gunpowder Mill, with branches to the potash works. The colliery is a drift mine and the rails run directly to the coalface. At the other end it enters the mill itself – you'll remember that, Sir James – and provides internal transport. Despite its age it's a most effective system – there's no double handling. The gauge was chosen so trains can fit in the main door of the mill."

"Why not widen the door?"

"Not allowed to."

"Who said so?"

"You did."

"I did?"

"The mill is a listed historical building and no alterations of any kind are permitted. We applied for permission to the Ministry of Works between the wars to enlarge the doorway, but this was categorically denied. By coincidence, I have the letter of refusal." He fumbled in his briefcase. "Here you are – absolutely forbidden to carry out any alterations. Dated 21st July 1930 and signed by someone called Ratcliff."

"Extraordinary coincidence," murmured Sir James. "Well, at least we can replace the rolling stock."

"I'm afraid not. Owing to the danger of explosion, which was a matter of concern to you personally, if I recall, in both the powder mill and the pit, the only form of prime movers permitted are fireless locomotives. They're filled with high-pressure steam from the special plant near the coal mine. Very efficient, since the coal for the boiler is dug on the spot! Anyway," continued Charles, "nobody will manufacture fireless locomotives of that gauge, so we build and maintain them ourselves. The whole system is thus totally self-contained and independent."

"What does it carry?" asked Fanshawe, desperately endeavouring to recover some status in the eyes of his superior.

"Coal, sulphur and potash from the mines to the mill, and gunpowder from the mill to the mines. Oh yes, and workmen to and from both locations. And the odd load of spindle wood to the house – it makes a lovely fire."

At the mention of the house a seraphic smile came over Ratcliff's face. "Pure Queen Anne," he said softly.

* * * * *

As usual, Ratcliff was equal to the challenge posed by the Pitchfield and Littleworth railway. Shortly after the discomfiture of Fanshawe, Charles received another of his letters.

> *Dear Mr Foster,*
> *In pursuance of our discussion of recent date, I am pleased to be able to inform you that it is no longer the government's intention to take your railway into public ownership. My research has revealed that the line was originally constructed as a private venture without an authorising Act of Parliament, and in such cases the Minister is empowered to exercise his prerogative to exempt the line from nationalisation. This decision may be reviewed in the light of future circumstances...*

The Fosters, from previous experience of dealing with officialdom, did not regard the threat of renewed government interest seriously, and life at Pitchfield settled back into its own idiosyncratic routine. There was a brief alarm in December when an official envelope arrived, but it transpired that it was nothing more than a Christmas card from Ratcliff, naturally a reproduction of an abstract painting. Thereafter he sent one every year. The Fosters responded to their fairy godmother, and as is the custom with people who correspond very seldom, the opportunity was taken to include little snippets of news with the seasonal greetings. Soon they were on Christian name terms, and over the years the cards were transformed into fairly lengthy letters.

6. A Merry Christmas, 1959

Dear James,

Well, another year has passed uneventfully and here we are thinking of Yule logs (spindle, naturally!) and roast turkey. This may be the last card we write in our capacity as the denizens of Pitchfield Powder Mill. Charles has always cherished the idea of studying for Holy Orders and he has been accepted as a mature student at the nearby Theological College. It seems that the Church is short of recruits to the priesthood and welcomes some older students who have gained experience in other walks of life. We have managed to keep the mill going thanks in no small part to the generous assistance of the government (you will know this better than anyone), but have reluctantly decided to call it a day. Since we have no children there are no more Fosters to keep it running in any case. In fact, it is out of consideration for the remaining four employees that we have continued for so long.

Etc., etc.

Yours affectionately,

Charles and Elizabeth

7. *And a Happy New Year, 1960*

My dear Elizabeth and Charles,

Thank you for your card, containing as it does such momentous news. Promise me, I beg you, that you will give me first refusal if you decide to sell the house – you know how much I have always coveted it over the years. I have ambitious plans for the mill as well – I would convert it into an art gallery to house my collection of twentieth-century masterpieces, staging exhibitions in order to enhance public awareness of the merits of modern painting. In addition, I believe that I could offer security of employment to the residue of the mill staff. In order to encourage the continuance of painting in the modern context, I envisage the production of artists' materials at attainable prices from traditional ingredients, and the supply of high-grade charcoal forms an integral part of my plans.

Etc., etc.

Yours ever,

James Ratcliff

8. *Not Without Honour, 1961*

New Year's Honours List (extract)

Life Peers

Sir (Richard) James Cobb RATCLIFF, late Permanent Secretary, Home Office. He assumes the title of Lord Ratcliff of Pitchfield, after an estate he has recently acquired.

9. Important Points, 1962

Article in the *Railway Times*, issue 236, Feb 1962.

> *Fears for the future of the unique 3ft 7¾ gauge Pitchfield and Littleworth railway appear to have been allayed. Following the recent announcement that the gunpowder factory and associated mineral workings served by the railway have passed into new hands and that the production of explosives is to cease, it appeared that the railway system had no further function and that it would be allowed to decay, or worse, be dismantled for scrap. We are pleased to report that the entire line has been donated by the new owner to a local preservation society, who has dubbed the system the 'Guy Fawkes Line' after its erstwhile principal traffic. At a recent ceremony the three famous fireless locomotives were named* Rev Charles Foster, Lord Pitchfield *(former and present owners of Powder Mill House) and* Powder Puff. *Proposals to paint the locomotives in colours associated with these names aroused lively debate. It was suggested that clerical grey, mandarin orange and pink respectively should be applied; wiser counsels prevailed, however, and after a postal ballot of Society members it was decided by the narrowest margin to retain the traditional livery of Buckingham green, lined out in red and black. It is understood that ambitious plans are afoot for the introduction of a variety of rolling stock (which will necessitate re-gauging) and the operation of a passenger service. The colliery, known as Cuckoo Pit, has known reserves of coal, and unconfirmed reports state that it is intended to tap these as locomotive fuel if it proves to be of suitable quality. Existing workshop facilities in the vicinity of the old Nazareth potash mine will provide a very useful base for the new operator's activities.*

10. In the Eye of the Beholder, 1963

Extract from *The Times*, April 16th 1963:

MODERN ART

An exhibition of twentieth-century art is to be held at the Powder Mill Gallery, Pitchfield, by kind permission of the owner, Lord Ratcliff. It will be opened on 3rd January 1964 and will run for the whole year. On public view for the first time will be many twentieth-century masterpieces from Lord Ratcliff's own collection, featuring works by Squibb, Nagashakashuru, Meurde, von Wűrzel, Dmitri Laryngitis, Costas Halitosis, X Diabetes and the Kindynos School. In addition there will be a major retrospective of pieces by the French Algerian False Impressionist Mustapha Peaupeau.

Plans are advanced for the showing during the following year, for the first time in this country, of work executed by the sensational twenty-three year old Basque multi-media artist, Verucca Fluxx – painter, sculptress, glass blower and ceramicist. She is also a gifted musician and a renowned exponent of the Pyrenean bagpipes.

Looking further forward, Lord Pitchfield envisages major expositions to commemorate the one hundredth anniversary of the birth of both Abraham Moth and Bartolemeo Hoakes. Displays of such high calibre afford the prospect of an excellent future for the new gallery.

11

H_2O

It was essential for me to get a preview of those papers. My ingenious plan worked perfectly, but I had reckoned without the intervention of such a tricky substance as water.

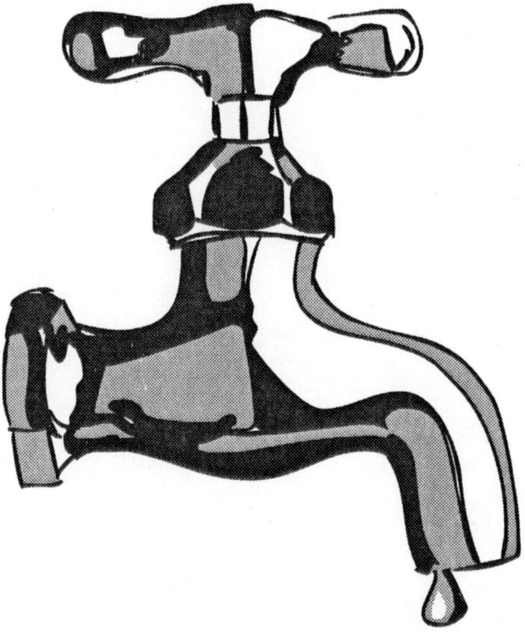

A very peculiar material is water. For a start, it is the only substance which is liquid at normal temperatures, except mercury, and you don't meet a lot of mercury in your day-to-day life. It also has a strong propensity to get into places where it doesn't belong. Something to do with molecular attraction, possibly. A heating engineer once told me that he had seen water escaping through a joint which was proof against quite high-pressure gas. I'm sorry for plumbers and people who work for public utility companies, as they spend their whole lives dealing with the stuff. In fact, it was the tendency for water to misbehave which almost had a decisive effect on the outcome of this story.

* * * * *

Most towns with any claim to antiquity have a ring of eighteenth and nineteenth-century houses round the historic core, and in many instances these are no longer occupied as dwellings, but have found new uses as offices. Ours was one such, being a three-storey Victorian house fronting West Street. It still retained its original high ceilings, sash windows and fireplaces, and although the latter no longer saw real fires, it provided a pleasant working environment for a firm of accountants. Apart from the principal rooms, the place was a bit of a rabbit warren, with odd passages and staircases and a rear door giving access to a paved courtyard and thence to a back lane. This layout was another factor in determining the course of events which I am about to narrate.

I was very young at the time and struggling to qualify in my chosen profession. That is a slight misnomer, since in the absence of any clear idea on my own part as to how I was going to earn a living, accountancy had been 'chosen' by my father on my behalf. That being the case, there was scope for conflict between the necessity to study in my spare time and the siren calls of the football pitch and the dartboard. When the time came for me to take a certain examination, therefore, I was less than confident in my own ability to do myself justice. The examination was to be conducted under the auspices of my own firm, and the examining body had sent the question papers directly to the senior partner in advance of the day appointed for the test. I knew this, and I also knew that the papers were securely ensconced in the senior partner's safe. Mr Carpenter was a bit of a martinet, and there was no prospect that he would drop any useful hints as to the area on which my last minute revision should be focussed. Prompted by this knowledge, and by some pointed references from my father concerning my ability to 'make my way in the world', I resolved on a desperate course of action. A glimpse of that examination paper would considerably enhance my chances of obtaining the elusive pass mark.

* * * * *

Gaining access to the offices out of normal working hours would not present me with any problems. As a junior member of the staff, it often fell to me to secure the premises at close of work, and in consequence I was well aware of the vagaries of old sash windows and worn door locks. The system was straightforward: when all internal doors, cupboards and so on were closed, the main key bunch was handed to a representative of a local security company, who would briefly satisfy himself that all appeared well, close and lock the front door and retain the keys until the following morning. Random patrols were carried out during silent hours, and on working days the door was opened at 7 a.m. to admit the cleaners. We did not keep any large amounts of cash on the premises; what we did have, however, was commercial information, which can itself be a valuable commodity. So the senior partner had an alarm system installed. This was switched on when the offices were vacated and had a link to the security company's own operational headquarters. My way of circumventing this was very simple, as will be seen. There was the little matter of the safe, of course. It was an old-fashioned model with a simple lock controlled by a four-digit code. In theory, nobody except the senior partner was privy to this, and in any event it was supposed to be changed monthly. In fact, once recently when Mr Carpenter had been away sick it had been necessary to access some papers and he had given the code to Bedford, a colleague of mine. I had been present when Bedford locked up, and he had casually revealed the code to me. When the cat's away, the mice will play, as the old adage goes. I could only hope that the senior partner had not been punctilious about entering a new code.

* * * * *

The chosen day dawned somewhat inauspiciously. When I arrived at the office for work, the area of the street immediately in front of our building was a hive of activity. Two vans with flashing orange roof-lights were parked at the kerbside. Barriers were everywhere. An air compressor was busy supplying power to the man with the pneumatic drill, and, above all, everything was running with water. It filled the gutters, ran all over the road and cascaded onto the pavements. We obviously had a burst water main.

* * * * *

At close of play that afternoon I shut the offices down and switched on the alarm system in accordance with the routine procedure. The security man was known to me and I did not anticipate any problem in that direction. Just prior to leaving, I made the excuse that I had accidentally left my briefcase in my own office – which was quite true, except that I had left it there on purpose – and went in to fetch it while the guard waited on the street. As I passed the alarm I switched it off. Outside, the water board had clearly performed some kind of miracle, as the flood had subsided, the vans, other paraphernalia and workmen had disappeared, and all that remained was a small barrier around a section of street which would need the surface restored. Bidding the security guard goodnight, I made my way home.

* * * * *

When I judged it opportune to do so, at about 9.30 p.m., I returned to the town centre. I made my way quickly and quietly along Mill Lane, which ran along the rear of the building. Nobody was in sight, so I shinned over the wall into the courtyard. Sheltered from the sight of any passer-by, I soon gained admission via the back door and made straight for Carpenter's office. This did not face onto the street, and a light was always left burning there, so my task was considerably facilitated. Preoccupied, I made straight for the safe. Then, to my horror, I saw the water. There was obviously some kind of leak in the roof, for there was a huge damp stain right across the ceiling. Water was trickling from the plaster rose, down the pendant cable, over the lamp-shade and onto the senior partner's desk. Any moment, I thought, and it would fuse the lights, explode or flood the entire building, or possibly all three. I now faced a fearful dilemma. It was imperative that action be taken at once to stop this water. On the other hand, if I intervened, how could I possibly explain my presence in the office? Self-preservation is the strongest instinct, they say, and in this case 'they' were absolutely right. Turning towards the door, I noticed another dribble of water running down the banisters of the staircase in the hall. I suddenly recalled the purpose of my clandestine visit. Stiffen the sinews, as Shakespeare said.

I went across to the safe and spun the wheel, using the code given me by Bedford. Good old Bedford, must buy him a drink. The door refused to open. In my near panic I must have misdialled. I tried again. No response. That imbecile Bedford! I stood up and walked over to the desk. On the sodden blotter was a yearly calendar. 'Year 84. Week 40' caught my eye. I returned to the safe and dialled 8-4-4-0 and the door opened as sweetly as you could wish. You would be surprised how unimaginative even erudite people are when it comes to this sort of thing. Half of them use their wife or girlfriend's name or their date of birth as computer passwords. I seized the large envelope, which, mercifully, Carpenter had opened. It was the matter of a moment to take the question paper to the general office, copy it – the photocopier always played up if it was switched off, so it was always left on; thank God for the shortcomings of modern technology – replace it and shut the safe door. I ran to the back door. Immediately, a fearful cacophony broke out – obviously the water had reached the alarm and short-circuited something. I left by the way I had entered and walked down Bridge Street. I had the satisfaction of seeing the security patrol van, light flashing, heading for the office. I had always meant to leave the alarm off, as it was the habit for either the security man or the cleaners to switch it off first thing in the morning. Each would think the other had done it. Familiarity breeds carelessness. Now there was no problem with the alarm – it had done its job and the flood would be discovered and stopped. If the security man noticed that the alarm was off he was not going to make any fuss, as it was his job to make sure it was on. My visit had left no trace.

* * * * *

It transpired that the hole in the road, allied to the antediluvian (pun intended!) plumbing in our offices combined to cause the flood. A small piece of gravel had entered the main in the course of the repair work, finding its way to the header tank in our roof. It wedged the ball-valve open, and the water kept coming, even though the tank was full. The overflow pipe was inadequate and half-choked, with the result that our offices got rather wet. The alarm system saved the day.

* * * * *

Two days later, as I was about to sit the examination, Carpenter called me into his office. “Ah, there you are, Robert,” he began. “Today’s the great day!” He outlined the examination arrangements and wished me the best of luck. I think he probably meant it – he wasn’t such a bad old stick, really. “By the way,” he continued, “we’ve had quite a kerfuffle with the examination paper.” I froze with horror. He seemed not to notice. “Apparently, there was some suggestion that its confidentiality had been compromised. Not locally, of course. Somewhere in Leeds. They had to devise a fresh one at short notice.”

* * * * *

This all took place some time ago. I suppose you could say it’s all water under the bridge. My guardian angel did not desert me and the paper seemed quite reasonable. I am now qualified and a partner in another firm. My current assignment is the development for a water company of a system for assessing the true cost of leaks from main pipes.

12

ARRIVEDERCI

The Whittaker family had strong connections with Italy. A trivial matter such as a world war was not allowed to interfere with this arrangement.

One of Henry Whittaker's most treasured possessions was a penknife, given to him on his tenth birthday by his Italian grandmother. It was slim and elegant and fitted unobtrusively into a lad's trouser pocket. Any boy will tell you that a penknife has a myriad of uses and Henry never went anywhere without it. It was engraved with the date and the message 'Buon Compleanno', and this was a constant reminder of his grandmother, of whom he was very fond. Grandmother and penknife were among the reasons for the love of Italy and things Italian which he was to retain until the end of his life, which, I am pleased to say, has not yet arrived, as this year there is going to be a family get-together to celebrate his attaining the age of eighty-five.

* * * * *

Major Henry Whittaker was a General Staff Officer (Grade II) with Military Intelligence at the War Office, and he was well aware of the deteriorating situation in Europe in the summer of 1939. He had broached the idea of taking his wife and son to Lake Garda for the holidays in conversation with the Brigadier, who had remarked, "If you want to go, Whittaker, you had better go quickly. You know well enough it's probably your last chance. I don't know how long you'll be there, mind."

* * * * *

The blow, when it fell, was not unexpected. Giuseppe, the proprietor of the hotel where they always stayed, ran across the courtyard separating the main house from the old coach and stable block. "Ecco, un telegramma!" he cried. Henry had no need to read the contents: 'ALL LEAVE CURTAILED. RTU FASTEST MEANS'.

"Bad news?" asked his wife Mildred.

"Afraid so, dear; start packing up. We must get the Paris express from Milan tonight."

Possessions were crammed into suitcases, straps pulled tight and the luggage piled in the courtyard. Henry and his wife bade a solemn farewell to Giuseppe and Sophia with promises to return as soon as circumstances permitted. Alessandro, the fifteen-year-old son of the house, and boon companion of their own boy Hugh who was the same age, piled the cases into the taxi, and all at once they were on their way to the lake steamer jetty. They crossed the lake to Desenzano, where porters from the railway station met the boat with handcarts and pushed the luggage the half-mile through the streets to the main rail line. There they boarded the train for Milan and home. Later that evening, the express plunged into the Alpine tunnel with a shriek, symbolically shutting out the Italian sunshine and entering a new age of darkness.

* * * * *

"I think it's time for a Commandant's parade, Sergeant Major," said Henry Whittaker. "I want to cast an eye over this latest lot and it will give them something to do."

"Something to grumble about, more like, sir."

"All the better. The devil finds work for idle hands."

Henry stepped out onto the level dusty patch of North African desert which passed as the parade ground and walked slowly along the assembled ranks of dispirited prisoners of war. After going to France and being evacuated at Dunkirk, he now found himself Commandant of an Italian prisoner of war camp. At forty-three he was a little over the age at which men were normally given command of a front-line regiment, and his knowledge of Italy and its language made him an ideal candidate for this post.

He paused here and there and said a few words to selected individuals. For the most part they seemed to be relieved to be out of the firing line. At one juncture he stopped, looked hard at a young man and asked him, "Come si chiama?"

"D'Agostino, Alessandro," came the reply. (In those days, if you asked an Italian his name he would give his surname first. Some older Italians still do.)

"I'll have this man as my batman, Adrian," said Colonel Whittaker to his adjutant. "Have the Sergeant Major bring him to my office when the inspection is over."

"Very well, sir."

* * * * *

At the close of these proceedings, Henry made his way to the Commandant's 'office' – a slightly more commodious version of the standard tent – and was seated at his 'desk' – a six-foot folding table – when he heard a knock on the tent-pole.

"Yes," he called.

"Your batman, sir."

"Thank you, Sergeant Major. That will be all for now."

"Sit down, Alex," he said, in Italian, motioning the youth into a canvas chair. "How are the family?"

"Very well, Signore, thank you. And yours?"

"Hugh is a soldier now, too. I haven't heard from him for a while. And we had better speak Italian. Some of your compatriots might get suspicious if they hear you using English."

"They are happy to be out of this stupid war."

"You are going to be my batman. And behave yourself, or I'll tell your father when next I see him."

"What are my duties, Signore?"

"You can start by making two cups of coffee."

* * * * *

The best chance of escape afforded to a prisoner of war occurs immediately after his capture, especially if this has taken place following some military action. Men on both sides alike may be tired, excited, confused or scared. The very number of prisoners may well constitute an embarrassment, and the mechanism for looking after them probably does not exist. The captors have urgent priorities concerning defence works, casualties, communications, supplies and further operations; prisoners can be an unwanted liability. An escapee who is bold, resolute (and lucky) has good prospects.

One such was Lieutenant Hugh Whittaker when he fell into German hands in Northern Italy in 1944. Radio conditions were extremely difficult in the mountainous country bordering Lake Garda, and his unit was widely dispersed. He had encountered no enemy during his reconnaissance patrol, and first contact with the opposition came when he walked straight into a force much larger than his own, well dug in on a wooded hillside. He at once decided on an orderly retreat and the other members of his group made their getaway, he alone having the misfortune to be taken prisoner. Once he had been disarmed, nobody seemed very interested in or to take much notice of him, so he resolved to escape. His opportunity soon arose when a sudden increase in activity presaged a move to a new location. Hugh edged his way towards the periphery of the site and quietly and deliberately walked uphill and to the north, in what he fondly believed was the opposite direction to that which an escaper might be expected to take. When he was clear, he climbed an oak tree, which provided surprisingly thick cover from the ground below. Just then, far to the west, the setting sun illuminated an arm of the lake with a metallic glint. "That's it," he decided, "I'll go and finish my holiday at Garda."

He descended from his tree and made a wide detour around the position where his captors had been. He had no idea whether they had left, and if so in what direction. If pressed, he could probably not have justified his decision to head for the lake – at the time it seemed a good idea. The night was clear. Keeping the North Star on his right, he headed steadily towards the west, and after some hours felt that the ground was perceptibly falling away. The forest was thinner, with small cultivated patches. At dawn he concealed himself amidst some rocks and remained there all day, sleeping fitfully. At dusk he set off again towards the lake.

Cold, tired and hungry, he eventually came across a small streambed tumbling downhill and, reasoning that it could only flow into the lake, followed its course. Quite suddenly he encountered the main lakeside road and realised that he was on the outskirts of Garda town. He sat behind a bush and considered his situation. Reaching in his breast pocket, he felt the outline of a slim penknife. His father had given him this as a lucky talisman, with strict injunctions to take care of it, when he left home. He cut the stitching around the map pocket of his battledress trousers and tore it off. He next did the same with the obviously military breast pockets of his blouse. The remnants of khaki material and his beret having been hastily buried in the sandy soil, he felt that with luck he would not attract too much attention. He was light-headed from hunger and fatigue and cast any remaining caution to the wind. The town looked deserted – was there perhaps a curfew? Avoiding lighted places, he made his way to the lakeside. In those days there was little more than the steamer jetty and a fishermen's wharf behind the small railway station. If you go there now you can enjoy a stroll along a most attractive paved promenade, although unhappily the railway has succumbed to the motorcar.

Presently, he was on the rough beach between the waters of the lake and the rear boundaries of large houses fronting the main road. He recalled with relief and gratitude his boyhood excursions around these by-ways with Alessandro. How different was his situation now! After some hundreds of yards, a narrow lane, scarcely more than a footpath, ran at right angles from the beach between wooded gardens and gave onto the main road directly opposite the hotel entrance. Hugh made his way along the path. Somewhere in the distance a dog barked, but there was no other sign of life. Reaching the road, he paused, considering his next move. As he did so an army lorry filled with helmeted German soldiers swung out of the hotel drive and turned down the hill towards the town. He waited for an agonising hour. Nothing else happened, so summoning the last of his resolve, he sprinted across the road, scaled the wall, dropped into the familiar garden and lay still. Lights and activity were apparent in the main building, but the old stable annexe seemed quiet apart from a dim light on the ground floor. The rear door was locked. He fumbled in his pocket and took out the penknife. It was the work of a moment to slip the worn catch and enter the house. Under the kitchen door was a sliver of light. He knocked softly, pushed on the door and called, "Eh, Mama, it's me, Hugh." Gieseppe and Sophia stared in disbelief. "Ho fame – I'm hungry," explained Hugh.

Two fat tears rolled down Sophia's brown cheeks. "You boys always are," she said.

* * * * *

When Hugh was acquainted with the situation, he realised that he had jumped out of the frying pan and into the fire. There was a lot of German military activity in the area of Garda, and in fact the main building had been commandeered as a tactical HQ. Mercifully, they had plenty to occupy them and had left the family in the coach house to their own devices. It was resolved that Hugh would remain in concealment in one of the capacious attics for the time being.

"This stupid war will soon be over," Giuseppe had said. "Meanwhile, you stay with us."

There was a brief alarm the following morning when two German officers accompanied by an Italian policeman called at the coach house. Hugh observed them from the small skylight in his attic roof. Giuseppe made no mention of the event to Hugh, who, realising that the Italian had his own compromises to make, did not raise the matter.

* * * * *

Hugh kept a check on the days by carving a small notch each evening in one of the heavy wooden roof trusses with his father's penknife. One evening as he was engaged in this task, he heard a sudden disturbance in the yard below. Raised voices, the noise of vehicle engines and a general hubbub ensued. He laid the knife on the flat beam top and peered through the glass of the skylight. A jeep flying the

Union Jack was parked below. Lieutenant Hugh Whittaker, posted as 'missing', had been found.

* * * * *

When peace finally came, the world was never to be quite the same place, and the Whittakers were not exempt from the all-pervading ethos of change. Career exigencies, new places to visit, the vagaries of life in general combined to keep them away from Italy. Henry never lost his affection for the country and its people and was never happier than when regaling his grandson, also named Henry, with stories about life there before the war. Henry junior, Hugh's son, shared not only his grandfather's Christian name but also his birthday. The old man, in consequence, had always taken an interest in his grandson, one manifestation of which was his desire to share his pleasure in things Italian with his namesake. Finally, this propaganda bore fruit in the form of a decision by young Henry and his wife Christina to take a family holiday on Lake Garda. They had liked the look of the Hotel Bella Vista and the notion was swiftly transformed into action. No steam engines roaring through Alpine passes for them – in less than two hours they were at Verona airport.

They were greeted at the reception desk by the proprietor, a stocky man of about Henry's father's age. "Your room is in the annexe, Signore and Signora," he explained. "There is plenty of space in the old building for the children and it is next to the garden. It's also quieter than the main hotel and overlooks the lake."

"Thank you," replied Henry. "You speak very good English."

"I was British prisoner of war," replied Alessandro proudly. "I was Commandant's batman. Very important and trustworthy job."

* * * * *

One day, the Whittakers had taken a trip on the lake and caught the hydrofoil back to Bardolino, the next town to Garda, with the intention of walking the mile back to the hotel. There is a level road on the course of the old railway, and halfway along there is a curious, isolated, tall wooden building which now functions as a restaurant. They sat by the water's edge, sipping their drinks and listening to the chatter of birds in a swathe of reeds and sedge growing along the lake margin.

"This must be the old signal box!" exclaimed Henry suddenly. "The one that Father told us about. The engine drivers always whistled here so that people in Garda knew the train was coming. He said you could hear it from where they used to stay." Hugh had always played down the episode of his captivity, but the cheery locomotive whistle was one of the factors in his keeping a grip on reality in the attic.

At the end of the promenade they walked along a gravel beach between the lake and the rear fences of large houses facing the main road. After a while, a narrow lane, more of a footpath, ran at right angles from the beach between wooded gardens and gave onto the main road directly opposite the hotel entrance.

"Safer this way," said Henry junior. "Keeps us away from the traffic on the main road." For some quite inexplicable reason the lane seemed familiar, although of course he had never been there in his life.

* * * * *

The following day, sunny Garda belied its name and it rained hard. Someone was carrying out some maintenance on the old coach house roof, and in the children's bedroom a ladder stretched enticingly though a trapdoor and into a capacious attic. Henry was irresistibly drawn to clamber up and entered the dusty loft. By the light of a small window set in the tiles, he noticed a series of notches cut into one of the transverse roof beams, resting on which was a slim silver penknife. Something prompted him to pick it up and put it in his pocket. On later examination he observed the inscription and date. There was also an old framed sepia photograph of the hotel, with a caption 'Hotel Paradiso, 1939'. Henry descended. "What was the name of the hotel that Grandfather is always talking about?" he asked Christina.

"Paradiso," chipped in his son David, at nine years of age the fount of all knowledge.

* * * * *

Grandfather Henry's eighty-fifth birthday party was a resounding success. Members of the family had gathered from the four corners of the earth; the sun shone on the marquee erected in the garden. Henry senior was in very good spirits and naturally keen to hear about the family venture to Italy. Then it was time to cut the cake and open the presents. The last one was a small, slender package, scarcely four inches long, securely wrapped in Italian gift paper. Henry fumbled at the cover. "Buon Compleanno 1909," he murmured, reading the salutation on the penknife.

* * * * *

Nearly everyone had gone home, leaving the two Henrys and Hugh sitting on canvas chairs outside the tent, glasses in hand.

"How was the hotel, then, Henry?" asked the old man.

"Marvellous. We stayed in the old coach house annexe. Main building was full of Germans."

"It always was," said Hugh.

13
REMEMBER, REMEMBER

The annual bonfire ceremony was the highlight of the year in the ancient town of Market Bradbury. On this occasion, however, there was a pall of gloom rather than smoke over the event, which would be memorable for the wrong reason.

Market Bradbury is an example of what are sometimes called 'decayed towns'. This is not a reference to their state of dilapidation, quite the contrary, reflecting the fact that they have lost status and importance over their long history. They have also declined in population generally. At the last census, Market Bradbury was credited with having 3,206 inhabitants, rather less than half the number living there at the turn of the nineteenth century. Bradbury was granted its first charter by Edward I in 1279, conveying the right to hold markets and fairs, and for many centuries it returned two Members of Parliament. Changing economic patterns have altered all this, and it is many years since Market Bradbury actually held its own market. It no longer elects its own Members of Parliament, and has lost its status as a borough. Main roads and railways passed it by, and its position on a hilltop ruled out the existence of a canal or navigable river.

Such decayed towns can, nevertheless (or perhaps as a consequence), be remarkably pleasant places in which to live. It has what is reputedly the largest square in the country, a magnificent church and many fine houses. It was never fully urbanised, its old buildings were not demolished in the name of progress, and it is generously endowed with mature trees and open spaces. It retains several of the old shops and inns, and the capacious square means that visitors and residents alike can park their cars in the main street, a facility envied by many a larger town.

A relic of the great annual fair persists in the form of the November Bonfire Night ceremony, characterised by firework displays, processions and, of course, culminating in a magnificent conflagration, lit in the middle of the square itself. It seems that the custom of lighting the fire has its origins in the great Christmas beast market, at the conclusion of which all the waste straw, broken hurdles and other debris were piled up in the square and burned, a spectacle much enjoyed by the participants in the proceedings and accompanied by the liberal consumption of ale. This apparently dangerous procedure has never caused any difficulties, given the large space available, and efforts to have the fire sited elsewhere have, down the years, been successfully resisted.

Indeed, it was the practice for long years to accumulate fuel for the fire in an old stone animal pound in the square, but this tended to become unsightly and attract rubbish, so materials are now collected in a field on the edge of the town and the fire is built by the bonfire committee in the square a day or so prior to the event. Some decades ago there occurred a regrettable incident when the fire was lit two days before the scheduled evening, ostensibly by a carelessly discarded cigarette end. This was one of the causes of the removal of the combustible material to Farthings (the mediaeval field names are still in use in Bradbury).

* * * * *

By vagrant standards, the figure walking along the lane towards Market Bradbury appeared really quite respectable. He was clad in what once had been an army greatcoat, the effect of which was somewhat marred by the verdigris on the brass buttons and the length of rope encircling the wearer's middle. A trilby hat, corduroy trousers and serviceable boots completed the ensemble. He proceeded at a stately and measured pace, pushing before him a battered perambulator containing his worldly possessions. He was a stranger in the district, usually operating in the adjoining county some fifty miles further north, but for some reason his peregrinations had brought him to Bradbury. In fact, tramps in general are a diminishing asset in the district. They once were to be seen patrolling the lanes, occasionally seeking casual work, and sleeping in barns where a sympathetic or tolerant farmer raised no objection. In recent years the countryside has become less hospitable, and the opportunities for casual work have all but vanished. Even the itinerants have not escaped the soft embrace of the welfare state, so that they lack the imperative to seek a livelihood on the open road.

It had been a fine autumn day, but at sundown the sky clouded over and a steady drizzle began to fall. The vagrant was passing the field known as Farthings when he spotted the large pile of bonfire material, covered with a tarpaulin, at the edge of the meadow. His long experience with ricks indicated a weatherproof shelter, and he made his way across to the pile. He burrowed expertly into the dry centre of the heap and settled down for a pleasant night's repose.

* * * * *

Some one and a half miles away from Market Bradbury, at the bottom of the hill, lies the twin village of Low Bradbury. Keen rivalry has long existed between the two communities. Because of its convenient location, Low Bradbury attracted the attention of the railway builders in Victorian times. The arrival of the iron road was followed by the establishment of various industries such as a sawmill and a sand quarry, so that the importance and population of Low Bradbury tended to increase as those of Market Bradbury declined. This competition extended to personal relationships, and within living memory it was a bold lad living in either village who would contemplate courting a girl resident in the other. People travel more nowadays, and are as a result much less parochial in their outlook, so this sense of isolation is far less marked. Nowadays it surfaces only occasionally. The railway, unhappily, has disappeared, along with the sand quarry.

The ancient antagonism, if that is not too strong a word, between the Bradburys was revived by the vagaries of fate, in the shape of the draw for the County Association Football Intermediate Cup. Both villages had teams, which normally played in different leagues and hence in the usual course of events never opposed each other on the field of play. This year's cup draw, pairing Market Bradbury with Low Bradbury, generated keen local interest, and a good crowd gathered in the hilltop town to witness the encounter. Low Bradbury was strongly fancied to prevail, and it was a matter of considerable surprise when Market Bradbury ran out the winner by three goals to one. It was, in truth, a vicarious triumph, since no member of the winning team actually lives in the town; several, in fact, come up the hill from Low Bradbury, an irony not lost upon the disgruntled members of the losing eleven. The match took place on the day of the tramp's arrival, the Saturday before the annual bonfire celebrations, and at the conclusion of the game, members of both teams along with a considerable number of spectators adjourned to the Chequers Inn in the market place to fortify themselves with pints of Tadpole, the ferocious local real ale. This is a time-honoured tradition in Bradbury, a recent variant of which, in consequence of more enlightened licensing laws, has been that the participants now use the front door of the inn rather than the rear one.

There was naturally a good deal of discussion and some light-hearted chaff concerning the match. One lad who appeared to feel the defeat keenly was Ben Godfrey, who played in goal for Low Bradbury and had been thought by some observers to have been partly responsible for two of the Market Bradbury goals. He sat on one of the old wooden settles flanking the great fireplace, looking gloomily into his beer and saying little except for a few monosyllables to his friend and teammate Brian. After an hour the throng in the bar began to thin out, and the two men left the inn and collected their motorcycles from the car park at the rear, setting out for Low Bradbury and home. On such excursions it was a matter of honour to reach home first, and Ben jumped on his machine, shot across the square and disappeared down East Street, past the old brewery, heading for Bradbury Lane; his way took him past Farthings. His companion decided on the alternative route along the bottom of the square and down Windmill Hill. There was little to choose from in terms of distance between the two ways, and their motorcycles were well matched. Brian was surprised, therefore, to find himself in Low Bradbury with a clear two minutes advantage, but never gave the matter any further thought.

* * * * *

It had been a dry autumn and the bonfire heap contained some excellent material. The current fashion for replacement plastic window frames had thrown up a quantity of well-seasoned wood, which had considerably enhanced the yearly supply. Fanned by the rising wind, the flames gained hold with remarkable speed. Farthings lay in a little hollow on the far side of the town. It has been noted that it was a dark and unwelcoming evening and the few people who were out of doors were still in the Chequers. It was no surprise, therefore, that nobody was aware of the conflagration until it was a veritable inferno. Some extensive layering of over-grown hedges was being undertaken around the town and burning of the trimmings was a regular occurrence. Smoke and smell therefore attracted little attention.

* * * * *

Extract from the Millington and Wolds Gazette

TRAGIC DEATH OF INTINERANT AT MARKET BRADBURY

At an inquest held on 20th December at Millington, a verdict of Accidental Death was returned in the case of sixty-four-year-old George Hogg, a vagrant who perished when a pile of bonfire material in which he was sheltering ignited prematurely. Medical evidence revealed that his body had been charred beyond recognition and that the precise cause of death could not be adduced; asphyxiation was considered probable. The Station Officer of the county brigade at Murton described the events of the fateful evening. The fire service was alerted by a passing motorist, but not until the fire was well alight, and there was little to be done except damp down the embers, which had been fanned by a vigorous wind. There was no suggestion of human involvement and in view of the location and the nature of the fire, the appliance left when the area was considered safe from further outbreak. One member of the fire crew later recalled seeing what appeared to be the remains of a perambulator at the scene, and reasonably assumed that someone had used the site to deposit litter. The tragedy was discovered the following morning when investigations into the cause of the conflagration commenced. A fire officer, accompanied by a police constable and member of the Market Bradbury Bonfire Committee, carried out an inspection of the area. In the course of this the nature of the fatality became apparent. There was no evidence of any accelerant, or as to how the pile had been ignited. In the Station Officer's view the recent closure of the Market Bradbury fire station, a cause of much public concern, had not significantly affected the outcome.

PC George Hopkins gave evidence of identification. On searching the site he had discovered two round metal discs, distorted and discoloured by the heat, but bearing the legend '22306622 HOGG DG A POS CE'. It transpired that these were army identification tags and the information they contained enabled the deceased's antecedents to be established. Very persistent enquiries had failed to produce any living relatives of the unfortunate man. It appears that he spent many years in the army and at the termination of his service he returned to his hometown of Pitchfield, but had been unable to acclimatise to a settled existence and so had taken to the road. His motive in visiting Market Bradbury remains a mystery.

Summing up, the Coroner commended the actions of all concerned and expressed his sympathy for the unfortunate man's family, should there be any. In the absence of any other information, it should be presumed that the careless use of a cigarette was the most likely cause of the accident. The Coroner also noted his approval of the decision not to proceed with the usual celebrations at Market Bradbury as a mark of respect for the deceased.

The incident generated much macabre interest, and as is usual in such cases, was widely reported. One evening shortly after the publication of the inquest findings, two men were discussing the affair in the White Hart Inn at Pitchfield, the dead man's hometown.

"Dreadful business about old Hogg. I used to see quite a lot of him around the place. Never did anyone any harm."

"You're quite right; he was always known as 'hedge-hog' from his habit of sleeping in hayricks or ditches. Funny thing, though, Billy, I've known him since I was a boy and I've never seen him smoking."

14
MAXIMUM REMISSION

The County Village Cricket Cup Final was the most important occasion in the history of Bumblethorpe Cricket Club. The last thing they needed was the enforced absence of their best batsman.

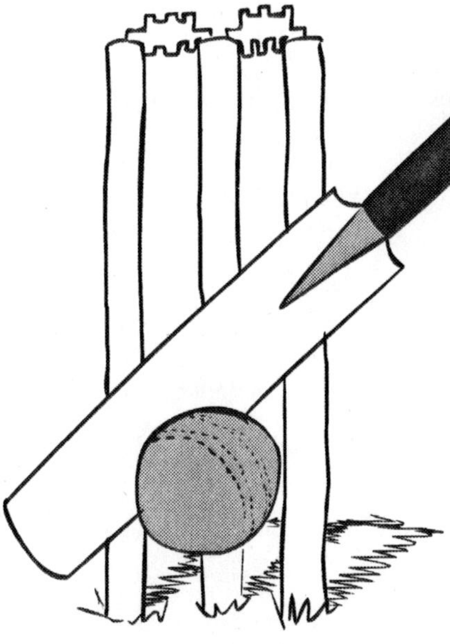

A shaft of strong late summer afternoon sunlight was shining through the upper stained-glass windows of the Victorian magistrates' court, picking out the bright colours and forming a kaleidoscopic pattern on the polished wooden furniture of the room. As befitted its status, the magistrate's chair was delineated in regal gold, while the dock, appropriately, was illuminated in a sepulchral and pessimistic grey-green. The occupant of the chief magistrate's seat was the distinguished holder of that august office, Colonel Sir Piers Edwin Malpas Egerton, DSO, OBE, MC, JP etc. The Colonel was one of the old school, noted for the severity of his punishments and a distinct lack of sympathy for the accused person appearing before him. These attributes, let it be said, were a major contributory factor in the low rate of petty crime in the district. For its own part, the dock was occupied by a male figure, of little more than medium height, square shouldered and of stocky build, with sharp eyes and a resolute expression. He was not yet forty and, in accordance with his appearance, was noted for his sporting achievements. When he was younger he had been a hard and skilful boxer, and was still recognised for activities entailing keen sight and powers of concentration, being a feared opponent on the dartboard and the star batsman in the Bumblethorpe village cricket team. He was of Gypsy extraction and rejoiced in the name of Ezekiel Smith, or Zeke to all and sundry. His present brush with the law arose out of various offences concerning vehicle insurance and MOT certificates. Zeke was self-employed as a dealer in scrap metal, logs or any other saleable commodity. His past record was lamentable and he had on this occasion been warned that a finding of 'guilty' could result in a custodial sentence.

This was a serious prospect, not only for Zeke but also for the Bumblethorpe cricket team, of which it will be recalled he was a vital component. The team had enjoyed a most successful season and had reached the final of the county village knockout competition for the first time in its history. Their opponents, Great Umbridge, were an unknown quantity, as that village is located some distance from Bumblethorpe, on the far side of the river, and the teams had never previously met. The final was to be played on neutral ground on the following Saturday, and Bumblethorpe could ill afford the absence of their star player. It was with great trepidation, therefore, that the verdict of the magistrate was awaited.

"I find that you are guilty as charged on all counts, Smith," intoned the Colonel. "You have already been warned of the likely outcome of such a finding. In this instance I am remanding you until next Monday pending the receipt of reports, upon which you will be sentenced. You may stand down until 11 a.m. on Monday."

These words were greeted by those present in the courtroom with absolute incredulity. Colonel Egerton had no truck with such things as reports, and was accustomed to hand out sentences at the conclusion of the case with little or no delay. The magistrates' clerk, the local reporter, the court usher, Smith's supporters from the cricket team and various hangers-on were dumbstruck. Whatever could this mean?

At dusk the solitary figure strode purposefully along the lane and approached the wicket-gate at the side entrance to the Old Rectory. He was somewhat above medium height, well built with square shoulders, sharp eyes and a resolute chin. He moved surprisingly lightly for a man of such stature and appeared to glide along on his toes, like a cat. The wicket-gate was freshly painted white, with ironwork picked out in shiny black, had well-oiled hinges and a small brass plate bearing the legend 'PEM EGERTON Tradesmen's Entrance'. The figure closed the gate behind him and made his way along the edge of the tennis court and through the immaculate gardens towards the house. In the complete absence of any alteration, the latter bore the same appearance as on the day it was built some three hundred years earlier, except, of course, that it had matured.

The day of the cricket final dawned bright and sunny. All concerned made their respective ways to Ficklebury, the neutral venue situated about halfway between Bumblethorpe and Great Umbridge. Rumours and speculation concerning the supposed merits of the two elevens and the likely outcome were naturally rife. The extraordinary means by which Zeke had evaded incarceration was high on this agenda. It also appeared that Great Umbridge had their own secret weapon in the form of a demon fast bowler. Well, their progress to the final had seen them take some notable scalps, including those of Low Scumble, Dry Stapleton and Utterby Magna, all of these teams having been finalists in recent years. The bowler who had wrought such havoc was none other than Police Constable Alan Michael Bush, who was a new arrival in the district and had rapidly acquired the sobriquets of 'Ambush' and 'Fuzz', for obvious reasons. To raise the stakes even further, it was

Bush who had been the chief witness at Zeke Smith's trial. This was clearly going to be the Day of Reckoning.

The captains were on the pitch. Great Umbridge won the toss and elected to bat first. They reached the respectable total of one hundred and sixty-one in their thirty-five overs, thanks largely to an unbeaten seventy by Fuzz, who as well as being a feared bowler was clearly no slouch with the bat either. He rapidly showed his mettle with the ball by dismissing three of Bumblethorpe's top batting order with only thirty-one runs on the board, and it began to appear that the longed-for fairy-tale ending to the season would turn out to be a nightmare. Smith was the next man in. He walked from the pavilion to the wicket with his light, casual gait, a confident smile on his face.

"Middle and leg," he asked.

He had to face the first ball of a new over from Bush, who summoned up every last ounce of his power and venom, took a twenty-yard run and launched a ferocious full-length ball, pitching on Zeke's toes. The latter, completely at ease and with apparently all the time in the world, took a full pace outside off stump and, with hardly any perceptible effort, hit the ball over the longest boundary and into the pond, causing panic among the assembled coots. Bush's next ball was short, whizzing past Zeke's ears and receiving the same treatment as the first. The third ball was despatched all along the ground to the pavilion. A rope had been placed around the boundary and the ball hit this, leapt into the air and landed on the table occupied by the Great Umbridge scorer, knocking over his glass of beer and landing painfully in his lap.

"Did you get that one, George?" enquired his opposite number from Bumblethorpe solicitously.

Zeke took twenty-one runs from the first over, contriving a single off the last ball in order to keep the bowling. Bush had only one over left from his allotted seven, so he retired wounded, donned his police motorcyclist's helmet and took up his fielding position at short leg, where he remained. Obviously, Smith could not contrive to monopolise the bowling for the entire innings, and at the other end a steady procession of wickets fell. The climax approached with the Bumblethorpe score of one hundred and fifty with eight wickets down and one over left. It was now or never for both sides. Zeke cut the first ball of Bush's over – they had kept him in reserve for just such a contingency – very late, and despite the fielder's despairing dive it hit the boundary rope – one hundred and fifty-four. The next one ran down the hill to fine leg and the batsman scampered a single – one hundred and fifty-five. The Bumblethorpe tail-ender now had the unenviable task of facing Fuzz at his most virulent. He groped wildly with his bat in the direction of the ball, which fortuitously missed not only the wicket but also evaded the wicketkeeper's glove.

"Run!" yelled Zeke and the batsman took two byes – one hundred and fifty-seven.

But no! The Great Umbridge umpire called, "One short," meaning that the score remained at one hundred and fifty-six with three balls to go and five runs needed.

Disaster struck. Bush shattered the wicket of Smith's partner with his fourth ball, bringing the last man in with two balls remaining. Somehow, Bumblethorpe's forlorn hope managed to get his bat to the ball and they ran a single. This made the score one hundred and fifty-seven with one ball left. The only way in which they could lift the cup outright was for Zeke to hit the last ball for six. Four runs would result in a tie.

Total silence fell over the ground as Bush pounded up to bowl. Zeke, bat lifted, had shuffled two paces down the wicket, intending to heave the ball full toss over the boundary. At the last second, Bush realised what was happening and bowled slow, low and short. Unable to get the requisite elevation, Zeke hit the ball with all his power off the centre of the bat. It sped along the ground at lightning speed. The square-leg umpire saw it coming and just in time leapt to his left. There was a loud report when the ball struck the policeman's helmet, which had been on the ground behind the square-leg umpire, who called "Obstruction on the pitch – five runs." Bumblethorpe's name was on the cup.

On the following Monday morning the saga of the court case resumed. The presiding magistrate, Colonel Egerton, announced his decision.

"I have studied the relevant reports and in the light of their content have decided that the appropriate sentence in this case will be two hundred hours community service. It is in the public interest that you be gainfully employed for this period rather than be idling your time in a prison cell. You are free to go."

That evening, Zeke was in his accustomed place at the bar of the Three Horseshoes in Bumblethorpe, accompanied by a number of his cronies.

"How did you pull this one, Zeke?" asked one.

"Easy, mate. You probably know that the Colonel is President of the Bumblethorpe Cricket Club? He and I made a pact. He said that the offences were worth three months in jail, but that he would knock off one day for every run I scored in the final. Once I reached ninety-two I knew I was safe."

"Taking a bit of a risk, weren't you, dealing with him?"

"Not at all. The Colonel is a gentleman, and a gentleman's word is his bond. We shook hands on it and we sealed it with a drop of his best whisky."

"What's all this about reports?"

"The only report he wanted to see was the report of the cricket match."

"And what about this community service lark?"

"You remember those gales last autumn – knocked down a lot of trees over by the common. I'm going to clear them up for the public benefit. Some decent oak logs there, too. The Colonel will get a couple of tons and the rest are mine."

"What about Ambush?"

"Oh, he'll be all right. He's new around here and hasn't settled down yet. I had a drink with him after the game and he tells me he has his eye on a cottage in Bumblethorpe. I'll drop him a few logs for his house-warming. I also suggested he plays his cricket locally next season. We could do with another bowler since Arthur left."

15
SAFE DEPOSIT

The ancient tower on the town walls appeared to provide the answer to the search for a new home for the Tourist Information Bureau. Although long disused, it still had the capacity to spring a surprise.

It has been claimed that tourism is now the world's greatest industry. Whether this is the case or not, it is certainly true that the number of people visiting the picturesque ancient town of Haversham has been steadily growing over the past few years. As one consequence, it was recently determined that the town needed a larger and more up-to-date Tourist Information Office, and the search for suitable premises was immediately initiated.

The town has a long, varied and interesting history. The Romans established a fort protected by earth ramparts around AD 120, and owing to its position at the estuary of a navigable river and the possession of a sheltered harbour, this grew into the town of Cerastium. Gardeners will recognise this name as that attributed to the garden flower known commonly as 'Snow in Summer', and its scientific title is believed to be derived from the fact that it grows profusely in the district. In modern times the harbour has silted up and is no longer accessible to the larger vessels now in use. When the railway arrived in 1857, an embankment was constructed to carry the tracks across the river mouth with a system of sluice gates in the main channel to enable the river water to drain into the sea. Likewise, these can be closed, retaining the high tidal water in a large lagoon. This facility has made Haversham a Mecca for boating, since it remains connected to the national river and canal system and further adds to the town's popularity.

In due course the town defences were reconstructed in stone, and over succeeding centuries they were frequently enlarged, altered, repaired or robbed out as historical events dictated. The walls were penetrated by various gates, two of which remain. The gate situated on the river wharf was known as the Water Gate for obvious reasons, and at some stage the gateway was blocked, leaving a solid square tower with crenellations and other defensive embellishments. This tower was extended or rebuilt many times, and in the more peaceful climate obtaining in the period since the English Civil War it has seen a great variety of uses – among them a brewery, the town jail, a butcher's shambles and a blacksmith's shop. Evidence of the latter lasted for years in the form of two forges and wooden beams festooned with old horseshoes. In more recent times it has remained empty and was at one stage under threat of removal in the interests of road traffic. This proposal naturally aroused vociferous opposition, since the tower has symbolic associations with the whole town, and it was not pursued.

It became apparent, however, that the Water Gate tower would be the ideal location for the Tourist Information Bureau, and since it extends to several storeys, the upper floors would make the logical home for the museum, the establishment of which has been mooted for many years. It was not immediately clear who owned the tower, but following a public enquiry, freehold was vested in perpetuity in the name of the town, and management in the town council. Help was sought and obtained from the Heritage Lottery Fund and this enabled work to begin.

A prerequisite was the complete survey of the building to ascertain its condition and to prepare detailed plans for the alterations which were envisaged. This was by no means straightforward, since the tower was a veritable warren of thick stone walls, chambers small and large (some without windows and many of irregular shape), cellars, spiral staircases, passages and vaults. As far as could be established, no earlier plans existed and the surveyors were starting from scratch. Eventually, they were able to create some order out of centuries of chaotic development and retired to their offices to discuss what they had discovered. After some time it became apparent that there was something wrong with their recorded dimensions, which literally did not add up. There seemed to be either something erroneous in the measurements, or some aspect of the building which they had overlooked. There was an area of about ten feet square in the centre of the tower at the first-floor level which could not be accounted for. The obvious assumption was that a hidden chamber existed.

The two men hurried back to the tower. A narrow crooked staircase extended from the first to the second floor, ending in a small landing. At this point, one wall was covered with dark wooden wainscot, studded with square-headed handmade iron nails. Something prompted the younger surveyor to examine these closely. On so doing he discovered that one was loose and could be extracted fairly readily to the extent of a couple of inches, whereupon it formed a kind of handle. When this was turned, a section of the panelling swung inward, giving access to a space behind the wall. A dank, musty smell was detected, reminiscent of a church crypt.

Peering into the darkness, he shone a small torch, which he habitually carried for use during survey operations, down into a cavernous chamber. “My God!” he cried. “We need a ladder, Chris, and a stronger light.”

* * * * *

The sole occupant of the tower, hearing a knock on the heavy street door, shuffled along the gloomy passage, peered through a grilled spy-hole and, apparently satisfied by what he saw, drew the iron bolts and admitted the visitor, carefully securing the door again. The newcomer, from his dress, appeared to be a foreigner. The proprietor signalled him to follow and the pair entered a chamber on the ground floor, where a cheerful fire burned in a massive grate, illuminating the bare stone walls. The guest proffered a leather bag to the old man, who examined the contents by the light of the fire and an oil lantern. Motioning the stranger to remain seated, he took a lighted candle and left the room, ascending a narrow staircase which opened onto a small landing on the second floor, one wall of which was covered with wooden panels. He glanced briefly over his shoulder, then manipulated a square iron stud nail set in the wainscot, upon which a small door opened inwards. Reassuring himself once more that he was alone, he entered the chamber, lit two further candles placed in sconces, and prepared to descend a rickety ladder which stretched down to the floor. As he attempted to close the hidden door it was wrenched out of his hand by the visitor, who had crept surreptitiously up the staircase behind him. A brief scuffle ensued, during which the intruder inadvertently closed the door behind him, and half-sliding, half-falling, both men found themselves at the foot of the ladder. The chamber was some ten feet square and of similar depth, and windowless; standing along one wall were four large wooden chests, reinforced with iron straps and secured with padlocks. The old man’s candle had been extinguished in the struggle and the only light available radiated dimly from the two candles at the head of the ladder; the corners of the room were in virtual darkness. No word had been spoken during the whole proceedings. The old man then seized a heavy wooden stave lying on one of the chests and advanced menacingly upon the visitor, whose hitherto-concealed dagger glinted in the candlelight. The old man swung the club with all his power, forcing his adversary to retreat into the shadows of the far corner. As he did so there was a loud metallic clang and an audible crack of bone, followed by a cry of agony from the intruder as the sprung mantrap closed on his leg. He dropped the dagger. The tower proprietor picked it up and stabbed wildly at his opponent, eventually penetrating his neck. He fell, bleeding profusely. The old man turned to climb the ladder and make good his escape, intending to leave his adversary to die. He had already mounted the first few worn wooden rungs when the robber mustered his final desperate lunge and succeeded in grasping the old man's cloak. Their combined weight proved too great for the decrepit ladder, which was wrenched from its fastening and fell to the floor, disintegrating in the process. Later, the flame of the remaining candle, burnt low and guttering, finally sank. A red glow briefly marked the stub of the wick and a thin wisp of smoke ascended into the eternal darkness.

* * * * *

Dr RJK Armitage was born in Haversham and following a distinguished university career had returned to his native habitat, quickly establishing a reputation for himself in the town. He was not a doctor of medicine, but of some obscure academic subject, was a gifted teacher and had also found time to qualify as a solicitor. He was never happier than when haranguing an audience on any topic you care to name. He specialised in local history and rapidly became the acknowledged authority on anything concerning the town and its rich, colourful and varied background. He was, in addition, the local coroner, and had been the logical choice for the post of curator for the proposed new museum.

Following the revelation of the grisly secret chamber in the tower, the police rapidly established that whilst a crime had clearly been committed, this was historic and that no formal investigation on their part was called for. Further, as their statement indicated, "They were not looking for anyone in connection with the matter." For the coroner, this was too good an opportunity to miss, so he decided that since there had occurred two deaths in suspicious circumstances, an inquest was necessary. Another matter falling under his jurisdiction was that of treasure trove, in view of the contents of the chests discovered in the tower, whose ownership could not be established and which clearly had been concealed. Since the person best qualified to unravel the historical mystery was Dr Armitage himself, he was placed in a compromised position; he could hardly adjudicate on his own evidence. He resolved the matter by the simple process of handing the case to his deputy, and then taking centre stage.

When the inquiry got under way, the two surveyors briefly testified to their discovery of the hidden chamber, the broken ladder and the existence on the floor of two skeletons. One had a dagger wedged in the neck vertebrae and a mantrap closed over a broken shinbone. In the remains of a cloak which the other deceased had been wearing was a heavy bunch of keys which fitted the locks on the banded chests containing large quantities of precious metals and stones. The atmosphere in the room was extremely stale but quite dry, and the wooden and cloth relics were remarkably well preserved with little sign of rot or insect damage. Extensive paper records were also in existence, protected inside the airtight chests. Also discovered was a small drawstring bag made of wash leather, which contained several jewelled finger rings.

For his part, Armitage began by confidently asserting that he knew the identity of the resident of the tower. He explained: "Official population censuses did not begin in the United Kingdom before 1801, and these men met their deaths prior to that date. I therefore had recourse to the Pipe Rolls, which as is generally known were instituted during the reign of Henry II, continuing until the abolition of the Pipe Office in 1834." Armitage was warming to his theme. "The Pipe Rolls were the means by which county sheriffs accounted to the exchequer for the revenues raised on behalf of the Crown. Much information can be gathered, therefore, concerning who had paid taxes. There are parallels to the present-day tax system. I discovered that prior to 1776 one Solomon Tulk, a citizen of this town carrying on business as a pawnbroker, moneylender and dealer in precious metals and stones, had regularly paid tax to the Exchequer, but from that date onwards such tributes ceased. Now Tulk was a well-known figure in Haversham and there are many references to him in other documents, not least those discovered in the tower chamber, but no record of his moving nor yet of his death. No evidence exists of his interment in the old Jewish cemetery in Pillory Lane.

"From his occupation as a pawnbroker he was known locally as Uncle Solomon, which does not imply that he was a benevolent elder member of the family. The term is said to derive from the Latin 'uncus', meaning a hook, a device used by pawnbrokers to lift items before the spout was invented."

The whole affair had aroused great interest, nationally as well as locally, and there was a sizeable press presence throughout the court proceedings. Armitage was a perfectionist, and noted for his antipathy towards the editors of newspapers carrying reports of his proceedings if he deemed them to be inaccurate, too brief, or misleading. Upon Armitage's last pronouncement, the reporter from the *Pitchfield Post* muttered to his compatriot from the *Haversham Herald*, "What on earth is he talking about, George?"

"Not the faintest idea, mate. I'm going to leave that bit out."

Armitage now had the bit between his teeth. This was his finest hour and he was resolved to make the most of it. "The term 'Uncle', now universally applied to pawnbrokers, is first recorded in connection with Uncle Solomon, and I'm further satisfied that he perished in the tower in November 1776. This is borne out by the dates of coins contained in the chests, and on documents lending further support also found in the chamber. Now, as regards the other victim, I'm persuaded that he had visited the tower in order to do business with Solomon and had resolved to rob him. He had reckoned without the security measures which the pawnbroker had installed. The dagger is decorated on its hilt with amber, a substance widely obtained in the Baltic, so it appears that he originated from that area, assuming that the dagger was his, naturally. In the past, Haversham was a member of the Hanseatic League, one of only three cities in this country to have that distinction." The two reporters exchanged glances and shrugged. "Since that time, trade has been maintained with northern European countries. We cannot say for certain what took place inside the chamber, but it seems most probable that an accident prevented Solomon Tulk from leaving, and that he starved to death, whereas the injuries from the mantrap and the dagger were the likely cause of the other's demise."

Unsurprisingly, these opinions were subsequently endorsed by the deputy coroner, who also, in a separate ruling, declared that the valuables contained in the chests were treasure trove. They consisted in the main of coins and jewels to the total value at present-day prices in excess of £33 million. Under the rules which govern such things, those items became the property of the Crown, and the two lucky surveyors who unearthed them were the recipients of very substantial rewards. Naturally, these remarkable finds aroused the newspaper editors' power of invention, and sensational headlines such as 'Uncle Solomon's Mines' and 'The Haversham Hoard' were the order of the day.

The Crown gracefully consented to the long-term loan of many of the items in the treasure to the town, to form the centrepiece of the new museum. They are displayed in the old secret chamber, where appropriate security measures are established. Health and Safety officials have, however, placed a bar on mantraps. The Tourist Information Bureau is kept busy informing tourists (who come in increasing numbers) about the remarkable history of the town and the tower in particular, and the latest touch-screen interactive video interpretation has been installed. On the second floor there is an attractive and popular restaurant specialising in the local seafood delicacies. To popular acclaim it was named 'Solomon's Prawnshop'.

16
NOT WANTED ON VOYAGE

The would-be merchant seaman proved to be of vital importance on his first trip aboard the ocean liner.

The confluence of the two rivers lies some eight miles from the sea proper and the waters flow in a broad, straight and deep channel down to meet the ocean. The site is tidal and sheltered with convenient banks for the construction of wharves and, not surprisingly, has been a port for at least two thousand years. The continuous process of dredging allied to the building of improved docks has ensured that the largest ships afloat can still call – not only tankers and cargo boats but also ocean liners, replaced in the modern era of air travel by cruise ships. About halfway along the eastern shore a tributary stream joins the main waterway, wide at the juncture and with extensive mudflats at low tide. This presented a barrier to the construction of the railway, as it had done to the earlier roads, and the chosen solution in both cases was to cross the side stream some miles from the mouth. The effect of this was the delineation of a large triangle of land whose sides were formed by the main channel to the west, the secondary river to the north and the main road and railway to the east; this was poorly furnished with communications and remained strangely remote and cut off from the surrounding areas of much more intensive development. There were a few small farms, some market gardening activities and small-scale quarrying of sand and gravel, the geological legacy of the area's formation. No large settlement had been established and the population was scattered.

I lived there as a boy in the hamlet of Coxheath and knew the area intimately. It offered excellent opportunities for bird's-nesting and similar activities now proscribed in our more enlightened times. I had naturally been familiar with the procession of ships passing to and from the port and had resolved that one day I should pursue a career as a merchant seaman. Fortunately, my father supported me in my juvenile aspirations and, being acquainted with the captain of a passenger vessel, had arranged that I should travel on a certain voyage as a supernumerary crew member to gain what nowadays would be described as 'work experience'. I am not sure whether my father thought that such an undertaking would prove to be a deterrent to my ambitions; if so, in the event it had the opposite effect. It was thus that I joined the ship's company of the passenger liner *Paradise* for the journey which took me to Cape Town and back and the biggest adventure of my young life.

The Captain was a kind-hearted man and was true to his promise to my father that he would keep an eye on me during the voyage. I became a sort of messenger-boy and odd-job man and was kept very busy running errands and helping out all over the ship, in the process finding my way around an ocean-going vessel and discovering a great deal about how it functioned. As we approached our home port on the return leg of the journey I happened to take the Captain's afternoon coffee up to the bridge. On my arrival I noticed that he was not alone, but was in earnest conversation with the ship's doctor. I hesitated to disturb the great man, who was obviously dealing with something of importance, so I lurked behind the door, within earshot of the two officers' conversation.

"I'm afraid there's no doubt about it, Skipper," said the medical officer. "It's typhoid and, barring miracles, he's a goner."

"All right, Jonathan, keep me posted, will you?"

"Aye, aye, sir." And the doctor was gone.

As I have said, I had succeeded in ingratiating myself with the Captain and by the end of the voyage had free run of the bridge. After all, he was a family friend, and since I was not a true crew member he could probably relax with me to an extent that naval discipline precluded with the members of the ship's company. Shortly after the incident with the doctor he told me to go to the ship's radio room to collect an urgent message that had been transmitted over the radio-telegraph. In those days, communications had not achieved their present level of sophistication and we received written missives on a sort of teleprinter. The radio officer was as familiar with me as the Captain and handed me a large printed sheet without bothering to seal it. Naturally, I read the text avidly. It emanated from the shipping line HQ and the contents were at once exhilarating and alarming.

> *'An outbreak of typhoid has been confirmed in West Africa,' it ran. 'International rules provide that all vessels calling at Freetown must be inspected and receive clearance from the Port Health Authority before docking in the United Kingdom. Failure to comply will result in ships being placed in quarantine. No disembarkation will be permitted until authority obtained. Pilot joining* Paradise *for the final approach will convey further information.'*

I ran to the bridge and handed the signal to the Captain, who at once convened a meeting of the ship's officers. In the confusion, my presence in the Captain's cabin was overlooked.

"What's the situation with your patient?" he asked the doctor.

"I was on my way to see you, Skipper. Died at 3.36 p.m."

"We have a major emergency on our hands," announced the Captain, and he briefly outlined the facts. "I've experienced this sort of thing before. They'll anchor the ship in the roads and check every nook and cranny. All persons on the passenger and crew manifest must be accounted for and their state of health verified. If this ship is quarantined we'll have three hundred and sixty-seven disgruntled passengers on board who are unable to disembark. Quite a number of them are not in the best frame of mind following that lively crossing of the Bay of Biscay."

I didn't gather from any of this how long quarantine would last in such cases, but recalled reading in a book that originally it was forty days (the term 'quarantine' derives from the Italian word 'quaranta', meaning forty). Four days would be too long, let alone forty. We were supposed to set sail to Buenos Aires next Thursday.

"Has anyone any intelligent suggestions?" continued the Captain. "I exclude throwing the corpse overboard from that category," he added.

My moment of glory had arrived; I stepped out of my half-concealment behind a pillar. "Yes, sir. We pass close to the shore at Coxheath. Take him ashore and bury him." My sudden appearance, my extreme youth and the extraordinary remark caused a near-uproar.

"Just calm down," interposed the Captain. "Out of the mouths of babes and sucklings, as the Good Book says. How do you propose to achieve that, young fellow?"

"Easy. They can't be everywhere at once, and while the upper decks are being inspected and the passengers checked, slip ashore from the baggage port on H deck forward."

"But motorboats make a noise."

"Not all of them," I replied. An eccentric inventor had designed a ship's tender driven by battery-powered propeller. The range was strictly limited by battery life, but a short trip was all that we needed. As pure luck would have it, the shipping line had agreed to take such a boat on board, but no serious attempt had been made to employ it, although providentially the batteries had been kept charged. The 'Lightning Launch' was just the thing.

"What will you do when you reach the shore?"

"Leave that to me, sir. I know every inch of this coast."

"This is total madness," protested the Bosun, an old-fashioned disciplinarian who had been at sea for forty years and clearly disapproved not only of the scheme but also its originator.

"I'll think it over and decide what to do," announced the Captain. "Meanwhile, it goes without saying that you are all sworn to absolute secrecy, in the interests of the ship and all who sail in her. Wait here, my lad," this last to me as the officers dispersed. "Assuming that I agree to this lunatic plan, how would you dispose of the … er, evidence?"

"Two of us go ashore. There are trenching tools in some of the larger lifeboats. The soil is very sandy and we can have him underground in no time. There will be nothing to identify him or link him with us. We can get back to the ship easily before she's allowed into harbour."

And bizarre as it sounded, that is exactly what happened. We picked up the pilot at sundown near the entrance to the sound and he directed the ship to drop anchor some five miles up the estuary, right opposite Coxheath. A team of customs men, coastguards, police, medical officers and Lord knows who else swarmed all over the liner. The unfortunate decedent, sealed in a canvas bag and tied across a stretcher purloined from the sickbay, was surreptitiously slipped into the electric launch accompanied by myself and another person, whom I to this day could not identify, armed with pointed spades. The little boat shot away as silently as a ghost into the darkness and minutes later it grated on the sandy shore close to where a small tributary added a fresh trickle to the mighty ocean. The boat was secured to a convenient tree, and the burden carried up a track ascending the low sandy cliff. I knew exactly where I was going – into a small irregularly shaped field formerly used as grazing for a couple of horses. The old owner had moved away from the area a year back and the pasture lay neglected and untouched, surrounded by overgrown hedges. Under the light of a friendly full moon, our desperate efforts made short work of concealing the dead man in a shallow grave under a canopy of hawthorn and bramble. Our elation at the success of our mission was shattered when, making our way cautiously down the rough track giving access to the shore, we were abruptly confronted by a human figure. In the bright moonlight the buttons on his policeman's uniform were quite unmistakable. I had no doubt as to his identity; we only had one policeman in the district. Everyone knew him and he knew everyone else. There was no possible way that anyone on shore could have been privy to our plan and we were clearly the victims of some extraordinary coincidence. Perhaps he was on the lookout for poachers. A notorious local character had developed a remarkable skill with a bow and arrow, which it will be recalled does not make the same noise as a shotgun. Known for obvious reasons as Robin Hood, he was the plague of the local landowners' stock of pheasants.

All three of us froze for an instant. Whilst we were no longer carrying a corpse, to be discovered on a moonlit night on the seashore in possession of a stretcher and two spades was, to put it mildly, suspicious. To our complete amazement, the policeman neither challenged us nor indeed paid us any particular regard, but walked off in the opposite direction to that taken by us.

* * * * *

Brambles grow at a prodigious rate and in a short time the neglected pasture was a tangle of vegetation. Ash, oak and elder saplings gained hold and in a few years the field was completely overgrown. Nearly three decades after my adventure the peace of this remote corner was disturbed once more. Owing to a building boom in the district, the possibility of further mineral extraction was being investigated, as it was realised that there were still substantial reserves of suitable sand and gravel available. Thus it came about that the field was cleared of the untrammelled growth of bushes and trees. One day a man walking his dog near the workings noticed what appeared to be a human skull in soil recently disturbed by mechanical diggers – it is a remarkable fact that nearly all dead bodies are recorded as being found by 'a man walking his dog'; the government must actively encourage dog ownership as a cost-effective means of tracing missing persons.

The brass band played merrily on the quayside and the sun shone brightly on the festive proceedings. The brand new cruise ship *Paradise Two* was dressed in flags and bunting for her introduction to the public prior to embarking on her maiden voyage. I had the honour as Senior Captain and Commodore of the company's fleet to be appointed to command the gleaming leviathan. A large and august company had been invited to the unveiling, among these being the recently appointed Chief Constable of the county. He was a local man, having begun his career as village constable in nearby Coxheath some thirty years previously. After distinguished service he had come full circle to lead the county constabulary. We greeted each other on the upper deck.

"Long time no see," he remarked.

"Congratulations on your appointment," I said.

"Likewise to you," he replied.

"Funny business about that skeleton out at Coxheath," the Chief Constable continued.

I looked at him warily. Just making conversation, I thought.

"No one reported missing and no sign of identification. Couldn't be local. Wonder where he came from?"

"Well, if it wasn't from the land, perhaps it was from the sea," I ventured, immediately regretting my words.

He looked sharply at me in his policeman's fashion, but the subject had now taken on a horrible fascination. "Wondered about that myself. Any ideas?"

"Is this a formal enquiry?" I asked tentatively.

"No," he said. "If you'll pardon the mix of metaphors, when you have a skeleton in your cupboard you don't rock the boat, nor anyone else's boat for that matter."

His manner had become conspiratorial and I knew instinctively what he meant. I took the plunge and gave him a quick synopsis of the events. "What were you doing out by the beach on that night all those years ago, then?" I queried. "Looking for poachers?"

"No," said the policeman. "At the material time I was chasing after a girl. She lived with her father in an estate cottage on the Earl of Greystoke's property. He was a gamekeeper or some such. He hated the sight of me and had forbidden his daughter to have anything to do with me. Said she was too young. We had an assignation that night and I couldn't afford to be seen by anyone in that area, whatever their business was. A couple of days later I was suddenly posted to Littlebury at the other end of the county and never came back until three weeks ago. I think the Superintendent used to go shooting on the estate and her father had a quiet word with him. I never even had the chance to explain to her why I didn't show."

"Why don't you go and do so right now?" I asked. "She's over there, in the pink hat."

"How on earth do you know that?"

"We've been married for twenty-five years, old boy. That trip ashore had far-reaching consequences."

He took two paces across the deck, turned and came back. “What’s your first cruise destination?”

“Cape Town.”

“Will you be calling in West Africa?”

“Not this time.”

“One final thing. How come they never traced the missing person on the ship’s passenger and crew lists?”

“There’s one category of traveller who doesn’t appear.”

“What?”

“Stowaways,” I replied.

17
WATCH THE BIRDIE

The town was plagued by a persistent thief, who acquired the nickname 'The Cat' from his silent, stealthy activities. He was finally brought to book in a most unexpected fashion.

The B6622 crosses the river by a picturesque four-arch brick bridge with pedestrian refuges built into the pillars set into the riverbed, favourite places for observing the trout in the clear water or for hoping to catch a glimpse of a kingfisher upstream. The road meanders for twenty miles across country as far as Allbury. Just on the far side of the river, Sandy Lane leads off to the left and ascends a gentle slope into the trees. In prehistoric times this formed the edge of a large lake, and Sandy Lane is well named: the soil hereabouts consists of a light and well-drained stratum of loam on top of pure sand. During the 1930s a number of dormer bungalows were erected on the south side of Sandy Lane, and there has been no further residential development since. In those days, houses were blessed with much larger gardens than is the fashion nowadays, so they enjoy considerable privacy. The conditions favour the growth of trees and the gardens have naturally matured to a considerable extent. The houses themselves have been enlarged and improved, so that what once was considered an area somewhat beyond the pale has now become a highly sought-after location. Sandy Lane itself leads nowhere in particular and so the passing traffic is minimal. Many of the residents are retired and the large gardens present a challenge to people who are no longer as active as they once were. This combination of circumstances presents opportunities to a new breed of entrepreneur – the jobbing gardener, equipped with a second-hand van or a trailer, a couple of motorised mowers and sundry hand tools.

One such gentleman, whose vehicle bore the legend 'Green Fingers' and a cartoon-style representation of a hand with only three digits depicted in green paint on the side panels, had several regular customers among the population of Sandy Lane. He was aged about fifty, from his accent was not indigenous to the area and had been carrying on his business for three or four years. He was reserved and quietly spoken and had gained a deserved reputation for reliability. The lawns were cut, the shrubs trimmed and the weeds attacked at prescribed intervals and to an agreeable standard. Introductions to new customers, appointments to undertake work and other arrangements were all made verbally. Payment for his services was invariably made in cash, and the only written record of any transactions appeared to be kept in a well-thumbed red notebook residing on the dashboard of his ex-post office van.

He was referred to as 'Jim', and nobody could recollect hearing his surname or having any awareness of where he lived. He was such a familiar figure that nobody questioned his presence in anyone's back garden and he would frequently carry out his tasks in the householder's absence. Apart from grateful acceptance of a cup or two of sweet tea, his communication with his customers was limited to matters concerning business or the occasional comment upon the weather. He was singularly well equipped, therefore, to observe the inhabitants of Sandy Lane or, for that matter, any other location where he obtained work, and to note their habits and style of life. He knew who owned a dog and which houses had security lighting or burglar alarms; he was acquainted with people's movements and knew who was on holiday or went every Thursday afternoon to visit her sister and who played bowls on Wednesday evenings during the summer. He also knew where folk stored their ladders, steps and suchlike and where they hid the spare keys to their houses, garages and outbuildings. Whilst such information was of little horticultural significance, it had great value in the pursuance of Jim's other career, that of a professional house burglar.

Of course, he observed certain hard and fast rules. For instance, he never used the familiar 'Green Fingers' van after dark – people do not cut lawns nor root up stinging nettles at night. He would never target a house where he was currently employed, lest his presence there might be associated with a theft taking place around the same time. He stole only cash or small portable items of high value. His thefts were planned to the smallest detail and with the utmost care. He never robbed the same house twice. Under no circumstances would he inflict any damage apart from effecting forced entry. So thorough were his methods that he had been able to conduct his clandestine activities for over two years without any serious risk of detection. After all, who would associate that quiet, hard-working, sober, reliable and pleasant man with such a thing?

Major and Mrs Balding had resided at number 17 Sandy Lane for a number of years. They were a delightful retired couple who loved country life and in particular were keen amateur ornithologists. The area was absolutely ideal for such a hobby, as it was noted for the rich variety of birdlife inhabiting the locality. Such species as spotted flycatcher, long-tailed tit, gold crest, nuthatch, tree creeper, nightingale and blackcap were almost commonplace in the Baldings' garden, which was a veritable bird's paradise of ponds, nesting boxes, feeding stations and all the other paraphernalia favoured by the bird fancier. It goes without saying that cats were strictly banned.

One morning, Jim was working in the rear garden belonging to Mrs Pritchard, a widow living alone in Sandy Lane a short distance away from the Baldings, with whom she was on friendly terms. It so happened that the bird enthusiasts had called on Mrs Pritchard for morning coffee, which was taken in the lounge with the patio doors wide open onto a balmy spring day. The hostess was profoundly deaf and since she usually neglected to use her hearing aid, conversation was addressed to her at a very high volume. She, for her part, assuming that everyone else shared her affliction, shouted back. It was not difficult, therefore, for Jim, bent and apparently engrossed over his weeding, to overhear their conversation, during which the Baldings indicated that they would be away from home for a fortnight commencing next Sunday. His next victims had been selected.

At 8.30 a.m. on the Monday morning he parked his van at some remove and surreptitiously made his way to the Baldings' rear garden. It was well grown with trees and shrubs and enjoyed total privacy. The visitor was, of course, aware that there was no intruder alarm or light triggered by movement detected around the house, and that nobody had been deputised to feed any cats. He also knew where Major Balding stored his ladders. It was the work of a moment to ascend the steps up towards the dormer window. As he drew close to his target he observed a bird-nesting box affixed to the side of the house. When he was young, Jim had been an avid collector of birds' eggs and he instinctively paused to observe the box. Major Balding manufactured his own to a high specification, with a hinged lid, enabling the box to be cleaned at the end of the nesting season. Jim lifted the lid, to observe that it was occupied. A characteristic nest of vegetation and feathers was filled with a large clutch of tiny white eggs with red spots, partially hidden under the moss. Forty years ago or more he would have promptly removed a couple and placed them in the tin full of cotton wool which he kept for that purpose in his jacket pocket.

"Great tit," he muttered to himself. "It's illegal to take wild birds' eggs nowadays. Wouldn't do to break the law, Jim-boy. I've my reputation to think of!" His mind briefly dwelt on his juvenile bird's-nesting proclivities, which still struck a chord in his mind. "The commonest bird," he mused, "especially in urban areas, is the ubiquitous house sparrow. Curiously, very few people have ever seen a sparrow's nest or handled one of the grey and white eggs. They build in nooks and crannies under the eaves and their nests are virtually inaccessible. This probably accounted for their success. Nowadays, with all those plastic windows, soffits and bargeboards, there's nowhere for them to go and their numbers have diminished dramatically." Closing the nestbox lid, he diverted his full attention to the job in hand.

He was a skilled and tidy worker and opening the window was rapidly achieved without occasioning undue damage or noise. His depredations sometimes passed unnoticed until the luckless occupant discovered that something was missing. This often made it difficult to ascertain the time of the crime and lessened the chances that it would be attributed to him.

* * * * *

Inspector Watts, stationed at Poppleby, was a weary and disillusioned man. The district had been plagued for a couple of years by the most elusive housebreaker, who had thereby earned the sobriquet of 'The Cat'. Last night, as on previous occasions, he had mounted a stakeout on a certain area of the town which had recently endured the attentions of the thief, but had found nothing and caught nobody. He called at his office to have a cup of tea and read through the night duty staff book prior to going home for a few hours' rest. As chance would have it he was acquainted with the Baldings through a shared interest in ornithology. He was also involved in the trials of a revolutionary new CCTV surveillance system employing miniature cameras linked by satellite to the control room located in his office. While consoling himself with a cup of hot sweet tea, he switched on the monitoring unit.

"I wonder how the great tits are getting on," he thought. What he saw caused him to leap out of his chair, totally forgetting the tea, which flooded over his table. Cramming on his hat, he departed headlong to the operations room.

Minutes later, four policemen had surrounded the Balding residence, two at the front and two at the back. The ladder having been removed, all they had to do was wait for the jobbing gardener, totally engrossed in his painstaking search of the house and unaware of their presence, to appear at the dormer window.

The following account of court proceedings subsequently appeared in the *Poppleby Argus*:

> *'CAT' FINALLY CAUGHT BY A BIRD*
>
> *A bizarre case has been concluded at Poppleby Crown Court. The infamous 'Cat Burglar', named as William MacPherson, aged fifty-three, of Meadow Street, Ashwick, appeared for sentence. He had pleaded guilty at a previous hearing to one charge of housebreaking and asked for twenty-one other counts to be taken into consideration. He has eluded all attempts to catch him for more than two years, but was finally trapped whilst robbing the home of Major and Mrs Balding in Sandy Lane. The couple are well-known ornithologists and had installed a miniature camera inside a nesting box attached to their house in order to observe the nesting cycle of a pair of great tits. It appears that MacPherson had been filmed by this camera*

in the act of entering the house in the owners' absence via an adjoining window. It was whilst he was engaged in searching the house that his arrest was effected. Full details of the video surveillance system were not revealed, as the equipment is both novel and commercially sensitive. Sentencing MacPherson, who used several aliases and ran an ostensibly respectable business as a gardener, to seven years' imprisonment, His Honour Judge Kilworth told the accused, "You advertised yourself as 'Green Fingers', but it appears from your record that 'Light Fingers' would have been more appropriate."

The great tits successfully raised nine young.

18
COUNT YOUR BLESSINGS

An allegory

I had reached the stage in my life where my view of the world tended to be retrospective rather than forward-looking. At times I was inclined to ask myself some unanswerable questions: why did I elect to take history when I didn't even like the subject (this, of course, was schoolboy-speak for

'I didn't like the history master', although in the final analysis it probably came to the same thing); why didn't I spend a bit more time looking for a new house; why did I allow myself to be persuaded to drink whisky – I can't stand the smell of the stuff; why did I ever attempt to drive two hundred miles when snow was threatened; what made me agree to that; why was I induced to lend money to him, of all people; why did I turn right and not left? Hindsight is a wonderful thing, and like everyone else (I suspect) I would love to have the opportunity of living my life over again and avoiding all the stupid mistakes that I made first time round. Of course, the consequences of some unwise actions are minimal, consisting of nothing more than a headache, a difficult journey or a temporary shortage of funds, but in other cases they can be life altering. Probably, given the chance, I would respond differently in only half a dozen situations.

One day, reflecting along these lines, I happened purely by chance to glance at an advertisement in a magazine which I do not normally read. I was in the dentist's surgery and had got bored watching those highly coloured fish in the tanks which are installed in such places, presumably to deflect the victim's attention from the forthcoming ordeal. The text was brief and cryptic, and appeared in small print at the bottom of the page. I shall never forget it and can quote it verbatim. It was headed 'Recapture the Joy of Youth with Ayurvedic Medicine', and continued, 'You too can be a Time Traveller. For details of his truly amazing technique simply call…' and gave a freephone number. I am not a gullible person, but for some reason this extraordinary claim commended itself to me. Usually I consign junk mail to the recycling bin and hang up on unsolicited telephone callers, but this time I paid a little more attention.

When I reached home after the visit to the dentist I rang the number and, as anticipated, was greeted with a message recorded in a sing-song accent which sounded Indian. "Please to listen meticulously to the following options and select your preferred one by using the numbered buttons on your handset: 1, correspondence courses in Sanskrit, Pushtu, Punjabi or Gujarati; 2, The Potential for Time Travel; 3, Doctor Maharashtra's Magic Curry Recipe Book; 4…" I could not contain my impatience and pressed '2' to end the flow of verbiage. The response was a request for my full name, title, date of birth, Zodiac sign (if known) and address details, not forgetting postcode and daytime telephone number. I reflected on the wisdom of adding my name to yet another database, but consoled myself with the thought that the call had been free and that most likely I would hear nothing further.

To my surprise, the following morning I received a plain envelope, addressed by hand in copperplate writing, in the mail. It was addressed to me by my full name, but nothing about it distinguished it from the tide of unwanted communications to which we are subjected. I opened it surreptitiously and discovered that the contents were indeed a mysterious pamphlet purporting to emanate from one Doctor Maharashtra. The only indication of its origin was a telephone number, and on looking up the area code I discovered that this was allocated to Market Harborough. I will quote some of the wording in order to convey an impression of its contents:

> *Time has fascinated mankind since he first discovered its concept. It is often referred to as the Fourth Dimension. Many authors have speculated about the possibilities of travel within this dimension and have even produced works detailing actual or supposed movement within its boundaries. The clock is one of the earliest examples of highly developed technology and skilled engineering. Prehistoric monuments such as Stonehenge and the Egyptian pyramids have clearly established links with celestial movements and the rotation of the seasons. Numerous legends exist concerning men who do not perish but live forever, much of which folklore has been incorporated into the world's leading religions. Which among us has not wished to revisit earlier phases of this life in order to correct mistakes or to seize opportunities which he let slip?*

Now, owing to astonishing discoveries and techniques perfected by the Great Guru, Doctor Maharashtra, of Allahabad, India, you too can travel in time. And, further, The Avatar is the advent to earth of a deity in visible form. The Ten Avatars of Vishnu are the most celebrated, the most memorable being the Eighth Avatar in a child named Krishna, who performed numerous miracles. Follow the path of Krishna to your desired destination. The Great Guru, Doctor Maharashtra, will receive aspirants at the Shrine to Vishnu. Please telephone for details; all calls are dealt with on a personal basis.

My immediate response was one of mixed amusement and mild irritation at having exposed myself to such gibberish. It was clearly designed to extract money from unwary people. Typically, no demand for payment was contained anywhere – that comes later, after you have signed up! There is no point in living to my age if you haven't learnt in the process to throw rubbish like this straight into the dustbin. I resolved to have nothing to do with this nonsense. I would probably have paid regard to my own counsel had I not received an unexpected further communication from the learned doctor; a couple of days later the telephone rang just as I was passing it, so I picked up the receiver. At first I assumed that it was just another random approach from some call centre in India, since I was addressed in my own name in a heavily accented voice. It sounded vaguely familiar, and after a moment's reflection I connected it with the recorded message I had heard when I called in response to the Great Guru's advertisement.

"Thank you for your interest in my work. If you would like to make an appointment this would be an opportune moment. I have several dates available, as it happens."

'No' is one of the shortest words in the English language and at the same time one of the most powerful. To my sorrow, in my life it has not been employed frequently enough. This was the principal reason for my wish to revise certain details of my prior existence. I shall never know what prompted me to do so, but the matter had now assumed such proportions in my mind that I accepted his offer of an interview. I needed a pretext before I disappeared for a day and one was conveniently provided by my hobby as a railway enthusiast. For some time I had been angling to visit the Nene Valley Railway and seized upon this as a convenient excuse. So it was that I drove to Market Harborough to locate the Guru's establishment. The latter was situated in a disused village railway station on the closed line between Market Harborough and Northampton. This was finally abandoned sometime after the mass closures of the Beeching vandalism but all traces had not been eradicated. The station buildings remained in situ and had been let out to various small local enterprises, for example a potter, a silversmith and a manufacturer of humane mousetraps, who doubled as a tattooist, besides, of course, Doctor Maharashtra himself. I walked along the remaining platform, beyond which lay the weed-grown vestige of the tracks, and discovered a blue door bearing his name on an enamel plate. Invited to enter in response to my knock, I went in and found myself in a small stuffy square room furnished elaborately in an oriental style, with carpets, silk wall hangings, silver-framed photographs of odd bearded figures, camphorwood chests, ivory elephants, Benares brass trays and spittoons, lamps, jade paperweights, filigree silver screens, a hookah, ginger jars, Chinese porcelain plates, teapots, a ceiling fan and so on. I could not take it all in. The great man motioned me to take a bamboo cane chair with fat cushions, whilst he remained seated in a carved armchair behind a heavy polished mahogany desk. He appeared to be of late middle age and wore European dress. The most striking features of the man were his dark, luminous eyes. We shook hands. He wasted no time in getting down to business.

"Welcome to my humble abode, my dear friend. I understand that you wish to learn more about my work and in particular how it may enable you to shake off your shackles and move freely through the Fourth Dimension which we call Time. You have come at a most propitious juncture, since I have made demonstrably great progress. Let me first say that Time itself cannot be altered in any way – it remains constant, and passes inexorably at a predetermined speed; it may not be stopped, nor can it be reversed or diverted from its course in any way whatsoever."

Despite myself, I had become totally absorbed in these words, drawn willy-nilly by the mesmeric light in his eyes.

"What I can offer you," he went on, "is the ability to dissociate your ego from the present and return to any time of your choosing. When you do so you will retain full consciousness and total cognizance of all your acquired knowledge, and will possess the attribute most desired by all men – hindsight. You will consequently have the option of avoiding all those errors and misjudgements which have occasioned loss or suffering in your previous existence and will, as a result, attain your personal Nirvana, your final release into absolute blessedness. A word to the wise, into which privileged classification I hope that you may be included: our scientific knowledge is not finite, but evolving. Our methods are empiric, relying on experience rather than theory, and not everything is always predictable—"

"You mean you proceed by trial and error?" I interposed, in a futile last attempt at self-assertion.

"Error is not a term associated with me, my friend. What is certain is that your own understanding will be enlarged in the passage of time, if you will excuse the pun. You can rest assured that I shall evince the greatest personal interest in you and that you may explicitly rely on me for advice in any way whatsoever." He went on to say that I should implement the plan by embarking on a course of medicine, taken in the form of pills, to enable me to manipulate my position in the time and space spectrum. An adequate supply of those medicaments would be furnished, together with instructions regarding their administration.

It later became only too obvious that I should have asked a great many more questions, such as the action to be taken to remedy the situation if something had gone wrong, for example an excessive dose of the pills, or my arrival at a point in time not of my choosing. At the outset, however, I had been completely taken in by the deception and could only focus on beginning the treatment as soon as possible.

Any remaining doubts were dispelled when I received a letter from the TV Licensing Authority in Bristol demanding to know why I was using television-receiving apparatus without having remitted the requisite fee. I duly coughed up, considering this a small price to pay for having shed a few years and thereby obtaining proof of the efficacy of the Great Guru's treatment. I persisted with the pills. Sometime later I received another letter, this time from the Teachers' Pensions Authority. This brought some unwelcome news:

> *An internal audit has revealed that your entitlement to a terminal gratuity and pension was miscalculated owing to confusion concerning your date of birth. The effect will be the immediate withdrawal of your pension. Your retirement grant need not be repaid at this stage, but an equivalent amount will be deducted from the sum due when you eventually reach the qualifying age. Meanwhile, interest on the lump sum paid in error will be due from you and will be calculated at the current Bank of England rate plus 0.5 % and this will be deducted in due course.*

Something similar happened with regard to my army terminal benefits. In that case the explanation was that approval for me to take Premature Voluntary Retirement had been rescinded owing to a growing shortfall of service manpower. In a brief period I had travelled backwards in my army career as far as my early days as a young NCO. One morning, the company runner, one Private Webb, arrived in haste at my barrack block and informed me that my presence was required at the company office.

"What on earth for?" I demanded.

"No idea. Don't shoot the messenger," and with that he mounted his green army bicycle and pedalled off on his next errand. He was a National Serviceman, distinguished by the way in which he waddled like a duck in his size twelve boots. He was therefore known to all and sundry as Webb Feet. He did not resent this in the slightest, since the attribution of a nickname was considered a mark of approval and acceptance. On my obeying the summons, I was ushered by the CSM into the Company Commander's office.

"You have to see the Commanding Officer on orders at 1100 hours," the latter informed me. Disciplinary business was dealt with at 0900 at company level, whilst the CO held his court two hours later in order to process cases remanded to him on the same day – an admirable example of the administration of justice without undue delay. The call was entirely unforeseen and I had never been in the Commanding Officer's inner sanctum before. Dressed in best battledress and best boots, I stood before a large polished desk. The Company Commander, Adjutant and RSM were all assembled in a row behind the Colonel, who was brief and to the point.

"You have been ordered to appear before me on the grounds of false enlistment," he began. "You are under age for military service and in accordance with the Queen's Regulations this constitutes grounds for instant dismissal. You will hand in your equipment and leave tomorrow morning. This is a regrettable business, as you have been the subject of favourable reports, but rules are rules and cannot be flouted. March out, RSM."

I did as I was bidden, receiving the balance of pay due to me and a railway warrant home.

It was now glaringly obvious that something had gone seriously wrong with the time travel treatment. I had lost control over where I wanted to be and how long I wished to remain there. The only common factor was that I was growing progressively younger, but the steps were unequal and the timings arbitrary. It was true to say that at any point in time – which time? – I could not with any assurance predict how old I was going to be. I urgently needed to consult with the Great Guru on my predicament – but how was I to reach him? I had a telephone number that was all too clearly modern. Not long ago, before the days of subscriber trunk dialling, every town and village had a physical exchange, a building with a real person inside it. The earlier manual exchanges still had extension numbers of one, two or three digits and to call outside your immediate area you had to be passed through a whole series of operators. The number I possessed had no meaning in earlier ages.

I was, naturally, in a state of great confusion. If I could not contact my mentor by telephone the only way was to pay another visit in person. As luck would have it I had been stationed quite close to Market Harborough, so I made my way there by the first available train. The Guru's lair was located some way from the town. In those days there was a bus from everywhere to everywhere else every hour, so I caught the United Counties from the town into the village. I approached the old railway station by the inclined road from the main street. During that period even small wayside railway stations had a proper range of buildings and facilities such as a waiting room, ticket office and staff. As I walked onto the platform I was confronted not with a vista of decay and tangled vegetation such as I had seen on my previous visit, but two shiny sets of rails. In the distance I distinctly heard a locomotive whistle and saw a plume of steam. There was a rattling sound of signal wires from the loom under the platform and the heavy clunk of a semaphore signal being pulled off. Around a bend in the track appeared an elderly 0-6-0 tender engine pulling a short rake of mixed wagons.

I heard a voice at my elbow. "07.22 pick-up goods from Stratford-on-Avon," offered the porter-cum-booking clerk, presuming that I was a railway enthusiast. The awful truth dawned on me. The Guru's den was located on a disused railway station and this one was patently anything but disused. The only place where I could seek salvation did not yet exist. The locomotive entered the station with a clank of connecting rods and steam leaking from various orifices. On the tender, beneath a thick layer of grime, the letters 'LMS' were only too clear. The railways had just been nationalised and they hadn't got around to repainting this one, and probably never would.

I walked along the platform to where the Guru's shrine was located. The building and the blue door were there all right, but the room was locked. The railwayman had followed me, and said, "Nothing for you in there, my son. That's the lamp room." Those signals had red and blue glass spectacles on the inner end of the arm, and in order that the appropriate aspect could be seen at night, oil lamps were situated behind the glass. Every station or lone signal-box had a lamp room where oil was kept and the lamps themselves were maintained.

"I was hoping to meet someone here," I said lamely.

"No one here. Will you be travelling? There's a train to Market Harborough in ten minutes."

I hesitated, but realising that retreat was my only option, I replied, "Yes."

"Come round to the ticket window. Single or return?"

"Single, please."

"Will that be adult or half fare?" I remained silent, unable to offer a coherent reply. "How old are you?" Seeing my confusion, the booking-clerk-cum-porter, who was a kindly chap, gently teased the daydreaming boy. "Well, since you're half awake, we'll make that a half, shall we? That'll be tuppence-ha'penny, my lad."

He took one of those cardboard Edmonson tickets that were once so familiar from his rack and punched it twice in a date-stamp device resembling a vertical torpedo.

"Look sharp, over the bridge and platform two. She'll be here in just a minute."

The goods train had recessed into a fan of sidings to allow the passenger to pass and was engaged in some desultory shunting.

* * * * *

I went home. By chance it was the school holidays, so it was a couple of weeks before I needed to present myself there and pick up the threads of my education. I was quite looking forward to it. After all, I had done it all before and once I had read this year's set books it would simply consist of revision. Now at last was my chance finally to accomplish one of my chief objectives – to work harder and obtain better results at school. On the first day I walked over the familiar route and made my way directly to the sixth-form classroom; I was the first to arrive and sat in my old chair.

Soon afterwards a fellow pupil entered the room, and on seeing me exclaimed, “You shouldn’t be in here, young fellow. Aren’t you a junior boy? Have you just joined? This is the sixth form and you ought to be in the second – across the corridor, in that classroom there.” He spoke kindly but with undeniable authority, and I realised that I had undergone yet a further stage in the de-aging process.

At this point things grew appreciably worse. It was downhill all the way. It was compulsory for all pupils to wear uniform whilst at the grammar school, and the outfitter in the town appointed to provide the requisite clothing could not supply a blazer small enough to fit me. In consequence I was expelled. I was likewise excluded from junior school on the grounds that I was unable to tie my shoelaces or put my coat on the correct way round. The final blow soon followed. I had made a dental appointment with the objective of studying that magazine closely to determine whether I had missed something. On approaching the tank for the ostensible purpose of admiring the tropical fish, I searched the tables and the paper rack. It goes without saying that there was no sign of it. The ultimate humiliation was administered by the dentist, who declined to see me on the (not unreasonable) grounds that I had no teeth.

* * * * *

My next recollection was of lying in my perambulator in the back garden. A hot sun was burning my face, as I had not been provided with a shade. I closed my eyes against the glare. For the rest of my life I had an antipathy to strong light, whether indoors or out, and I attribute the fact to my early exposure to that sunshine.

For some time my parents had been hoping to have a child and had decided that this was a good time to start.

One evening at about 10.30 my mother said to my father, “I’m going to bed, dear. Don’t be long.”

"All right, I've nearly finished the crossword. I'll be up in a couple of minutes." He bent over his newspaper, concentrating hard. Eight down. Six letters. Cryptic clue. "Doctor in the past mixed up unborn offspring." How apt, he thought. Must just finish this. He puzzled over the clue for several minutes. He never was much good at crosswords anyway. I don't know why he wasted so much time on them, especially when there were more important matters on hand.

"EMBRYO, you idiot", I shouted. "MB is a doctor, ERYO is an anagram of YORE, time past."

People, particularly those living together for years and with the same approach to life, often develop an uncanny ability to synchronise their thoughts. Of course, I could not communicate with my father. Who ever heard of a telepathic relationship with an egg? Meantime, my mother settled in the warm, comfortable bed and soon began to feel drowsy. After a few moments she reached out to her bedside table and extinguished the lamp. My father struggled for fully twenty minutes, threw down the paper, placed the guard in front of the fire, switched out the light and went upstairs. Mother was fast asleep.

Suddenly, I experienced a blinding flash of enlightenment, although not of the kind that the Great Guru had promised. I saw the enormous irony of my embarking on the biggest mistake of my life in the vain hope of correcting all the minor ones. I had been hypnotised and plied with hallucinogenic drugs and, in all probability, had my bank account emptied by means of an elaborate plot. How, at my age, could I have been so credulous? The bogus 'Great Guru' was not an Eastern mystic with supernatural powers, but probably a former milkman from Stoke-on-Trent with previous convictions for fraud. Then, abruptly, everything was plunged into eternal darkness, and I knew as my consciousness ebbed away that I was dead even before I had been born.

I awoke with a start and carried out a quick count of the occupants of the bed: myself, one wife, one dog, one cat. Four. All present and correct. For my part, I had a slight headache, which was unusual, as I am not prone to such ailments. My wife opened one eye.

“I think I’ve had an out-of-body experience,” I said.

“What you need is an out-of-beddy experience,” she retorted. “Get up and make the tea.”

The dog stretched herself luxuriantly, pulling the duvet off my legs. I did as I had been bidden. Drawing the kitchen curtains, I saw that it was an absolutely beautiful autumn day and that the sun was already strong, illuminating a pair of goldfinches in the birdbath. Despite the lateness of the season there were still quite a few flowers in bloom in the garden. Later, the postman delivered my bank statement, and I gave it a cursory glance. It seemed to consist mainly of credit entries – army pension, lecturer pension, guaranteed minimum pension, bank interest, investment income, winter fuel payment, Christmas bonus, and just a sprinkling of small direct debits for utilities. No mention of TV licence, and most certainly no mysterious withdrawals from the account.

On consulting the household diary I noted that I had an optician’s appointment the same afternoon.

“I’ll catch the 2.45 into town,” I told my wife. “No point having a bus pass if you never take advantage of it.”

The eye test, naturally, was free. Whilst in town I called at the surgery to collect my repeat prescription for eye-drops.

“Sign here,” asked the receptionist, “nothing to pay.”

It occurred to me then that increasing age has considerable benefits to commend it, and that we cannot, nor should we wish to, turn the clock back. Nobody has ever succeeded in doing so, at least. We all make mistakes – they are part of life. What is important is to learn from them. Acknowledging them makes us better people.

19
THE OLD MASTER

The retired schoolmaster lived contentedly in his cottage, occupied with his books and his garden. He and his companion, a little dog, were very close; practically, one might say, blood brothers.

There was never any doubt that Edmund Langridge was destined to become a schoolmaster. Whilst in the second form he was the only boy in living memory who actually liked Latin. At afternoon break, while a disorderly horde escaped from the classrooms and spilled all over the playing field to engage in impromptu games of football or cricket, he remained at his desk, engrossed in the tasks set that day to be carried out as homework. By the time his classmates clattered back along the corridors, the evening's work had been virtually completed. After school, on the way home, the others would temporarily abandon their usual pursuits of mocking an old man seated in his cottage doorway down the street or purloining a few apples from a convenient orchard and solicit his assistance.

"You've done your homework, Language," the name which he had rapidly acquired. "What does this mean?" they would ask, indicating a passage in Virgil's *Aeneid.* He never raised any objections to such requests, his manner didactic, not to say pedantic, as he patiently explained at length and to the manner born the mysteries of irregular verbs of the third conjugation.

And so it proved. On completing his education he acquired a post as classics master at a well-known public school, where he remained for the next forty years. On his being persuaded, against his will, that he should take retirement, he returned to his native village and purchased a small cottage facing the green. Since he had never had time or inclination to get married, he obtained a small Jack Russell terrier to be his companion. The dog was named Canis Minor, to reflect his master's lifelong interests in Latin and astronomy. The pair was inseparable and the little dog invariably accompanied Edmund wherever he went, never on a lead, but always trotting along at his master's heels. The duo became one of the familiar sights in the village and was referred to affectionately as 'Me and my shadow'. His usual form of dress was plus fours, a tweed jacket with leather buttons and elbow patches, stout brogues and a cap. Another of the schoolmaster's preoccupations was gardening, and he spent many hours tending his hedges and flowerbeds, which were an attractive feature of his cottage. He had a pet aversion to the presence of broad-leafed weeds in his lawns and invariably carried a clasp knife about his person. On spotting an offender, not only on his own property but also on the village green and in particular in the vicinity of the cricket square, he would mutter, "Ah, a dandelion," or, "There's a plantain," rummage in his side pocket, produce the knife, open it and proceed to decapitate the unfortunate plant. The detritus thus produced went back into his pocket along with the knife, eventually to find its way onto his compost heap. This treatment was highly effective, and the garden, the village green and the cricket pitch were notably weed-free. His method was invariably the same – gather up all the horizontal leaves of the offending plant into a whorl and cut across the tap root about an inch below ground level, then slit the root vertically downwards as far as the blade would reach, thereby inflicting maximum damage. On one particular day, observing a large thistle growing perilously close to the square-leg umpire's normal stance, he set about it in the customary manner. As he did so he revealed a large black and yellow bumble bee among the spiny leaves. The insect, disturbed by his actions, promptly crawled upon his finger. Recalling that a bee sting was the most painful affliction he had ever suffered during his life, he quickly withdrew his hand and shook off the threatening creature. In his haste he cut his finger on the clasp knife, the blade of which was always kept sharp. Nothing daunted, he despatched the thistle, sucked the wound, made his way back to the cottage, the little dog ambling along behind, and repaired the damage with a strip of sticking plaster. Edmund was a hands-on gardener who never wore gloves; his nails were chipped, and removing thorns or splinters from fingers, thumbs or palms was a commonplace occurrence. He gave the matter no further thought.

Edmund Langridge had an elder brother, Wilfred, who did not share his academic bent, but was by nature much more worldly. He assumed control of the family business when his father died at a comparatively young age. There were no other children and their mother remained a widow for more than twenty-five years, during which time she continued to reside at the family home. She finally passed away shortly before the events related here. Edmund had been much closer to his father than to his mother, and it was his father's encouragement and support which had been instrumental in his pursuing a career befitting his cerebral nature.

Edmund was a disappointment to his mother, who was made in the same mould as her elder son; in consequence he had less and less contact with her, a situation exacerbated by the fact that his school was located at a considerable distance from his mother's home. It probably would have helped if Edmund had married and had children, but this was not to be. On his mother's demise, Wilfred and his second wife Nanette, considerably younger than her husband, had inherited the family home along with the business. Edmund kept any disappointment at this arrangement to himself, and appeared quite content with his cottage, his dog, his books and his weeds. As a man of wide culture and knowledge, he was in demand as a speaker at such organisations as the University of the Third Age or the Women's Institute, and still undertook some private tutorial work when the occasion demanded.

In due course, Wilfred and Nanette occupied the old house. It was a venerable building and had been the subject of much alteration and renovation over the years. Whilst carrying a table into the house, the removal men, faced with an awkward corner, had accidentally broken a small pane at the bottom of a glass-panelled door giving access to a corridor at the rear of the house. It so happened that this occurrence passed unobserved by the new owners, and some quick work with a dustpan and brush removed the shards of glass. In the general confusion which accompanies house moves, the workmen's error was overlooked, and they pocketed their cheque and made good their escape.

Wilfred had decided to hold a house-warming party as soon as the move had been effected. There had been some delay in finalising the actual removal, and as the house-warming had been notified well in advance, precious little time was available for the requisite arrangements to be made. Trivial things like a broken pane in a dark corridor went unnoticed. All surviving family members, local notables and business associates were invited. Despite his misgivings, as he was not an avid partygoer, Edmund naturally accepted the invitation to join the merriment. Apart from the occasion of his mother's funeral, he had not set foot in the house for a number of years. The great lounge was thronged with people, as invariably occurs on such occasions, all talking at the tops of their voices whilst looking over the shoulder of the person with whom they were ostensibly in conversation at someone else on the far side of the room. Edmund knew hardly anybody.

Quite suddenly, the hubbub ceased and a shrill voice cried, “I say, is that your little doggie, Nanette?”

“No, certainly not; I can’t stand the things! All that beastly hair and dirty footprints – can’t tolerate them! I don’t know whose it is – get rid of it, Wilfred, darling!”

Edmund, to his dismay, caught sight of poor little Canis Minor, who had evidently succeeded in escaping from the cottage and traced his master as far as the Tower of Babel.

“I’m sorry, he actually belongs to me,” he admitted. “He doesn’t like being left out of things. I’ll just pop him back home.”

The noise returned to its previous level, while Edmund restored his friend to the safe haven of the cottage. When he got back, the din had diminished somewhat, as people were making their way to the dining room to attack the buffet supper. He had the opportunity to look round the living room with its beams, great fireplace and leaded windows. His view was suddenly arrested by a picture, at first sight not very prepossessing, only about two feet by one in a plain frame. He immediately crossed the hearth, took the picture down and examined it closely. How could he possibly have forgotten this? He turned it over. On the back was a note, in his father’s distinctive handwriting: ‘Attributed to Jan van Eyck, circa 1430. This is said to be a preliminary study for the completion of the great triptych now located at St Bavo’s Cathedral in Gent’. Memories of his boyhood flooded back. His father had promised that this picture would be passed down to him. When his father had died, his mother and brother were executors of the will. Of course, everything concerning the business would have passed to the eldest son, and his mother would have enjoyed use of domestic property for the remainder of her life. He had no awareness of any of the provisions of his parents’ wills.

Noticing his preoccupation with the picture, a small group formed around him, curious to know what he was studying so intensely. Someone ventured to ask. Grateful for an audience, Edmund adopted his schoolmaster mode.

"This is ascribed to the Flemish master Jan van Eyck, although the true provenance has never been confirmed and the picture itself remains unsigned. It is believed to have been a cartoon or first sketch for what subsequently became acknowledged as a masterpiece, the folding altar screen located in Flanders. One school of thought is persuaded that van Eyck finished the screen begun by his brother. It depicts biblical allegories and is remarkable for the freshness of the colours, given its great age. It belonged to my late father for many years, although I have no knowledge of whence he obtained it."

"Must be worth a few thousand," remarked his interlocutor.

"If this really is by van Eyck, you can add three noughts to that," responded Edmund. This intelligence naturally caused a great stir. He replaced the picture on its hook and went in search of a cheese sandwich.

The house-warming took place on a Saturday, and on the following Monday morning the lady of the house reported the loss of the painting to the police. Because of the supposed value of the missing item, the case at once assumed great urgency, and two members of the local CID arrived promptly. A thorough examination revealed two significant details which had previously been unnoticed by the family in the general confusion of house-moving and house-warming: the broken glass panel in the rear door and some spots of blood on the carpet inside the adjoining corridor. Having ascertained that as far as could be determined nothing else had been stolen, the police requested the particulars of all persons who had been present at the party. The existence of this picture was virtually unknown, as no record of it appeared in any catalogue or book concerning the artist's work. After Mr Langridge senior had died, nobody in the family had paid any attention to it nor advertised its presence. The obvious inference was that somebody at the house-warming, having been alerted to its possible value, had returned to the house the following day and helped themselves to it. In the circumstances, all guests were asked to supply a sample of DNA to eliminate them from the search for the individual who had left the bloodstains adjacent to the broken glass. Nobody was to be omitted.

It would clearly be highly embarrassing to ask Edmund Langridge to produce such a sample, and this delicate task was delegated to the young Constable, Greenwood by name, who lived in the police house in the village, on the grounds that he knew the gentleman concerned and could be relied upon to tread lightly on his sensibilities. This officer thereupon telephoned Edmund and asked him to call at the police house at his convenience, which he duly did, accompanied inevitably by Canis Minor. The policeman apologised profusely for the matter, briefly outlining details of the broken window and bloodstains indicating the likely means of entry.

"Of course, you're not under suspicion, Mr Langridge. But it's standard practice to eliminate as many people as possible so that we can concentrate on the real business of finding the perpetrator. I've got a kit here. It only takes a minute – would you like to sit in my office?"

He gave Edmund a sealed packet. On being opened, the latter revealed a plastic stick with a cotton-wool bud attached, rather reminiscent of the things people used to employ to remove wax from their ears (before such practices were discouraged) or to clean out the creases in babies.

"Just rub it round the inside of your cheek for a couple of minutes. Fairly vigorously—" The policeman was interrupted by the sound of the radio of his police car, parked outside. "Excuse me, won't be a moment, Mr Langridge."

Edmund, seated in a chair, held the simple device in one hand and glanced at the instructions printed on the packet. At that moment, his little dog, ever present, caught a glimpse of the plastic stick and grabbed it in his jaws. Playing with sticks was one of his favourite pastimes. A brief tug-of-war ensued, during which the cotton wool was vigorously rubbed on the inside of the dog's mouth. As his master retrieved the stick. PC Greenwood re-entered the room.

"Ah, that's fine, sir. I'll just get this sent off for analysis." For once in his life, Edmund was at a total loss. He could hardly confess to the fact that the DNA sample emanated from his dog. He consoled himself with the thought that he had recently read somewhere that the higher mammals share most of their genes with us – after all, they test human medicines on apes or even mice, don't they? In any case, he had certainly not broken into his brother's house nor stolen his picture.

He was awakened from this reverie by the policeman, who had been fussing the little dog. "He's got a nasty wound on his ear, haven't you, boy?"

Edmund, who had failed to observe this, replied, "Oh, he's always diving into hedges chasing imaginary prey. It'll soon clear up. I'll have a look at him when we reach home."

"Both been in the wars, haven't you?" continued PC Greenwood, indicating Edmund's plastered finger.

"Yes, cut myself on my knife, you know. Getting careless."

Accompanied by his canine friend, the schoolmaster made his way home. Musing on the events of the last couple of days, he was suddenly brought down to earth with a violent shock. He had completely overlooked something. On the Saturday evening his dog had appeared, uninvited, at his brother's party. In the fuss engendered by the incident he had totally failed to ask himself how the little chap had gained entry to the house, since there was no access open to him. All the doors were closed. He must have gone to the rear of the house, jumped through the broken pane, catching his ear in the process and bleeding onto the carpet.

Chief Inspector Percival was presiding at the briefing conference held daily in his office at 0900 hours to review the state of the case of the stolen masterpiece. Those present at the Langridges' house-warming had been very co-operative and a total of seventeen samples had been sent away for scientific analysis. The latest information received from the laboratory caused, to put it mildly, a great sensation. From all appearances, the blood on the carpet matched the sample supplied by none other than Mr Edmund Langridge. This was not absolutely clear-cut, the Inspector explained. It appeared that there were some small and inexplicable discrepancies in the specimens provided, possibly due to contamination or some imperfections in the new computer software recently installed, but in the circumstances, where the investigation was merely trying to establish blood details and nothing more complex, there were reasonable grounds for proceeding with the next stage of the investigation. There were, after all, other factors pointing towards the schoolmaster. By report and observation, the police were aware of Edmund Langridge's great interest in the missing picture, its alleged high value, and the cut on his finger: circumstantial maybe, but evidence nonetheless. Percival summoned Greenwood and the pair at once proceeded to Mr Langridge's cottage to confront him with the accumulated evidence and interrogate him further. On their arrival they discovered that he was out, presumably taking his dog for the customary morning walk. He was a man of regular habits and a familiar figure around the village footpath circuit. It was a pleasant day, so the two arms of the law walked across the village green, through the kissing gate and down the path towards the watermill.

"You don't think he did it, do you, sir?" asked the village policeman. "It's just not possible."

"Never judge a package by its wrapping, young man; crooks come in all sorts of guises. If you had gone to Doctor Crippen with a sore throat he would most likely have been very helpful."

They soon spotted their quarry walking towards them. As they drew near they observed that the little dog was barking in an agitated manner at what appeared to be a white object located in the hedgerow at head height alongside the path.

"Just a moment, Greenwood," said the Chief Inspector, detaining his subordinate by the sleeve of his jacket. As they watched, Langridge produced a clasp knife from his side pocket, reached into the bushes and cut the brambles entwined around a plastic supermarket shopping bag.

"What's he up to?" wondered Percival.

"Let's have a look, governor," replied the Constable.

Recognising the two men, the teacher said, "How opportune is your arrival, gentlemen. It appears that your case has solved itself." From the bag he drew out a framed picture, two feet by one foot, obviously of some antiquity, and depicting biblical scenes and characters.

"It can't have been there long, as it's bone dry, and we've had a couple of wet days recently. Couldn't get out into my garden."

"Please don't handle it, sir. It'll have to go for forensic examination," said Percival, extending his hand and relieving Edmund of the plastic bag containing the painting.

Suddenly, proceedings were interrupted by the shrill note of the Chief Inspector's mobile telephone. He engaged in a brief and cryptic conversation, answering in monosyllables. "Yes. Yes. Where? When? OK. No. Yes. Now. All right, now." He beckoned to his comrade and walked away a few paces. Percival spoke urgently, sotto voce. "I'm scaling down this investigation with immediate effect. Say nothing to Langridge; let him cook. The picture was clearly dumped or left on view intentionally. Let all concerned know. The uniformed branch, by which I mean you, Greenwood, are handling this case from now on. I have bigger fish to fry – a murder over at Whittlebury."

"Very good, sir. The picture ought to be valued."

"Excellent idea. Let me know what happens, my lad. I'm off."

Nothing useful was produced by the examination of the old picture. Naturally, it had been handled recently by various people in the course of the house move and Edmund's own examination. Rather more revealing was the report of the art experts commissioned to identify it. Scientific analysis of the paints and canvas proved that it was a nineteenth-century fake, albeit very skilfully executed, of small value. This came, naturally, as a major disappointment to Nanette; not that she was in any sense attracted by the intrinsic worth of the supposed masterpiece – she was not religious, had never heard of van Eyck, did not know what a triptych was and had never been to Gent. She would have offered it to Edmund, but was reluctant to discuss such a subject, about which she was totally ignorant, with her brother-in-law. She was almost afraid of Edmund, and mistook his preoccupation and aloofness for contempt. To make matters worse, he was one of very few men to be unmoved by her considerable charms. The task of disposing of the picture therefore fell to Wilfred. Edmund was pleased to be reunited with his old friend, and to this day it has pride of place on the wall adjacent to his fireplace. The family notified the police that they had no wish to proceed further with the matter. Most of those concerned had valid private reasons for letting the whole thing drop – Edmund's deception over the sample, the dog for aiding and abetting, PC Greenwood's failure to supervise the sampling process, Wilfred for not respecting his late father's wishes with regard to its disposal, the removal men for breaking a glass panel.

The schoolmaster's finger and the dog's ear both healed without any scar.

20

ONE FOR THE ROAD

A satire

The latest addition to Britain's burgeoning motorway network has been formally opened with due ceremony. The M1000 encapsulates the very best of modern practice and includes many novel facilities not heretofore seen in this country. It has eight lanes and is a genuine all-weather road, equipped as it is with under-surface heating to offset the effects of adverse weather. Electric elements are incorporated under the tarmac for the entire sixty-seven miles of the new carriageways. The provision of adequate power at competitive cost necessitated the erection of one hundred and forty-eight wind farms on both sides of the new road. Clearly, such a massive undertaking required considerable time and investment in order to comply with planning regulations and establish essential way leaves, entailing the compulsory purchase of no less than 2,417 acres of prime farmland, since the M1000 runs exclusively through agricultural districts. A further source of delay was entailed by the discovery, some five years after work had commenced, that the turbines do not produce electricity on calm days. As a result, three nuclear power stations were needed as a backup. In the light of these factors, the opening of the motorway was a mere eleven years late, and the eventual provisional cost has been set at 7.68 times the original budget. Her Majesty's government regards this as exceptional value for money, when the full benefits are taken into consideration.

Originally, the inauguration of the new highway was to have been marked by the Queen driving a party of European royalty and other heads of state down the motorway in a luxury coach. As can be imagined, there were difficulties in choosing a date suitable to such a wide variety of participants, all with their own official obligations to fulfil. A time was finally agreed upon, but was cancelled at the last minute when Buckingham Palace announced that Her Majesty had inadvertently allowed her PSV licence to lapse. The M1000 has already been in public use for some time.

A feature of the new motorway is the double hard shoulder, whereby there are twin surfaced lanes provided on the inside of the main running road proper. The outer hard shoulder serves the usual purpose of a refuge for broken-down vehicles and can be used as a running lane when traffic conditions render this advisable. The inner hard shoulder is not intended for normal travel, but furnishes a means of immediate access for emergency vehicles. Like all innovative improvements, this has suffered a few teething problems. As explained by Sir Jasper Petterell-Head, Minister for Roads, in his response to a parliamentary question, certain members of the travelling public have been mistakenly using the inner hard shoulder as a picnic site or for riding quad bikes and horses, with consequent difficulties. The Minister gave details of a £21 million publicity campaign to enhance people's awareness of the problems, and early indications point to the success of this effort, as evidenced by the fact that there have been no reported sightings of joggers or cyclists on the motorway in the last ten days.

A work of this magnitude inevitably has its detractors, and one of the more controversial issues concerned the demolition of several mediaeval villages which lay in its preferred path. In particular, much heat was generated over the destruction of what a government spokesperson referred to as 'that row of verminous fifteenth-century almshouses' situated near the halfway point of the motorway. There was no physical problem with their removal, which was secured with explosives experts' assistance using the latest techniques, but the fact that the dwellings were still occupied drew undue attention to the episode. The fifteen aged inhabitants were eventually rehoused, but unfortunately it proved impossible to keep them all together in one group and they were dispersed around the country. Some personal antipathy was aroused among three wives separated from their husbands of upwards of sixty years, but as the government bulletin explained, 'you can't make an omelette without breaking some eggs'.

The re-arranged formal opening of the road was signified by the despatch of the first of the new 'Muggernaut' lorries, the introduction of which has triggered a massive new wave of road-building projects. It is hoped that when work has been completed to strengthen bridges, widen roads and open up pinch points such as market towns, the blessings offered by the new super-lorries will be extended to all corners of the land. Provisional estimates for the work involved are quoted variously as £750 to £2,000 billion for the first phase. Our reporter is accompanying the driver of the pioneering vehicle and the following is an account of the extraordinary experience thus undergone.

The Muggernaut pulls away from the start-line, snapping a ribbon festooned with plastic bags and empty lager cans to symbolise the break with the old and the historic dawn of a new, more enlightened, era. It is a vehicle like no other seen so far on our roads, having twenty-eight axles, all steerable, and being 122 feet in length. It is powered by two 3,000 horsepower, gas-cooled, V16 two-stroke turbo diesels, with electro-hydraulic transmission. There are thirty-two forward and four reverse gears, all fully automatic, in-cab 40-channel TV, DVD, CD, digital radio, satellite navigation, two-way short-wave citizen's band wireless, telephone, ice-making machine, electronic fault detection system, broadband wi-fi Bluetooth internet access and, as can readily be imagined, the cab resembles the cockpit of a Concord, with the addition of a king-sized bed and air conditioning.

The driver reveals that this lorry can carry five full-length ISO shipping containers. This particular cargo consists entirely of stuffed toys manufactured in China, reputedly to the quantity of 7.7 million (although on being pressed he admitted that he had not actually counted them) – one for every child in the country, he claims with sentimental pride and the merest suggestion of a tear in his eye.

About halfway along the new motorway the traveller encounters an illuminated red neon sign with the legend 'M1000 Megalopolis – Seven Star Service Station – only ten kilometres to go'. This information is repeated at the five and one-kilometre points, and after passing the latter the driver prepares to pull in and sample the delights of the new station, built in conjunction with the road itself. On approaching the entry slip road, he effortlessly goes down through the gears from twenty-fourth to eleventh and pulls over into the exit lane. As he does so, the short-wave radio hisses and announces: "Welcome to the Four S complex. Please follow the signs to the CVRA [Commercial Vehicle Reception Area] – the road is marked out in illuminated green cats' eyes."

Having complied, the driver is further told to proceed to Bay 136. He stops his vehicle. At once, a uniformed male attendant approaches the driver's door. He is a young man, dressed in page-boy jacket with brass buttons and a pill-box hat, such as one might see in a hotel in early black-and-white American films. He accosts the driver and asks for the vehicle keys.

"What can I do for you, sir?"

"Just fill her with diesel. Use this fuel card."

"We have red diesel for agricultural vehicles, black diesel, blue diesel for boats, green diesel made from oilseed rape, or yellow diesel made from sugar cane."

"Black, please."

"Anything else, sir?" pursues the youth. "Oil change and filter? Full lube? Check all lamps? Tyre pressure? Coolant? Screen washers? Full shampoo and polish?"

"Just tyres. Sixty all round," replies the driver.

"We can download latest details of roadworks, diversions, traffic light failure and weather warnings onto your satnav, if you wish."

"Have it your way, son."

"Very well, sir. You may pick up your vehicle from EMZ [Exit Marshalling Zone]. The keys will be at the Marshal's office, docket number 1046." The youth hands the driver a yellow token. "Have a nice day."

Approaching the main entrance to the complex, one passes through perpetual-motion revolving doors into a magnificent glass atrium, soaring up to the full height of the six-storey building, crowned with an octagonal lantern, clearly inspired by Ely Cathedral, and topped with a mast, from which the European Union flag proudly flutters.

We are now spoilt for choice. A broad avenue curves away to the right. It is labelled 'Grub Street' and contains every kind of food outlet that the most discerning gourmet could ever want. Traditional fish and chips rub shoulders with Peking Cuisine and Turkish kebab, beyond which lie Le Bistro and La Trattoria. Opposite are Miguel's Tapas Bar, the burger bar, snack bar, fish bar, sandwich bar, sushi bar and coffee bar. Elsewhere can be found the nail bar and the heel bar. No bars are barred, evidently. There are Joe's Café, the Taj Mahal Curry Parlour, the Olde Englishe Tea Rooms, Auntie Elsie's Front Room, the Great English Breakfast, Hank's Diner, the Cavendish Restaurant, the Corner House, the chippie, the choppie, the Cavern, the Salt Cellar, the Pepper Pot and the Mustard Bath. In the other direction can be detected the casino, the cloakrooms, the baby-changing facilities, the Roman baths, the jacuzzi and four Finnish saunas lined with Carrara marble – male, female, mixed and indeterminate (in order to comply with European legislation on gender discrimination). A signpost indicates the shower rooms, gymnasium and fitness suite, ironing cubicles, cycle hire, herbal medicinal and acupuncture clinics, tattoo parlour, public telephone, fax bureau, internet café, cash points, bureau de change, police station, pharmacy, photographic booth, smoking area and tobacconists, newsagent, betting shop, interpreters in all languages and help point. We can also consult with the medical centre and first-aid point should the need arise. Lifts, stairs and escalators will take you to the supermarkets, department stores and hotels. Underground lie the ice and roller-skating rinks, tenpin bowling alley, boxing ring and squash courts. On the mezzanine floor are located the estate agents, solicitors, citizens' advice and marriage bureaux, travel agents and health and safety advisors, undertakers, jewellers and watchmakers and pet shop and poodle parlour, ethnic souvenirs etc.

Our lorry driver is seemingly unimpressed by the blandishments to sample all these earthly delights, and walks purposefully along the main avenue to the far end, where an automatic door gives access to the rear of the magnificent main edifice. Outside lie the manicured grass tennis courts (racquets for hire) and bowling greens, beyond which can be detected the long, low, ranch-like equestrian centre, containing the livery stables and pony-trekking enterprises. In the far corner, behind the artificial ski slope, we glimpse the garden centre, ornamental lake and the quarantine kennels. These he ignores, passing through a wicket-gate into a small copse marked 'Nature Reserve'. A narrow muddy pathway leads through birch and oak scrub and brambles, finally giving onto a tarmac road, which had evidently been the main traffic thoroughfare prior to the construction of the motorway. It now lies silent, sad and abandoned, with the vegetation already encroaching on the verges. Turning left, a few paces bring him to a gravel drive-in, heavily pock-marked with muddy puddles. Set back some thirty yards from the old road a ramshackle single-storey building is situated. This had begun life as the bottom deck of a Huddersfield Corporation tram, had subsequently been employed as a chicken shed and ultimately come to rest in its present location, where it had been extended to form a traditional roadside transport café. A creaking signboard announces 'Mike's – Good Pull In'. Our driver negotiates the larger puddles and enters, being greeted by the proprietor.

"Hello, mate. Breakfast?"

"Yes, please. Double egg, bacon, sausage, tomatoes, fried bread, mushrooms and baked beans, and some toast with marmalade."

The seating is of two patterns – the first, folding wooden chairs of military vintage known in army circles by the designation 'Chairs, GS, fold-flat', once the universal fashion in all such establishments as well as in the majority of village halls and cricket pavilions; the second, their modern replacement: stacking chairs with a steel frame and covered in a plywood monocoque seat and back. Our driver avoids the latter, as they appear to have been vandalised by the removal of the rivets securing the seat to the frame. The unwary sitter can sustain a very nasty pinch by such an object.

He feels under an obligation to comment on the state of this amenity. "Had trouble with bikers?"

"No, mate," replies mine host, "bikers are well behaved. This lot was done by the Ghoulthorpe Hunt after their Boxing Day meeting. They hadn't managed to kill anything except a couple of their own horses, a hunt saboteur and a rabbit with myxamotosis, so they were in a nasty mood." He fills a large, cracked china mug with scalding tea. "Sugar?"

"Yes, please," says the driver. "Three spoonfuls."

21
OFF THE RECORD

What's in a name? In this instance, a very great deal.

Once upon a time, I followed the profession of White Van Man. This is an endangered and imperilled species, to whom all manner of misdemeanours are unfairly attributed. He is indelibly associated with breaches of the Highway Code, exceeding the speed limits, reckless driving, illicit parking, ill-considered overtaking, staying too close to the vehicle in front, proceeding in the wrong direction down one-way streets, and a catalogue of other failings too numerous to mention. In fact, he is the victim of his employers' excessive expectations and the subject of totally unrealistic delivery schedules. If you have ever tried to reach the remote village of Pigsthorpe Underhand before 11.24 a.m., as I have, you will know that regardless of your start point, this is quite impossible. To forestall your next question, it is near Burnham on Crouch – I will rephrase that: it is not exactly *near* anywhere, but that will give you the general picture. In point of fact, my van was not white at all, but an ecologically friendly shade of green, but the same principles apply. It was while I was serving in the capacity of courier that the events described took place.

On the day in question I had to deliver a consignment of documents to the National Broadcasting Centre in London. As it happened, I had never been there before but I knew the place by its reputation, which was anything but favourable. The original building dating from between the two world wars had been the subject of constant change since it was erected, reflecting the advance and spread of broadcasting activities and technological development and so had been extended and altered internally innumerable times. The net result was a vast labyrinthine warren of offices and studios which were forever changing their names and functions as well as their staff. In consequence, nobody knew where anything was, whether it still existed, what its new title was and what its purposes, if any, might be. In short, it was the courier's pet nightmare. It was comparable in these respects to the average industrial estate, another bugbear for the unfortunate deliveryman on a tight timetable. These places are typically an anonymous collection of identical buildings scattered around what once had been a railway yard. There is a one-way traffic system, generally ignored, and streets named Jubilee Way or Millennium Avenue, the nameplates for which have been flattened by frustrated lorry drivers. The premises, in theory, have numbers, few if any of which are visible, and those which are in view are not contiguous and have no logical relationship. There is a location board at the exit gate (never at the entrance) but the small firms occupying these buildings have a habit of moving somewhere else on the estate at short notice to take advantage of lower rents or a supposed better position. If you have ever been to one of these places you will know exactly what I mean.

My first duty on that fateful day was to deliver a packet of documents to an office in the radio facility, part of the Broadcasting Centre. People employed in the media lead adventurous lives, travelling all over the globe, frequently in war zones, and generally becoming involved in extreme activities. A major consideration, therefore, lies in the matter of the insurance of these individuals' persons and their expensive equipment. An enterprising gentleman named Desmond Ireland had set up an insurance agency in-house, and this had subsequently been taken over by the Broadcasting Commission itself. They thus became in effect their own insurer and saved considerable sums of money in resultant lower premiums. This company was known from the outset as Desmond Ireland Risks, a deliberate play on the name of a celebrated radio programme chosen to attract publicity, which in fact it did, as the company also acquired an external client base. The name, however, had unfortunate consequences, as we shall see.

In the absence of any authorised parking spaces, I left my van on the customary yellow lines and entered the building. At a reception desk I encountered an extremely young and inexperienced girl, who, in response to my query, "Desmond Ireland Risks?" replied, "Yes, sir, they're waiting for you. Room 217K. The lift is down there. Eleventh floor."

I was a little surprised to hear that I was expected, but supposed, if I thought about it at all, that they were waiting for some urgently needed documents. I reached Floor K and with some difficulty located Room 217. The door stood open. An outer room contained another receptionist who greeted me with evident relief.

"Ah, here you are, the producer will be pleased." She pressed a button on her desk, whereupon a door marked 'Private' was thrown open. There emerged an extraordinary personage, tall, thin and dressed in a pair of floral trousers, a T-shirt, sandals and a baseball cap. He sported a ponytail hairstyle and wore a large name-badge. As he advanced towards me I examined the latter. It bore a legend in a florid italic script which was quite difficult to interpret. I eventually made out the words 'Producer. Crispin Murchison-Prebend'.

He followed my glance, proffered a soft, flabby hand, shook my own and said, "Don't worry, everyone calls me Bunny, darling."

I was still clutching my bundle of documents and the receptionist came to my rescue. "Shall I look after these?" she said, relieving me of the package.

Bunny began to talk rapidly. "We're in a frightful tizz today, my dear. We normally record these programmes well in advance but we've had difficulties that I won't bother you with, and this one is going out live. Haven't done that for years. Miss Crawley is extremely uptight, I ought to warn you, and she can be quite sharp. Sorry I wasn't here when you did the rehearsal and the script conference, but I'm sure that Malcolm looked after you and that you know precisely what to expect. I've been on an exchange posting with Japanese TV and just got back from a kibbutz in Argentina. You know what that entails, darling."

Darling had not the faintest idea what that entailed, nor the smallest notion of what he was talking about. At this point it dawned on me that there had been some horrendous communication failure and that things had gone very, very awry. I tried to summon up the will to interrupt him in full flow and extricate myself before it got any worse, but somehow I simply could not.

"Never mind," Bunny rabbited on. "Here's your script. You know all the general background, so just stick rigidly to this and we'll do fine. I'll lead the way." Mesmerised, I followed him into an inner room.

A large table equipped with microphones occupied centre space. There were four chairs around this, with nameplates – 'Lou Crawley', 'Guest', 'Producer' and 'Engineer'. There was all manner of technical equipment spread round the walls and two or three people who were evidently operators of some kind. The producer motioned me towards the 'Guest' chair and sat in his own seat. A third person occupied the position allocated to 'Engineer', leaving the fourth seat vacant. In front of each plate except mine was a folder. I realised that these were the scripts Bunny had referred to and that I had already been given mine. I glanced at it. It was labelled 'Script: Desert Island Discs' and a date. Underneath the title was printed 'Marmion Walmsley-Smythe', which eminent personage was evidently today's contributor. A door on the far side of the studio opened, admitting Lou Crawley, who without preamble occupied the remaining chair.

"Script, everyone, please," called Bunny.

I opened my folder, which contained a surprisingly large number of A4 sheets of paper. Glancing at these, I soon realised that the entire dialogue had been prepared in advance, down to the last question and response and even to the very punctuation marks. In my total ignorance I had always believed that there was an element of spontaneity, of improvisation, of action and reaction, of the evincing from the participants of ideas and emotions. Evidently, this was totally untrue. The whole thing was scrupulously predetermined and nothing had been left to chance.

The producer called, "Three, two, one, zero," whereupon the engineer depressed a large switch located on the table and a box on the facing wall glowed red with the words 'ON AIR'.

Miss Crawley at once launched into the introduction, in a cut-glass accent and with the extremely deferential manner which had transformed numerous complete nonentities, whom no one had ever heard of, into instant celebrities, and which had thereby earned her the sobriquet of 'Creepy Crawley'. "My guest today is regarded as the standard-bearer for avant-garde music not only in this country but also throughout Europe, to North America, Japan, Brazil and beyond. Author, composer, conductor, musicologist, inspiring teacher and acknowledged expert in his field, I have the greatest pleasure in welcoming…" Here she paused, closed the script folder and read his name off the front cover. I had the distinct impression that she had forgotten who he was. "Marmion Walmsley-Smythe." She addressed herself to me in a sycophantic tone. "You obviously come from a musical family?"

In my shock and confusion, I entirely forgot about the script and tried to give an honest and factual reply. "Well," I faltered, "my father used to play the mouth-organ in the village pub on Saturday nights."

The response to this ill-judged sally was instantaneous and terrifying. Her hand shot across the table and switched off the 'ON AIR' notice. Her large, liquid eyes contracted to narrow slits and glittered like fragments of marcasite. Her voluptuous lips became hard and as narrow as whipcord and her face was contorted with rage. "Don't get smart with me; follow the script or you can forget your fee," she hissed. These words were punctuated with Anglo-Saxon oaths and delivered in an accent somewhere between Mid-Atlantic and Middlesbrough. She threw the transmission switch, her eyes opened, her features softened and a beatific smile played upon her full lips. The accent returned to Cheltenham Ladies' College with a fashionable hint of the Scottish Highlands in the vowels.

It was clearly too late for me to make a clean breast of the unintended deception; I was completely hypnotised, overwhelmed by the experience, and, I must admit, influenced by the prospect of receiving a fee.

I had to admire the way in which the hostess kept the show on the road despite this initial setback. Soon it was time for me to choose my pieces of music and here I was confronted with another challenge – that of keeping a straight face when reading the appalling rubbish contained in my script, and of enduring the subsequent 'music'. "For my opening record I have chosen an excerpt from the exciting ballet entitled *The Darts Match* by the gifted young Polish composer Yevgeny Malinovski. This is a remarkable violin solo entitled 'Cataclysm on the Mataclysm' and occurs when the players are throwing their initial darts at the bullseye in order to determine who will begin. It has become a very popular piece in its own right and has become known in popular parlance as 'Fiddle for Middle'."

This was just a foretaste of what was to come. Mercifully, I cannot recall much of the interview, which in retrospect appears as a hideous nightmare. With enormous relief, I heard the sycophantic voice intoning, "And now for your final piece?"

"I've gone back to continental Europe," I replied, or more properly, the script replied, "to the tragic opera by the enormously talented young German Hans Otto von Schleimburger entitled *Das Schneeweissmadchen und die giftige Zwerge*, the usual English translation being *Snow White and the Poison Dwarfs*. The Snow White exemplifies the beautiful daughter of a village innkeeper, who is the butt of unwelcome attentions from soldiers of a Scottish regiment stationed in an adjoining barracks and noted for their anti-social behaviour in the local indigenous community, hence the appellation 'Poison Dwarfs'. Notification has been received that the unit is being relieved by another and the music reflects the villagers' joy. Tragedy is never far away from Hans-Otto's work, however, and it transpires after the arrival of the new regiment that the girl has surreptitiously absconded with the English cook corporal. The celebratory tone of the piece is harshly interrupted when this fact becomes known. The composer simulates the events by adding eleven saucepan-beaters to the standard orchestra and they create a fearsome cacophony with these implements, which epitomise the tools of the cook corporal's trade. The passage in question occurs at the climax of the opera at the conclusion of the fourth act and is often known as 'Cymbalismus', with echoes of the revelry of the witches on the night of Saint Walpurga, who died in AD 779. No finer paradigm of the continuity of musical thought has ever been devised."

I made no attempt to conceal the irony in my voice on reading this nonsense, but took great care to avoid Miss Crawley's vitriolic gaze, with the recollection of the previous five-second demolition that I had undergone. I even contrived to pronounce 'cacophony' as 'cook-oveny', upon which I heard a sharp hiss of breath exhaled between clenched teeth. I braced myself for the attack, which never came.

"And if you could take just one record, which would it be?" asked Lou Crawley.

After nearly half an hour of such pretentious drivel my spirit had begun to rebel. I paused. Miss Crawley shot me a venomous glance. This, plus the small matter of the fee, won the day; chastened, I returned to my script. "Oh, the Schleimburger. He has no equal," I added, for the first time speaking the truth.

"And one book, aside from the Bible and Shakespeare?"

"Tolstoy, *War and Peace*, in the original language. Plus the largest Russian dictionary money can buy. I shall need something to while away the lonely hours."

At last the monstrous experience came to its end. Bunny indicated that the receptionist would deal with the matter of my fee. The last I saw of him, poor wretch, was when he was being dragged by his ponytail through the rear door of the studio by Lou Crawley, who was berating him soundly in her harshest voice.

"I want a word with you, Bunny," I heard her snarl. "Where did you get that cretin from? And why was he not properly briefed?"

The girl at the desk was much more accommodating. I realised that I had left my package in her care and in answer to my query she was most reassuring. "Oh, the insurance people sent someone over to collect it. It happens all the time. They get our mail and we get theirs. It's those daft names."

I fished out of my pocket my electronic notepad, which I had been clutching throughout the whole ordeal, and forged a signature for the parcel.

"Here's your cheque," the helpful girl continued. I was astonished to see that it was made out in the sum of £2,500. I also observed that the payee's name had been omitted. "Just fill it in yourself," she continued. "So many people use stage names, or have numbered bank accounts, or remit their money through financial advisers that we never know what to put."

I thanked her profusely and made my escape as rapidly as possible. As I reached the lift, the doors opened and an individual emerged. I knew instinctively that he was the real Marmion Walmsley-Smythe. He scampered up to the reception desk and I just had time to overhear his opening gambit before the lift doors closed behind me.

Breathless, he wheezed, "Desperately sorry to be so late. Been on a symposium in Bratislava, communication failure…"

I selected 'Ground Floor' and made my dash for freedom.

On reaching the street, it dawned on me that I had totally forgotten about my van, which had been illegally parked for the best part of an hour. At best it could be covered with parking tickets, at worst clamped or towed away. To my amazement, it had not suffered any of these indignities, and I was just about to unlock it and drive away when I spotted, directly opposite on the other side of the street, a small, rather tatty shop displaying a plastic signboard – 'All Cheques Cashed'. I immediately crossed the road and entered a bare room with a few chairs scattered round the walls and a cashier's window behind a security grille. A cheerful individual greeted me.

"What you got there, mate?" he asked.

I produced the cheque. "Whom shall I make it payable to?" I asked.

"It's quite OK; I'll take care of that. We get a lot of these from the broadcasting place. Never bounce – public money, you see. Just a minute." He counted out £2,400 in grubby notes. "£100 commission, guvnor," he said.

"That's fine," I replied, took the money and drove away. I have never been to Broadcasting Centre since that day.

22
CAST OFF

With his usual insight, the Inspector unravels the mystery from the bare bones of the facts.

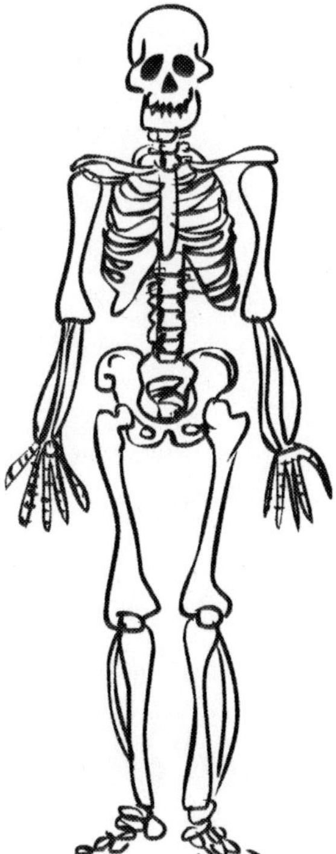

The last coach party of the day emerged from Spookey Hole and straggled across the road to the car park. They had spent a couple of hours wandering around the vast subterranean caverns which riddle this part of the Sheepdip Hills, marvelling at the wonders of nature – lofty chambers, open spaces large enough to accommodate hundreds of people, narrow contorted passageways, and everywhere the stalagmites and stalactites formed over countless thousands of years by the slow, patient drip, drip of water which had penetrated the fissures in the limestone layers overhead. Parts of the cave systems were ingeniously lit to highlight extraordinary shapes, whilst others remained dark and gloomy. The guide counted off her flock as they mounted the steps of the coach and subsided wearily into their comfortable seats. Tourism is extremely hard work.

"All here, Sarah?" inquired the driver from his seat, folding his newspaper and adjusting one of his outside mirrors.

"One to come – ah, here she is. Always seems to be last, but is never actually late."

The person referred to – seat number 45 – was a lady in late middle age, of genteel appearance, expensively but unobtrusively dressed and carrying what appeared to be a large knitting bag. Fellow travellers had noted that she was indeed in the habit of clicking needles to produce some unspecified object during the journey, which on this occasion had lasted for four days. She seemed very preoccupied and only spoke when addressed directly, invariably with extreme politeness and in a cultured voice. She appeared on the courier's nominal roll as 'Mrs Simpson'.

Later the same evening there was a tremendous thunderstorm over the Sheepdips accompanied by torrential rain of unprecedented volume and duration. The watercourses draining into the cave systems became overloaded; modest trickles of water turned into rushing streams and many of the caves were flooded. The whole site was closed for several days in deference to public safety concerns and when the water flow moderated, careful inspections were necessary to ensure that nothing untoward had occurred and that no danger existed before visitors were again admitted. The passage of the floods had left considerable debris made up of sand shoals and small stones, and amongst this detritus the policeman who accompanied the tourism official and safety expert made a startling discovery in the form of a human skull. The attendant publicity sparked a furious debate amongst archaeologists, historians and other academics, as it had long been believed that the caves were the site of prehistoric burials. On closer examination it emerged that the skull was marked with small incisions evidently carved into the bone with a sharp instrument. These consisted of straight lines, a curved line and what appeared to be a right angle. Many theories as to their significance surfaced, the interpretations ranging from proto-Celtiberian hierographs to Old Icelandic runes. In all cases some religious connection was presupposed. The speculation intensified in academic circles until a twelve-year-old Eton schoolboy, one Joshua Prigg, pointed out in a letter to the editor of *The Times* that the markings on the bone bore a close resemblance to Roman numerals. No further abstract theory appeared; the earlier advocates, especially of the more abstruse explanations, keeping their heads well below the parapet until the public derision abated.

Further light was shed when the skull was submitted for official forensic examination. It appeared from radiocarbon and other tests that the relic was not in fact prehistoric, but appertained to a Caucasian male who had died during the twentieth century at an age set between thirty and forty years. Moreover, there was some deformation of the lower area where, in a complete skeleton, the skull would have met the vertebrae. One explanation proposed that the head had been mounted on a pole, with connotations of witchcraft or ritual murder. These discoveries removed the matter at one stroke from the sphere of archaeology or anthropology into the area of a police investigation. Further, the bones were discoloured not merely by the aging process but by what seemed to be a coat of varnish of some kind. Despite intensive enquiries, nothing was discovered that would link the skull to any missing person, and in the normal course of events the matter would probably have remained a local curiosity.

However, three days later came another revelation. At the end of a very busy day at Fastbuck Abbey, where an anniversary of the completion of the building in 1938 was being celebrated, the bones forming a complete human hand were discovered behind an altar cloth. The numerous small individual constituent pieces had been skilfully joined to form a complete hand, which had what appeared to be a threaded socket at the wrist, presumably to enable it to be affixed to an arm. The most telling factors were, however, the realisation that marks resembling Roman numerals were inscribed on the assembly, and the whole had clearly been coated in some kind of lacquer.

On the following day, two lads fishing off a canal towpath found two round bone objects concealed in the brickwork of a farm bridge, which, it transpired, were human kneecaps. The pattern, now becoming familiar, was followed – bones varnished, screw attachments and Roman numerals. In this instance, the numbers were followed by the letters 'D' and 'S' respectively. Because of possible foul play, the police were notified at once. It fell to the redoubtable Chief Inspector Corse of the local constabulary and his assistant Sergeant Brewis to investigate. By now the whole matter was a cause celebre in the newspapers and the two policemen were already aware of the other chance discoveries. They took possession of the objects and retired to their office to ponder on the affair.

"You know, Brewis, I have an odd presentiment that I've seen something like this before," mused the Inspector, "but for the life of me I can't think where."

"What about an exhibition," offered Brewis, "or a medical school?"

Corse leapt to his feet, removed his coat from its hanger on the office wall, seized his car keys from the hook near the door where they invariably hung – he was a most methodical man – and exclaimed, "Come on, Brewis, we've got to see Lady Molly; for once you've said something useful."

In the car, Brewis sought an explanation. "Who's Lady Molly then, sir?"

"The widow of Sir Christopher Maudsley. Lives at Haxton Manor."

"Who's Maudsley?"

"Who was, Brewis. He was a leading surgeon and an internationally known expert on anatomy. Lectured all over the place. Died a few months back."

"And how do you know her?"

"Chris and I used to meet socially."

"Freemason?" asked Brewis with a sly grin.

Corse favoured his subordinate with a contemptuous glance. "We were members of a musical appreciation society and shared a common interest in the works of Gustav Mahler. He had an amazing brain. Could hum or whistle the entire Mahler first symphony, note perfect."

"How did he manage those drum beats in the finale?" queried Brewis, tongue-in-cheek.

"Used to thump his desk," replied Corse, seemingly unaware of the younger man's sarcastic tone.

Arriving at Haxton Manor, a sixteenth-century stone house in a beautiful garden, Corse strode up to the front door, which lay ajar. He was evidently on familiar terms with the good lady, as evidenced by his failure to telephone in advance, and he knocked briefly and walked into the hall, a large square room lit by two windows and furnished with a great fireplace.

"A word of warning, Brewis," muttered Corse sotto voce, "keep your mouth shut. She doesn't know why we're really here."

Neither do I, reflected Brewis, but did as he had been bidden.

Beside the hearth was a black marble plinth, empty.

"I thought so; Pedro's not here," murmured Corse.

At that moment, a lady of late middle age, genteel appearance, expensively but unobtrusively dressed, pushed the door open and entered. "I thought it was your car, Corse," she said in a cultured voice. Everyone called Corse by his surname; his first name, if he had one, remained a secret.

"Hello, Molly, my dear. We have some business in this area, so I thought I would steal ten minutes and call on you. How are you getting on?"

"I suppose that 'as well as can be expected' meets the bill," she said graciously. "Can I offer you some coffee, gentlemen?"

"Thank you; that would be very nice. I don't think you've met my assistant Brewis, have you?"

After coffee, served in beautiful antique porcelain, and some desultory chat, Corse suddenly remarked, "Why, where's Pedro?"

Lady Molly, usually so precise, sounded uncharacteristically vague. "Oh, someone borrowed him. Christopher was inordinately proud of Pedro and he often went on his travels."

"Where's he gone this time?"

"I really have no idea. It was a long-standing arrangement and Christopher dealt with all the details as normal. I just moved him to an outhouse so they could collect him whenever they called. What with the funeral and one thing and another I haven't given it much attention, I'm afraid."

Corse let the matter drop and, not wishing to trouble the bereaved lady, they soon left.

"Who on earth is Pedro?" Brewis demanded back in the privacy of the car.

"A skeleton, no less," replied his superior. "Maudsley used it as a very effective training aid for his lectures. He assembled all the small bones into functional groups and fixed the principal parts in such a way that it could be dismantled, either for transportation or for instructional purposes. The bones were all numbered, in Roman numerals, naturally."

"So why the 'D' and 'S' on those kneecaps?"

"Dexter and Sinister – Latin for right and left. There's no doubt that what has been popping up all over the place is none other than Pedro."

"I can see the point of numbering the bits – more than two hundred bones in the human body."

"How did you know that, Brewis? I didn't have you down as a specialist in ossification."

"I'm not. It came up in the pub quiz last week. Anyhow, where did Maudsley get him from?"

"No one really knows. But you know how ruthless some of these medical people are. I suppose that earning your living cutting people up hardens the attitude. Rumour had it that he was a convict, killed during a prison riot in Brazil. Fortunately – if you can apply such a word in a case like this – the bullets entered soft tissue and his bones remained intact. He was a perfect specimen and so ideal for the job he had to perform. Some people even claim that they left his body out for the birds and ants to eat the flesh. Maudsley certainly used to go to South America, that much I do know."

"But what's the point of pinching him, or borrowing him, and spreading him all over the place? Very elaborate practical joke. Some crank opposed to surgery? Private feud against the family?"

"Who knows?" replied Corse thoughtfully.

Since it was now obvious that the discoveries were in fact the constituent parts of a skeleton that belonged in his area, and the additional circumstance of his knowing their owner, Corse was appointed by agreement to co-ordinate the whole case. If Lady Molly didn't yet know about the discoveries, she obviously soon would, as they came thick and fast on the heels of the kneecaps, if that is not a contradiction in terms. A shoulder blade in the gardens near the waterfall at Ratsworth House, a ribcage here, a foot there, a femur somewhere else. It is certainly true that there is safety in numbers and that one person can easily conceal themselves and their actions amidst a multitude of people. In any event, many of the finds occurred in areas frequented by tourists, whether by accident or design was unclear.

Thus in a fairly short time, Pedro had reappeared in his pristine glory, and with the aid of one of Sir Christopher's admirable textbooks it was possible to reconstruct him, making use of the Roman numerals and their cross-reference to the diagrams. Corse took it upon himself to personally escort the skeleton to Haxton Manor and to place him with due ceremony upon his marble plinth. Lady Maudsley expressed her warm gratitude for the efforts of all concerned in his recovery and undertook to ensure that he would not go astray again. There would be no more loans and he would be kept under strict surveillance – after all, he was her late distinguished husband's pride and joy.

"Have you any plans, Molly?" enquired Corse at the informal supper party arranged to commemorate Pedro's safe return home.

"I'm thinking of one or two trips abroad, as a matter of fact. Christopher was forever flying off round the world and I usually stayed at home. Now it's my turn."

"You don't mind flying?"

"Oh, no, I shan't go that way. I always resent some foreigner x-raying my luggage at an airport – it's an intrusion into one's privacy. No, there are some perfectly nice coach trips around Europe these days. As it happens, I'm off on Monday to the Black Forest and Lake Lucerne. I shall travel light; just take my knitting and a good umbrella."

On the Sunday evening, Molly packed her modest luggage. She unscrewed Pedro's head (catalogue number CLII) rolled it in a half-finished woollen scarf and dropped it into her knitting bag. Next she slipped a humerus (XCVII) inside her large furled umbrella. "God, how I hate that bloody thing," she said aloud. "They won't find it this time."

23
LOOK BEFORE YOU LEAP

Thirty days hath September,
April, June and dull November.
All the rest have thirty-one,
Excepting February alone,
Which hath twenty-eight days clear,
And twenty-nine in each leap year.

The Reverend E. Cobham Brewer, in his admirable *Dictionary of Phrase and Fable, Classic Edition*, informs us of the following fact:

In 1228 an Act of the Scottish Parliament provided that:

> *[It is] ordained that during the reign of her most blessed majesty, Margaret, any maiden lady of both high and low estate, shall have liberty to approach the man she likes. If he refuses to take her to be his wife, he shall be fined in the sum of one hundred pounds, or less, as his estate may be, except and always if he can make it appear that he is betrothed to another woman, then he shall be free.*

I have anglicised and modernised the spelling, without, I hope, distorting the underlying meaning. Brewer omits to record how long this decree lasted before being repealed, or whether it was rigorously enforced. It would be most interesting to study the reactions of present-day Scottish gentlemen in the event that their new parliament took it upon itself to reintroduce such a measure today.

The modern equivalent would appear to be the tradition that ladies have the prerogative of proposing marriage during leap years, and that Leap Year's Day, 29th February, is when males are most at risk. This is the background to our tale.

* * * * *

Christopher Wilkins had attained the age of forty years without venturing to enter the state of wedded bliss. He had nothing against marriage, and indeed regarded it as the normal condition of life, accepting that one day he would undertake such a step. He was, however, shy and diffident in his dealing with members of the fair sex and had never had what could be described as a real girlfriend. He owned a very successful company, which he had created literally from nothing, and was totally engrossed in business affairs. As a very young man he had received a modest inheritance from his grandfather and with this had purchased a semi-derelict quarry located near to his home. There were very considerable reserves of good quality building stone and he rapidly discovered that there was a ready market for this product waiting to be exploited. He expanded the business to include the winning of sand and gravel and then mixed concrete. Subsequent booms in the construction of roads and houses combined to make him a very rich man. Apart from the favourable outcome of his initial purchase, he was possessed of sound business acumen. He never borrowed money or issued shares to raise new capital, but financed expansion purely from current profits. As a result he retained personal control over all his assets and was at no risk of losing his company to a hostile take-over by one of the large conglomerates that soon began to beat a path to his door. He steadfastly resisted all offers to buy him out, largely out of loyalty to his employees, whose hard work had created his own personal wealth, added to the fact that the concern was effectively his life's purpose.

It so happened that Christopher had been born on 29th February, and in consequence had a 'real' birthday only once every four years. He did not feel in any way disadvantaged by this state of affairs, as he took no notice of birthdays in any event. Since by this time both his parents were deceased and he had no siblings, there was no pressure from any immediate family member to acknowledge what is considered a key milestone in a human life, the fortieth birthday. He was taken completely by surprise (a rare occurrence in his well-ordered life) when his long-serving secretary, Ruth Lander, entered his office abruptly, without being bidden and without notice or ceremony.

"Whatever is it, Ruth?" he asked, observing her flushed face and agitated manner. "Is the place on fire?"

"No, Christopher," she stuttered, "the place isn't, but I am! Do you know what date it is?"

He glanced at his desk calendar. "29th February. You haven't come in here to tell me that, have you?" he asked, half facetiously and half convinced that she had lost her reason. She had never previously called him Christopher, as he had never endorsed the 'modern' trend towards the universal use of first names.

"It's Leap Year's Day. On this day it is a woman's prerogative to propose marriage." She spoke in an uncomfortable, forced manner, as if she were a member of an amateur dramatic society reading the script for the first time of a play which she did not like. He made no answer, merely because he could not for the life of him think what reply could be required. "I'm here to propose marriage to you," she blurted out. "I've known you for years, and you must be aware of my feelings for you by now!"

Christopher was dumbfounded and sat motionless in his chair. This total lack of reaction merely served to increase Ruth's agitation, and unable to control her emotions, she burst into tears.

He pulled himself together with a gigantic effort. "Please don't upset yourself. I'll go and get a cup of coffee." This mundane act was the only possible solution he could imagine.

He returned with two cardboard cups of what the automatic dispenser optimistically and somewhat untruthfully described as 'Magic Bean blend coffee', by which time Ruth had regained a little of her composure.

They remained silent for some minutes, tentatively sipping the tasteless acidic black liquid. Ultimately, he regained his wits sufficiently to make some kind of conversation. "I'm sorry that I was so slow to react, Ruth. I was taken rather by surprise." That was the most masterly understatement possible. "I really had no idea – it must have taken a very great deal of courage to do what you have done. What would have happened if I had simply laughed, or taken it as a bad joke? I think that the best thing is that you should take the rest of the day off. I'll try and muddle through without you. When you've calmed down we can talk about it further."

She brightened considerably. "You don't think I'm mad?"

"Of course not. I admire your honesty. We'll discuss it properly. After all, we aren't exactly strangers, are we?"

Ruth repaired the damage to her face as best she could and disappeared. Christopher felt the need for some fresh air and an opportunity to put his thoughts in order, so he left his office, after deputing one of the staff to sit in for the departed Ruth, and went for a walk down to the stonemasons' workshops. This was one of his favourite places. He had always appreciated the wonderful natural quality of stone, one of the reasons for his acquisition of the run-down quarry all those years ago, and took particular interest in the intricate work executed by his craftsmen in that medium. The exercise stimulated his thought processes, as it always did. Perhaps this apparently bizarre suggestion was not so crazy as it first seemed. He was not blind to feminine charms, and Ruth was undeniably an attractive girl. As she had stated, they had worked together for ten years and knew each other's peculiarities extremely well. He had always assumed that he would marry one day, and that whilst he was in good health, forty was a significant marker and he wasn't getting any younger. If he wanted a wife he would be spared all the agony, uncertainty and excruciating embarrassment of finding a willing candidate. Most eligible women were already spoken for. She thoroughly understood what his work entailed (a very strong point, this last). His analytical business mind mentally wrote down the pros and cons just as if he were considering the purchase of a sand quarry or investing in a concrete-mixing plant. The only factor not taken into account was the human factor – flesh, blood and emotion. By the time he had got back to the office his virtual balance sheet had been drawn up. He would accept.

A complication arose in the matter of Christopher's forthcoming trip abroad. For some time past he had been contemplating expanding his activities in Europe and possibly beyond. With customary caution and thoroughness he would do nothing precipitate, but proposed to go and have a long look himself. 'Due diligence' was his motto in everything that he undertook, with the possible exception of marriage. A brief visit, an expensive consultant's report and a possibly disastrous investment were not on his agenda. He had therefore arranged to go away for six months and make a scrupulous personal investigation into any company he might consider absorbing – the local market, labour relations, financial implications, properly audited accounts and so forth. Whilst he was away he would delegate the day-to-day running of his empire to a trusted friend and colleague, Andrew Talbot. Andrew was the company solicitor and financial director, and knew as much about the business as he himself. He derived considerable benefit from profit sharing, so had vested interests, and Christopher could rely on his integrity and judgement.

On 1st March promptly at ten o'clock, Ruth came into Christopher's office for the customary daily conference. On this occasion she was visibly nervous at revisiting the scene of the preceding day's events, and Christopher wasted no time in putting her at ease. "Feeling better?" he asked solicitously. Without waiting for a reply, he continued. "I've thought over the little chat we had yesterday, and will not delay in putting you out of your misery, if that's the right word for such a matter. I'm honoured to accept your proposal. Just one thing," he added quickly, as she jumped like a scared rabbit out of her chair, made as if she would run out of the room and then sat down again heavily. "You know I'm going away for six months. I know a great deal about quarry products, but less than nothing regarding wedding arrangements. If we're going to do this, we should do it reasonably quickly. What do you say? Do we go for a small private ceremony?"

"You can safely leave all of that to me, Christopher. My mother is the world's prime expert on weddings. I've got three sisters, remember, and she has launched them all in considerable style. I know she's longing to do the same for me, being the only one remaining at home. And you know that Daddy is going to be the next mayor, don't you? Mummy will pull out all the stops, I know."

If Christopher had any misgivings about all the stops, he kept them to himself. The pragmatic side of his nature took over. He had no time for ostentation, but it was something he wouldn't need to bother about. It only lasts a few hours, anyway. And if it pleased Ruth, why not? All her sisters had had showy weddings, and it was unreasonable to expect her to be any different.

"Shall I ask Andrew to be best man?" he ventured.

She could hardly voice any objection, even if she had wanted to. It was all over bar the shouting.

Christopher called Andrew and asked him to come over to the cottage that same evening. They were accustomed to meet there on occasions when there was something important to discuss, as it afforded a calm and private refuge away from the hurly-burly of the workplace. He wasted no time in apprising Andrew of this novel situation and the latter readily assented to act as best man. Any reservations about the wisdom of his friend's actions remained unexpressed.

"Do you know the Landers, Ruth's parents?" asked Christopher.

"Oh, yes. She's a great socialite and will be in her element. I'll arrange to see her as soon as possible, as you're away in a few days' time. I'll keep a watching brief and let you know what's going on. We'll be in contact a couple of times a week in any case."

Shortly afterwards, Christopher departed for foreign climes, leaving Andrew in full charge of both business and private affairs.

A couple of weeks later, when the two were having their bi-weekly telephone conversation, Christopher asked, "How are the wedding preparations?"

Andrew paused before replying in what he hoped was a light and reassuring tone. "She's got the bit between her teeth, make no mistake. All principal males to be in top hats, tail coats and cravats; live orchestra, champagne; hired a large hall; limousines; all sisters to be maids of honour; no children allowed in the vicinity. This is the last daughter she has left and she's totally single-minded on this one."

"Well, I suppose it's only natural," Christopher said consolingly, although he was not entirely sure whom he was endeavouring to console.

They passed on to more mundane matters concerning sand and gravel.

A month later, the messages emanating from home were assuming an alarming tone. "It's spiralling out of control. Guest list now totals one hundred and fifty-three. Talk of a horse-drawn carriage. Bride's father to wear mayoral regalia. Local TV station alerted. Wants the police to close half the roads. Special peal of bells – 88 changes. Trying to get the Bishop to officiate. Thank God it only happens once!"

In the absence of an adequate reply, Christopher contented himself with a query about the business.

"Piece of cake by comparison, and not wedding cake, either."

The great day dawned at last, with the bonus of fine, settled weather. Christopher had returned from his travels a few days previously and just had time to be measured for his hired finery, which was duly issued.

In response to Andrew's question regarding the matter of expanding the company's activities abroad, he was very emphatic. "Game's not worth the candle. All manner of minefields – currency exchange rates, political unrest, European regulations, language difficulties, taxation regime, environmental considerations. Recipe for disaster. Wouldn't touch it with a bargepole."

"I think you're absolutely right," replied his assistant, and the whole matter was dropped.

He was so preoccupied with business affairs that he had hardly seen or spoken to Ruth, who had in any case left work. Naomi, Ruth's mother, had specifically warned him to stay away from her daughter immediately prior to the wedding to avoid bad luck. They met briefly at a somewhat perfunctory rehearsal at the church, at which Naomi took the most prominent role.

The service before a packed congregation passed without incident, or appeared to do so to Christopher, who by this time was reduced to a state resembling an automaton. An interminable photography and video session ensued at the church door.

After a couple of shots of the bride and groom, Naomi Lander assumed command. "Bride and attendants; bride and bride's mother; bride and father; bride and both parents; parents and four daughters; bride's mother; mayor in robes and chain of office; bride's maternal grandmother…" The list seemed endless.

Christopher began to feel a distinct sense of being marginalised, but such was his temperament and state of mind that this did not trouble him unduly. Finally, Naomi appeared satisfied that the event had been suitably commemorated for historical purposes and they entered the cars. (At the eleventh hour the horse-drawn carriage had been ruled out – something, it was rumoured, to do with foot and mouth disease preventing the free movement of animals.) Thus they made their way in stately procession to the reception.

The place was absolutely jam-packed with people, none of whom Christopher recognised. In the main hall, waiters in eighteenth-century dress and powdered wigs were dispensing champagne to all and sundry. Naomi had ruled out a formal seated breakfast on the grounds that people should be free to circulate and meet everybody else. The real reason was that the building could not accommodate the large throng she had invited. The guests helped themselves from an enormous and exotic buffet laid out on side tables.

Ultimately, some form of order was established and speeches, mercifully brief, were delivered from a raised dais, followed by numerous toasts, proposed by the town crier, specially engaged because of his elaborate costume and loud voice. Dancing began, led by the bride and groom. Hardly had Christopher and Ruth accomplished one circuit of the room than the bride's father excused him. All and sundry followed, everyone wishing to dance with the bride. Champagne flowed like water. The noise level rose in tandem. Christopher found himself wedged in a corner adjacent to a fire door and was quite unable to extricate himself. Once or twice he examined the mechanism of the fire door, but concluded that it hardly seemed appropriate to escape that way.

He caught the occasional glimpse of his new wife whirling past in the general maelstrom, and saw that she appeared very flushed from the heat of the room, the crush, the emotional nature of the proceedings and the quantity of champagne which she had evidently consumed. She clearly had not eaten sufficient to counteract the effect of the drinks that were pressed upon her from all sides. After an eternity, the crowd was perceptibly thinner, and Christopher, released from his corner, went in search of his new bride; he was dismayed to find her clinging helplessly to her mother's arm, supported on the other side by her sister Penelope, her veil and tiara askew, and quite intoxicated.

Mother was consolatory. "Come along, darling, we'll just get you home and you can change your clothes and have a little rest."

Ruth mumbled something indistinct about "my husband", whereupon Naomi replied acidly, "Husband! Not very attentive, is he!"

He last saw her half-carried out of the back door of the hall and whisked surreptitiously away. She appeared to have been sick over her dress, and was clearly in no condition to go anywhere except to bed.

By this time the hall was almost empty. Andrew was nowhere to be seen, and who could blame him? An elderly gentleman, the worse for drink, accosted Christopher, seized him by the arm and said, "Fine looking woman, that!"

"Who?"

"Why, the bride, you fool, the bride."

"Yes, I think so," replied the bridegroom as the old man staggered off.

Christopher had previously arranged for them to spend a few days in the country at an old inn after the wedding. This was one matter which he had kept strictly under his personal control, and absolutely nobody knew where the lucky pair was going. He made his way rapidly to where he had left his car, conveniently close to the hall, drove directly to his cottage, divested himself of his borrowed finery and dressed in comfortable casual clothes. He carefully packed the wedding suit into the cardboard containers in which it had been delivered and placed these in the unlocked garage. He telephoned the hire company and left a message asking them to collect them. Picking up his bag, previously prepared, he locked the house, got into the car and proceeded directly to the country hotel, some two hours distant. During the journey he had ample time and opportunity to reflect on the day's events. It was all too obvious that the whole affair was a creature of Naomi's, and that in all probability it was she who had induced her daughter to propose to him. He was, after all, by any token an excellent catch. The day was a celebration of Naomi Lander, and nothing else.

The country hotel was a long, low stone-built edifice of some considerable antiquity. It lay back from a secondary road, was surrounded by attractive gardens and what once had been a moat or monastic fishpond. Following the events of the day it appeared to be a haven of tranquil normality. This impression was reinforced when Christopher entered the building. A small reception area led into a large inviting lounge with leaded windows, beams, heavy carpets, fat armchairs, wooden panelling and, most inviting of all, a bright log fire in the great hearth at the far wall. It was by now late summer and the evenings could be chilly.

The room was empty, but as he entered he heard a voice behind him. "Good evening. You must be Mr Wilkins – I heard the car. Do you want any help with your luggage?"

"Yes to the first, and no to the second, thank you. I've only a small bag. Incidentally, there's only one of me. Family crisis, you know." I suppose that's true, he thought.

"Would you like to sign in at the desk? You're in number four." The speaker was a woman of about his own age, and her voice was clear and mellifluous; after the hysteria of the earlier part of the day, it was very reassuring. He entered his particulars in the book at the reception desk. "Would you like some dinner, Mr Wilkins?" the soothing voice continued.

"I would love some, thank you. Would you be Mrs James? I think I spoke to you when I made my reservation."

"Yes, although people call me Rose; short for Rosemary."

He was struck by her direct and open manner, which was in sharp contrast to the pretence, side and insincerity which had characterised everyone at the wedding.

"I'm called Chris, for Christopher." He could scarcely believe that he had made such a remark to a complete stranger, but somehow it seemed appropriate and natural.

"What time do you want to eat? Here's a menu."

"I don't stand on ceremony. When it's ready, and whatever you have handy."

She smiled. "Well, you're easy to please, Chris. I'll show you your room. There's a telephone there if you need it."

"That's the last thing I need. Anyway, nobody knows I'm here. I have a very busy life and I'm taking a break."

He appeared to be the only guest; he ate a hearty supper alone and went to bed, where he slept like a log.

After breakfast next morning he went to explore the garden. Pausing to admire the huge golden carp in the pond, he became aware that he was not alone. Rose had followed him in his perambulations and at once opened a conversation. "Did you sleep well?"

"Absolutely wonderful. Superb restful place you have here."

"What's the agenda for today?" she asked, again in a straightforward matter-of-fact way.

"I want to see some local points of interest. The old post mill at Flaxton, for example. I believe it's the oldest mill of its kind still in existence."

"Oh, yes, it's very worthwhile. I haven't been up there for years. Have you got a large-scale map? There's a maze of lanes around here and we don't want to lose you, do we?"

He astonished himself by his next remark. "Why don't you come with me to avoid that unhappy eventuality? I presume you can leave the hotel?" He had never made such a proposition to a woman in his life.

"What a good idea. Yes, I do have some help in running the place."

He had arranged to stay at the inn for four days, and had then hired a narrowboat on an adjacent canal. He had been canal cruising a couple of times as a young lad and knew the fundamentals. On his last evening he went to the bar for a glass of beer after dinner. Rosemary was behind the counter, and there were only a couple of locals seated in front of the fire. These soon departed and the pair was alone.

"You aren't quite yourself, Chris. Something bothering you?"

"Very much so. My time is up and I don't want to go."

"Then stay." He explained about the canal trip. "Won't that be difficult with only one person on board? What about locks and mooring?"

"You sound very knowledgeable, Rose. Have you ever been on a narrowboat?"

"As a matter of fact I have. I enjoyed it."

At this juncture he finally took leave of his senses. "Why don't you come with me? The boat is forty-five feet long and there's lots of room, so I shan't invade your privacy."

"Wait just a minute," she said, and disappeared into the reception area. He could hear her on the telephone, but not sufficiently well to ascertain the drift of her conversation. "You've got yourself a crew, Captain," she said on her return. "I was due to have a week off in any case."

They arrived at the boatyard and while Chris reported in, Rose went to the local store to buy a week's supply of food.

"Ah, hello, sir," said the man behind the desk. "You've changed from Ruth to Rosemary, haven't you?" Christopher froze in horror. He hadn't spoken to anyone around there and no one knew who he was. He had a private mobile phone but even Andrew was not privy to the number. The boatman appeared not to notice his confusion. "Yes, but *Rosemary* is three feet longer and a different layout. She's a much newer boat, though. *Ruth* developed engine trouble and we didn't manage to contact you regarding a substitution."

Glancing out of the window, Chris saw that all the boats had girls' names. "What an incredible coincidence! Seems like predestination," he mused.

The problem with hiring a canal boat for a week lies in the fact that you have to deliver it back to where you started. A careful itinerary must be drawn up with details of where to find the water taps, where to locate good overnight moorings, where to turn the boat around, what to do if you lose time because a lock is closed for repairs without warning, and so on.

Three days out, and Chris was once again assailed by incipient gloom. Ever sensitive to his moods, Rose asked him, "Well, what is it this time?"

"I don't want to go back yet."

"What about extending for a week, if it isn't already booked for someone else?"

Chris at once telephoned the boatyard; unbelievably, his luck held.

"That'll be fine sir. We've got your card details. Call at the Three Oaks Marina, that's twenty miles up from where you are now. We have an arrangement with them – they'll pump you out, fill you up with diesel and check your gas canisters. There's also a shop there selling groceries. You got lucky – it's the end of the summer season and you were the last booking. In any case, we're getting rid of her."

"What on earth for? It's nearly new."

"We've merged our concern with Bittern Cruisers and we're rationalising the combined fleet."

"You're selling Rosemary?"

"Not at the moment – you're on her for another ten days."

"Give me first refusal – put my name on her."

"Very well, sir. Suits both of us."

"What have you done?" asked Rose, who had heard sufficient of the conversation to pick up the gist of it.

"Booked another week. We got lucky."

"I think there's more to it than that," said Rose with a penetrating look.

"There's a very great deal more to it," confessed Chris, "and I was scared witless about telling you the whole story, because the inevitable outcome would be that I would lose you." The unfortunate man had fallen in love for the first time in his life, at the age of forty, on his wedding day, and with the wrong woman.

"Have you ever been married?" she asked, with characteristic perspicacity.

He recognised what he already knew, that she had remarkable empathy, that she could invade his mind and know what he was thinking before he had even clarified his own thoughts. "I was married once," he began, "but now it seems an awfully long time ago."

"I was married too," she said, without elaborating, and by way of encouragement, "but not any longer. You might as well come clean."

So he told her the whole sorry story, culminating with the fact that he intended to sell his business and was now, literally, afloat.

"What a coincidence," she said, "I've decided to get rid of mine. One of those hotel chains has been pursuing me for ages. Lend me your telephone, Chris."

Christopher telephoned Andrew that evening. "Listen carefully, old fellow. I'm selling the business, lock, stock and barrel, and pulling out. Amalgamated Asphalt has been bothering me for the past two years and has put a very tasty price on our head. Tell them I accept, on two conditions. One, the whole thing is done at once and in total privacy; two, they keep you on under a cast-iron contract as chief executive, if you want to stay, that is. If not, neither of us ever needs to work again for the rest of his life. You have total discretion. Got that?"

"Very clear. Now I've some news for you. Lander is in trouble. Naomi is being dunned for a lot of money from caterers, hall owners, wine merchants, dressmakers, florists, car hire people and numerous others. She overdid the wedding slightly."

"Fine," said Chris. "Buy them off. Pay all the debts as part of the purchase price for his assets – he's got a transport concern. That would fit in nicely with our firm. Put it about that it's a merger, but in reality none of the Landers will have anything to do with the company in future."

"Good. What about Ruth? By the way, she's gone to ground. Allegedly in Wales with her sister Lucinda."

Christopher was about to ask how Andrew knew this, but thought better of it. On that score least said, soonest mended. However, there remained the tricky affair of his marital status.

"Have a word with one of your lawyer friends who specialises in divorce. There must be something called constructive desertion or failure to fulfil contractual obligations for what happened. One other thing, Andrew; pop round to the cottage and make sure that the monkey suit has been collected from the garage. I'll be in touch."

* * * * *

At this point the canal runs for some distance alongside the river, but at a slightly higher elevation, being cut into the side of a low hill. The view from the towpath across the valley is extremely attractive, embracing water meadows with small distributary streams controlled by ancient wooden sluice gates, and in the background the counter-slope well covered with deciduous trees. In spring and summer the scene is enlivened with birdsong and fragrant with the perfume of wild flowers. I had been walking under a hot sun for some distance and was glad to encounter a log seat, thoughtfully placed in the shade of a row of beech trees, where a mooring furnished with bollards had been established. I subsided gratefully onto the bench, admiring the outlook and enjoying the solitude. Presently I noticed the snub nose of a narrowboat approaching very quietly along the waterway. The only visible occupant was a man of some sixty years of age, and evidently a skilled and experienced boater, as he cut the engine and brought the boat extremely gently close into the bank side without making contact with dry land. The vessel was virtually motionless when he came ashore with a quick and agile step, holding the stern rope, which he looped deftly twice around a bollard in a rapid and practised movement. I wondered idly how he would secure the other end of the narrowboat, which had drifted about a foot towards mid-stream. I was not left long in doubt. The boatman emitted one shrill whistle, upon which a small terrier leapt from the prow onto the towpath, the end of the bow-rope in his jaws.

"Good boy, Toby!" exclaimed his owner, who seized the rope's end and secured the boat in an instant. "Shall we go for a walk?"

The dog scampered to the stern of the tethered narrowboat, vanished abruptly down the cabin steps and in a trice reappeared with a worn leather lead held in his mouth. The man nodded to me and the pair set off along the towpath in the direction from which they had arrived.

"Just up to bridge 64, Toby," he said to his companion. "It's your dinnertime!"

In ten minutes they returned, Toby still carrying his lead, and the dog rushed headlong down the cabin steps.

I was level with the boat and noticed that the superstructure was embellished in an ornate cursive script, surrounded with emblematic paintings of flowers, with the name 'Rosemary'. I had been so fascinated by the whole mooring process that I could not forbear to make some comment. I looked at the boatman and saw that he was indeed in late middle age, tall, upright, with a healthy suntan under his hat, from which wisps of unkempt grey hair revealed themselves.

He smiled in an amicable manner and, encouraged, I remarked, "You've done that before."

"A few thousand times," he said.

"Are you alone on the boat?" I asked.

"Oh, no, we have a crew of four. I'm the navigator, Toby is the bosun and Felicity is in charge of security and rodent management." He indicated a female tabby cat as he spoke.

I had not previously observed her lying on the cabin roof between a trough containing geraniums and a pile of small logs. "That's a happy name," I ventured. "Has she got a temperament to match?"

"That's a requisite for living afloat," he replied, "but she started life with us named Felixstowe. It was a play on words, you see," he said in response to my unspoken question. "Felis is Latin for cat, and she crept on board one night when nobody was looking. Stowed away, as it were. Hence Felis and Stow. My grandfather came from Felixstowe, so there was a family connection."

"Why did you alter it?"

"Well, Felix is a boy's name and she turned out to be a girl."

"How did you know? I believe it can be notoriously difficult to tell with young cats."

"The four kittens were a fairly strong hint," he replied, laughing. "We had her doctored and rechristened after that."

"What about the kittens?" I asked, fearing the worst in view of the proximity of the unlimited amount of water.

"Got them all jobs on other boats. We monitor their progress from time to time as we cruise around the network."

"How does she maintain security?"

"She watches the cabin door, and if anyone gets near it she calls the dog. He does the rest."

"You said you had a crew of four?"

"Oh, yes, the other one is Rose, the captain. She's down in the galley making some tea. Would you care to join us?"

"That's extremely civil of you. My name is David."

"And we are Chris and Rose aforementioned."

"Do you live aboard permanently?"

"Most of the time, hence the flowers and firewood. Had the old girl twenty years. Still got a cottage on terra firma, of course. Sometimes the canals are closed in the winter, especially for heavy maintenance like replacing lock gates or repairing leaks, and the boat herself has to have her bottom blacked and suchlike. But we regard the boat as our first home. Come aboard; the tea should be ready."

I descended the steep wooden steps, with Toby's permission, and entered the cabin. This was exquisitely furnished and decorated, cosy and comfortable in the extreme. A wood-burning stove stood in the corner. "What a wonderful home!" I exclaimed. "How did you come to be living on a narrowboat?"

"It's quite a story," replied Rose. "How long have you got? How did you get down here?"

"My car is about a mile away at the next lock, only twenty or thirty minutes' walk."

"Well, don't try walking along the towpath after dark. I'll give you the bare bones of the story," which she proceeded to do, clearly omitting some details.

"And what happened to Ruth?" I queried when she had finished.

"When the dust settled, she and Andrew got married in a registry office with seven people present, including the happy couple and the registrar. Apparently, he had always been sweet on her, and he considered it his final duty as the original best man to tidy up the loose ends."

"What did her mother think of this?"

"Nobody told her until it was over. Once bitten twice shy, you might say."

"And Andrew – did he remain at work?"

"Just retired as chairman of the parent company on a pension of £1.4 million a year. Very astute fellow, Andrew."

"That's absolutely fascinating. Why don't you write a book about it?"

"Nobody would believe it," said Chris.

24
CAVEAT EMPTOR

Lottie had spent her entire long life living in Tunnel Cottage. It would be extremely difficult for her to leave and to contemplate the thought of someone else in the old familiar house.

Tunnel Cottage was very appropriately named. It stood guarding the cavernous black entrance which admitted boats into the hole bored directly through the great sandstone bluff known as Mount Piggle, and which obstructed the bold onward march of the Midland and North Western Union Canal. The curious name was said to derive from a dialect word signifying gorse, which grew in profusion and for most of the year imparted a bright yellow blaze of colour all over the hill. Despite its name, it was hardly a mountain, attaining scarcely nine hundred feet above sea level. Canal tunnels were notoriously difficult and expensive to construct, but the engineer resolved to dig this one to avoid a lengthy and tortuous diversion around the obstruction, which, apart from the opposition of local landowners, would have entailed an extended journey time along the waterway. In addition, the tunnel was only some seven hundred and fifty yards long and was cut through fine-grained hard sandstone which would not necessitate a brick lining. The stone itself was of good building quality, so some of the material recovered could be put to use in structures on the canal itself or sold for use elsewhere. A considerable quantity was quarried and there were side-galleries and wide stretches under the hill which apart from yielding stone enabled ready passage of boats. A flight of five locks lowered the waterway to the entrance level.

The cottage was built in 1777 when the canal was constructed and was occupied by the tunnel and lock-keeper. It lay at the head of a kind of natural rift or valley about a hundred yards deep, which was the logical place to start tunnelling.

When the tunnel was bored, a towpath was provided to enable draught animals to be employed. The path was narrow, and although boats could pass, horses could not, and a system was adopted whereby traffic could flow in one direction during the odd hours and in the reverse direction during the even hours. With the coming of the railways, commercial traffic underwent a serious decline and there were insufficient resources to allow proper maintenance, so the structures of the waterway fell into disrepair. In the name of 'rationalisation', the towpath was removed, since powered boats had become the norm in any case. When the canals were nationalised, the Midland and North Western Union was put into the so-called remainder category, meaning that it had neither commercial nor leisure potential and that limited maintenance would be carried out. The future appeared gloomy, but two factors combined to ensure its survival. It was realised that a canal can usefully function as a water carrier, and it found a new use as a feeder to a large reservoir which had been built some sixty miles further on. One effect of this was that the canal had a constant current. In addition, some local heritage enthusiasts formed a preservation society which raised funds and undertook voluntary work on the canal structures. They also succeeded in having Tunnel Cottage classified as a Grade II listed building, as externally it was in original condition and hence of historical interest. In recent years there has been a substantial increase in pleasure boating, so the Midland and North Western seems to have an assured future.

Meanwhile, what of Tunnel Cottage? For many years the lock and tunnel-keeper was one Walter Atherton, who lived there with his wife and only child Charlotte, known to all and sundry as Lottie. She had been born in the cottage and never lived anywhere else. She had no siblings and her mother died when she was still young.

When her father retired, a new keeper was appointed, Timothy Sage by name, and Lottie wasted no time in marrying him. Naturally, Walter stayed there also, occupying his time by tending the garden, which flourished in the sheltered valley, for the rest of his life. In the fullness of time, Walter passed away, leaving Timothy and Lottie with a collection of pets, in charge of the cottage, the garden, the tunnel and the locks. As Timothy approached retirement age, the couple became increasingly preoccupied with the matter of where to go and what to do when the axe fell. Their dilemma was solved by the Waterways Authority, who made it known that in view of the ever-increasing need to economise, the keeper would not be replaced, and that furthermore they had carried out an assessment of their property portfolio, as a result of which they intended to dispose of Tunnel Cottage. As a long-serving tenant, Mr Sage had the option of purchase on his home at a favourable price. Years of frugal living, and the fact that her late father had been a life assurance addict, enabled them to take advantage of this offer, and thus their life continued in much the same way as it had always done for years past. Timothy carried on as unofficial custodian of the locks and tunnel, whilst the preservation society had done much valuable work in replacing lock gates, so the whole structure was in a good state of repair. Unhappily, Timothy did not live long to enjoy his retirement and it transpired that before she was sixty years of age, Lottie was the sole occupant of Tunnel Cottage.

Having known nothing else since she was a child, it did not occur to her to go anywhere else or to undertake anything different. She became well known among the frequenters of the waterway and the leisure boaters who now passed Piggle in burgeoning numbers, and was always ready with practical help or useful advice to people less familiar with the ways of life on a canal. She sold the produce of her orchard and garden to passers-by; by this time this included new-laid eggs from a few chickens. Blackberries grew prolifically over the hill and each year her homemade jam was in great demand. Lottie was always ready with her windlass to speed progress through the locks, or to accompany nervous beginners through the tunnel, on many occasions taking the tiller herself. No one knew that tunnel better than Lottie did – she had frequently walked the towpath with her father before it was removed, and had accompanied the men on inspections, often rowing the rubber dinghy used on such occasions.

The usually benign Piggle Tunnel had, however, a trick up its sleeve. Millions of years ago, during the formation of the earth in its present shape, the sandstone beds forming Mount Piggle had been laid down by alluvial action and compressed by the inestimable weight of the material above. It so happened that this process had occupied three phases, the two hard layers being separated by a thinner stratum of a softer mudstone. This created a giant rock sandwich. Later, a cataclysmic upheaval and folding of the earth's crust had stood the sandwich on its end, with the sandstone outermost and the filling in the centre. When the tunnel was bored, a ventilation shaft was sunk from the surface down to the future water level, and the most expedient way to achieve this was to excavate down through the mudstone layer.

When the towpath was removed, a track was constructed over the top of the hill, rejoining the canal at the north portal, to enable the horsepower to be led past the tunnel. Meanwhile, the boats had to be propelled by humans through the bore. Very little use was ever made of this, as by the time the towpath was demolished, horse-drawn boats had virtually disappeared. The path had its uses, however, and the tunnel keepers had kept it open. It was of especial value for leisure boaters, where nervous passengers, human or canine, could simply enjoy a walk in the fresh air while the boat was in the bowels of the earth.

In a prominent position at the tunnel mouth, adjoining the moorings for boats waiting to enter, was a noticeboard, painted white and carefully maintained by Lottie. Behind the glass were all manner of informative snippets, such as the tide times for the lower section of the navigation, where the canal joined a tidal river, details of any planned stoppages for maintenance and so on. What caught the eye was a poster informing the public that following the removal of the crane and weighbridge, no further freight facilities would be available at Jericho Wharf, to be effective as of 1st March 1947, by Order of the Secretary of State. This was left on display as a historical document. Like all the rest, it was fastened with brass drawing pins to avoid the ravages of rust.

One fine late summer afternoon, when Lottie had been living alone for almost ten years, she made her way up the horse path, through the gorse, to the summit of the hill. It was blackberry harvest time and this year there was a plentiful crop. At one point she turned off onto a secondary track which led towards the upper end of the ventilation shaft. It was her practice to visit this spot on such occasions, as the fruit on one particular bush in that area was invariably large, sweet and succulent. She paused near the small round tower marking the shaft, her eye caught by two lizards sunning themselves on the greenish stone. As she approached they made no move to escape and she was able to examine them closely. Eventually, aware of her presence, the animals scuttled off into the vegetation. Lottie then noticed that the stone blocks forming the shaft cap were acutely worn and weathered and that sizeable flakes had broken off. The iron grille covering the orifice, some ten feet in diameter, was heavily rusted and in places the expanding movement of the corrosion had split the stones and pulled the framework out of its sockets. Two centuries of hot sun, severe winter frost and exposure to wind and rain had done their work. The structure was clearly damaged and appeared liable to collapse into the void beneath. Plainly, no one had examined the shaft for years. Given its status as a remainder waterway, very little attention had been paid by the responsible authority to such things – a desultory inspection once every couple of years by boat was all that could be expected. The onus for checking the tunnel lay with the keeper, and his post had long since been abolished. Any detritus falling into the canal from the shaft would be carried away – the canal was used as a reservoir supply feeder, and at the bottom of the shaft the tunnel was narrow, creating a pinch point where the current was appreciably stronger.

* * * * *

Time and tide wait for no man, and the years rolled inexorably past. Despite her iron will and wonderful constitution, Lottie had at last begun to feel her age. The house was far too large for a single occupant and the upkeep of the garden was now proving very burdensome. The gate paddle windlass now hung, unused, with the other ornaments on the great stone fireplace in the kitchen, and the blackberry jam had vanished, along with the chickens and the cats. On her eightieth birthday she finally admitted to herself that she needed some help with domestic chores. Accordingly, she placed an advertisement in the local newspaper, and at once received a response from Mrs Fulton, a resident of the nearby village. Thus it came about that Lottie was no longer alone in Tunnel Cottage, as Mrs Fulton would spend a couple of hours twice a week with the vacuum cleaner, the duster and the ironing board. She could also, if need arose, help with the shopping or any other errands. Inevitably, 'Mrs Fulton' soon became 'Dawn', and since Lottie was congenitally unable to sit down and do nothing, on many occasions there was no housework that demanded Dawn's attention, enabling the latter to sit in Tunnel

Cottage and drink a cup of coffee, prepared, naturally, by Lottie. One day, the matter of garden maintenance arose.

"I really need some help with things like cutting the grass and pruning the shrubs," admitted Lottie.

"That's easily arranged," replied Dawn. "My Ed can take care of it."

Dawn's Ed had at one time worked in a local stone quarry, until some mysterious ailment curtailed this activity, and he now earned a living as a jobbing gardener and general factotum.

The morning coffee group now numbered three. In the cosy environment of the cottage kitchen, Dawn and Ed set about the realisation of the plans they had evolved privately.

"You're very independent, aren't you?" said Dawn on one occasion when the kitchen committee was in session.

"I had to be," replied Lottie. "My mother died when I was only fifteen and I became cook, bottle-washer and housekeeper to my father. My husband was quite a few years older than me and after he retired he developed dementia, so I was responsible for everything."

"Did that cause any problems?"

"No, because I had what's called power of attorney and was enabled to make any necessary decisions about financial matters and so on."

This led naturally to Dawn's next question. "What will happen when you go? Have you got any family?"

"None at all, as far as I've ever known. But I was born in this cottage and I shall die in it," insisted Lottie.

"But what's going to happen to the house?"

Lottie made no reply and the matter was dropped, for the time being at least.

Dawn returned to the attack whenever the opportunity presented itself. On one occasion the conversation had got around to Lottie's late husband and his disability.

"What are you going to do when you reach the point where you can't manage your affairs properly? Will you have one of those attorneys acting for you?" queried Dawn.

"Oh, no, it won't happen to me. I'm made of sterner stuff than those men," retorted Lottie defiantly.

"But this house is much too large for you; it's not convenient for things like shopping, and it's very lonely in winter," pursued Dawn. "Have you thought about selling it? You know that Ed and I are very fond of the place, and we know how everything runs here. It would suit us down to the ground if you gave us first refusal."

Lottie would not be drawn and contented herself with the usual reply. "I was born in this cottage and I shall die here."

One Thursday, the two women had gone into town, as was customary, to do the shopping and had made their way to the upstairs room of the Tea Cosy Café in the market place for morning coffee. They were seated in the usual place near a large sash window which commanded a wide view over the activity taking place in the square beneath. Suddenly, Lottie's attention was caught by the sight of a familiar figure emerging from a building on the far side. It was unmistakeably Ed, framed in the doorway of a garish red plastic shop-front, the premises of Partridge and Hare, Estate Agents, Valuers and Auctioneers. Any lingering doubts in her mind were at once dispelled, but she kept her own counsel.

"The agent is coming next Thursday at eleven o'clock," said Ed, in the privacy of the Fulton residence. "Keep her out of the way as long as possible. Have lunch or something."

An envelope franked 'Partridge and Hare' duly arrived at Dawn and Ed's abode.

"Well," exclaimed Dawn impatiently, "what does it say?"

Ed pursed his lips and whistled. "Listen to this, Dawn. 'Tunnel Cottage, Piggle. A late eighteenth-century canal house in original external condition, but with modern facilities. Grade II listed building. In view of its unique position and historical value, this property should be marketed in the sum of £350,000’. Signed by Augustus Hare, Senior Partner. The old girl is sitting on an absolute fortune and probably doesn’t even know it. If we can get hold of this we’ll be made for life.”

“But I thought you didn’t like the place.”

“I don’t. Wouldn’t live in that rat-hole; I’m scared of that tunnel with all those bats flying about. We pay her a knockdown price and immediately sell it for market value. We’ll offer £150,000 – she won’t know the difference. Probably paid tuppence-ha’penny for it all those years ago. This is a chance to make some serious money. We don’t want to live there. I’d rather be a bit nearer the pub.”

“But we haven’t got any money now. Where are you going to get the cash?”

“I’ll borrow it on the security of the house. That bloke in the estate agents’ suggested that something could be arranged between us. Won’t take long to sell it in the present market.”

“What if she won’t sell?”

“Keep working on her. She’s already past the age when she should be in a nice little retirement bungalow with no stairs or garden.”

The determinant of Lottie’s future at the cottage was her doctor, who advised that she should give up driving. She, most reluctantly, decided to comply with his recommendation and to seek alternative accommodation closer to amenities, finally settling on a small retirement bungalow located in a warden-assisted complex on the edge of the town, and subsequently parting with her beloved twenty-year-old car. These events precipitated Dawn’s persistent attempts to get her employer to agree to sell the house, and at this stage, sums of money were being mentioned for the first time.

* * * * *

The navigation was closed from October until Easter for essential maintenance, although it was still functioning as a feeder to the reservoir further downstream. The summer ramblers were huddled over their fireplaces, and the area of Piggle

Locks and Tunnel reverted to its winter solitude. The only noise emanated from the harsh staccato of the jackdaws, soaring along the rocky face of the escarpment.

On the day of her final departure from Tunnel Cottage, Lottie rose early, dressed and had breakfast. Collecting her walking stick at the door, she set out for the last time to walk up the horse path and pay a sentimental visit to her favourite blackberry bush. Slowly and painfully, but resolutely, she made her way up the gravel path to the summit, turning off towards the ventilation shaft. The deterioration which had been evident on her previous visit, now twelve years ago, had increased markedly. The iron grille had broken away around much of its circumference and was hanging forlornly down into the shaft. The coping stones were split and one or two had vanished altogether. The blackberry bush had run riot over the ruinous structure and appeared to be the only thing holding it together. All around was atrophy and decay. Lottie turned away and made her way back down the hill for the final time, pausing frequently for a rest.

The essentials for living had previously been moved into the new bungalow, and Lottie made one last tour of the house to ascertain whether anything remained that should have been transferred. She selected two favourite ornaments and lastly took the windlass off its hook as a memento of her prior existence.

Dawn accompanied Lottie to her new home and helped her arrange a few trivia around the small but neat and cosy living room.

Finally, Dawn said, "Well, we've done it. I know you'll be comfortable here. Come and see me out."

Lottie made her way to the front door but suddenly laid a detaining hand on Dawn's arm. "I've been thinking it over. I've just got to face facts. Nothing goes on forever, not even Tunnel Cottage. I've decided to accept your offer, Dawn."

"Well, that's wonderful news, my dear. Ed will be delighted. I'll dash off and tell him right away. We won't forget you, Lottie, and will see you soon."

"Goodbye, Dawn."

"It's not goodbye, Lottie! Whatever do you mean?"

It was a windy day and a sudden gust blew Lottie's reply away.

Dawn and Ed spent a convivial evening in the Plume of Feathers, celebrating the fruition of their carefully laid plans.

At closing time, Ed said, “Let’s go and look at our new property. Got to keep an eye on our investment, haven’t we? Just a minute.” He obtained a large bottle of whisky from the landlord. “We’ll have a house-warming.”

The pair made their way to Tunnel Cottage, got a good fire going in the kitchen, closed the heavy curtains to shut out the noise of the squally rainstorm and settled down to discuss the whisky and their good fortune. At midnight they decided to stay in the cottage rather than face a wet journey home, which in any event they were in no condition to undertake, so they went to bed.

The first flash of lightning struck the ventilator shaft tower, melting the lead seals around the grille joints into the wall like butter and shattering the coping stones. The grille, broken loose, fell vertically down the shaft like a giant portcullis, embedding itself into the clay puddle in the canal bottom. A great cascade of rock, shale, clay and a tangle of vegetation followed, sealing the canal as effectively as a purpose-built dam. The lightning was accompanied by thunder and rain in unprecedented volume. Ordinarily, the canal could have carried such a volume of water, as it had spillways enabling any surplus to run off into natural streams, but once past the bottom lock the only exit was through the tunnel. The tunnel was blocked and the water had in consequence nowhere to go. With astonishing rapidity, the level rose until it was lapping the front door of the cottage, seeping under the door and into the kitchen. Having extinguished the fire, it continued to rise, creating an air pressure that broke several windows, allowing the surging tide to rise unhindered. The couple upstairs lay in a drunken stupor, and by the time they became aware of what was happening it was much too late. By dawn the cottage was submerged.

Clearing the blockage in the tunnel presented a considerable problem. It was not obvious what had caused the inundation and the matter of ascertaining the reason for the flood and devising a solution presented significant difficulties. Characteristically, the tunnel, which had occasioned the flood of its own accord, chose to resolve it. A further dramatic collapse of the remaining blocks at the shaft top brought a fall of massive stones directly onto the top of the grille, tipping it sideways. The pressure of thousands of tons of water, pent up by the improvised dam, swept all the detritus clear. Silt, rocks, vegetation, stone blocks, branches were borne along by the raging current and deposited beyond the tunnel portal for the distance of a mile.

As rapidly as the water level in the valley had risen, it dropped and within twelve hours the damage occasioned to Tunnel Cottage could be determined. Windows and doors were smashed, ceilings brought down and a section of the roof had collapsed. It was not until the following day that the full horror became apparent with the discovery among the chaos of two corpses. The local reporter had recourse to his thesaurus in order to convey the scale of the disaster, and the newspaper lovingly described the affair in such terms as 'cosmic forces', 'biblical scale', 'Nature at her most savage', 'latter-day Noah's Flood', 'calamitous' and suchlike. A careful assessment revealed that the cottage was damaged beyond repair and it was demolished. Most curiously, the one thing which appeared unharmed was the noticeboard, still standing on its legs and with the glass unbroken. It remains as a link with the past. It is still possible to make out, in a certain light, on a faded and water-stained piece of paper, the words 'Jericho Wharf'.

The inquest into the two deaths was held in due course. Lottie was certified by her doctor as not well enough to give evidence in person, so her written statement was entered into the court proceedings. She confirmed that the two deceased had been in her employ and that they had been charged with keeping an eye on Tunnel Cottage following her departure. Their presence was consequently completely in accordance with her wishes. This was the sum total of her evidence, as no one thought that she could have anything else to contribute to the enquiry, which declared the deaths as accidental, the flood being an Act of God. The ventilation shaft was quietly closed top and bottom and there is now scant evidence that it ever existed. The blackberry bushes and gorse have completely grown over the cap, and a brick arch halfway along the tunnel attracts no attention from passing boaters. No evidence was adduced concerning the grille, the cause of the episode, which lies flat, concealed in the soft mud of the canal bottom, under three feet of water. The waterway authority adopted a masterly policy of saying as little as possible and succeeded in keeping the matter of maintenance, or the lack of it, off the agenda. Piggle has given no trouble since.

Jericho Wharf has seen an upturn in its fortunes. A magnificent leisure boat marina has been constructed there, and the guest of honour at the opening ceremony was Lottie, who commemorated a personal milestone by cutting a cake, especially baked in the shape of a tunnel, on the occasion of her 100th birthday.

25
THE ROAD TO DAMASCUS

It is an old adage that there is no zealot like the neophyte.

Chapter 1 – Yesterday in Parliament

In pursuance of his cabinet reshuffle, the Prime Minister yesterday announced a further ministerial appointment. It will be recalled that on the preceding day, two posts had received new incumbents. Lord Candlestick now occupies the position of Energy Secretary, with special responsibility for electricity generation, whilst in deference to the ethnic minorities quota policy, and following the admirable precept of 'set a thief to catch a thief', a self-confessed former house burglar elevated to the peerage as Lord Ali Baba became Justice Minister, bringing with him a panel of forty special advisers.

The most recent nomination, that of Minister for Education, has been Dr Gavin Bernard Hopton Trendie, PhD, MA, Dip Ed etc, the celebrated (or notorious, depending on one's point of view) headmaster of No. 1176 Regional Government Comprehensive Academy, which at the last count had approximately 3,011 pupils. This remains an estimate, as nobody really knows how many are enrolled, and they have never all been there at the same time. Dr Trendie, known to his many friends as GBH, was, in common with the other recent nominees, not an elected Member of Parliament and hence has been created a Life Peer, taking the title of Laird Trendie of Auchtermuckpyll in the Kingdom of Fife, after the former colliery village where he was born in 1962.

Chapter 2 – In Full Flight

Dr Trendie took to politics and his new job like a duck to water. He has implemented all his cherished ideas across the whole school population with astonishing alacrity, and it is claimed by his supporters that his appointment has ushered in a golden era in our long educational history.

He is best known for his advanced views on education, many of them garnered from the United States, where he spent three years on an exchange secondment to a college in South Carolina. His last post as headmaster of the largest school in Britain (and, incidentally, in Europe) strengthened his adherence to the mantra that 'big is beautiful'. He was aided in this onerous task by no fewer than seventeen deputy headmasters and one hundred and ninety-two teaching staff, plus an unspecified number of auxiliaries. It has been unkindly said of him that he could not possibly have remembered even the names of all his assistants, and some teachers claim (unofficially) never to have met him. Dr Trendie was quick to defend his regime, and in his last annual report to the governors stated that he was proud of the improved disciplinary situation obtaining at the school over the year under review. "Only eleven playground murders," he states in the report's preamble. In this regard the opening of a dedicated police station on the campus has had a beneficent effect.

One innovation for which he was responsible was the replacement of the miscellany of school buses with imported American Chevrolet vehicles, left-hand drive and painted yellow. Most people will be familiar with these from the cinema or television screen. It is claimed that the introduction of these vehicles has had a calming effect on the pupils with consequent amelioration in their behaviour. It must be said that there are factors other than the yellow colour and the transatlantic ethos, however. The driver sits in a caboose, physically separated from the passengers, furnished with bulletproof glass and an ejector seat. There are also two armed guards on each vehicle, and this has helped considerably in the lowering of the incidence of hijacking of their bus by the children themselves and their subsequent use in ram-raids on cashpoints and post offices.

Another area of particular interest for Dr Trendie lies in the establishment of school clubs. On discovering that many less fortunate pupils are despatched to school without having partaken of a nourishing meal, he has been quick to set up a breakfast club to remedy this deficiency. This obviously entailed assembling the children much earlier than the accustomed 9 a.m. start to lessons so that they could be fed before the day's instruction. It was not all plain sailing, as children living at some remove from his school were obliged to catch the school breakfast bus as early as 7 a.m., and on winter days this naturally took place in total darkness. At the other end of the academic day it was evident that children of working parents were going home to empty houses, and so he pioneered the creation of homework clubs. The children remain at the school and carry out their homework under supervision in a warm and secure environment, with computer access, ensuring their safety and freeing their parents from any responsibility for ensuring that homework tasks are in fact carried out.

A logical development of this idea led to the setting up of evening recreational pursuits, indoor or outdoor as weather and the season of the year dictate. Some of these activities continue until fairly late in the evening, and this raises the issue of pupils who left home before daylight returning after nightfall. The natural corollary has been the institution of the sleepover clubs, allowing children to remain in the protective envelope of the school overnight, and obviating the need to catch the school bus at an untimely hour in the morning. Since sex education now begins at the age of five in progressive establishments, it has been found advisable to segregate the boys and girls of the age of four years and upwards in the dormitories to lessen the danger of unauthorised practical experimentation.

Dr Trendie has always been very preoccupied with the matter of computers in schools and was instrumental in forming the policy that each child should have a laptop for his exclusive use in the classroom. In pursuance of this worthy ideal, he has been prominent in obtaining the release of funds to enable the same child to have an identical computer at home, the two being connected by ultra-fast broadband wireless links, so that the home computer mirrors the activity of the school computer and vice versa. This system offers two distinct advantages – children are spared the labour of carrying a computer to and from school, and forgetting to bring one's computer to school at the start of the day is no longer a valid excuse for not having produced homework for evaluation by the teacher.

The Minister is very interested in the pioneering work done by Professor Max Pretzl at Zurich and by Dr Figelius Frijdegg of the University of Stellenbosch in South Africa concerning the pre-natal implications of computing. He has evolved a policy whereby children are given a profile on social networking websites before they are actually born, and thus come into contact with the concepts of computing at the earliest possible age. This is seen as a useful tool in influencing the child's development and shaping his characteristics, as anyone is welcome to add input into the process. Lord Trendie is known to be a devotee of Dr Maharashtra of Allahabad, India, who has done much useful early work in this evolving field.

Couples contemplating embarking on parenthood are strongly advised to access government sites www.friendofthefoetus.gov.uk and www.cyberchildren.gov.uk, where a great deal of valuable advice is obtainable. This is a purely voluntary activity at the moment, but the Minister has given broad hints of further legislation in this area.

Chapter 3 – Six of the Best

The recent landslide victory of the erstwhile opposition party in the general election has meant that along with all his colleagues of the same political persuasion, Lord Trendie has lost his job. Following some unpleasantness concerning allowances claimed by members of the House of Lords, Dr Trendie has renounced his Life Peerage and quit Parliament, stating that he intends to return to his true vocation and resume his career as a teacher. The policies of the new government being diametrically opposed to those of their predecessors, sweeping changes have been made in the field of education. It has now been resolved that all the town and village schools closed in recent decades will be reopened, using where possible the original premises, which, after all, were usually purpose built and in convenient locations.

The decentralisation of primary and secondary education has resulted in the disappearance of the yellow Chevrolet school bus, which had spread like wildfire right across the spectrum. Since all children live within walking or cycling distance of their school, these vehicles no longer have a function, and 17,500 of them have been sold. The resultant glut on the second-hand bus market resulted in very low prices being realised, and the majority of them went back to the United States. Data obtained under the Freedom of Information Act reveals that the loss to the taxpayer has been astronomical, and great public concern has been aroused. This has largely been allayed by claims that the savings effected on road tax, insurance, diesel fuel, drivers and security guards should ensure that the deficit is cleared during the life of the new parliament.

The re-opening of all these schools has also created a large number of job opportunities, and Dr Trendie rapidly secured for himself the headmastership at Utterly Dismal, a small market town in the depths of the Lincolnshire Wolds, where the school buildings had for the past seventeen years been used as a pig farm. No trouble or expense was to be spared in the rehabilitation of the school premises.

The contractor entrusted with the restoration of the pig farm to its pristine function as a school has adhered extremely closely to his remit. He was a former pupil from many years previously and hence had a good first-hand knowledge of the conditions which had prevailed there, and he had thus ensured that everything down to the finest detail reflected as closely as possible the appearance of the building as it had once been. The classrooms were equipped with blackboards, and this proved to be a revelation to the younger members of the newly appointed staff who had never used one, or in some instances never even seen one.

If you fall into that category it may be useful to digress for a moment. The blackboard is a most ingenious invention, combining great simplicity, low first cost and ease of use with admirable properties. All manner of information can be drawn on a blackboard; the user can write on it in any direction, using any script and it does not issue incomprehensible messages such as 'Error Code 127'. It is large and can in consequence be seen readily by all the pupils in the class. All information engrossed in chalk on a blackboard can be obliterated by the stroke of a duster. It can be prepared as far in advance as appropriate and, unlike a computer screen, does not need to be refreshed or protected. It is likewise entirely unaffected by power cuts, and has neither fiddly keyboard nor yards of trailing cable. It is totally freestanding and can be moved anywhere, indoors or out. It has no operating system or complex application software and therefore nothing to go wrong. There is not even a user manual, although doubtless someone somewhere will feel the need to write one. The teachers were overjoyed to encounter blackboards and, in consequence, they are now the chief medium of instruction. They are, incidentally, cheap to purchase and the only maintenance is a coat of paint during the long summer holiday.

As well as blackboards, the contractor responsible for the restoration of the school, who had begun his working life as a carpenter and joiner, had designed from memory a replica of the traditional desk, and the entire establishment was equipped with these.

Each room in the school, sometime pigsty, has been restored to the function which it had previously fulfilled, so that Dr Trendie's study was to become the headmaster's room. On first entering this, he noticed to his horror a stout bamboo cane hanging on the wall over the fireplace. This had been preserved as a memento during the interim period and had found a use as a prod for recalcitrant pigs. "I must dispose of this dreadful reminder of the past," he said to himself, removing the cane from its hook and making his way towards the refuse area at the rear of the premises. His way took him along the main corridor, and as he approached a swing door, a lad overtook him. To his great surprise, the boy did not barge past him but opened the door, held it and bowed his head.

"Good morning, sir," he said, nervously eying the implement of torture which the new headmaster was carrying.

Responding to this novel situation with customary aplomb, the good Doctor at once returned to his room with the cane and hung it carefully back in its place. This symbol of reaction and oppression would clearly be an influence for good. Dr Trendie henceforward never went anywhere without it.

Dr Trendie had decided that it was time for him to visit the hairdresser in order that he might look his best when taking up his new appointment. His accustomed hairstyle had always been to sport long, luxuriant curls over his collar, reflecting his modern image. By this time he was living close to the school and called at a small traditional barber's shop situated in a side street leading off the market place.

"How do you like it?"

"It's grown a little untidy, so just trim it up a little, please."

As was his custom, Trendie was engrossed in thought and paid scant attention to what the barber was doing, when abruptly something caused him to look down at the shop floor to see that the area around the barber's chair was littered with his carefully nurtured tresses. The barber evidently had a very different view of what constituted a tidy style. Thunderstruck, he was entirely unable to make any remark, and then caught sight of his image in the barber's mirror. That's incredible! I look at least ten years younger, he thought, and all that grey hair's vanished. "Fairly short back and sides," he said aloud to the barber.

Such was the pressure to get the school at Utterly Dismal into use that it was decided to proceed with the formal opening before the final decoration was complete. This led to a temporary classroom shortage and the headmaster decreed that pending final completion, classrooms would not be allocated to teachers but to classes, for the excellent reason that there were fewer classes than teachers.

This produced a quite astonishing outcome – it transpired that it is far quicker and infinitely quieter if the teachers went to the classes and not the other way round. Mahomet should go to the mountain, as it were. As a result, there are no vociferous crowds of children milling around the corridors from location to location when the bell is rung.

Vanished into oblivion are the school clubs, whose usefulness has been completely eroded by the other changes which the new regime has brought in its train. The school premises are open from 8 a.m. until 4.30 p.m. At close of afternoon lessons the pupils disappear as fast as their legs or pedals can carry them towards the safety of their own home. The internal functioning of the school has undergone a sweeping transformation. Each class has a permanent classroom, where the pupils remain throughout the working day unless they are undertaking sports or some such activity. Every child has a chair and nobody sits on the floor. The only computer in the school belongs to the administrative office. Pupils keep their schoolwork and impedimenta in a desk, the lid of which lifts to reveal a very useful storage space. Each desk has an inkwell, these vessels actually containing ink. An air of cloistered calm pervades the whole establishment, stimulated by the august presence of the headmaster, who can be seen frequently patrolling the corridors, exercise yard and playing fields sporting a military haircut and a three-foot cane. Children address all staff as 'sir' or 'ma'am'.

The effect of all these revolutionary changes has been most marked – last year seventeen children sat their GCSE examinations in English and maths three years early, all obtaining high marks. The buildings are characterised by a complete absence of vandalism and absenteeism is virtually unknown.

And finally, what of the great Doctor? The metamorphosis which he had undergone extended even to his signature. This had been relaxed, informal and expansive, but now has become sharp, incisive and authoritarian. At first glance one could think it reads 'Traddie'.

REPERES PRATIQUES NATHAN

CW00807479

Les Institutions de la France

B. de Gunten,
A. Martin, M. Niogret

NATHAN

Sommaire

ISBN 2-09-177683-1

Mode d'emploi

Divisé en six parties, l'ouvrage s'organise par doubles pages.
Chaque double page fait le point sur une question et, en général, fonctionne de la façon suivante :

Un repérage : les six parties de l'ouvrage.

Un titre : il annonce le sujet de la double page.

Quelques lignes présentent le sujet de la double page.

Les sous-titres : d'un seul coup d'œil on repère les grands points du sujet.

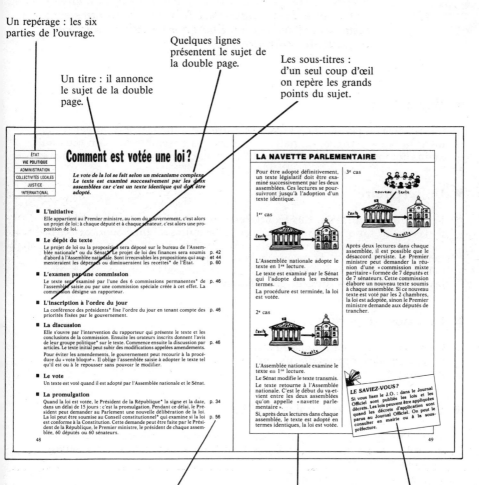

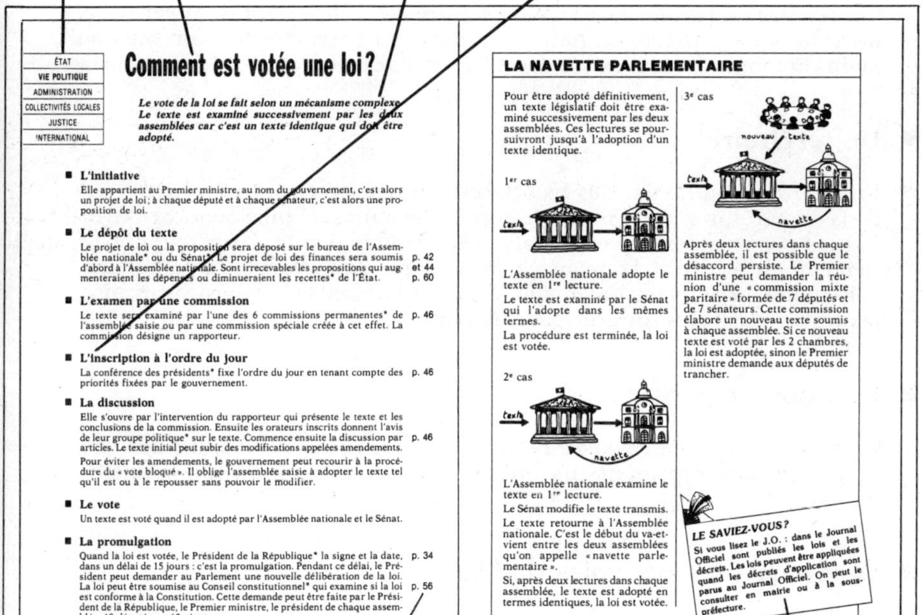

ÉTAT
VIE POLITIQUE
ADMINISTRATION
COLLECTIVITÉS LOCALES
JUSTICE
INTERNATIONAL

Comment est votée une loi ?

Le vote de la loi se fait selon un mécanisme complexe. Le texte est examiné successivement par les deux assemblées car c'est un texte identique qui doit être adopté.

- **L'initiative**

  Elle appartient au Premier ministre, au nom du gouvernement, c'est alors un projet de loi ; à chaque député et à chaque sénateur, c'est alors une proposition de loi.

- **Le dépôt du texte**

  Le projet de loi ou la proposition sera déposé sur le bureau de l'Assemblée nationale* ou du Sénat*. Le projet de loi des finances sera soumis d'abord à l'Assemblée nationale. Sont irrecevables les propositions qui augmenteraient les dépenses ou diminueraient les recettes* de l'État. p. 42 et 44 p. 60

- **L'examen par une commission**

  Le texte sera examiné par l'une des 6 commissions permanentes* de l'assemblée saisie ou par une commission spéciale créée à cet effet. La commission désigne un rapporteur. p. 46

- **L'inscription à l'ordre du jour**

  La conférence des présidents* fixe l'ordre du jour en tenant compte des priorités fixées par le gouvernement. p. 46

- **La discussion**

  Elle s'ouvre par l'intervention du rapporteur qui présente le texte et les conclusions de la commission. Ensuite les orateurs inscrits donnent l'avis de leur groupe politique* sur le texte. Commence ensuite la discussion par articles. Le texte initial peut subir des modifications appelées amendements. p. 46

  Pour éviter les amendements, le gouvernement peut recourir à la procédure du « vote bloqué ». Il oblige l'assemblée saisie à adopter le texte tel qu'il est ou à le repousser sans pouvoir le modifier.

- **Le vote**

  Un texte est voté quand il est adopté par l'Assemblée nationale et le Sénat.

- **La promulgation**

  Quand la loi est votée, le Président de la République* la signe et la date, dans un délai de 15 jours : c'est la promulgation. Pendant ce délai, le Président peut demander au Parlement une nouvelle délibération de la loi. La loi peut être soumise au Conseil constitutionnel* qui examine si la loi est conforme à la Constitution. Cette demande peut être faite par le Président de la République, le Premier ministre, le président de chaque assemblée, 60 députés ou 60 sénateurs. p. 34 p. 56

48

LA NAVETTE PARLEMENTAIRE

Pour être adopté définitivement, un texte législatif doit être examiné successivement par les deux assemblées. Ces lectures se poursuivront jusqu'à l'adoption d'un texte identique.

1er cas

L'Assemblée nationale adopte le texte en 1re lecture.

Le texte est examiné par le Sénat qui l'adopte dans les mêmes termes.

La procédure est terminée, la loi est votée.

2e cas

L'Assemblée nationale examine le texte en 1re lecture.

Le Sénat modifie le texte transmis.

Le texte retourne à l'Assemblée nationale. C'est le début du va-et-vient entre les deux assemblées qu'on appelle « navette parlementaire ».

Si, après deux lectures dans chaque assemblée, le texte est adopté en termes identiques, la loi est votée.

3e cas

Après deux lectures dans chaque assemblée, il est possible que le désaccord persiste. Le Premier ministre peut demander la réunion d'une « commission mixte paritaire » formée de 7 députés et de 7 sénateurs. Cette commission élabore un nouveau texte soumis à chaque assemblée. Si ce nouveau texte est voté par les 2 chambres, la loi est adoptée, sinon le Premier ministre demande aux députés de trancher.

LE SAVIEZ-VOUS ?

Si vous lisez le J.O. : dans le Journal Officiel sont publiés les lois et les décrets. Les lois peuvent être appliquées quand les décrets d'application sont parus au Journal Officiel. On peut le consulter en mairie ou à la sous-préfecture.

49

Le renvoi à la définition d'un mot, lorsque ce mot, cité dans le texte, présente une difficulté.

La page de droite : elle développe un point particulier, elle illustre une notion ou une explication de la page de gauche.

Une précision, une anecdote, ou un détail inattendu qui concerne le sujet exposé sur la double page.

Qu'est-ce qu'un État ?

« Chef d'État », « conflit entre États », « État souverain », autant d'expressions couramment employées. Pourtant la notion d'État est difficile à cerner car l'État représente un pouvoir lointain que le citoyen conteste ou réclame. Trois conditions doivent être réunies pour assurer l'existence d'un État : une nation, un territoire, un pouvoir politique.

■ Une nation

C'est-à-dire un peuple, lié par une histoire commune et parlant généralement la même langue. La nation est donc un ensemble humain plus ou moins homogène, car il existe des différences de dialectes et de croyances.

■ Un territoire

Un territoire limité par des frontières : un peuple sans territoire n'a pas d'existence étatique. Ce territoire peut être d'un seul bloc ou morcelé. La France possède des départements et territoires d'outre-mer* qui appartiennent au territoire français : la Martinique, la Guyane, la Guadeloupe, la Réunion, la Nouvelle-Calédonie, Wallis et Futuna, la Polynésie française, les terres australes antarctiques, Mayotte.

p. 10

■ Un pouvoir politique

La nation doit être organisée pour être reconnue. Elle se donne des lois, se choisit des représentants qui parlent au nom de la communauté humaine.

■ Quels sont les pouvoirs de l'État ?

Il est d'usage, depuis le XVIIIe siècle, de mettre en évidence trois pouvoirs qui sont indépendants les uns des autres. C'est le principe de la séparation des pouvoirs :

- le pouvoir législatif fait les lois ;
- le pouvoir judiciaire fait respecter les lois ;
- le pouvoir exécutif fait appliquer les lois.

■ État fédéral ou État unitaire

Il existe dans le monde un peu plus de 160 États. On peut schématiquement les classer en deux catégories selon la structure qu'ils se sont choisie : l'État est soit fédéral, soit unitaire.

ÉTAT FÉDÉRAL OU ÉTAT UNITAIRE ?

▲ L'État fédéral

En général, les États fédéraux sont des États à grande superficie où cohabitent parfois plusieurs races ou plusieurs langues.

Dans l'État fédéral, il y a partage de responsabilités entre les États membres et le pouvoir fédéral.

— **Les États-Unis** forment aujourd'hui une fédération de 50 États. Le gouvernement de Washington assure la défense, les relations internationales, la monnaie. Chacun des 50 États possède sa constitution, deux chambres et un gouverneur. Leur autonomie est grande en ce qui concerne la justice (la peine de mort), le système scolaire.

— **La République fédérale d'Allemagne** ou Allemagne de l'Ouest groupe 10 États ou Länder plus Berlin-Ouest. La politique étrangère, la monnaie, le système judiciaire sont du domaine fédéral. Les Länder assurent l'enseignement, la police, l'application des lois fédérales.

— **La Suisse** ou Confédération helvétique est un État fédéral formé de cantons ayant chacun leur constitution. Les autorités fédérales assurent la sécurité, les affaires étrangères, la monnaie et le droit. On parle en Suisse 4 langues officielles : l'allemand, le français, l'italien et le romanche.

▲ L'État unitaire

Un État est dit unitaire lorsqu'on n'y trouve qu'un seul centre d'impulsion politique. Les citoyens de l'État unitaire obéissent à une seule et même autorité.

— **La France** est un État unitaire car les lois et le système judiciaire sont les mêmes sur tout le territoire.

— **La Chine**, selon sa constitution, est un « État multinational uni », c'est-à-dire un État unitaire quoique composé de provinces.

L'ÉTAT C'EST MOI

« L'État, c'est moi » est un mot attribué à Louis XIV. A l'âge de 17 ans, il aurait prononcé ces paroles lors d'une séance du Parlement. Une autre tradition prétend qu'il aurait dit cela en conseil des ministres en 1661, après la mort de Mazarin. Vraie ou fausse, cette formule est citée comme devise de l'absolutisme royal sous l'Ancien Régime.

L'organisation politique de l'État

Qui dirige l'État ? Quel est le rôle des citoyens ? Dans certains régimes politiques les citoyens ne peuvent pas intervenir dans le choix de leurs dirigeants ; mais, dans d'autres régimes politiques, les citoyens désignent les responsables du pouvoir politique.
C'est cette participation, plus ou moins grande, de chaque citoyen qui permet de distinguer les différents régimes politiques les uns des autres.

■ Qui dirige l'État ? Monarchie ou république ?

— La monarchie est le pouvoir exercé par un seul (le roi), il se transmet de façon héréditaire.

— La république (res publiqua : la chose publique) : le pouvoir est la « chose » de tous, il y a des élections.

Actuellement certains monarques ont moins de pouvoirs, en Grande-Bretagne, en Suède, par exemple, que certains présidents de la République, en France ou aux États-Unis.

■ Quel est le rôle du citoyen ? Dictature ou démocratie ?

Le régime dépend des possibilités réelles de participation ou d'intervention des citoyens.

— La dictature : les citoyens ne participent pas à l'élaboration des décisions et ne peuvent contester. Il n'y a pas d'opposition qui puisse s'exprimer, la liberté d'expression* est restreinte. p. 20 Le pouvoir s'appuie sur une police qui applique aveuglément ses décisions et procède à des arrestations arbitraires. Le plus souvent la dictature maintient son pouvoir par la force.

— La démocratie : les citoyens participent à l'élaboration des décisions, soit directement, soit par leurs élus.

La démocratie libérale privilégie la liberté des individus et leur participation au pouvoir (plusieurs partis, élections*). p. 23

Dans la démocratie marxiste* p. 16 le poids de la société, dans son intérêt collectif, est le plus fort. Les libertés individuelles sont limitées. Il n'y a qu'un seul parti. La démocratie marxiste, comme la dictature, sont des régimes totalitaires.

POUR QU'UNE DÉMOCRATIE EXISTE

Tout le monde doit avoir le droit de voter. Seules conditions imposées : l'âge et la nationalité. En France, le suffrage universel est, pour les hommes, une réalité depuis 1848, pour les femmes depuis 1944.

Plusieurs partis doivent pouvoir exposer librement leurs conceptions et leurs programmes. Pour permettre au citoyen de choisir, ces partis doivent avoir accès à tous les moyens de communication : presse, radio, télévision...

Le citoyen doit pouvoir choisir librement, c'est-à-dire qu'il ne doit pas subir de pression de la part du gouvernement.

L'opposition doit pouvoir s'organiser, par exemple dans des assemblées. Elle doit pouvoir disposer des mêmes moyens d'information que la majorité.

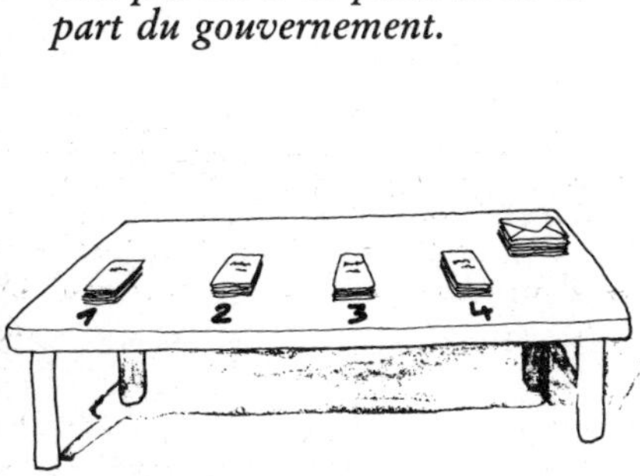

Le vote doit être secret. En France, les bulletins de vote doivent obligatoirement être imprimés sur du papier blanc et mis sous enveloppe, par chaque électeur, dans le secret de l'isoloir. Il y a un isoloir pour 300 inscrits.

L'État et les droits de l'homme

La Déclaration des Droits de l'Homme et du Citoyen de 1789 proclame les droits de l'homme libre et constitue une charte des libertés. Les droits de l'homme sont reconnus progressivement à la suite de luttes difficiles. La Déclaration Universelle des Droits de l'Homme de 1948 est un idéal en cours de réalisation, un but vers lequel les États devraient tendre.

Le contexte historique de la Déclaration des Droits de l'Homme et du Citoyen

— Le 5 mai 1789 : Louis XVI convoque les états généraux.

— Le 20 juin 1789 : lors du Serment du Jeu de Paume, les députés du tiers-état se proclament Assemblée Constituante.

— Le 14 juillet : le peuple de Paris prend la Bastille.

— Le 4 août 1789 : l'abolition des privilèges ébranle tout l'Ancien Régime.

— Le 26 août 1789 : l'Assemblée Constituante vote la Déclaration des Droits de l'Homme et du Citoyen.

Le contenu de la Déclaration des Droits de l'Homme et du Citoyen

— Ce texte reprend les grandes idées des philosophes du XVIIIe siècle, il énumère les droits essentiels de tout être humain*. p. 10

- la qualité d'homme libre;
- le droit à la sûreté de la personne;
- l'égalité en droits;
- la liberté de pensée et de culte;
- la liberté d'expression;
- la liberté d'accéder à tous les emplois.

— Le contenu de la Déclaration des Droits de l'Homme et du Citoyen n'a pas été immédiatement suivi d'effet, mais il a posé les principes auxquels nos constitutions modernes se réfèrent encore :

- le principe de la liberté individuelle* : un individu ne peut être arrêté qu'en vertu d'une loi existante; p. 10
- le principe de l'égalité devant la loi et devant l'impôt;
- le principe de la souveraineté nationale : la nation est souveraine, c'est elle et non Dieu qui donne son pouvoir au roi. Elle a le droit de demander des comptes;
- la séparation des pouvoirs : les trois pouvoirs, exécutif, législatif et judiciaire*, ne doivent pas être concentrés dans les mêmes mains; p. 4
- le droit de propriété : la propriété est reconnue comme un « droit inviolable et sacré ».

Le contexte historique de la Déclaration Universelle des Droits de l'Homme

Pour souligner l'importance historique de la Déclaration des Droits de l'Homme et du Citoyen de 1789, les nations membres de l'O.N.U.* décidèrent de tenir exceptionnellement leur assemblée générale à Paris, pour y discuter et y voter la Déclaration Universelle des Droits de l'Homme. p. 142

Le 10 décembre 1948 était adopté un texte d'une portée universelle, c'est-à-dire qui concerne tous les hommes sans distinction.

Cette déclaration intervient après la Deuxième Guerre mondiale qui a vu les droits de l'homme bafoués.

Le contenu de la Déclaration Universelle des Droits de l'Homme

La Déclaration Universelle des Droits de l'Homme se compose d'un préambule et de 30 articles.

— Les droits économiques et sociaux parmi lesquels figurent :
- le droit au travail (art. 23);
- le droit au repos (art. 24);
- le droit à un niveau de vie suffisant (art. 25);
- le droit à la sécurité en cas de maladie, invalidité... (art. 25).

— La protection internationale des droits : selon l'article 28, « toute personne a droit à ce que règne, sur le plan social et sur le plan international, un ordre tel que les droits et libertés énoncés dans la présente Déclaration puissent y trouver plein effet ».

— Les droits et les devoirs : la notion de droit est accompagnée d'une notion importante, celle de devoir envers la communauté.

— Le rôle de l'éducation : l'enseignement et l'éducation sont présentés dans le préambule comme les instruments nécessaires du progrès.

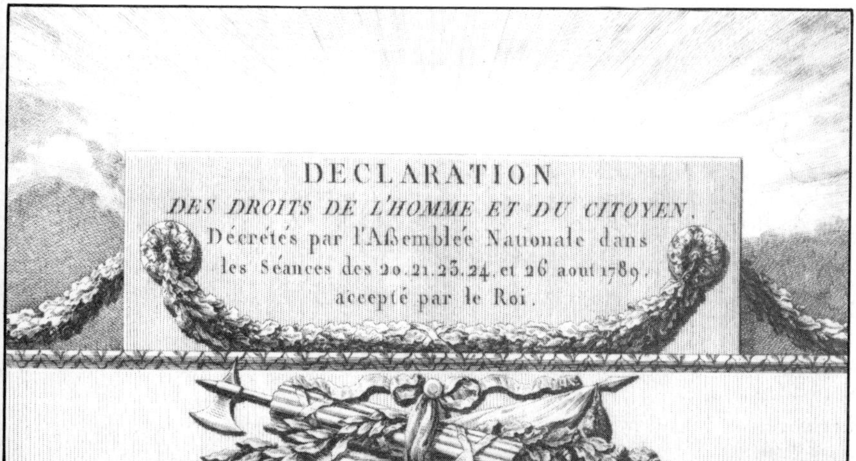

L'État et la liberté

Les libertés accordées à l'individu, ou libertés publiques, donnent à l'homme la possibilité d'agir sans contrainte dans les limites de la loi. La justice doit faire respecter ces libertés publiques. Cependant il peut exister des conflits entre l'intérêt individuel et l'intérêt général, d'où un certain nombre de restrictions.
On peut distinguer trois grandes catégories de libertés publiques :
les libertés de la personne ou libertés individuelles,
les libertés de la pensée,
les libertés économiques et sociales.

■ Les libertés liées à la personne

— La sûreté : elle protège contre des arrestations arbitraires. La loi délimite le permis et l'interdit. La personne soupçonnée doit avoir toutes les garanties pour sa défense.

Mais les personnes soupçonnées peuvent être gardées à vue pendant 24 heures, de même des témoins importants peuvent être retenus pour éviter des destructions de preuves. L'instruction doit prouver la culpabilité de l'inculpé.

— La liberté d'aller et de venir : c'est le droit de se déplacer et de choisir son domicile.

Mais, après une condamnation, il peut y avoir une interdiction de séjour sur une partie du territoire.

La circulation automobile est soumise à certaines règles (permis, papiers de voiture, code de la route).

Il peut y avoir des contrôles d'identité dans des recherches d'utilité reconnue.

Les étrangers sont soumis à certaines règles (permis de séjour, de travail).

— Le respect de la vie privée : le domicile est inviolable, on ne peut y pénétrer sans autorisation; il est interdit de poser des écoutes, de photographier pour un usage commercial.

Mais on peut perquisitionner pour les besoins d'une enquête*, il faut p. 121
être muni d'un mandat sauf en cas de flagrant délit ou pour les douanes.

On ne peut pénétrer chez une personne pour l'arrêter entre 21 heures et 6 heures.

— Le secret de la correspondance : nul n'a le droit d'ouvrir les lettres qui ne lui sont pas adressées.

Mais la correspondance peut être saisie par le juge d'instruction* ou p. 110
contrôlée dans des cas exceptionnels : pour les détenus, en cas de guerre.

— Le secret professionnel : ceux qui ont recueilli des informations de par leur profession (médecins, magistrats, journalistes) n'ont pas à les divulguer.

Mais il y a des exceptions pour les médecins experts ou pour ceux dont le secret, dévoilé, protège quelqu'un (victime de sévices).

Les libertés liées à la pensée

— La liberté d'opinion.

— La liberté religieuse.

— La liberté d'enseignement.

— La liberté de la presse et de l'audio-visuel. Mais elle est limitée par le nombre de canaux sur lesquels on peut émettre et par le rôle de l'État.

— La liberté de réunion. Mais elle est soumise à une autorisation préalable, si elle a lieu sur la voie publique.

— La liberté d'association. Mais l'association peut être dissoute si elle a un but contraire à la loi ou au gouvernement de la République.

Les libertés liées à la vie économique et sociale

— Liberté du travail (choix d'un emploi). Mais certaines professions sont strictement réglementées (notaire, huissier).

— Liberté syndicale.

— Droit de grève. Mais il est réglementé pour certaines professions.

— Droit de propriété. Mais la construction est soumise aux règles d'urbanisme et à l'autorisation du permis de construire. Certaines zones sont protégées. L'usage d'une propriété peut être limité pour respecter l'ordre public, le bruit qui gêne les voisins par exemple.

— Liberté de commerce et d'industrie. Mais certaines activités sont interdites (fabriquer du tabac par exemple).

Une monarchie constitutionnelle : le Royaume-Uni

Le Royaume-Uni pratique un régime parlementaire, c'est-à-dire que les pouvoirs peuvent agir l'un sur l'autre. Le gouvernement peut dissoudre la Chambre des Communes qui peut elle-même, par un vote de méfiance, obliger le gouvernement à démissionner.

■ Le pouvoir exécutif

Il est détenu par le Souverain et le Cabinet. L'ensemble des pouvoirs du Souverain constitue la Couronne.

— Le Souverain :

L'accession au trône est héréditaire. Elle est réglée par une loi de 1701 : les fils du souverain, puis les filles par rang d'âge. Les prétendants doivent appartenir à l'église anglicane.

— La Couronne :

La Couronne est une institution juridique. Cette institution possède un ensemble de pouvoirs appelé « la prérogative royale » ; nommer à certains emplois civils ou militaires, convoquer et dissoudre le Parlement, promulguer les lois, faire la paix ou la guerre, exercer le droit de grâce. Cependant ces pouvoirs sont, en réalité, exercés par le Cabinet.

— Le Cabinet :

Le Premier ministre est choisi par le Roi ou la Reine, mais ce doit être obligatoirement le chef du parti majoritaire de la Chambre des Communes.

Le Premier ministre choisit et forme son gouvernement.

■ Le pouvoir législatif

Le pouvoir législatif est exercé par le Parlement. Il est composé de deux Assemblées, la Chambre des Communes et la Chambre des Lords.

— La Chambre des Communes :

Les députés sont élus au suffrage universel direct*, au scrutin uninominal majoritaire à un tour, pour 5 ans. p. 20

La Chambre des Communes discute et vote les lois et le budget.

— La Chambre des Lords :

Composée de membres héréditaires ou nommés à vie par la Couronne, elle a vu son pouvoir diminuer au profit des Communes.

Actuellement elle n'a plus de pouvoir sur les textes de lois à caractère financier. Pour les autres lois elle n'a qu'un veto suspensif.

POUVOIR EXÉCUTIF ET POUVOIR LÉGISLATIF

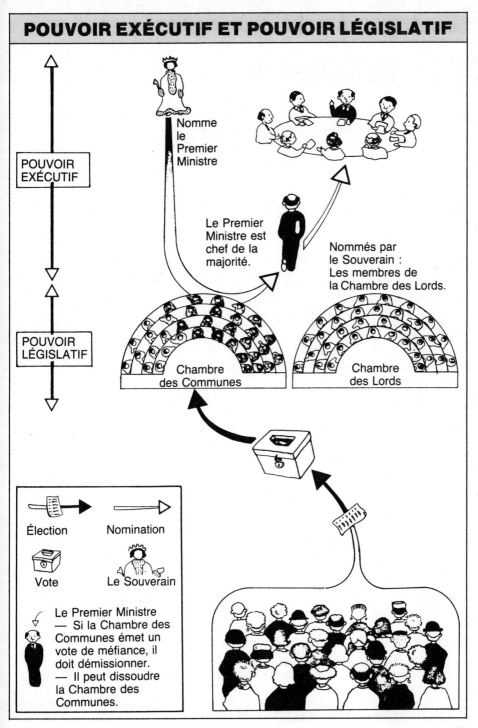

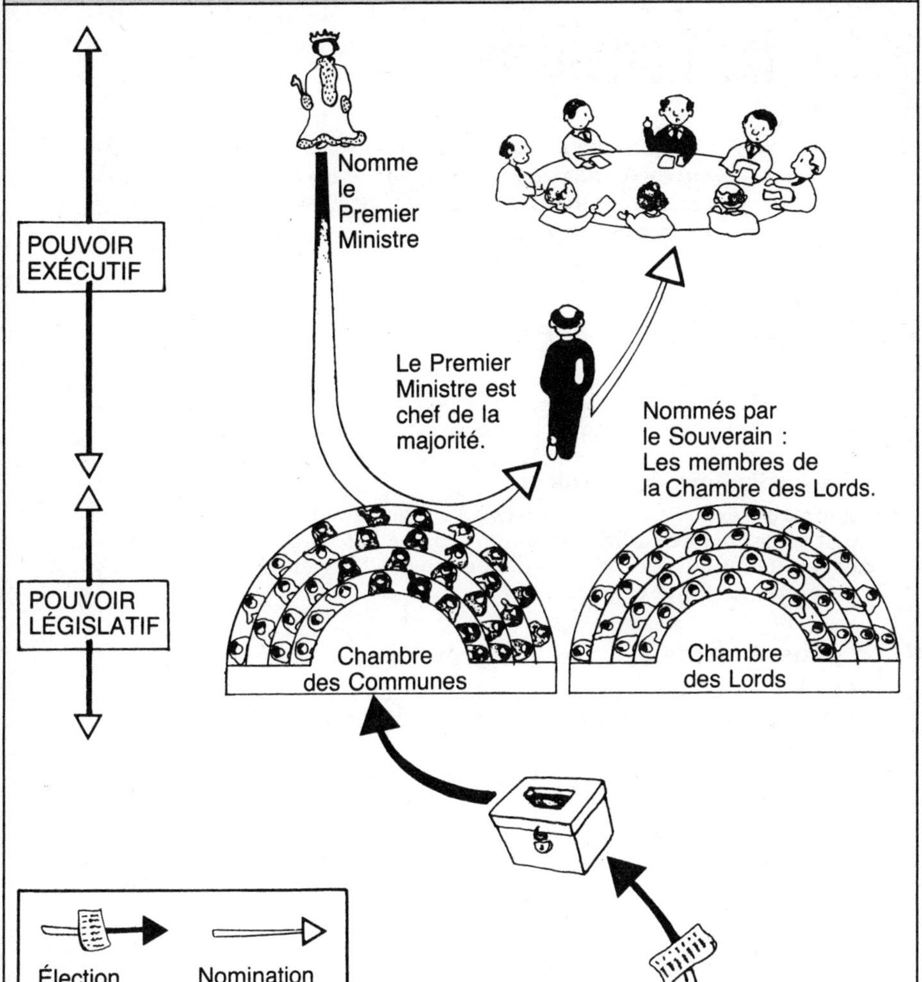
POUVOIR EXÉCUTIF
POUVOIR LÉGISLATIF
Nomme le Premier Ministre
Le Premier Ministre est chef de la majorité.
Nommés par le Souverain : Les membres de la Chambre des Lords.
Chambre des Communes
Chambre des Lords
Élection
Nomination
Vote
Le Souverain
Le Premier Ministre
— Si la Chambre des Communes émet un vote de méfiance, il doit démissionner.
— Il peut dissoudre la Chambre des Communes.

Un régime présidentiel : les États-Unis

Le régime présidentiel se caractérise par des pouvoirs séparés et n'ayant pas d'action l'un sur l'autre, le Président ne peut dissoudre le Congrès, et le Congrès ne peut renvoyer le Président.

■ Le pouvoir exécutif : le Président

— Le Président est élu, ainsi que le Vice-Président, pour 4 ans au suffrage universel indirect* par les grands électeurs, élus dans chaque État, au scrutin de liste majoritaire et n'est rééligible qu'une seule fois. p. 20

— Les attributions du Président :

Il nomme et révoque les Secrétaires d'État qui sont les agents de sa politique. Il est le chef de l'administration. Il possède le pouvoir réglementaire, participe à l'initiative de la loi et détient un droit de veto sur les lois votées. Il dirige la politique étrangère.

■ Le pouvoir législatif : le Congrès

— Le Congrès est élu au suffrage universel direct*, au scrutin uninominal à un tour. Le Congrès comprend la Chambre des Représentants et le Sénat. p. 20

— Les Représentants sont élus pour 2 ans, leur nombre varie en fonction de la population de l'État.

— Les Sénateurs sont élus pour 6 ans, à raison de deux par État (100 sénateurs). Le Sénat est renouvelé par tiers tous les 2 ans.

— Les attributions du Congrès :

— Le Congrès possède le pouvoir législatif*, le pouvoir constituant, et supervise les services publics. p. 4

Le vote des crédits et du budget appartient au Congrès; il peut ainsi bloquer des décisions du Président.

— La Chambre des Représentants décide du montant des impôts.

— Le Sénat contrôle la politique étrangère et donne son autorisation pour la nomination des membres de la Cour Suprême. Il est présidé par le Vice-Président des États-Unis.

■ La Cour Suprême : un tribunal de contrôle

Composée d'un Président et de huit juges nommés à vie par le Président des États-Unis, la Cour Suprême est chargée de contrôler la constitutionnalité des lois.

La Cour Suprême arbitre les différends entre les états, entre un état et l'Union, entre un citoyen et l'État fédéral.

POUVOIR EXÉCUTIF ET POUVOIR LÉGISLATIF

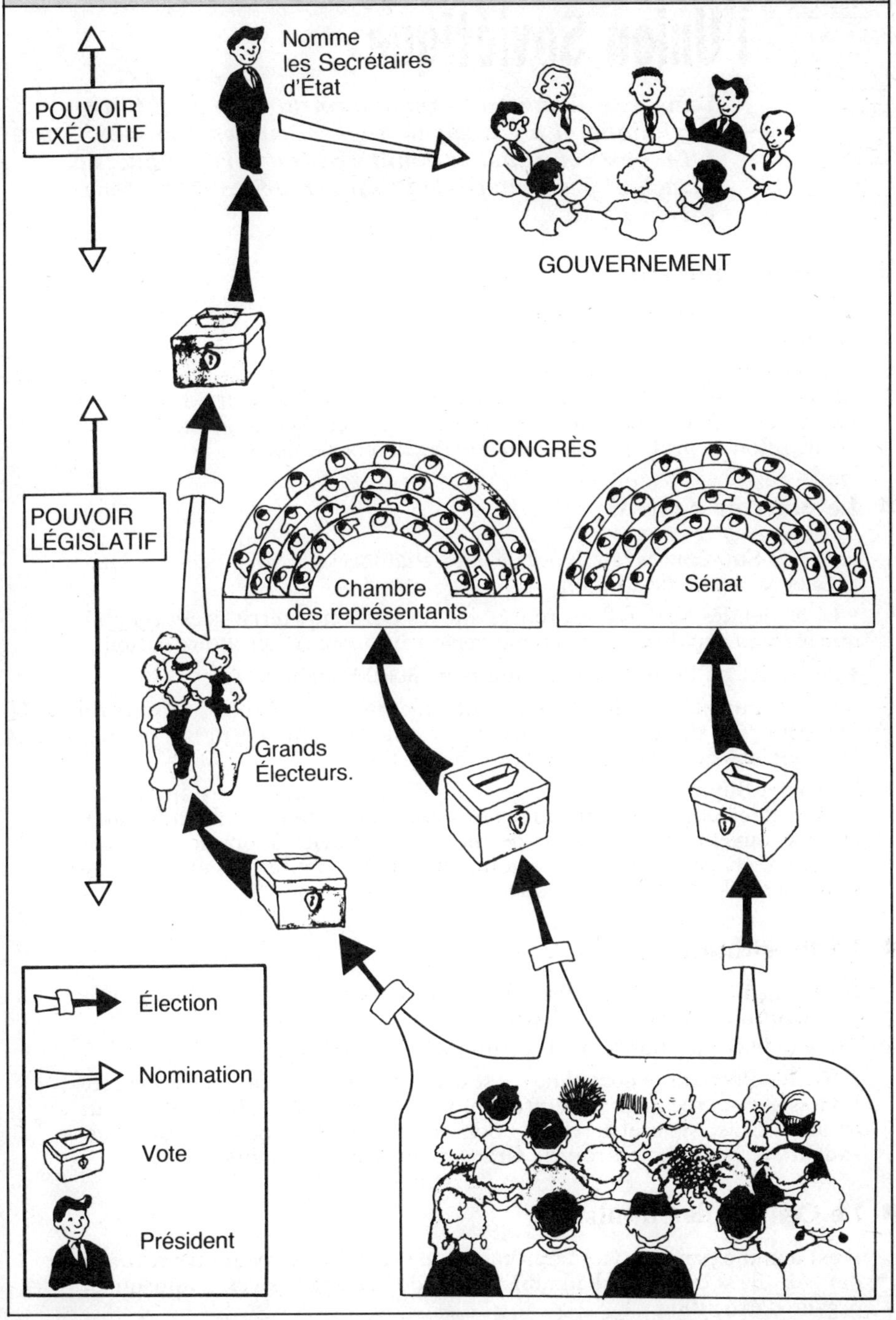

ÉTAT
VIE POLITIQUE
ADMINISTRATION
COLLECTIVITÉS LOCALES
JUSTICE
INTERNATIONAL

Une démocratie populaire : l'Union Soviétique

Dans une démocratie populaire du type de l'Union Soviétique, il n'y a pas de séparation des pouvoirs*. L'État est centralisé et dominé par un parti unique. Le principal personnage de l'État est le Secrétaire général du parti. p. 3

■ Un État centralisé

A tous les niveaux, de l'échelon local à celui de l'Union, le système est celui des Soviets.

Chaque soviet est un conseil élu au suffrage universel*, ce conseil désigne un comité exécutif. Le comité exécutif est responsable devant le soviet qui l'a désigné et soumis au comité exécutif de l'échelon administratif supérieur, selon le principe du « centralisme démocratique ». p. 20

■ Le pouvoir central

— Le Soviet Suprême est composé de deux chambres : le Soviet des Nationalités et le Soviet de l'Union.

• Le Soviet des Nationalités représente les différents territoires : république fédérée, république autonome, région autonome et territoire national.

• Le Soviet de l'Union : un député pour 300000 habitants.

— Les deux chambres sont élues au suffrage universel direct*, au scrutin majoritaire à deux tours*, mais il y a une liste unique présentée par le « Bloc des communistes et des sans-parti ». p. 20 p. 24

Le Soviet Suprême tient deux sessions par an. Il élit le Présidium, vote les lois et le budget. Mais la durée des sessions, une semaine au maximum, le plus souvent deux jours, ne permet pas au Soviet Suprême d'exercer son pouvoir, par contre le Présidium qui assure l'intérim entre les sessions possède la réalité du pouvoir.

■ Le Présidium

D'une façon générale « le Présidium exerce les pouvoirs établis par la Constitution et les lois de l'URSS ».

Élu par le Soviet Suprême, il comprend 39 membres.

Il fixe les élections et convoque les sessions du Soviet Suprême, interprète les lois et peut recourir au référendum, ratifie et dénonce les traités, peut annuler les décisions et arrêtés du Conseil des ministres, nomme les ambassadeurs et possède le droit de Grâce, peut déclarer la guerre.

■ Le Conseil des ministres

Il est nommé par le Soviet Suprême ou le Présidium et peut être révoqué par eux : il est chargé de l'administration de l'État et n'est en réalité qu'un organe d'exécution.

POUVOIR EXÉCUTIF ET POUVOIR LÉGISLATIF

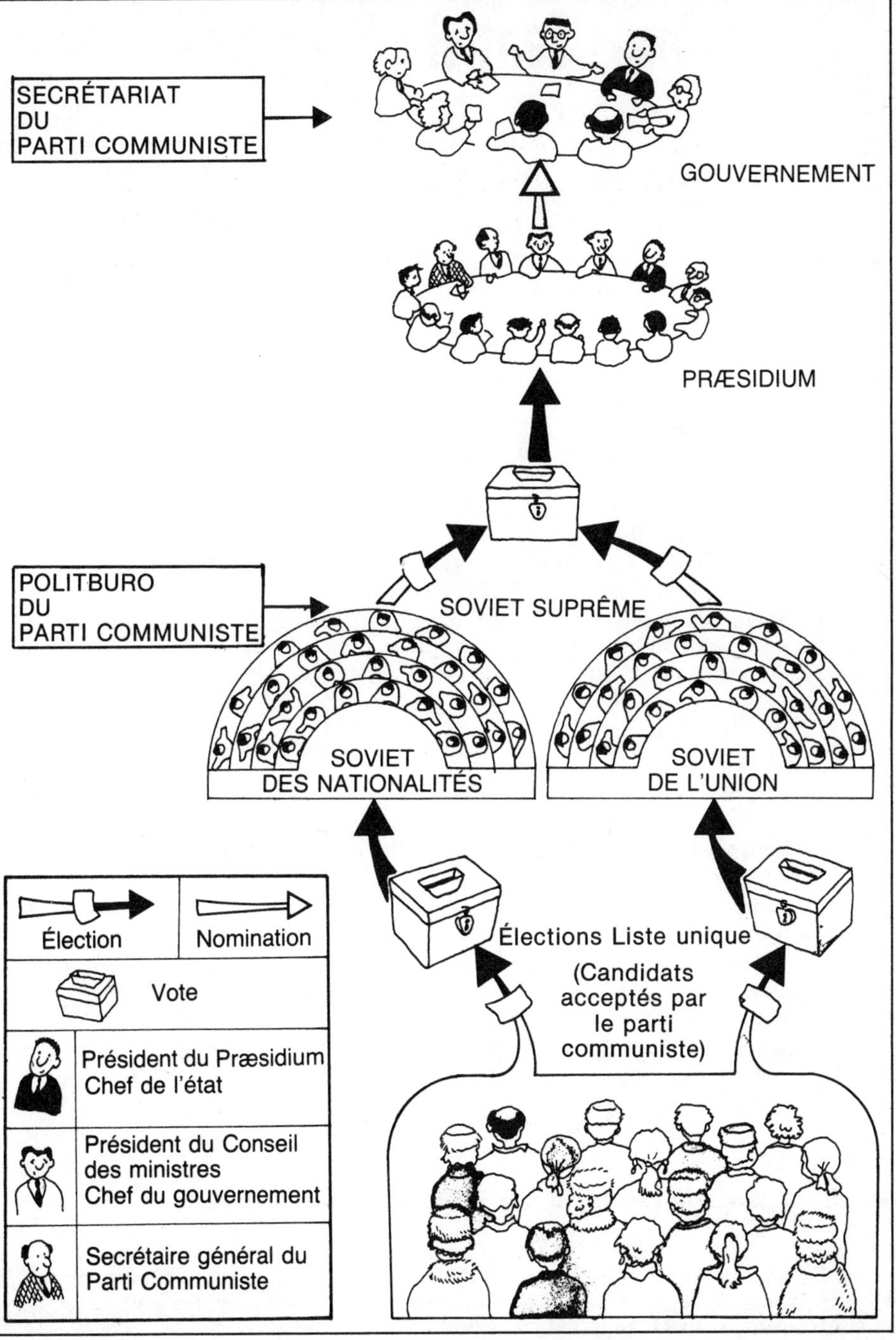

SECRÉTARIAT DU PARTI COMMUNISTE
GOUVERNEMENT
PRÆSIDIUM
POLITBURO DU PARTI COMMUNISTE
SOVIET SUPRÊME
SOVIET DES NATIONALITÉS
SOVIET DE L'UNION
Élections Liste unique
(Candidats acceptés par le parti communiste)
Élection
Nomination
Vote
Président du Præsidium Chef de l'état
Président du Conseil des ministres Chef du gouvernement
Secrétaire général du Parti Communiste

Un régime parlementaire et présidentiel : la France

Le Président de la République et le gouvernement partagent le pouvoir exécutif*. Le pouvoir législatif* est exercé par le Parlement. Le régime est parlementaire car l'Assemblée nationale peut renverser le gouvernement et le Président de la République peut dissoudre l'Assemblée. Il est présidentiel car le Président de la République ne peut être renversé. p. 4

■ Le pouvoir exécutif

— Le pouvoir exécutif est partagé entre le Président* et le Premier ministre*. p. 36 p. 38

— Le Président de la République : il est élu au suffrage universel direct pour 7 ans. Il a des pouvoirs importants : il nomme le Premier ministre; il préside le Conseil des ministres; il peut dissoudre l'Assemblée nationale, il peut recourir au référendum.

— Le Premier ministre est le chef du gouvernement. Il choisit les membres de son gouvernement et conduit la politique de la Nation. Il est responsable devant le Parlement. Il a l'initiative des lois et en assure l'exécution.

■ Le pouvoir législatif

— Le pouvoir législatif est exercé par le Parlement composé de l'Assemblée nationale et du Sénat*. p. 42 et 44

— L'Assemblée nationale est élue au suffrage universel direct. Les députés sont élus pour cinq ans.

— Le Sénat est élu au suffrage universel indirect par les conseillers municipaux, les conseillers généraux et les députés. Les Sénateurs sont élus pour 9 ans. Le Sénat est renouvelé par tiers tous les trois ans.

— L'Assemblée nationale et le Sénat votent les lois et le budget*. L'Assemblée nationale peut renverser le gouvernement par une motion de censure*. p. 60 p. 52

■ Un organe de contrôle : le Conseil Constitutionnel

Le Conseil Constitutionnel*, composé de 9 membres, nommés par les présidents de la République, du Sénat et de l'Assemblée nationale pour 9 ans, est chargé de veiller à l'équilibre des pouvoirs entre le législatif et l'exécutif et au respect de la Constitution. p. 56

POUVOIR EXÉCUTIF ET POUVOIR LÉGISLATIF

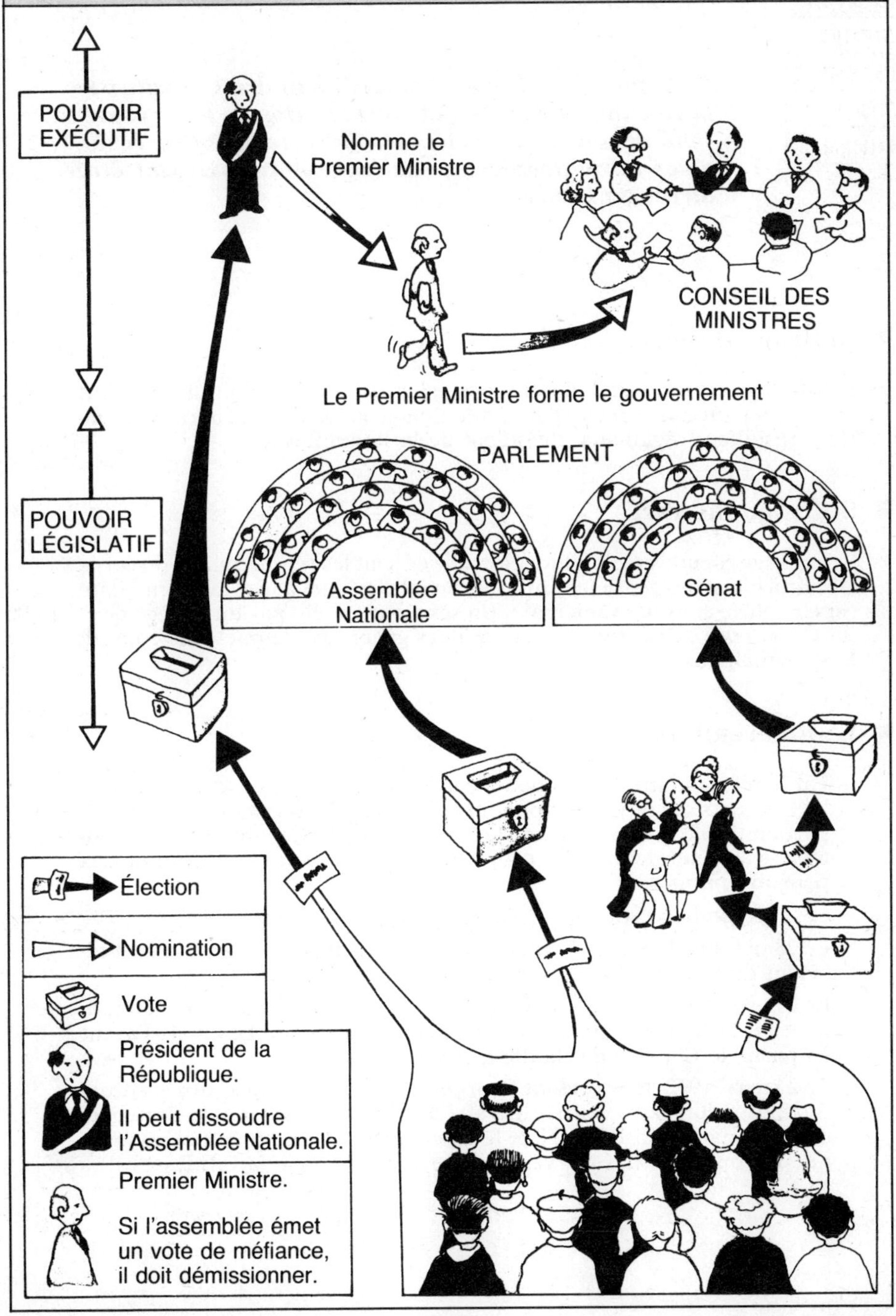

Les consultations électorales

En France, les citoyens exercent leur droit de vote par la voie du référendum et par l'élection de leurs représentants aux affaires locales, départementales, régionales ou nationales. Le suffrage universel peut être direct ou indirect.

■ Suffrage direct

Le suffrage est universel direct lorsque les électeurs élisent directement leurs représentants : conseillers municipaux, conseillers généraux, députés, conseillers régionaux, Président de la République.

■ Suffrage indirect

Le suffrage est universel indirect lorsque ce sont les représentants du corps électoral (donc des gens élus) qui deviennent électeurs à leur tour. Un maire est élu par le conseil municipal*. Un sénateur est élu par un collège électoral composé de députés, de conseillers généraux, de quelques conseillers municipaux.

p. 96

■ Le Référendum

— Par le référendum, le Président de la République consulte directement les électeurs qui répondent par oui ou par non à la question posée. Selon l'article 11 de la constitution, le Président de la République peut soumettre au référendum tout projet de loi portant sur l'organisation des pouvoirs publics.

— Les référendums sous la Ve République par exemple :

Le 28 octobre 1962, les Français se prononcent pour l'élection du Président de la République au suffrage universel direct.

Le 27 avril 1969, le Général de Gaulle propose aux Français un référendum sur la régionalisation et sur une réforme du Sénat. Le « non » l'ayant emporté, le Général de Gaulle a démissionné.

Le 23 avril 1972, le Président Georges Pompidou propose aux Français un référendum pour ratifier le traité d'adhésion de la Grande-Bretagne, du Danemark, de l'Irlande, de la Norvège à la Communauté Économique Européenne. (La Norvège refusera d'adhérer à la C.E.E.)

FRANCE : TOUTES LES ÉLECTIONS

▲ Élections municipales

Tous les six ans.
Élection des conseillers municipaux.
Suffrage universel direct.
Scrutin de liste selon un mode mixte.

▲ Élection des maires

Tous les six ans, après les élections municipales.
Élection des maires de chaque localité.
Suffrage indirect par chaque conseil municipal.
Scrutin uninominal majoritaire à trois tours.

▲ Élections cantonales

Élection d'un conseiller général par canton.
Le renouvellement du conseil général a lieu par moitié tous les trois ans.
Suffrage universel direct.
Scrutin uninominal majoritaire à deux tours.

▲ Élections régionales

Tous les six ans.
Élection des conseillers régionaux.
Suffrage universel direct.
Scrutin de liste à représentation proportionnelle.

▲ Élections législatives

Tous les cinq ans.
Élection des députés.
Suffrage universel direct.
Scrutin uninominal majoritaire à deux tours.

▲ Élections sénatoriales

Le Sénat est renouvelé par tiers tous les trois ans.
Élection des sénateurs.
Suffrage indirect.
Scrutin majoritaire à deux tours dans les départements de 1 à 4 sénateurs.
Scrutin à représentation proportionnelle dans les départements de plus de 4 sénateurs.

▲ Élections présidentielles

Tous les sept ans.
Élection du Président de la République.
Suffrage universel direct.
Scrutin uninominal majoritaire à deux tours.

▲ Élections européennes

Tous les cinq ans.
Élection des députés au Parlement européen.
Suffrage universel direct.
Scrutin de liste à représentation proportionnelle.

▲ Élections professionnelles

Elles ne concernent pas tous les électeurs mais seulement ceux qui exercent une activité professionnelle et qui remplissent les conditions d'âge et d'ancienneté. Élections des délégués du personnel, du comité d'entreprise, des conseillers prud'homaux, etc.

L'électeur et le vote

En France, voter est un droit mais pas une obligation, contrairement à ce qui se passe en Belgique ou au Luxembourg où l'abstention non justifiée est punie par une amende. Pour voter, il faut remplir certaines conditions et le vote se déroule suivant des règles précises.

■ Les conditions à remplir pour être électeur

— Être majeur : avoir 18 ans.
— Être français, ou naturalisé français, depuis plus de 5 ans.
— Jouir de ses droits civiques.
— Être inscrit sur la liste électorale. La demande d'inscription sur la liste électorale doit être faite en mairie, avant le 31 décembre.

■ La carte d'électeur

L'électeur inscrit reçoit sa carte d'électeur qui est renouvelée périodiquement.

Il est possible de voter sans présenter sa carte d'électeur. Il suffit de prouver son identité à l'aide d'une pièce officielle et de figurer sur les registres électoraux.

■ Le vote par procuration

— Il permet à un électeur (le mandant) de se faire représenter au bureau de vote, le jour du scrutin, par un autre électeur de son choix (le mandataire). Le mandataire peut représenter deux électeurs établis en France ou cinq électeurs établis hors de France. La demande de vote par procuration exige un certain délai.

— Qui est admis à voter par procuration ?
• toute personne éloignée de la commune en raison de ses activités : marins, militaires, mariniers, citoyens hors de France...
• toute personne ne pouvant se déplacer le jour du scrutin : invalides à 85 %, malades, femmes en couche...
• toute personne ayant sa résidence et son travail dans un autre département que celui de la commune d'inscription.

— Il convient de s'adresser soit au tribunal d'instance*, soit au commissariat de police, soit à la gendarmerie. Les Français hors de France s'adressent au consulat. p. 116

■ Le vote par correspondance

— Il a été supprimé en 1975 en raison des abus et fraudes auxquels il avait donné lieu.

PLAN D'UN BUREAU DE VOTE

LES DEUX ASSESSEURS : Ils sont désignés par les partis ou pris parmi les Conseillers municipaux.

LE PRÉSIDENT DU BUREAU DE VOTE : C'est le Maire ou un adjoint ou un conseiller municipal.

L'URNE : Elle est munie de 2 serrures ou d'un cadenas qui nécessiteront deux clés différentes.

LE SECRÉTAIRE DU BUREAU DE VOTE : Il tient le registre électoral où sont inscrits et signent les électeurs de la commune.

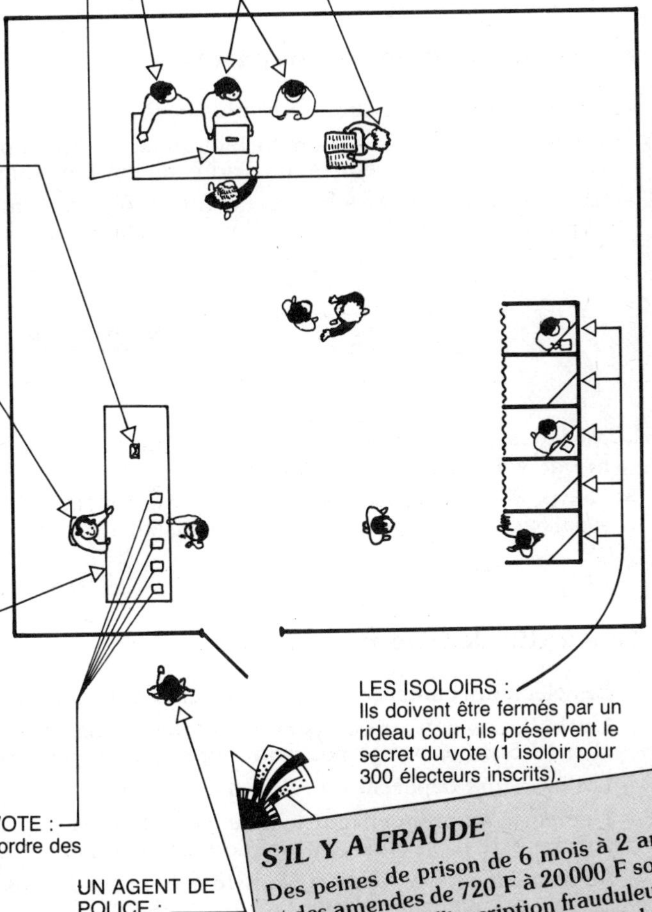

DES ENVELOPPES BLEUES : L'électeur glisse son bulletin de vote dans une enveloppe.

UN ÉLECTEUR DE LA COMMUNE VOLONTAIRE : Il donne les enveloppes bleues fournies par la préfecture. Il veille à ce que chaque tas de bulletins ait toujours la même hauteur.

LA TABLE DE DÉCHARGE : On y trouve les enveloppes bleues en nombre égal à celui des électeurs de la commune et les bulletins de vote.

LES ISOLOIRS : Ils doivent être fermés par un rideau court, ils préservent le secret du vote (1 isoloir pour 300 électeurs inscrits).

LES BULLETINS DE VOTE : Ils sont classés dans l'ordre des dépôts de candidature.

UN AGENT DE POLICE : Si le président du bureau de vote le souhaite. Il veille à ce que personne ne perturbe les élections.

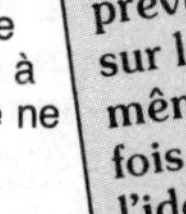

S'IL Y A FRAUDE

Des peines de prison de 6 mois à 2 ans et des amendes de 720 F à 20 000 F sont prévues en cas d'inscription frauduleuse sur les listes électorales. Sera puni de la même peine le citoyen qui vote plusieurs fois le même jour ou l'électeur qui prend l'identité d'un autre.

Le scrutin majoritaire

Dans le scrutin majoritaire est considéré élu le candidat ou la liste qui obtient la majorité des voix. La majorité absolue correspond à la moitié des suffrages exprimés plus une voix.

Le scrutin uninominal majoritaire

— Les électeurs choisissent entre plusieurs candidats.

Les bulletins de vote ne comportent qu'un seul nom puisque les électeurs n'auront à choisir qu'un seul candidat (uninominal : un nom).

— L'emporte au premier tour le candidat qui obtient la majorité absolue. Si personne n'est élu, on dit qu'il y a ballottage donc deuxième tour de scrutin.

$$\text{majorité absolue} = \frac{\text{suffrages exprimés}}{2} + 1$$

— Au deuxième tour, l'emporte le candidat qui obtient le plus grand nombre de voix ou majorité relative.

— Ce type de scrutin concerne l'élection présidentielle* et les élections cantonales où les électeurs élisent un conseiller général par canton. p. 34

Le scrutin de liste majoritaire

— Les électeurs choisissent entre plusieurs listes de candidats.

Les bulletins de vote comportent autant de noms que de candidats à élire (si 5 sièges sont à pourvoir, chaque liste comportera 5 noms...).

Les électeurs déposent une liste dans l'urne.

— L'emporte au premier tour la liste qui obtient la majorité absolue. Si aucune liste n'est élue, il y a ballottage et deuxième tour de scrutin.

— Au deuxième tour, l'emporte la liste qui obtient le plus grand nombre de voix ou majorité relative.

— « Liste bloquée » : dans un scrutin de liste, on parle de « liste bloquée » quand l'électeur ne peut ni raturer, ni modifier ni déposer une liste incomplète sous peine de voir son bulletin annulé.

— Ce type de scrutin concerne les élections sénatoriales* dans les départements qui élisent moins de 5 sénateurs. p. 44

10 000 ÉLECTEURS VOTENT

▲ Scrutin uninominal majoritaire. Exemple 1.

Résultats du 1er tour :

Candidat A	*Candidat B*	*Candidat C*
5 500 voix	*3 100 voix*	*1 400 voix*

Suffrages exprimés : 10 000 voix.
Majorité absolue : 5 001 voix.

Le candidat A est élu au premier tour : le nombre de voix obtenues est supérieur à la majorité absolue. Il n'y aura pas de deuxième tour.

▲ Scrutin uninominal majoritaire. Exemple 2.

Résultats du 1er tour :

Candidat A	*Candidat B*	*Candidat C*
4 500 voix	*3 600 voix*	*1 900 voix*

Suffrages exprimés : 10 000 voix.
Majorité absolue : 5 001 voix.
Aucun candidat n'est élu au premier tour, car aucun n'atteint la majorité absolue. Il y a ballottage. Au deuxième tour, sera élu le candidat arrivé en tête.

▲ Scrutin de liste majoritaire

Liste A	*Liste B*	*Liste C*	*Liste D*
1 700 voix	*5 200 voix*	*1 100 voix*	*2 000 voix*

Suffrages exprimés : 10 000 voix.
Majorité absolue : 5 001 voix.

La liste B est élue au premier tour : le nombre de voix obtenues est supérieur à la majorité absolue. Il n'y aura pas de deuxième tour.

Si aucune liste (ni A, ni B, ni C, ni D) n'avait obtenu la majorité absolue (5 001 voix), il y aurait eu ballottage. Au deuxième tour aurait été élue la liste arrivée en tête.

COMBIEN DE DÉPUTÉS ?

	1981	1986	1988
PC	44	35	27
PS + MRG	283	210	272
Divers gauche	6	5	6
RPR	83	157	129
UDF	61	132	130
Divers droite	11	6	12
F.N.		32	1
	488	577	577

Le scrutin proportionnel

Le scrutin de liste à représentation proportionnelle consiste à attribuer à chaque liste qui se présente, un nombre de sièges proportionnel à son score. Il n'y a qu'un seul tour de scrutin.

■ Le quotient électoral

— Pour répartir les sièges entre les différentes listes, il faut d'abord déterminer le quotient électoral. Il s'obtient en divisant le total des suffrages exprimés (donc ni les bulletins blancs ou nuls) par le nombre de sièges à pourvoir. Chaque liste obtiendra autant de sièges que son score contiendra le quotient électoral.

$$\text{Quotient électoral} = \frac{\text{total des suffrages exprimés}}{\text{nombre de sièges à pourvoir.}}$$

Exemple : total des suffrages : 10000 voix - Nombre de sièges à pourvoir : 3.
Quotient électoral : 10000 divisé par 3 = 3333.

■ La plus forte moyenne - Le plus fort reste

L'application du quotient électoral ne permet pas de distribuer tous les sièges. Pour attribuer les sièges restants, il existe deux méthodes de calcul.

— La méthode de « la plus forte moyenne » qui consiste à diviser le nombre de voix de chaque liste par le nombre de sièges obtenus + 1.

— La méthode du « plus fort reste » qui consiste à soustraire du nombre de voix de chaque liste le total des quotients électoraux qu'elle peut contenir, à comparer ensuite les voix restantes.

■ Quelles élections ont lieu à la proportionnelle ?

— Les élections sénatoriales dans les départements qui ont droit à 5 ou plus de 5 sénateurs.

— Les conseillers régionaux* sont élus à la proportionnelle. p. 82

Dans ces deux élections, la méthode de calcul utilisée est celle de la plus forte moyenne.

10 000 ÉLECTEURS VOTENT

Par opposition à la méthode de plus forte moyenne, la méthode du plus fort reste favorise les petites formations politiques.

▲ Dans une élection cinq sièges sont à pourvoir.

Quatre listes sont en présence.

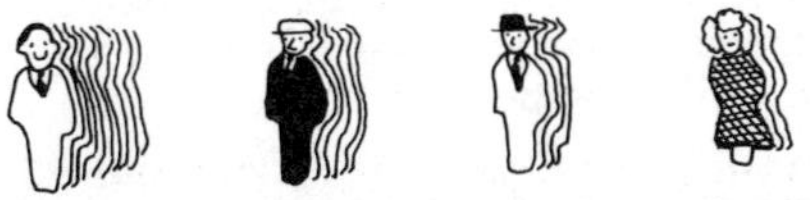

Liste A	*Liste B*	*Liste C*	*Liste D*
5 000 voix	*2 700 voix*	*1 200 voix*	*1 100 voix*

Total des suffrages exprimés : 10 000 voix.
Total des sièges à pourvoir : 5

▲ Méthode de la plus forte moyenne

— Quotient électoral : 10 000 divisé par 5 = 2 000. Donc 2 000 voix donnent droit à un siège.

Les différentes listes obtiennent :

Liste A	*Liste B*	*Liste C*	*Liste D*
$\frac{5\,000}{2\,000}$	$\frac{2\,700}{2\,000}$	$\frac{1\,200}{2\,000}$	$\frac{1\,100}{2\,000}$
= 2 sièges	*= 1 siège*	*= 0 siège*	*= 0 siège*

— 3 sièges seulement viennent d'être attribués, il en reste 2. Les listes ayant les plus fortes moyennes recevront, dans l'ordre, les 2 sièges non attribués. Pour calculer la moyenne de chaque liste, on divise son nombre de voix par le nombre de sièges qu'elle a obtenus auquel on ajoute 1, ce qui donne :

moyenne de la liste A : $\frac{5\,000}{2+1} = 1\,666$

moyenne de la liste B : $\frac{2\,700}{1+1} = 1\,350$

moyenne de la liste C : $\frac{1\,200}{0+1} = 1\,200$

moyenne de la liste D : $\frac{1\,100}{0+1} = 1\,100$

Les listes A et B auront un siège supplémentaire.

— Résultats définitifs

Liste A	*Liste B*	*Liste C*	*Liste D*

Trois sièges	*Deux sièges*	*Aucun siège*	*Aucun siège*

▲ Méthode du plus fort reste

— Si l'on reprend l'exemple précédent, les 2 sièges non attribués après la répartition avec le quotient électoral, auraient été donnés aux deux listes ayant le plus fort reste.

calcul des plus fort restes :
liste A : 5 000 − 2 (2 000) = 1 000
liste B : 2 700 − 1 (2 000) = 700
liste C : 1 200 − 0 = 1 200
liste D : 1 100 − 0 = 1 100

Les listes C et D ont les plus forts restes et se voient attribuer un siège supplémentaire.

— Résultats définitifs :

Liste A	*Liste B*	*Liste C*	*Liste D*

Deux sièges	*Un siège*	*Un siège*	*Un siège*

Le scrutin mixte

Le scrutin de liste selon un mode mixte combine le scrutin majoritaire et le scrutin à représentation proportionnelle. Il est prévu deux tours de scrutin.

■ Si une liste obtient la majorité absolue au 1er tour

Une liste obtient au premier tour la majorité absolue (c'est-à-dire la moitié des suffrages plus une voix) : elle occupera la moitié des sièges à pourvoir. (On arrondit, si c'est nécessaire, au chiffre supérieur.)

Le reste des sièges est réparti entre toutes les listes, y compris celle qui arrive en tête. Cette répartition se fait à la représentation proportionnelle, selon la méthode de la plus forte moyenne.

Il n'y a qu'un seul tour de scrutin, le second tour ne se justifie pas.

■ Si aucune liste n'obtient la majorité absolue au 1er tour

Aucune liste n'obtient au premier tour la majorité absolue (c'est-à-dire la moitié des suffrages exprimés plus une voix) : il y a un deuxième tour de scrutin.

Au deuxième tour, la liste qui obtient la majorité relative (c'est-à-dire le plus grand nombre de voix) recueille la moitié des sièges et le reste des sièges est réparti à la proportionnelle entre toutes les listes.

■ La barre des 10 %

Seules les listes qui ont obtenu au moins 10 % des voix au premier tour du scrutin sont autorisées à se présenter au deuxième tour. Les listes ayant recueilli moins de 10 % des suffrages doivent se retirer du scrutin (elles pourront, toutefois, se représenter lors d'une autre élection).

■ Quelles élections ont lieu selon un mode mixte ?

Les élections municipales*, dans les communes de plus de 3 500 habitants, p. 94 ont lieu selon le mode mixte.

10 000 ÉLECTEURS VOTENT

▲ Exemple 1

15 sièges à pourvoir, chaque liste comporte donc 15 noms.

Résultats du 1er tour :

Liste A *6 100 voix* — *Liste B* *2 800 voix* — *Liste C* *1 100 voix*

Suffrages exprimés : 10 000 voix.
Majorité absolue : 5 001 voix.

— Commentaire des résultats

La liste A, dont le score est supérieur à la majorité absolue, obtient la moitié des sièges, soit

$$\frac{15}{2} = 7{,}5 \text{ soit 8 sièges.}$$

Il reste 7 sièges à distribuer entre les 3 listes, à la proportionnelle.

Calcul du quotient électoral :

$$\text{quotient électoral} = \frac{10\,000}{7} = 1\,428$$

Distribution des sièges à l'aide du quotient électoral :

liste A : 4 sièges
liste B : 1 siège
liste C : 0 siège

Il reste 2 sièges à distribuer selon la méthode de la plus forte moyenne.

La moyenne pour la liste A est de :

$$\frac{6\,100}{4+1} = 1\,220$$

$$\text{la liste B est de : } \frac{2\,800}{1+1} = 1\,400$$

$$\text{la liste C est de : } \frac{1\,100}{0+1} = 1\,100$$

Les listes A et B qui ont les plus fortes moyennes prennent chacune un siège.

— Chaque liste obtient :

Liste A	*Liste B*	*Liste C*
8 sièges	*1 siège*	*0 siège*
+ 4 sièges	*+ 1 siège*	
+ 1 siège	*2 élus*	
= 13 sièges		
13 élus		

▲ Exemple 2

— 15 sièges à pourvoir.

Résultats du premier tour.

Liste A *3 300 voix* — *Liste B* *4 000 voix* — *Liste C* *2 700 voix*

Suffrages exprimés : 10 000
Majorité absolue : 5 001.
Aucune liste n'atteint la majorité absolue, il y a donc un deuxième tour.

— Résultats du deuxième tour.

Liste A *3 000 voix* — *Liste B* *3 900 voix* — *Liste C* *3 100 voix*

Suffrages exprimés : 10 000
On attribue la moitié des sièges à la liste B qui a la majorité relative.
Le reste est distribué à la proportionnelle entre les trois listes.

— Elus

Liste A *2 sièges* — *Liste B* *10 sièges* — *Liste C* *3 sièges*

Les partis politiques

La vie politique française est animée par de nombreux partis politiques. Quelques-uns seulement ont une audience importante et sont représentés au Parlement. Chaque parti politique exprime un courant de pensée.

■ La liberté politique

Chacun est libre d'adhérer ou non à un parti politique.

Chaque électeur est libre de voter pour élire un candidat appartenant à tel ou tel parti politique.

L'âge d'adhésion et le montant de la cotisation varient d'un parti à l'autre.

La liberté politique est reconnue dans la constitution de 1958. Elle reconnaît que « les partis et groupements politiques concourent à l'expression du suffrage. Ils se forment et exercent leur activité librement. Ils doivent respecter les principes de la souveraineté nationale et de la démocratie ».

■ L'expression des partis politiques

Pour faire passer leurs idées, les partis politiques s'expriment par voie d'affiches, de tracts, de journaux. Leurs leaders participent à des émissions de radios ou à des débats télévisés.

■ Majorité-opposition

Aucun parti politique ne rassemble suffisamment de voix pour être majoritaire au Parlement. On assiste à des alliances entre partis.

• On appelle « partis de la majorité » les groupements politiques qui, ensemble, ont un nombre de députés qui atteint la majorité absolue* à p. 24
l'Assemblée. Les partis de la majorité soutiennent le gouvernement* p. 40
en place.

• On appelle « partis de l'opposition » l'ensemble des partis politiques qui n'ont pas la majorité à l'Assemblée et qui s'opposent à l'action du gouvernement en place.

■ Gauche-droite

• Le terme « gauche » désigne, dans les assemblées parlementaires, les élus qui prennent place sur les bancs situés à gauche du Président.

• Le terme « droite » désigne les élus assis à la droite du Président.

LES PRINCIPAUX PARTIS POLITIQUES EN FRANCE

▲ Le PCF ou Parti Communiste Français

siège : 2, place du Colonel-Fabien Paris 19e
objectif : la conquête du pouvoir par les masses populaires, la transformation de la société capitaliste en une société sans exploiteurs ni exploités.

▲ Le PS ou Parti Socialiste

siège : 10, rue de Solférino 75333 Paris Cedex 07
objectif : engager le pays sur la voie de la démocratie socialiste, par étapes et par des moyens démocratiques.

▲ Le MRG ou Mouvement des Radicaux de Gauche

siège : 195, boulevard Saint-Germain Paris 7e
objectif : attachement au radicalisme authentique et à l'idéal d'un socialisme humaniste.

▲ Les Verts - parti écologiste

siège : 90, rue Vergniaud Paris 13e
objectif : mettre en place un projet de société écologiste.

▲ L'UDF ou Union pour la Démocratie Française

siège : 42 bis, boulevard de la Tour-Maubourg Paris 7e

L'UDF regroupe :
le Parti Républicain (PR)
le Centre des Démocrates Sociaux (CDS)
le Parti Radical Socialiste
les Clubs Perspectives et Réalités
le Parti Social Démocrate.

objectif : parvenir à une société libérale, de responsabilité et de solidarité.

▲ Le RPR ou Rassemblement pour la République

siège : 123, rue de Lille Paris 7e
objectif : rassembler, comme le Général de Gaulle, le peuple français par l'extension des libertés et un redressement économique.

▲ Le Front National

siège : 11, rue Bernouilli Paris 8e
objectif : combattre les socialistes et les communistes. Revenir à plus de fermeté dans les domaines de la justice et de l'immigration.

L'ORIGINE DES EXPRESSIONS DROITE ET GAUCHE

**Le 11 septembre 1789, les partisans de la monarchie se groupèrent à la droite du Président de l'Assemblée nationale Constituante. Donc, à l'origine, la «droite» rassemblait les défenseurs de l'ordre et de la tradition et faisait figure de parti plus conservateur.
Depuis, les expressions «droite» et «gauche» ont vu leur contenu évoluer.**

Les syndicats de salariés

Un syndicat est une association de personnes exerçant la même profession ou des métiers similaires. Il a pour objet la défense des intérêts économiques et professionnels de ses membres.

■ La liberté syndicale

Chacun est libre d'adhérer ou non à un syndicat.

Pour adhérer, il suffit d'être salarié, d'avoir plus de 16 ans, sans distinction de sexe ou de nationalité. L'adhérent s'acquitte d'une cotisation.

Une personne syndiquée peut se retirer librement de son syndicat.

■ Le droit syndical dans l'entreprise

— Il est reconnu par la loi du 27 décembre 1968 dans toutes les entreprises de plus de 50 salariés.

Un syndicat, reconnu sur le plan national, peut créer, dans l'entreprise, une section syndicale.

— La section syndicale dispose du droit d'affichage. Elle peut distribuer des tracts syndicaux aux heures d'entrée et de sortie.

Au-delà de 200 salariés, un local est mis à la disposition de la section.

— Le délégué syndical représente la section auprès du chef d'entreprise.

Le délégué doit avoir au moins 18 ans et travailler dans l'entreprise depuis un an. Il dispose d'un certain nombre d'heures pour exercer ses fonctions (ex. : 10 heures au moins si l'entreprise emploie de 50 à 150 salariés).

■ Les attributions d'un syndicat

— Il négocie avec les représentants patronaux, avec les représentants de l'État.

— Il passe des contrats concernant la profession (ex. : conventions collectives).

— Il peut décréter la grève.

— Il peut aller en justice pour défendre ses intérêts.

— Il présente des candidats aux élections des délégués du personnel et du comité d'entreprise.

— Il informe ses adhérents, défend leurs intérêts professionnels et matériels.

— Il crée des œuvres sociales.

LES GROUPEMENTS SYNDICAUX

Plus un syndicat réunit de membres, plus il est représentatif et capable de défendre leurs intérêts.

A partir de la section syndicale qui est la cellule de base, il existe plusieurs sortes de groupements :

— une union est une association de plusieurs syndicats, de métiers différents sur le plan local ou départemental.

— une fédération groupe des syndicats d'une même profession sur le plan national (ex. : la FEN ou Fédération de l'Éducation Nationale, la FNSEA ou Fédération Nationale des Syndicats d'Exploitants Agricoles).

— une confédération regroupe unions et fédérations sur le plan national.

Créée en 1944
Confédération générale des cadres

Créée en 1964
Confédération française démocratique du travail

Créée en 1919
Confédération française des travailleurs chrétiens

Créée en 1895
Confédération générale du travail

Créée en 1947
Force ouvrière

LA RECONNAISSANCE DU DROIT SYNDICAL

Le 21 mars 1884, la loi Waldeck-Rousseau autorise la création des syndicats. Le préambule de la constitution de 1946, repris par celle de 1958, affirme que «tout homme peut défendre ses droits et ses intérêts par l'action syndicale et adhérer au syndicat de son choix.»

L'élection du Président de la République

Le Président de la République est élu par tous les citoyens, ce qui renforce l'autorité du chef de l'État. C'est le plus haut personnage de la République française.

■ Qui peut être candidat ? Comment ?

— Il faut être âgé de 23 ans révolus au jour du scrutin.

— Une candidature doit être présentée par au moins 500 citoyens élus, membres du Parlement, des conseils généraux, du conseil de Paris*, des assemblées territoriales des Territoires d'outre-mer* ou maires. p. 102 p. 106

Les signatures des élus qui parrainent doivent provenir d'au moins 30 départements et Territoires d'outre-mer différents.

Les candidatures sont adressées au Conseil Constitutionnel*. p. 56

— Chaque candidat doit déposer auprès du Trésorier-payeur général une caution de 10 000 F qui lui sera restituée s'il a obtenu plus de 5 % des suffrages exprimés au 1er tour.

■ Comment est élu le Président de la République ?

— Il est élu au suffrage universel direct depuis 1962, c'est-à-dire que chaque citoyen vote pour un candidat à l'élection présidentielle.

— Le Président de la République est élu au scrutin uninominal majoritaire* à deux tours. Un délai de 15 jours sépare les deux tours de scrutin. Au 2e tour ne peuvent se présenter que les deux candidats arrivés en tête au 1er tour. p. 24

— Le Président de la République est élu pour une durée de 7 ans, c'est un septennat.

■ Que se passe-t-il quand la place de Président est vacante ?

Si le Président de la République démissionne ou décède en cours de mandat, l'intérim est assuré par le Président du Sénat, le temps d'organiser les prochaines élections.

Le Président du Sénat, Alain Poher, a assuré l'intérim en 1969, lors de la démission du Général de Gaulle et en 1974 lors du décès de Georges Pompidou.

Il y a suppléance et non intérim si le Président de la République est malade ou en déplacement à l'étranger. Le Premier ministre* peut alors le remplacer pour présider un conseil des ministres. p. 38

PARCOURS DU CANDIDAT

19 jours avant le 1er tour envoi des 500 signatures

16 jours avant le 1er tour publication des candidatures

Ouverture officielle de la campagne électorale

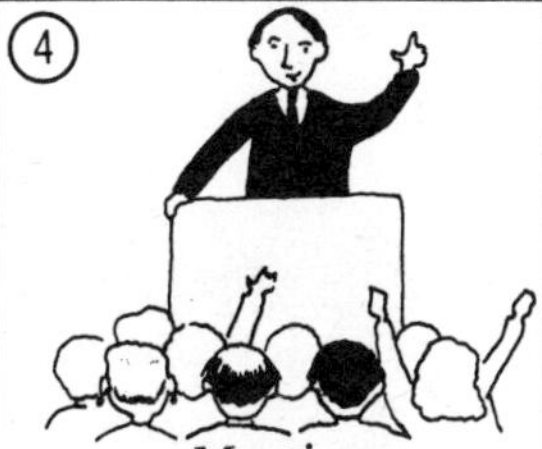

Meeting

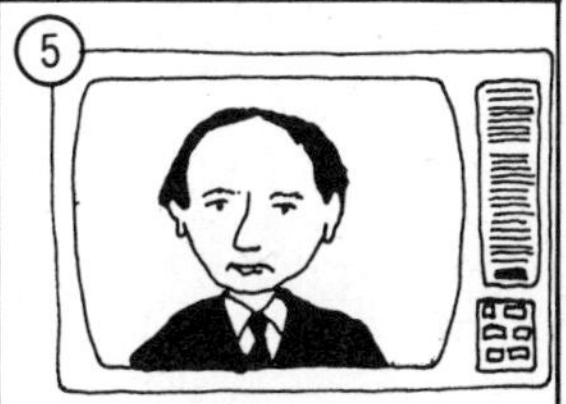

Allocution télévisée

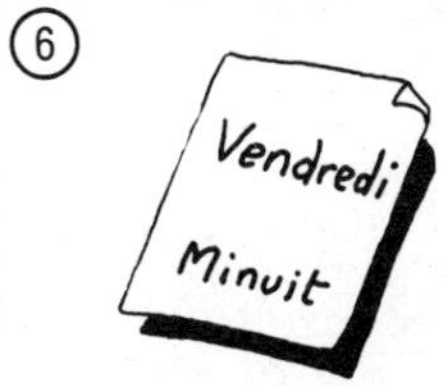

Fin de la campagne électorale

1er tour (dimanche)

2e tour (15 jours plus tard)

Proclamation des résultats

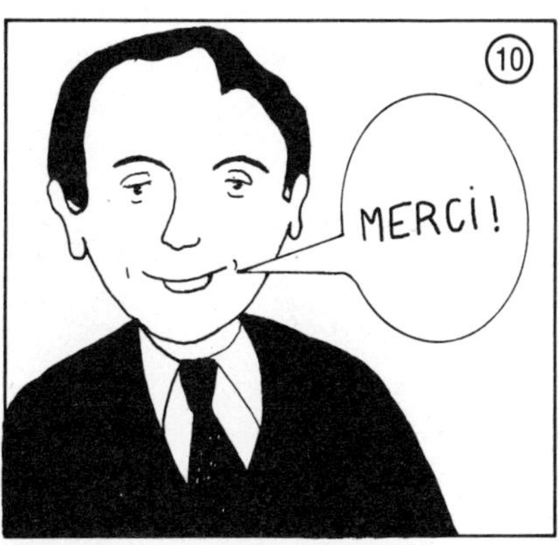

LES PRÉSIDENTS DE LA Ve RÉPUBLIQUE

Charles de Gaulle	1958-1965
	1965-1969
Georges Pompidou	1969-1974
Valéry Giscard d'Estaing	1974-1981
François Mitterrand	1981-1988
	1988-

Le Palais de l'Élysée est la résidence officielle du chef de l'État. Il se situe 55, rue du Faubourg-Saint-Honoré 75008 Paris.

Les autres résidences présidentielles sont :
— le château de Rambouillet
— l'Hôtel Marigny
— le fort de Brégançon (Var)

Les pouvoirs du Président

La Ve République donne au chef de l'État de nombreux pouvoirs. On distingue les pouvoirs traditionnels qu'il exerce en permanence et les pouvoirs exceptionnels qu'il prend dans des circonstances importantes ou graves.

■ Le Président et l'exécutif

— Il nomme le Premier ministre et sur proposition du Premier ministre*, p. 38 les autres ministres et met fin à leurs fonctions. Il préside le Conseil des ministres*. p. 40

— Il nomme aux hautes fonctions civiles et militaires de l'État (recteurs*, p. 77 commissaires de la République*...). p. 68

— Il est le chef des armées*. p. 72

— Il promulgue les lois (il signe et date). Il signe les ordonnances et les décrets délibérés* (décidés) en Conseil des ministres. p. 50

■ Le Président et la Constitution

— Il veille au respect de la Constitution. Si une loi ne lui paraît pas conforme à la Constitution, il peut demander l'avis du Conseil Constitutionnel*. p. 56

— Il nomme, pour 9 ans, trois membres du Conseil Constitutionnel, dont le Président de ce conseil.

■ Le Président et la diplomatie

— Il doit maintenir l'indépendance de la nation par rapport à l'étranger.

— Il négocie et ratifie les traités. Il nomme les ambassadeurs français à l'étranger et reçoit les ambassadeurs étrangers.

■ Le Président et la justice

— Il doit préserver l'indépendance de la justice. Les magistrats* ne p. 111 doivent pas subir de pression.

— Il préside le conseil supérieur de la magistrature.

— Il a le droit de faire grâce.

■ Le Président et le Parlement

— Il peut dissoudre l'Assemblée nationale*. p. 42

— Il ouvre et ferme les sessions extraordinaires du Parlement par décret.

■ Les pouvoirs exceptionnels

— Le référendum* : le Président peut consulter les électeurs par réfé- p. 20 rendum.

— Les pleins pouvoirs : en vertu de l'article 16, le Président peut prendre les pleins pouvoirs (exécutif + législatif) si le territoire est menacé ou envahi, si les institutions de la République sont menacées.

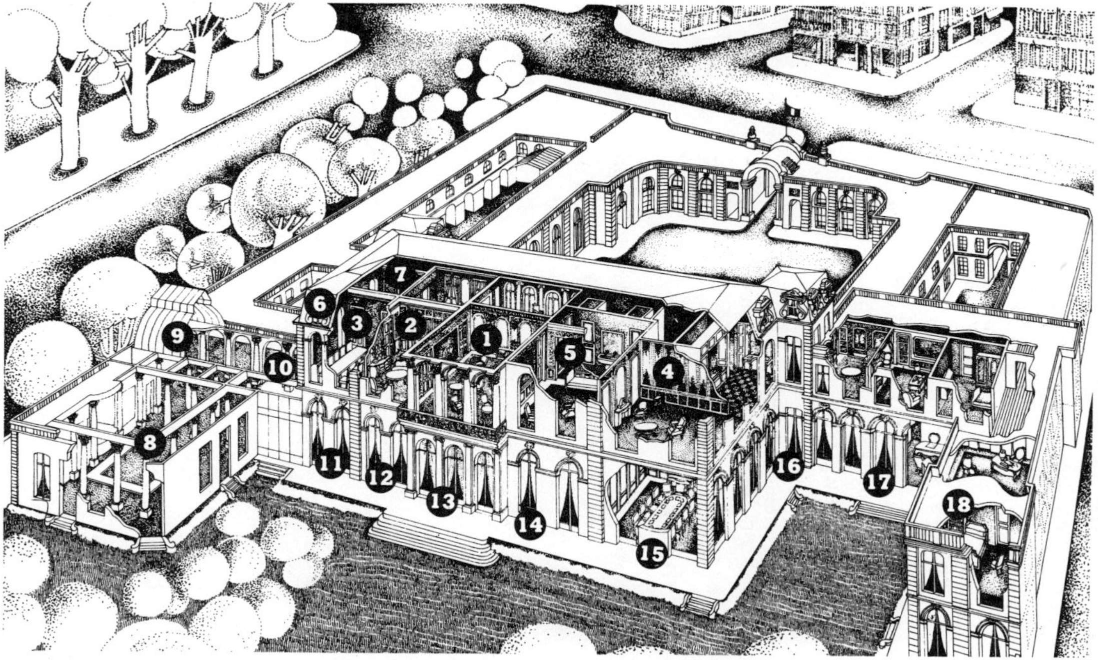

1. *Bureau du Président* (l'ancien bureau de Charles de Gaulle et Georges Pompidou).
2. *Bureau du Conseiller auprès du Président de la République* (les aides de camp de De Gaulle se tenaient là).
3. *Bureau du Secrétaire général* (la salle du conseil des ministres sous de Gaulle).
4. *Bureau du directeur de Cabinet* (l'ancien bureau de Valéry Giscard d'Estaing).
5. *Secrétariat particulier du Président* (c'est là qu'Alain Poher s'est installé pendant l'intérim de 1969).
6. *Bureau du porte-parole de la présidence.*
7. Le bureau traditionnellement réservé au chef de cabinet.
8. *Salle des fêtes* : en dessous de cette pièce rénovée en 1984, le Président a fait installer un studio de télévision d'où il peut intervenir sans qu'il faille mettre en place des installations spéciales.
9. *Jardin d'hiver*, refait en 1984.
10. *Salle à manger Napoléon III.*
11. *Salon Murat*, où se tient le conseil des ministres.
12. *Salon des aides de camp*, où ont lieu les déjeuners officiels avec un nombre restreint de convives.
13. *Salon des ambassadeurs*, où sont présentées les lettres de créance.
14. *Salon de l'hémicycle*, derrière lequel se trouve l'ascenseur réservé au Président.
15. *Salon des portraits*, où se déroulent les petits déjeuners de travail.
16. *Salon Cléopâtre*, qui sépare les appartements privés du Président de la République de la Présidence.
17. *Bibliothèque.*
18. *Les appartements privés*, rénovés en 1984.

Le Premier ministre

Nommé par le Président de la République, le Premier ministre est l'animateur de l'équipe gouvernementale. Sa résidence officielle est l'Hôtel Matignon.

■ Le Président et le Premier ministre

Le Président de la République* nomme le Premier ministre et, sur proposition du Premier ministre, les autres membres du gouvernement*. p. 36 p. 31

Le décret portant nomination du gouvernement est publié au Journal Officiel.

Le Président de la République met fin aux fonctions du Premier ministre sur la présentation par celui-ci de la démission du gouvernement.

■ Le rôle du Premier ministre

— Dès sa nomination, il propose la liste des ministres au Président de la République.

— Il dirige l'action du gouvernement.

— Il est, selon la Constitution, responsable de la défense nationale* p. 72

— Il assure l'exécution des lois.

— Il dispose du pouvoir réglementaire*, c'est-à-dire qu'il peut prendre des décisions appelées décrets et contresignées par le ministre chargé de leur application. p. 50

— Il nomme à certains emplois civils autres que ceux pourvus par le Président de la République.

— Il peut, si le chef de l'État le lui demande, présider un Conseil des ministres*, sur un ordre du jour déterminé. p. 40

— Il peut déléguer certains de ses pouvoirs aux ministres.

— Il peut, au nom du gouvernement, soumettre au Parlement des projets de loi*. p. 48

— Il peut proposer au Président de la République une révision de la Constitution.

— Il peut engager la responsabilité de son gouvernement devant l'Assemblée nationale en posant la question de confiance*. p. 54

— Il est consulté par le Président de la République avant la prise des pleins pouvoirs.

L'HÔTEL MATIGNON

Il est situé 57, rue de Varenne à Paris.
Sa façade est de style rocaille et son jardin est le plus grand espace vert de Paris.

- En 1721, Jean de Courtonne entreprend la construction pour le Maréchal de Montmorency et l'achève pour le comte Jacques de Matignon.
- En 1808, Talleyrand achète l'édifice qui changera plusieurs fois de propriétaire.
- En janvier 1888, l'hôtel Matignon devient ambassade d'Autriche.
- En janvier 1935, il est mis à la disposition du président du conseil. (Léon Blum sera le premier occupant).

LES PREMIERS MINISTRES SOUS LA Ve

1959-1962	Michel Debré
1962-1968	Georges Pompidou
1968-1969	Maurice Couve de Murville
1969-1972	Jacques Chaban-Delmas
1972-1974	Pierre Messmer
1974-1976	Jacques Chirac
1976-1981	Raymond Barre
1981-1984	Pierre Mauroy
1984-1986	Laurent Fabius
1986-1988	Jacques Chirac

Le gouvernement

Les ministres et les secrétaires d'État, ayant à leur tête le Premier ministre, forment le gouvernement. Nommé par le Président de la République, le gouvernement est responsable devant l'Assemblée nationale.

■ Nomination du gouvernement

Les ministres et secrétaires d'État sont nommés par le chef de l'État*, sur proposition du Premier ministre. p. 36

■ La fin du gouvernement

— Si le Premier ministre* remet au Président de la République la démission de son gouvernement, il y a changement complet de gouvernement. p. 38

— Si le Président de la République met fin aux fonctions d'un ministre ou si un ministre démissionne, il y a remaniement ministériel.

■ La composition du gouvernement

— Le nombre de ministres et de secrétaires d'État varie d'un gouvernement à l'autre. Il existe une hiérarchie ministérielle.

— Le Premier ministre est l'animateur de l'équipe gouvernementale.

— Les ministres d'État sont chargés d'un ministère jugé plus important ou d'un rôle de coordination.

— Les ministres à portefeuille sont chargés d'un ministère : économie, éducation, justice...

— Les ministres délégués dépendent du Premier ministre.

— Les secrétaires d'État ont un rôle plus restreint, on distingue :

— les secrétaires d'État autonomes
— les secrétaires d'État auprès du Premier ministre
— les secrétaires d'État auprès d'un ministre.

■ Le Conseil des ministres

— Il réunit le Premier ministre et les ministres sous la présidence du Président de la République. Les secrétaires d'État n'y participent pas de plein droit.

— Exceptionnellement, le Premier ministre peut présider un Conseil des ministres avec une délégation du chef de l'État et sur un ordre du jour déterminé.

— Le Conseil des ministres se tient habituellement à l'Elysée*, le mercredi. Il s'achève par un communiqué officiel. p. 37

Conseil de cabinet et comité interministériel

Le Conseil de cabinet réunit, exceptionnellement, le Premier ministre et les ministres alors que le comité interministériel, présidé par le Premier ministre, ne réunit que quelques ministres ou secrétaires d'État concernés par une même question.

Le rôle du gouvernement

Le gouvernement détermine et conduit la politique de la nation.

Il dispose de l'administration et de la force armée.

Avec le chef de l'État, il assure le pouvoir exécutif.

Le rôle d'un ministre

— Il joue un rôle politique en tant que membre du gouvernement. Il présente et défend le budget de son ministère devant le Parlement.

— Il joue un rôle administratif comme chef hiérarchique du personnel de son ministère.

Les incompatibilités

La constitution précise que les fonctions de membres du gouvernement sont incompatibles avec l'exercice de tout mandat parlementaire, de toute fonction de représentation professionnelle à caractère national et de tout emploi public ou de toute activité professionnelle.

Ainsi donc, on ne peut être à la fois ministre et député, ministre et sénateur ou encore ministre et dirigeant syndical.

La responsabilité du gouvernement

— La responsabilité politique :

Le gouvernement est responsable devant l'Assemblée nationale qui peut le renverser en votant une motion de censure ou en refusant la confiance.

Le Premier ministre est alors contraint de remettre la démission de son gouvernement au Président de la République.

— La responsabilité devant les tribunaux :

Un ministre est responsable civilement et peut, pendant l'exercice de ses fonctions, être condamné à verser des dommages et intérêts à des particuliers.

Un ministre est responsable pénalement et peut être déféré devant un tribunal pour un délit ou un crime.

L'Assemblée nationale

Le Parlement se compose de deux assemblées : l'Assemblée nationale et le Sénat*. L'Assemblée nationale vote les lois et contrôle l'action du gouvernement. p. 44

Où siègent les députés ?

Les députés siègent au Palais Bourbon. La salle des séances a la forme d'un demi-cercle, c'est l'hémicycle.

Combien de députés ?

Depuis mars 1986, l'Assemblée nationale comprend 577 députés (555 pour la métropole et 22 pour les départements d'outre-mer). L'assemblée précédente comprenait 491 députés.

Comment sont élus les députés ?

Les élections législatives ont lieu tous les 5 ans, au suffrage universel direct. Cette durée de 5 ans s'appelle la législature. Elle peut être écourtée en cas de dissolution prononcée par le Président de la République.

En mars 1986, le scrutin utilisé a été celui de la représentation proportionnelle départementale à un tour. Mais le scrutin majoritaire est rétabli.

L'âge minimum d'éligibilité est de 23 ans.

Quel est le rôle de l'Assemblée nationale ?

— Le domaine de la loi* : p. 50

Un député peut proposer un texte de loi qu'on appelle « proposition de loi »*. p. 48

L'Assemblée nationale vote les lois et le budget* de l'État. p. 60

— Le contrôle de l'action du gouvernement : un député peut s'informer de l'action du gouvernement en posant des questions.

Une question écrite : un député pose une question à un ministre qui répond dans le Journal Officiel.

Une question orale : un député pose, en séance publique, une question à un ministre qui lui répond oralement.

L'Assemblée nationale peut renverser le gouvernement en votant une motion de censure ou en refusant la confiance*. p. 52 et 54

— Les pouvoirs du Président de l'Assemblée nationale :

Il nomme trois membres du Conseil constitutionnel*. p. 56

Il est informé lors de la prise des pleins pouvoirs par le chef de l'État*. p. 36

LA SEMAINE D'UN DÉPUTÉ-MAIRE ET CONSEILLER GÉNÉRAL

	Matin	Après-midi
Lundi	**Conseil général** **Circonscription :** accueil des industriels, commerçants, etc.	**Conseil général :** séance plénière. **Circonscription :** permanences.
Mardi	**Circonscription :** rendez-vous avec les industriels, les commerçants, les professions libérales, etc.	
Mercredi	**Assemblée nationale :** réunion des commissions.	**Assemblée nationale :** questions au gouvernement.
Jeudi	**Assemblée nationale :** réunion des commissions.	**Conseil municipal :** réunions des différents services.
Vendredi	**Réunions diverses :** conseil d'administration du centre hospitalier, conseil local pour l'Emploi, etc.	**Mairie :** permanence.
Samedi	**Mairie :** permanence.	Participation aux **manifestations** locales, départementales ou régionales.
Dimanche	Participation aux **manifestations** locales, départementales et régionales. Courrier.	

Le Sénat

Le Sénat constitue la deuxième assemblée du Parlement. On l'appelle encore « chambre de réflexion ». Il est composé de sénateurs élus au suffrage universel indirect.

■ Où siègent les sénateurs ?

Les sénateurs siègent au Palais du Luxembourg.

■ Combien de sénateurs ?

On compte 317 sénateurs. L'effectif est de 318, un siège est non pourvu, c'est celui de l'ancien territoire des Afars et Issas.

■ Comment sont élus les sénateurs ?

— Ils sont élus au suffrage universel indirect*, pour 9 ans. p. 20

— Il y a des élections sénatoriales tous les 3 ans car le Sénat est renouvelable par tiers tous les 3 ans.

— Le scrutin varie selon le nombre de sénateurs que le département doit élire.

Dans les départements de 1 à 4 sénateurs, c'est le scrutin majoritaire* à deux tours. p. 24

Dans les départements de plus de 4 sénateurs, c'est le scrutin de liste à représentation proportionnelle*. p. 26

— L'âge minimum d'éligibilité d'un sénateur est de 35 ans.

■ Quel est le rôle du Sénat ?

— Le domaine de la loi : un sénateur peut proposer un texte de loi qu'on appelle « proposition de loi* ». p. 48

Le Sénat vote les lois et le budget de l'État.

Le Sénat, contrairement à l'Assemblée nationale, ne peut pas renverser le gouvernement.

— Les pouvoirs du président du Sénat :

Il est le deuxième personnage de l'État. Il assure l'intérim si la place de Président de la République est vacante.

Il nomme trois membres du Conseil constitutionnel*. p. 56

Il est informé lors de la prise des pouvoirs exceptionnels par le chef de l'État.

UNE SEMAINE D'UN SÉNATEUR EN PÉRIODE DE SESSION

Lundi	— Courrier. — Rendez-vous. — Règlement des affaires locales. — Réunion hebdomadaire avec adjoints et collaborateurs.
Mardi	— Réunion du groupe politique au Sénat. — Séance.
Mercredi	— Réunion de la commission sénatoriale. — Séance. — Rendez-vous.
Jeudi	— Réunion de la commission sénatoriale. — Réunion du groupe politique. — Séance.
Vendredi	— Courrier. — Rendez-vous. — Réunions départementales ou régionales.
Samedi	— Participation aux manifestations locales, départementales ou régionales.
Dimanche	— Participation aux manifestations locales, etc. — Courrier.

Le Parlement : sessions et débats

Le fonctionnement du Parlement est réglementé de façon précise. Les députés, qui siègent au Palais Bourbon, et les sénateurs, qui siègent au Palais du Luxembourg, se réunissent en sessions ordinaires deux fois par an. Députés et sénateurs peuvent aussi être convoqués pour une session extraordinaire.

■ Les sessions parlementaires

— Les sessions ordinaires : l'Assemblée nationale et le Sénat se réunissent de plein droit deux fois par an.

La session d'automne ou budgétaire s'ouvre le 2 octobre et dure au maximum 80 jours.

La session de printemps s'ouvre le 2 avril et dure au maximum 90 jours.

— Les sessions extraordinaires ont lieu à la demande du Premier ministre ou de la majorité des membres de l'Assemblée nationale et sur un ordre du jour déterminé. Si la session extraordinaire se fait sur la demande des députés, la session ne peut dépasser 12 jours.

Les sessions extraordinaires du Parlement sont ouvertes et closes par décret présidentiel*. p. 36

■ Le bureau des assemblées

— Il assure l'organisation du travail parlementaire, la présidence des débats et l'administration dans chacune des deux assemblées qui composent le Parlement.

— A l'Assemblée nationale*, le bureau comprend un président élu pour 5 ans, 6 vice-présidents, 12 secrétaires et 3 questeurs chargés de la gestion financière et administrative. Ils sont élus pour un an. p. 42

— Au Sénat*, le bureau comprend un président élu pour 3 ans, 4 vice-présidents, 8 secrétaires et 3 questeurs. Vice-présidents, secrétaires et questeurs sont élus pour 3 ans. p. 44

■ Les groupes politiques

— Les groupes politiques : les parlementaires sont le plus souvent groupés par affinités politiques. Il faut 30 députés apparentés au même parti* pour constituer un groupe politique à l'Assemblée nationale, il faut 15 sénateurs au Sénat. p. 30

Chaque groupe politique élit son président de groupe.

La conférence des présidents

La conférence des présidents comprend à l'Assemblée nationale comme au Sénat : le président de l'assemblée, les vice-présidents, les présidents des groupes parlementaires, les présidents des commissions, un représentant du gouvernement. La conférence des présidents fixe l'ordre du jour des travaux parlementaires.

Les commissions permanentes

Il en existe 6 à l'Assemblée nationale et 6 au Sénat. Elles étudient les textes de loi* avant leur vote par les assemblées. p. 50

— Commissions permanentes à l'Assemblée nationale :
  Affaires culturelles, familiales et sociales.
  Affaires étrangères.
  Finances, économie générale et plan.
  Défense nationale et forces armées.
  Production et échanges.
  Lois constitutionnelles, législation et administration générale de la République.

— Commissions permanentes du Sénat :
  Affaires culturelles.
  Affaires étrangères, défense et forces armées.
  Affaires économiques et plan.
  Affaires sociales.
  Finances, contrôle budgétaire et comptes économiques de la Nation.
  Lois constitutionnelles, législation, suffrage universel, règlement et administration générale.

— Les commissions spéciales : si un texte de loi ne correspond à aucune des 6 commissions permanentes, le gouvernement ou les assemblées parlementaires peuvent demander la création d'une commission spéciale pour examiner ce texte de loi.

Les séances

— L'essentiel de l'activité parlementaire a lieu en séance plénière. Les séances des deux assemblées sont publiques. Les tribunes sont réservées au public mais en nombre limité. Le compte rendu intégral des débats est publié au Journal Officiel.

Comment est votée une loi ?

Le vote de la loi se fait selon un mécanisme complexe. Le texte est examiné successivement par les deux assemblées car c'est un texte identique qui doit être adopté.

■ L'initiative

Elle appartient au Premier ministre, au nom du gouvernement, c'est alors un projet de loi ; à chaque député et à chaque sénateur, c'est alors une proposition de loi.

■ Le dépôt du texte

Le projet de loi ou la proposition sera déposé sur le bureau de l'Assemblée nationale* ou du Sénat*. Le projet de loi des finances sera soumis d'abord à l'Assemblée nationale. Sont irrecevables les propositions qui augmenteraient les dépenses ou diminueraient les recettes* de l'État. p. 42 et 44 p. 60

■ L'examen par une commission

Le texte sera examiné par l'une des 6 commissions permanentes* de l'assemblée saisie ou par une commission spéciale créée à cet effet. La commission désigne un rapporteur. p. 46

■ L'inscription à l'ordre du jour

La conférence des présidents* fixe l'ordre du jour en tenant compte des priorités fixées par le gouvernement. p. 46

■ La discussion

Elle s'ouvre par l'intervention du rapporteur qui présente le texte et les conclusions de la commission. Ensuite les orateurs inscrits donnent l'avis de leur groupe politique* sur le texte. Commence ensuite la discussion par articles. Le texte initial peut subir des modifications appelées amendements. p. 46

Pour éviter les amendements, le gouvernement peut recourir à la procédure du « vote bloqué ». Il oblige l'assemblée saisie à adopter le texte tel qu'il est ou à le repousser sans pouvoir le modifier.

■ Le vote

Un texte est voté quand il est adopté par l'Assemblée nationale et le Sénat.

■ La promulgation

Quand la loi est votée, le Président de la République* la signe et la date, dans un délai de 15 jours : c'est la promulgation. Pendant ce délai, le Président peut demander au Parlement une nouvelle délibération de la loi. p. 34
La loi peut être soumise au Conseil constitutionnel* qui examine si la loi est conforme à la Constitution. Cette demande peut être faite par le Président de la République, le Premier ministre, le président de chaque assemblée, 60 députés ou 60 sénateurs. p. 56

LA NAVETTE PARLEMENTAIRE

Pour être adopté définitivement, un texte législatif doit être examiné successivement par les deux assemblées. Ces lectures se poursuivront jusqu'à l'adoption d'un texte identique.

1er cas

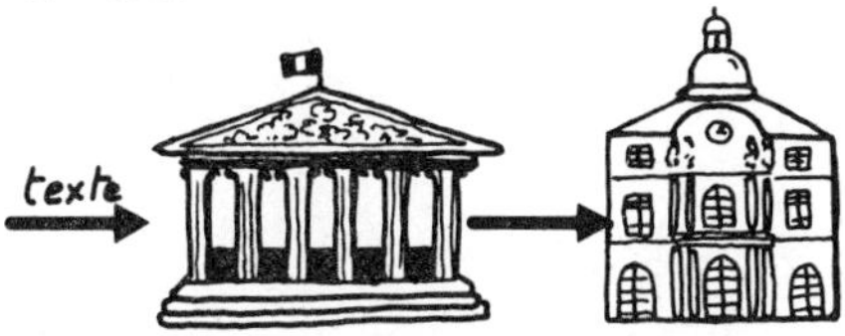

L'Assemblée nationale adopte le texte en 1re lecture.

Le texte est examiné par le Sénat qui l'adopte dans les mêmes termes.

La procédure est terminée, la loi est votée.

2e cas

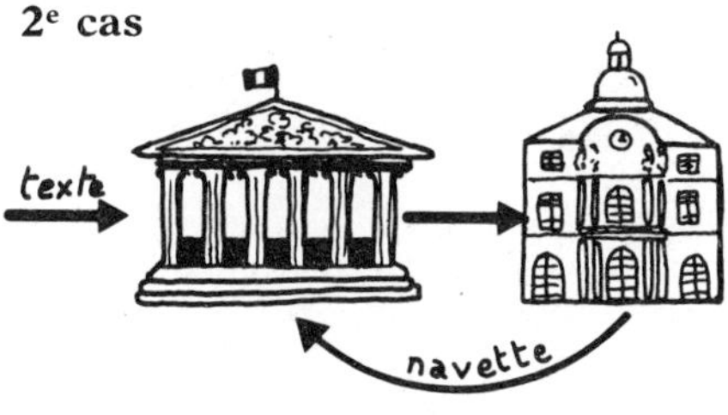

L'Assemblée nationale examine le texte en 1re lecture.

Le Sénat modifie le texte transmis.

Le texte retourne à l'Assemblée nationale. C'est le début du va-et-vient entre les deux assemblées qu'on appelle « navette parlementaire ».

Si, après deux lectures dans chaque assemblée, le texte est adopté en termes identiques, la loi est votée.

3e cas

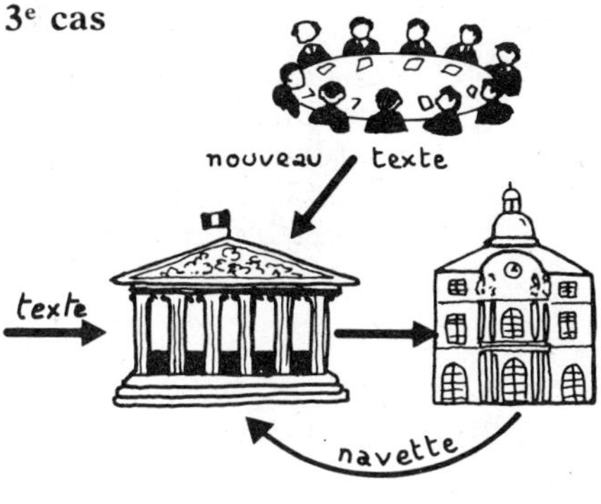

Après deux lectures dans chaque assemblée, il est possible que le désaccord persiste. Le Premier ministre peut demander la réunion d'une « commission mixte paritaire » formée de 7 députés et de 7 sénateurs. Cette commission élabore un nouveau texte soumis à chaque assemblée. Si ce nouveau texte est voté par les 2 chambres, la loi est adoptée, sinon le Premier ministre demande aux députés de trancher.

LE SAVIEZ-VOUS ?

Si vous lisez le J.O. : dans le Journal Officiel sont publiés les lois et les décrets. Les lois peuvent être appliquées quand les décrets d'application sont parus au Journal Officiel. On peut le consulter en mairie ou à la sous-préfecture.

ÉTAT
VIE POLITIQUE
ADMINISTRATION
COLLECTIVITÉS LOCALES
JUSTICE
INTERNATIONAL

Lois et règlements

Le Parlement fait des lois dans des domaines qui sont énumérés par la Constitution. Le pouvoir exécutif (Président de la République et gouvernement) prend aussi des décisions qui s'imposent à tous les citoyens. Ces décisions s'appellent des règlements.

■ Les lois ordinaires

— Les lois ordinaires ou parlementaires constituent l'essentiel de l'activité du Parlement qui assure le pouvoir législatif. Les lois votées peuvent modifier les droits civiques, les libertés publiques, le service national, la nationalité, les régimes matrimoniaux, la détermination des crimes, des délits, des peines, la procécure pénale, l'amnistie, les juridictions, le statut des magistrats, la fiscalité, les nationalisations, le régime électoral, l'organisation et la compétence des collectivités locales, l'enseignement.

— Les lois de finances déterminent les recettes et les dépenses* de l'État. p. 60

— Les lois de programme fixent les objectifs économiques de l'État.

■ Les lois organiques

— Ce sont des lois qui précisent ou complètent la Constitution. Par exemple, une loi organique fixe le nombre de membres de l'Assemblée nationale et du Sénat.

— Les lois organiques sont soumises au Conseil constitutionnel* et votées p. 56 comme des lois ordinaires. Toutefois, en cas de désaccord entre les chambres, l'Assemblée nationale doit les adopter à la majorité absolue de ses membres.

■ La loi constitutionnelle

Chaque article de la constitution est une loi constitutionnelle. Elle est adoptée par référendum* ou par le Parlement réuni en congrès (réunion des p. 20 députés et des sénateurs). Le texte doit alors être adopté à la majorité des 3/5.

La loi constitutionnelle est la plus importante car toutes les autres lois (ordinaires ou organiques) doivent lui être soumises.

■ Les règlements

Le Président de la République* et le gouvernement peuvent prendre des décisions dans tous les domaines qui ne sont pas réservés au Parlement. Ce sont les décrets, les arrêtés, les ordonnances et les circulaires. p. 36

— **Les décrets :**

• Le Président de la République prend des décisions appelées décrets présidentiels. Il nomme le Premier ministre* par décret. Le chef de l'État signe également les décrets pris en Conseil des ministres, il y aura alors contreseing (signature) du Premier ministre et des ministres intéressés. p. 38

• Le Premier ministre prend des décisions appelées décrets ministériels pour l'exécution des lois votées par le Parlement. Il dispose également d'un pouvoir de décision autonome; par décret, il peut décider que tout fonctionnaire engagé dans une procédure disciplinaire a le droit d'obtenir la communication des documents contenus dans son dossier.

— **Les arrêtés :** ce sont des décisions prises par une autorité administrative* : p. 64

• un arrêté ministériel est élaboré et signé par un ministre (un arrêté ministériel fixe la durée hebdomadaire de la scolarité à l'école primaire).

• un arrêté rectoral est élaboré et signé par un recteur d'académie.

• un arrêté préfectoral est élaboré et signé par un commissaire de la République* (par arrêté préfectoral, les chiens ne sont pas admis dans les magasins d'alimentation). p. 68

• un arrêté municipal est signé par le maire*. p. 96

— **Les ordonnances :** le Parlement peut autoriser le gouvernement à prendre, par ordonnances, des mesures qui sont normalement du domaine de la loi. Les ordonnances, assimilées à des règlements, entrent en vigueur quand elles sont signées par le Président de la République et quand elles sont publiées. Elles deviennent cependant « caduques » (sans effet) si un projet de loi de ratification n'est pas déposé devant le Parlement dans un délai fixé.

— **Les circulaires :** ce sont des textes internes à une administration et qui ne concernent que son personnel.

La motion de censure

Le gouvernement est responsable de son action devant les députés. L'Assemblée nationale peut mettre en cause la responsabilité du gouvernement par le dépôt d'une motion de censure qui, si elle est votée, entraîne la démission du Premier ministre et de l'équipe gouvernementale.

■ Le mécanisme de la motion de censure

La motion de censure est l'acte par lequel les députés* mettent en jeu la responsabilité du gouvernement et cherchent à le renverser. Cette initiative de l'Assemblée nationale porte le nom de motion de censure offensive. p. 42

Pour être adoptée, une motion de censure doit franchir trois étapes :

— Le dépôt : la motion de censure doit être déposée par au moins 1/10e des députés qu'on appelle alors signataires.

— Le délai de réflexion : un délai de 48 h, appelé délai de réflexion, doit s'écouler entre le dépôt et le vote.

— Le vote : pour être adoptée, la motion de censure doit obtenir la majorité absolue des membres composant l'Assemblée nationale. Seuls sont recensés les votes favorables à la motion.

$$\text{nombre de oui} \geq \frac{\text{nombre de députés composant l'Assemblée}}{2} + 1$$

Pour le vote d'une motion de censure, les députés se déplacent à la tribune.

■ Les effets du dépôt d'une motion de censure

— Si la motion est votée, le Premier ministre* est contraint de remettre au Président de la République la démission de son gouvernement*. p. 38 p. 40

Le gouvernement est renversé.

— Si la motion de censure est rejetée parce qu'elle n'a pas atteint la majorité absolue des membres de l'Assemblée nationale, le gouvernement reste en place et les membres signataires ne peuvent proposer une autre motion de censure offensive dans la même session*. p. 46

SCRUTIN DE NUIT

Un scrutin clos à zéro heure treize :

Vote sur la motion de censure.

M. le président. Je vais mettre aux voix la motion de censure.

En application des articles 65 et 66, paragraphe II, du règlement, il doit être procédé au vote par scrutin public à la tribune.

Le scrutin va avoir lieu par bulletins.

Je prie Mmes et MM. les députés disposant d'une délégation de vote de vérifier immédiatement au bureau des secrétaires, à ma gauche, si leur délégation a bien été enregistrée à la présidence.

Je vais tirer au sort la lettre par laquelle commencera l'appel nominal.

(Le sort désigne la lettre T.)

M. le président. Le scrutin va être annoncé dans le Palais.

. . . .

M. le président. Afin de faciliter le déroulement ordonné du scrutin, j'invite instamment nos collègues à ne monter à la tribune qu'à l'appel de leur nom ou de celui de leur délégant.

Je rappelle à ceux de nos collègues disposant d'une délégation qu'ils doivent remettre à MM. les secrétaires, non pas un bulletin ordinaire, mais une consigne écrite sur laquelle sont portés le nom du délégant, le nom et la signature du délégué.

Je rappelle également que seuls les députés favorables à la motion de censure participent au scrutin.

J'invite donc MM. les secrétaires à ne déposer dans l'urne que les bulletins blancs ou les délégations « pour ».

Le scrutin est ouvert.

Il sera clos à zéro heure treize.

Messieurs les huissiers, veuillez commencer l'appel nominal.

(L'appel a lieu. — Le scrutin est ouvert à vingt-trois heures vingt-huit.)

. . . .

M. le président. Personne ne demande plus à voter ?...

Le scrutin est clos.

J'invite MM. les secrétaires à se retirer dans le cinquième bureau pour procéder au dépouillement des bulletins.

Le résultat du scrutin sera proclamé ultérieurement.

M. le président. La séance est suspendue.

(La séance, suspendue à zéro heure quinze, est reprise à zéro heure trente-cinq.)

M. le président. La séance est reprise.

Voici le résultat du scrutin :

La question de confiance

Le gouvernement peut, de lui-même, engager sa responsabilité devant l'Assemblée nationale. Il pose ce que l'on appelle la question de confiance sur son programme, sur un débat de politique générale ou à l'occasion d'un projet de loi.

■ La question de confiance sur un programme ou sur une déclaration de politique générale

— Le Premier ministre*, après délibération en Conseil des ministres, peut p. 38
engager la responsabilité de son gouvernement* sur son programme p. 40
ou sur une déclaration de politique générale.

— Le vote de confiance a lieu à la majorité simple des membres de l'Assemblée nationale*. p. 42

• Si la confiance est votée, le gouvernement reste en place.

• Si la confiance est refusée, le gouvernement est renversé et le Premier ministre remet la démission de son gouvernement au Président de la République*. p. 36

■ La question de confiance à propos d'un texte

— Après délibération en conseil des ministres, le Premier ministre peut engager la responsabilité du gouvernement devant l'Assemblée nationale à propos d'un texte ou projet de loi*. p. 50

— Dans ce cas, les députés peuvent avoir deux attitudes :

• si les députés ne déposent pas de motion de censure* : le gouvernement estime avoir la confiance de l'Assemblée et le texte de loi est considéré comme adopté, sans vote. p. 52

• Les députés peuvent déposer une motion de censure (dite défensive). Elle sera signée par 1/10ᵉ des députés et le vote aura lieu après le délai de réflexion de 48 h.

Si la motion est votée, le gouvernement est renversé et le texte de loi est refusé.

Si la motion de censure est rejetée, le gouvernement estime avoir la confiance de l'Assemblée nationale et il reste en place, le texte est considéré comme adopté.

— Cette procédure de la question de confiance à propos d'un texte permet au gouvernement d'obtenir qu'un texte soit rapidement adopté.

QUAND LE PREMIER MINISTRE UTILISE LE 49-3

C'est l'article 49 de la Constitution, alinéa 3, qui autorise le Premier ministre à engager la responsabilité de son gouvernement, devant les députés, à propos d'un texte.

- *1re possibilité*

Le Premier Ministre engage la responsabilité de son gouvernement à propos d'un texte.

→ *pas de motion de censure*

Les députés ne déposent pas de motion de censure.

Le gouvernement reste en place et le texte est adopté.

- *2e possibilité*

Le Premier ministre engage la responsabilité de son gouvernement à propos d'un texte.

→ *dépôt d'une motion de censure*

1/10e des députés déposent une motion de censure.

La motion est votée

⇩

Le gouvernement est renversé, le texte est rejeté.

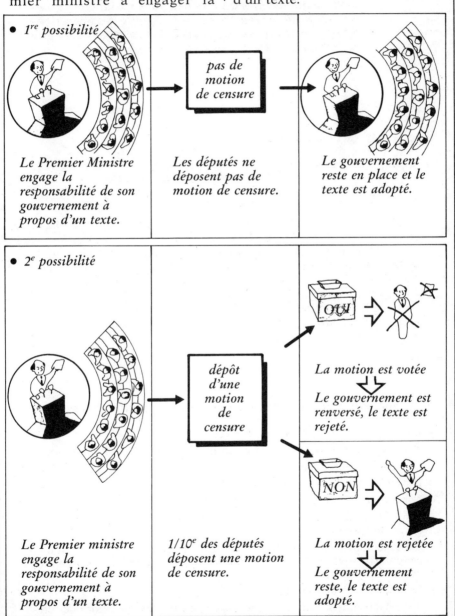

La motion est rejetée

⇩

Le gouvernement reste, le texte est adopté.

Le Conseil constitutionnel

Il est chargé de veiller au respect de la Constitution : c'est lui qui déclare que les lois votées sont conformes aux institutions. Il s'assure de la légalité des opérations de vote et il est consulté dans des circonstances graves. Il siège à Paris, au Palais Royal.

■ Quelle est sa composition ?

— Il comprend 9 membres : trois de ses membres sont nommés par le Président de la République* ; p. 36

trois membres sont nommés par le président de l'Assemblée nationale* ; p. 42

trois membres sont nommés par le président du Sénat*. p. 44

— Le président du Conseil constitutionnel est nommé par le Président de la République et a voix prépondérante en cas de partage des voix lors d'un vote.

— En plus des 9 membres, font partie de droit et à vie, les anciens présidents de la République.

— Le Conseil constitutionnel se renouvelle par tiers tous les 3 ans. Le mandat des membres est de 9 ans.

■ Quel est son rôle lors des consultations électorales ?

— Lors des élections présidentielles* : p. 34

Il veille à la régularité de l'élection du Président de la République.

Il examine les réclamations.

Il proclame les résultats du scrutin.

— Lors des élections législatives et sénatoriales*: p. 21

Il statue en cas de contestation sur la régularité de l'élection des députés et des sénateurs.

Tout électeur peut saisir le Conseil constitutionnel s'il estime qu'une irrégularité a été commise. Il dispose de 10 jours pour demander l'annulation de l'élection.

— Lors d'un référendum* : p. 20

Le Conseil constitutionnel veille à la régularité des opérations de référendum et en proclame les résultats.

Quel est son rôle en ce qui concerne les lois ?

— Les lois organiques, avant leur promulgation, et les règlements des assemblées parlementaires avant leur mise en application, doivent être soumis au Conseil constitutionnel qui se prononce sur leur conformité à la Constitution.

— Les lois ordinaires peuvent être envoyées au Conseil constitutionnel avant leur promulgation par le président de la République, le Premier ministre, le président de l'Assemblée nationale, le président du Sénat et depuis la réforme constitutionnelle adoptée par le Parlement réuni en congrès le 29/10/1974, par 60 députés ou 60 sénateurs.

Le Conseil constitutionnel statue (donne sa décision) dans un délai d'un mois.

La saisie du Conseil constitutionnel suspend le délai de promulgation.

— Le Conseil constitutionnel peut trancher entre le gouvernement et les assemblées pour déterminer la frontière entre le domaine réglementaire et le domaine de la loi.

Que fait-il dans les circonstances exceptionnelles ?

Il constate l'état de vacance de la présidence de la République.

Ce fut le cas en 1969 après la démission du Général de Gaulle et en 1974 après le décès de Georges Pompidou.

Le Conseil constitutionnel est consulté avant la prise des pleins pouvoirs par le Président de la République. Ce fut le cas en 1961 lors du putsch d'Alger. L'avis motivé du Conseil constitutionnel est publié au Journal Officiel.

Le Conseil économique et social

Le Conseil économique et social siège à Paris, au Palais d'Iéna. Il conseille le gouvernement et participe à l'élaboration de la politique économique et sociale du pays.

■ Le gouvernement consulte le Conseil économique et social

— Il le consulte obligatoirement pour tous les projets de loi*, de programme ou de plan. p. 50

Exemple : projet de loi programme sur l'enseignement technologique et professionnel,

— Le gouvernement consulte éventuellement le conseil pour tout sujet économique ou social.

Exemples : la présence française à l'étranger,
informatique et emploi,

■ Le Conseil économique et social émet des avis

— Chaque semestre, il émet un avis sur la situation économique des six mois précédents et sur les perspectives du semestre suivant.

— Il peut de sa propre initiative appeler l'attention du gouvernement sur des sujets très divers.

Exemples : les foires, les expositions et les salons spécialisés,
la protection et la mise en valeur des espaces naturels,
la qualité de la vie dans les banlieues des grandes villes,

■ Qui siège au Conseil économique et social ?

— Le Conseil économique et social comprend 230 membres nommés pour une durée de cinq ans.

— 70 % des membres sont désignés par l'organisation qu'ils représentent : organisations syndicales, professionnelles, organismes de la coopération et de la mutualité, associations familiales.

— 30 % des membres sont nommés par le gouvernement : représentants des entreprises publiques, des Français établis hors de France, des personnalités qualifiées...

■ L'organisation du Conseil économique et social

— Le bureau : 14 à 18 membres élus au scrutin secret pour deux ans et demi ; il fixe l'ordre du jour des travaux.

— Les sections spécialisées : dans leur spécialité, elles préparent les rapports et les avis. Au nombre de neuf, chaque section de 27 membres couvre un secteur d'activité.

— L'assemblée plénière : réunie en séance publique (une à deux fois par mois), elle vote les avis préparés par les sections spécialisées.

LE TRAVAIL DU CONSEIL ÉCONOMIQUE ET SOCIAL

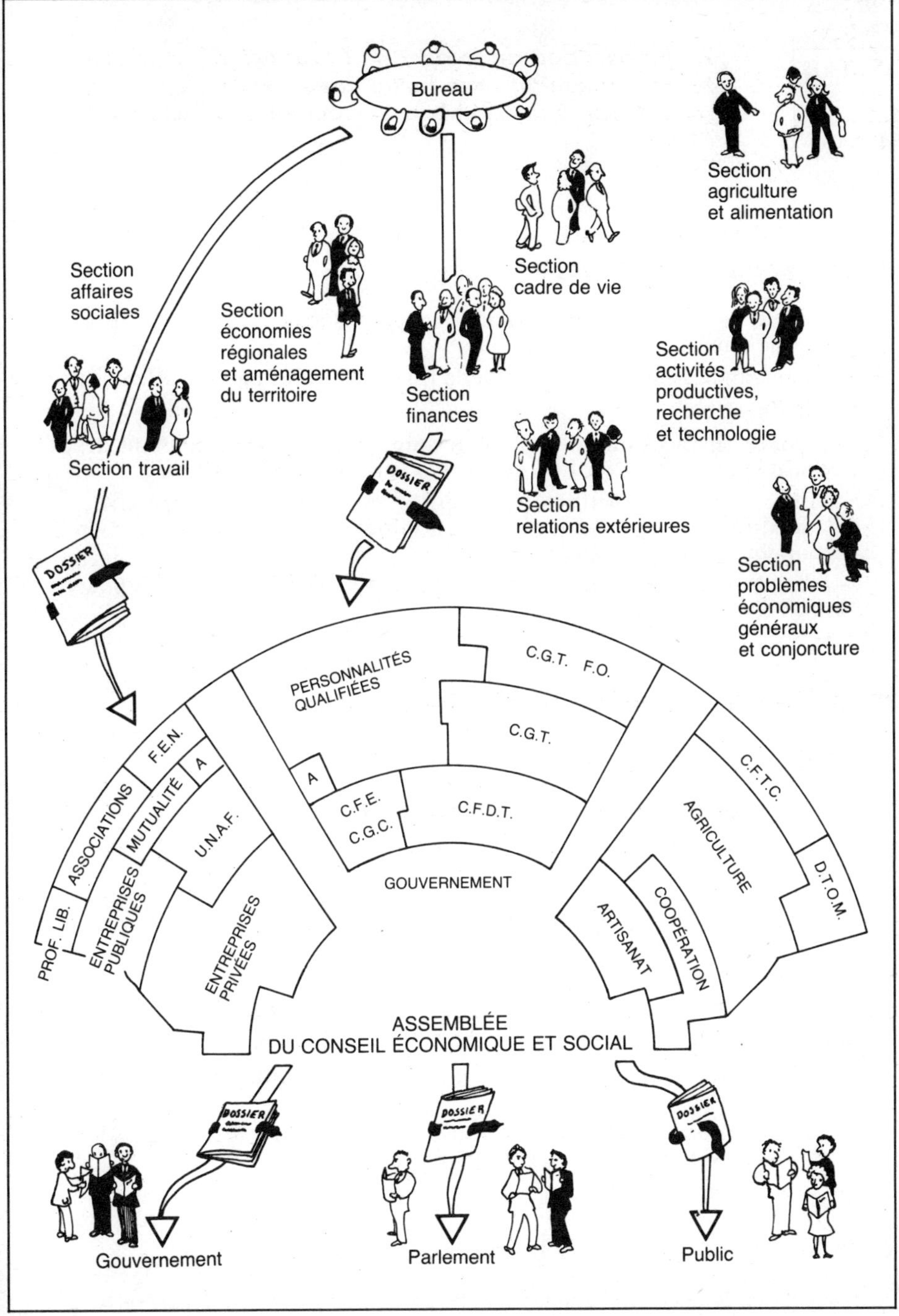
Bureau
Section agriculture et alimentation
Section cadre de vie
Section affaires sociales
Section économies régionales et aménagement du territoire
Section finances
Section activités productives, recherche et technologie
Section travail
Section relations extérieures
Section problèmes économiques généraux et conjoncture
DOSSIER
PERSONNALITÉS QUALIFIÉES
C.G.T. F.O.
C.G.T.
A
C.F.E. C.G.C.
C.F.D.T.
F.E.N.
A
ASSOCIATIONS
MUTUALITÉ
U.N.A.F.
PROF. LIB.
ENTREPRISES PUBLIQUES
ENTREPRISES PRIVÉES
GOUVERNEMENT
C.F.T.C.
AGRICULTURE
D.T.O.M.
ARTISANAT
COOPÉRATION
ASSEMBLÉE DU CONSEIL ÉCONOMIQUE ET SOCIAL
Gouvernement
Parlement
Public

La préparation du budget

La préparation du budget de l'État est effectuée par le gouvernement avec l'aide des services de tous les ministères. Elle consiste à recenser les besoins de l'État.

■ Qu'appelle-t-on budget ?

Le budget de l'État est la prévision des dépenses et des recettes de l'État pour une année.

Il est conçu dans le cadre d'une loi de finances* votée par le Parlement. p. 50

On distingue :

— la loi de finances initiale : elle détermine la nature et le montant des dépenses et des recettes. Elle est votée avant le début de l'année.

— la loi de finances rectificative : appelée aussi « collectif budgétaire ». Elle modifie en cours d'année le budget initial en fonction de l'évolution économique et des besoins ressentis.

— la loi de règlement : elle constate les résultats financiers définitifs pour l'année écoulée.

■ Le budget se prépare en plusieurs étapes

La préparation du budget de l'année (n) s'échelonne sur toute l'année précédente (n – 1).

— Recensement des besoins et arbitrage du Premier ministre*. p. 38

Chaque ministre effectue des propositions qui comprennent :

• la reconduction des moyens prévus au budget précédent (exemple : traitement des fonctionnaires, dépenses courantes de la défense nationale, des services de police). Ces sommes représentent plus de 90 % de l'ensemble du budget.

• les dépenses nouvelles correspondant aux actions nouvelles que chaque ministre désire entreprendre dans le cadre de la politique définie.

— Le Conseil des ministres approuve le projet de loi de finances.

— Le projet de budget est adressé au Parlement avant le premier mardi d'octobre.

L'Assemblée nationale* doit se prononcer en première lecture dans les 40 jours; le Sénat* dans les 20 jours. p. 42 p. 44

■ Qu'est-ce qu'un déficit budgétaire ?

Il y a déficit budgétaire lorsque les dépenses sont supérieures aux recettes.

LA STRUCTURE DU BUDGET DE LA FRANCE

On distingue les opérations à caractère définitif et les opérations à caractère temporaire. Les premières sont constituées par des dépenses définitives et non remboursables de l'État; les secondes sont constituées par des opérations remboursables.

▲ Les opérations à caractère définitif

— LE BUDGET GÉNÉRAL : il comporte :

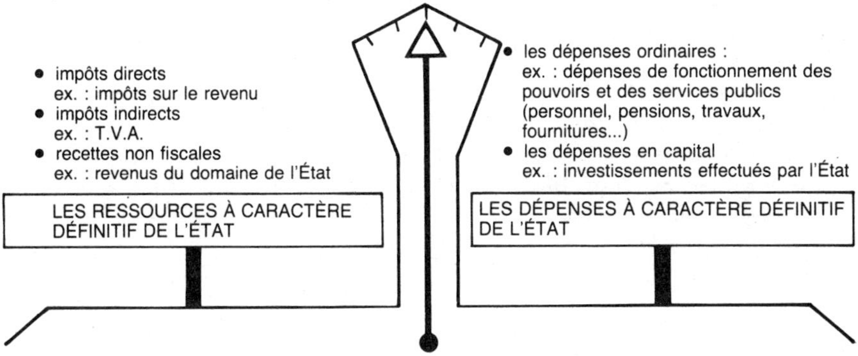

• impôts directs
ex. : impôts sur le revenu
• impôts indirects
ex. : T.V.A.
• recettes non fiscales
ex. : revenus du domaine de l'État
LES RESSOURCES À CARACTÈRE DÉFINITIF DE L'ÉTAT
• les dépenses ordinaires :
ex. : dépenses de fonctionnement des pouvoirs et des services publics (personnel, pensions, travaux, fournitures...)
• les dépenses en capital
ex. : investissements effectués par l'État
LES DÉPENSES À CARACTÈRE DÉFINITIF DE L'ÉTAT

— LES BUDGETS ANNEXES : ils font apparaître les recettes et les dépenses des services de l'État dont l'activité a un caractère commercial. Le montant de ces budgets annexes représente plus de 25 % du budget général.

Il existe huit budgets annexes :

- les Postes et Télécommunications : ce budget représente 70 % de l'ensemble des budgets annexes
- l'Imprimerie nationale
- le service des Monnaies et Médailles
- le service de la Navigation aérienne
- le service des Journaux officiels
- le budget annexe des Prestations sociales agricoles (B.A.P.S.A.)
- les budgets annexes de la Légion d'Honneur et de la Libération.

▲ Les opérations à caractère temporaire

Il s'agit des avances et des prêts consentis par le Trésor à des entreprises ou collectivités publiques et à certains pays étrangers.

50 KG DE PAPIER

Le Budget et ses annexes, c'est :

- 159 fascicules budgétaires soit 24 à 25 000 pages, une pile de 2,3 m de haut et un poids de 50 kg.
- il faut 90 tonnes de papier pour assurer l'ensemble de sa diffusion : 280 000 fascicules.
- 200 personnes travaillent à temps complet à la Direction du Budget.

Le budget de l'État : son application

Après son vote par le Parlement et après sa publication au Journal Officiel, le budget de l'État est mis en application. On perçoit alors les recettes et on engage les dépenses prévues.

■ Exécution de la recette publique

1. L'administration fiscale évalue les impôts dont elle pourra disposer. Elle détermine ce que l'on appelle l'assiette de l'impôt.
2. L'administration fixe le montant de l'impôt à payer.
   Cette opération s'appelle la liquidation de l'impôt : à partir des revenus déclarés, l'administration fiscale calcule le montant de l'impôt.
3. L'administration envoie les avis d'imposition.
   Elle émet un titre de perception envoyé à chaque contribuable.
4. Les comptables du Trésor sont chargés de procéder au recouvrement de l'impôt.

■ Exécution de la dépense publique

1. L'engagement de la dépense.
   Il est décidé de procéder à une dépense, ceci pour une mesure précise : accord pour la construction d'une route, nomination d'un fonctionnaire, etc.
2. La liquidation.
   On détermine le montant exact de cette dépense.
3. L'ordonnancement.
   L'ordre de payer est donné au comptable public.
   Qui donne cet ordre ? Celui que l'on appelle un ordonnateur : c'est-à-dire un ministre, un Commissaire de la République, un chef de service départemental.
4. Le paiement.
   Le versement est effectué par le comptable public.

■ Le Trésor public

Il enregistre toutes les opérations de recette et de dépense, il veille à ce que les dépenses coincident avec les recettes. Il assure la gestion des emprunts publics à court et moyen terme.

RECETTES ET DÉPENSES DU BUDGET DE LA FRANCE

▲ Où va l'argent ? Les dépenses

■ **26 % Services généraux du pays**

— Services publics
— Justice
— Police
— Diplomatie, etc.

■ **23 % Affaires sociales Santé et Travail**

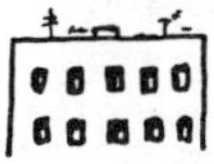

— L'emploi
— Le logement, etc.

■ **22 % Éducation**

— Salaire des enseignants
— Universités, recherche scientifique

■ **16 % Défense**

— Armée de terre
— Marine
— Armée de l'air
— Gendarmerie

■ **12 % Action économique**

— Reconversions
— Projets scientifiques et économiques

■ **1 % Culture**

— Maisons de la culture
— Théâtres, musées, cinéma

▲ D'où vient l'argent ? Les recettes

■ **44 % Taxe sur la valeur ajoutée**

— Elle varie suivant la catégorie de produits

■ **18 % Impôts sur le revenu**

■ **7 % Autres impôts (enregistrement, timbre, impôt sur les opérations de Bourse...)**

■ **9 % Impôts sur les sociétés**

■ **8 % Taxe intérieure sur les produits pétroliers**

■ **7 % Recettes non fiscales**

LE SAVIEZ-VOUS ?

Vous cherchez à obtenir une réponse à une question sur votre impôt ? Votre centre des impôts pourra y répondre.

Vous désirez un délai de paiement pour le versement de votre impôt ? Adressez-vous à la Recette perception dont vous dépendez (ou à la Recette des finances).

L'administration

L'administration permet au gouvernement de conduire sa politique. Tout pouvoir politique dispose d'une structure administrative pour mettre en application ses décisions.

■ Les structures administratives

— Au niveau de la Nation :

• Le Président de la République* nomme les fonctionnaires de haut rang. p. 36 Il est assisté d'un Secrétariat général de l'Elysée composé de collaborateurs et de conseillers chargés de suivre les questions de politique intérieure et extérieure du pays.

• Le Premier ministre* possède un Secrétariat général du gouvernement p. 38 qui coordonne l'ensemble de l'activité des différents ministères.

• Chaque ministre* dispose de l'ensemble des fonctionnaires de son p. 40 ministère qui est composé d'une administration centrale* à Paris et p. 66 d'une administration locale répartie sur tout le territoire.

— Au niveau des collectivités locales :

Chaque collectivité territoriale dispose de services administratifs pour mettre en application les décisions prises par les élus :

le Conseil régional* possède les services administratifs de la région; p. 82
le Conseil général* possède les services administratifs du département; p. 88
le Conseil municipal* possède les services municipaux. p. 96

■ Les moyens de l'administration

Toute administration dispose de moyens :

— Juridiques

Elle fixe les modalités de mise en application des lois et règlements* p. 50
ex. : arrêté municipal pour réglementer la circulation.

— Budgétaires

Elle donne les ordres nécessaires pour exécuter un budget
ex. : passation d'un marché pour matériel de bureau.

— Matériels

Elle utilise des locaux et du matériel
ex. : les services municipaux sont installés dans une mairie ou un hôtel de ville.

— Humains

Elle gère le corps des fonctionnaires mis à sa disposition
ex. : les élus locaux disposent des agents de la fonction publique territoriale (secrétaires de mairie, agents d'entretien...).

LES FONCTIONNAIRES

Un fonctionnaire occupe un emploi permanent dans une administration publique de l'État ou d'une collectivité territoriale.

▲ Recrutement

• le mode d'accès normal à la fonction publique est le concours ;

• le statut général des fonctionnaires prévoit l'organisation de deux types de concours :

— le concours externe réservé aux titulaires de certains diplômes ;

— le concours interne réservé aux fonctionnaires ayant une certaine ancienneté.

▲ Situation juridique des agents de l'État et des collectivités territoriales

— Le qualificatif de fonctionnaire ne s'applique qu'à un agent titulaire ayant fait l'objet d'un acte juridique de titularisation pris par un ministre.

— Les stagiaires sont des personnes recrutées dans un emploi permanent qui sont susceptibles d'être titularisées après une période de stage professionnel.

— Les auxiliaires, révocables à tout moment, sont employés pour une courte période.

▲ Les différentes catégories de fonctionnaires

Catégorie	Niveau diplôme	Fonctions	Type d'emploi
A	Licence au minimum	conception et direction	administrateurs civils professeurs
B	Baccalauréat	encadrement	contrôleur des impôts secrétaire administratif
C	Brevet	exécution spécialisée	secrétaire sténodactylo
D	Savoir lire et écrire	exécution	agent de bureau

L'Administration centrale

On retrouve sur tout le territoire français différents services administratifs (impôts, enseignement, police...). Ces services sont centralisés, organisés et coordonnés par une Administration centrale.

■ Le Premier ministre*, chef de l'Administration p. 38

Il est le chef de l'Administration.

Il définit, en fonction des choix politiques prioritaires, le nombre, la désignation et le rôle de chaque ministère.

■ Les ministres* sont responsables de leur domaine d'intervention p. 40

Chaque ministre est responsable de la mise en application des décisions du gouvernement dans le domaine qui lui est réservé.

- Il organise l'ensemble des services de son ministère, qui comprend :
  - un cabinet, composé de conseillers et de collaborateurs directs du ministre. La durée de leur mission est liée à celle du ministre.

    Le cabinet étudie et prépare toutes les décisions gouvernementales et administratives ;
  - plusieurs directions spécialisées, constituées de services très hiérarchisés qui traitent toutes les questions courantes relatives à leur domaine.
- Il a un rôle administratif important :
  - il dispose d'un pouvoir réglementaire : pour la mise en application des lois et décrets* il prend des arrêtés, et il élabore des circulaires p. 50 pour réglementer le fonctionnement de ses services ;
  - il est chargé de la gestion courante des différents services et de l'exécution du budget de son département ministériel ;
  - il est chargé de la gestion du personnel dépendant de son ministère.

■ Le ministre de l'Intérieur* p. 70

- Il est garant de la régularité des élections sur tout le territoire et de la coordination des attributions exercées par les Commissaires de la République.
- La Direction générale de l'Administration gère le corps des préfets et des administrateurs civils.

  Les moyens de fonctionnement des préfectures et sous-préfectures sont de sa compétence, ainsi que l'organisation des élections.

L'ADMINISTRATION CENTRALE DU MINISTÈRE DE L'ÉDUCATION NATIONALE

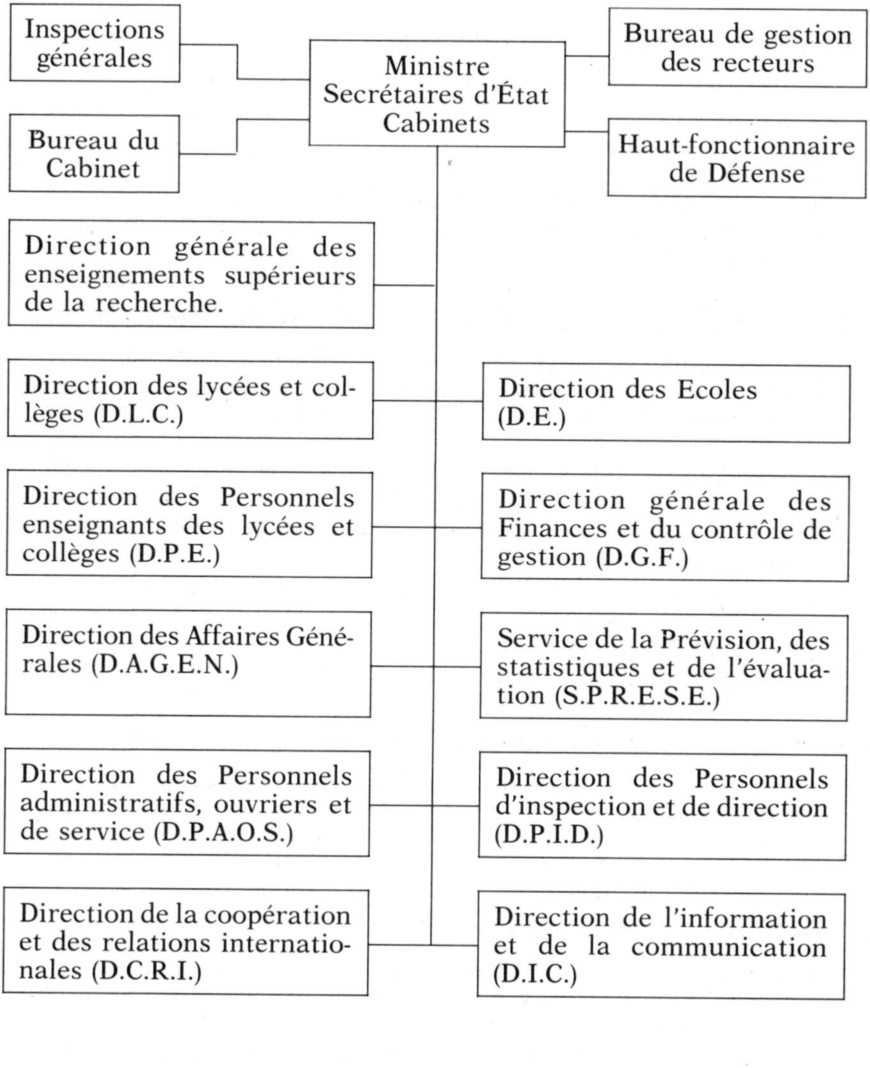

Inspections générales
Bureau du Cabinet
Ministre Secrétaires d'État Cabinets
Bureau de gestion des recteurs
Haut-fonctionnaire de Défense
Direction générale des enseignements supérieurs de la recherche.
Direction des lycées et collèges (D.L.C.)
Direction des Ecoles (D.E.)
Direction des Personnels enseignants des lycées et collèges (D.P.E.)
Direction générale des Finances et du contrôle de gestion (D.G.F.)
Direction des Affaires Générales (D.A.G.E.N.)
Service de la Prévision, des statistiques et de l'évaluation (S.P.R.E.S.E.)
Direction des Personnels administratifs, ouvriers et de service (D.P.A.O.S.)
Direction des Personnels d'inspection et de direction (D.P.I.D.)
Direction de la coopération et des relations internationales (D.C.R.I.)
Direction de l'information et de la communication (D.I.C.)

L'Administration territoriale

L'Administration territoriale couvre l'ensemble du pays. Elle doit agir de manière à résoudre les problèmes spécifiques à chaque région, tout en restant le plus près possible des administrés.

■ Le rôle du ministre de l'Intérieur

— Le ministre de l'Intérieur est chargé :

- de l'administration générale du territoire : il exerce son action sur l'administration du pays par l'intermédiaire des Commissaires de la République; p. 20
- des collectivités locales : le ministre de l'Intérieur élabore les textes qui permettent la réalisation d'un minimum d'unité dans l'administration locale.

■ Le rôle du commissaire de la République du département

— Le commissaire de la République du département est le représentant de l'État dans chaque département. Il a son siège à l'Hôtel du département (nouveau nom donné aux bâtiments de la Préfecture depuis la Loi de 1982 sur la décentralisation).

— Le commissaire de la République du département représente chacun des ministres* et dirige les services de l'État dans le département. p. 40

Il a la charge des intérêts nationaux, du respect des lois, de l'ordre public et du contrôle administratif.

Il assure le contrôle de légalité « a posteriori » sur les actes du Conseil général* et des communes. p. 90

— Le commissaire de la République est assisté, dans chaque arrondissement, d'un commissaire adjoint de la République.

■ Le rôle du commissaire de la République de région

— Le commissaire de la République de région est le représentant de l'État dans chaque région*. Il a son siège à l'Hôtel du département où se trouve p. 80 le chef-lieu de la région. Ses pouvoirs, au niveau de la région, sont comparables à ceux des commissaires de la République des départements.

■ L'Administration territoriale

— Les services extérieurs des différents ministères : pour étendre leur pouvoir sur l'ensemble du territoire, les différents ministères disposent de services administratifs appelés services extérieurs.

— Les administrations de collectivités locales : la région, le département, la commune.

Les collectivités locales possèdent un pouvoir de décision qui leur permet de disposer d'une liberté d'administration dans le cadre des lois de l'État.

LES DIVISIONS ADMINISTRATIVES FRANÇAISES

▲ Le territoire national

La France

55 586 714 habitants (54 334 871 en métropole et 1 251 843 dans les départements d'outre-mer).

▲ La région

La région Alsace

Collectivité locale qui regroupe plusieurs départements.
26 régions, dont 4 en outre-mer.

▲ Le département

Deux départements en Alsace :
le Haut-Rhin
le Bas-Rhin

Division administrative du territoire français.
101 départements dont 5 en outre-mer.

▲ L'arrondissement

Le département du Bas-Rhin se compose de 7 arrondissements.

Division territoriale qui regroupe plusieurs cantons.
Au chef-lieu d'arrondissement se trouve un commissaire de la République-adjoint.
337 arrondissements dont 12 en outre-mer.

▲ Le canton

L'arrondissement de Haguenau, du département du Bas-Rhin, se divise en 3 cantons.

Division territoriale de l'arrondissement. On trouve en général au chef-lieu de canton une gendarmerie et une perception.
3 838 cantons dont 124 en outre-mer.
(Le canton correspond parfois à une seule commune.)

▲ La commune

Le canton Bischwiller, situé dans l'arrondissement de Haguenau, rassemble 21 communes.

Unité de base de la division du territoire.
36 547 communes dont 114 en outre-mer.

Le ministère de l'Intérieur et la police

Pour assurer la sécurité des citoyens, l'État dispose, comme service public, de la Police nationale, qui intervient dans les villes de 10000 habitants et plus. Le maintien de l'ordre public dans les autres communes est assuré par la gendarmerie.

■ Le rôle du ministère de l'Intérieur

— Chargé de la sécurité de l'État et de celle des citoyens, le ministère de l'Intérieur doit maintenir l'ordre républicain et protéger les personnes* p. 10 et les biens.

— La protection de la vie et des biens est de la compétence de la Direction de la Sécurité civile dont la mission est double : la prévention et l'organisation des secours (plan ORSEC par exemple).

— La protection des personnes est assurée par la Direction générale de la Police nationale.

■ Les fonctionnaires de police des services actifs

— Comme tous les fonctionnaires*, ils sont recrutés par concours. Puis, p. 65 ils sont nommés dans l'un des services relevant de l'une des directions de la police nationale, soit à Paris, dans les services centraux* ou à la p. 66 Préfecture de Police, soit dans un service de province.

— Les commissaires de police : ils constituent le corps de commandement de la police. Ils assument d'importantes responsabilités dans les différents services de police (sécurité publique, police judiciaire, renseignements généraux, surveillance du territoire).

— Les inspecteurs de police : l'inspecteur de police, placé sous l'autorité du commissaire qu'il seconde, est particulièrement chargé d'enquêtes judiciaires et de missions d'information et de surveillance dans les différents services de police.

— Les officiers de paix : l'officier de paix exerce le commandement du corps des gradés et gardiens de la paix des services de police en tenue (corps urbains, préfecture de police et C.R.S.).

— Les gardiens de la paix : ils assurent la protection des personnes et des biens. Ils constatent les infractions aux lois et règlements et veillent au maintien de l'ordre public. Ils peuvent être promus brigadiers et brigadiers-chefs.

■ Les fonctionnaires de police des services administratifs

Pour effectuer toutes les tâches administratives, le ministère recrute des secrétaires administratifs, des commis et des agents de bureau.

L'ORGANISATION DE LA POLICE

Sous l'autorité de la Direction générale de la Police nationale, les fonctionnaires de police sont répartis dans les 9 Directions et Services actifs.

Inspection générale de la Police nationale (appelée « Police des Polices »).	Contrôler les services de police, enquêter sur les personnels, procéder à des études et enquêtes pour améliorer le fonctionnement des services.
Service central des polices urbaines.	Assurer le bon ordre, la sécurité et la tranquillité publique (exemple : intervention police-secours).
Direction centrale de la Police judiciaire (P.J.).	Lutter contre les activités criminelles (crimes, trafic de stupéfiants, d'armes, banditisme, vols...)
Direction centrale des renseignements généraux (R.G.).	Rechercher et centraliser des renseignements nécessaires à l'information du gouvernement.
Service central des compagnies républicaines de sécurité (C.R.S.).	Maintenir l'ordre public, surveillance des voies de communication, aérodromes, ports.
Service central de la police de l'air et des frontières (P.A.F.).	Surveiller la circulation transfrontière (2 875 km de frontières terrestres, 3 035 km de frontières maritimes et 116 aéroports).
Service des voyages officiels	Organiser les déplacements des personnalités officielles.
Direction de la surveillance du territoire (D.S.T.).	Lutter contre les activités de nature à nuire à la sécurité ou aux intérêts de la nation.
Service de la coopération technique internationale de la police.	Mener une action de coopération avec les pays qui en expriment le besoin (formation des policiers étrangers, conseils).

L'organisation de la défense

La défense a pour objet d'assurer en tout temps, en toutes circonstances et contre toutes les formes d'agression, la sécurité et l'intégrité du territoire ainsi que la protection de la population.

■ Les responsables de la politique de défense

— Le Président de la République*. p. 36

Il est garant de l'indépendance nationale, de l'intégrité du territoire et du respect des traités. Il est le chef des armées. Il peut donner l'ordre d'engager la force nucléaire.

— Le Premier ministre*. p. 38

Il est responsable de la défense nationale et coordonne l'activité de défense des différents ministères.

— Le ministre de la Défense

Il est responsable de l'exécution de la politique militaire. Assisté des chefs d'états-majors, il a autorité sur l'ensemble des forces et services des armées.

■ L'organisation permanente des armées

— L'état-major des armées (E.M.A.) : le chef d'état-major des Armées, conseiller militaire du gouvernement, assiste le ministre de la Défense. Il veille à l'emploi et à l'organisation générale des forces militaires.

— L'état-major de chaque armée est responsable de la préparation des forces armées.

— Les forces armées : forces nucléaires, stratégiques et tactiques, forces terrestres, forces maritimes, aériennes et gendarmerie.

■ L'organisation territoriale de la défense

— Le territoire métropolitain est divisé en six régions militaires, six régions de gendarmerie, quatre régions aériennes et trois régions maritimes couvrent le littoral.

Les DOM-TOM* sont divisés en quatre zones de défense : Antilles-Guyane, zone sud de l'océan Indien, Polynésie française, Nouvelle-Calédonie. Des unités stationnent en permanence dans chaque zone. p. 104, 105

— En cas de conflit, les six régions militaires deviennent des zones de défense territoriale à la tête desquelles :

• le commissaire de la République* est chargé d'assurer la défense civile et économique, p. 68

• le général commandant la région militaire exerce le commandement militaire.

ORGANISATION TERRITORIALE MILITAIRE

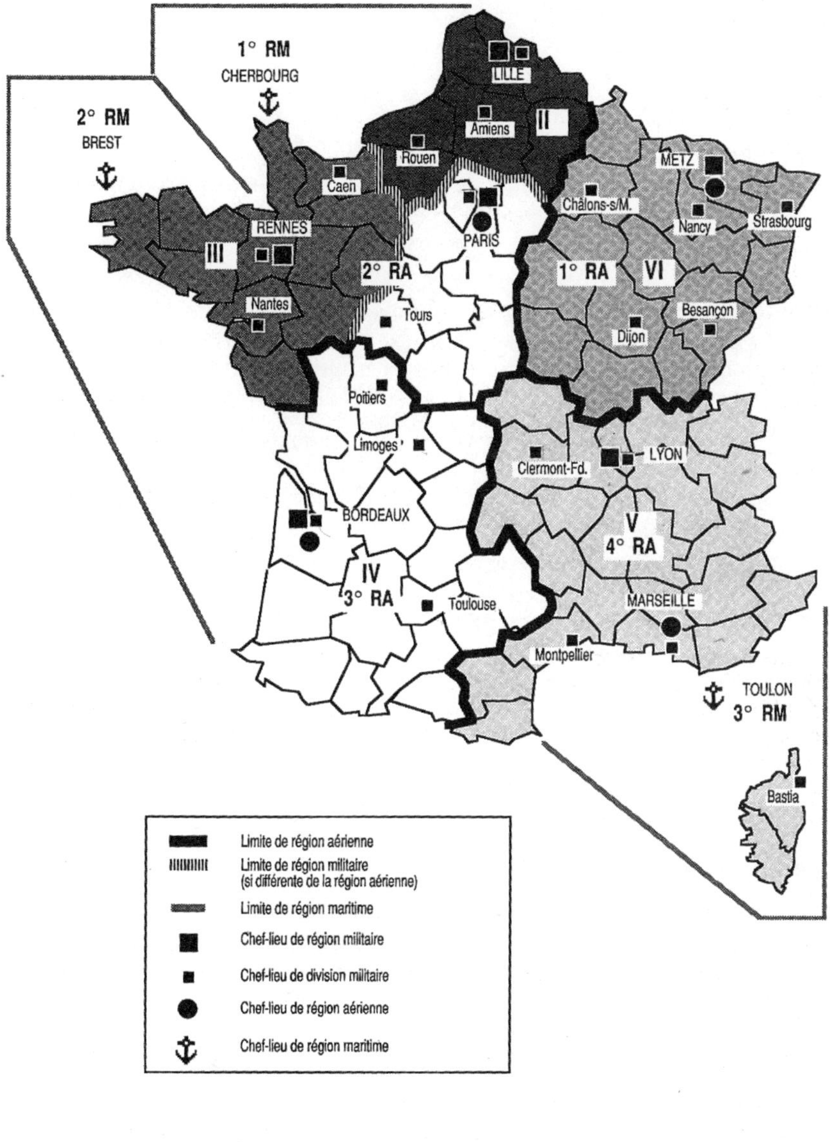

1° RM
CHERBOURG
2° RM
BREST
LILLE
Amiens
II
Rouen
Caen
RENNES
III
Nantes
PARIS
2° RA
I
Tours
METZ
Châlons-s/M.
Nancy
Strasbourg
1° RA
VI
Besançon
Dijon
Poitiers
Limoges
Clermont-Fd.
LYON
BORDEAUX
V
4° RA
IV
3° RA
Toulouse
MARSEILLE
Montpellier
TOULON
3° RM
Bastia
Limite de région aérienne
Limite de région militaire
(si différente de la région aérienne)
Limite de région maritime
Chef-lieu de région militaire
Chef-lieu de division militaire
Chef-lieu de région aérienne
Chef-lieu de région maritime

Les Forces armées françaises

L'effectif des Forces armées françaises s'élève à 500 000 hommes et femmes. Cet effectif se répartit entre l'Armée de Terre, l'Armée de l'Air, la Marine et la Gendarmerie.

■ Armée de Terre

305 000 militaires, dont 60 % d'appelés et 6 000 femmes.

Organisation :
- divisions blindées
- divisions d'infanterie
- forces stationnées en R.F.A.
- forces d'outre-mer

■ Armée de l'Air

99 000 militaires, dont près de 38 % d'appelés.

Organisation : • les forces aériennes stratégiques (F.A.S.) constituent, avec le Mirage IV et les missiles SSBS, la force nucléaire stratégique;
• la défense aérienne chargée de la surveillance de l'espace aérien dispose d'intercepteurs Mirage 2000 et Mirage F1 ;
• la force aérienne tactique (FATAC), équipée d'avions de combat Mirage et Jaguar;
• le transport aérien militaire dispose de Transall, DC 8, Mystère 20 et des hélicoptères Alouette, Puma, Écureuil.

■ Marine nationale

67 700 militaires dont 27 % d'appelés.

Organisation : • force océanique stratégique (forces nucléaires);
• forces classiques de surface, réparties en 2 escadres (Méditerranée et Atlantique) et des moyens régionaux en métropole et outre-mer : 3 porte-aéronefs, dont 1 porte-hélicoptères, 91 bâtiments de surface;
• forces sous-marines réparties en 2 escadrilles (Méditerranée et Atlantique), 17 sous-marins;
• Aéronautique navale (plus de 250 aéronefs).

■ Gendarmerie

77 000 gendarmes et 8 000 appelés du contingent.

L'implantation des brigades date de 1720. La Maréchaussée prend le nom de Gendarmerie nationale en 1791. La gendarmerie est chargée de veiller à la sûreté publique et au respect des lois. Elle participe à la défense militaire du pays.

Organisation : • brigades territoriales (3 675 regroupant 50 000 gendarmes);
• gendarmerie mobile (126 escadrons);
• groupement de sécurité et d'intervention de la gendarmerie nationale GSIGN);
• garde républicaine;
• formations spécialisées (gendarmerie de l'air, des transports aériens...).

GRADES ET INSIGNES

ARMEE DE TERRE

Chez les officiers, aspirants, majors, adjudants-chefs et adjudants, les insignes de grade apparaissent sur le képi et les épaules.
Chez les autres sous-officiers et les militaires du rang, les insignes de grade apparaissent sur les manches
Ce sont :

des broderies d'or
des étoiles d'argent ou d'or
et suivant les armes
des galons et des soutaches de métal or ou argent
et des galons de laine de diverses couleurs

OFFICIERS GENERAUX

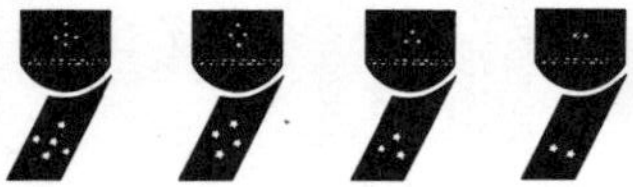

OFFICIERS SUPERIEURS

OFFICIERS SUBALTERNES

SOUS-OFFICIERS

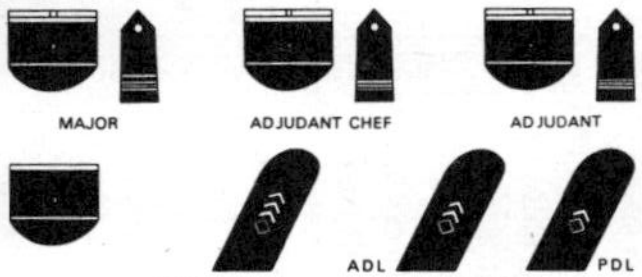

MILITAIRES DU RANG

MARINE NATIONALE

Les insignes de grade apparaissent sur la casquette et sur les manches
Ce sont :

des broderies d'or
des étoiles d'argent
des galons or ou argent
des galons de laine rouge

OFFICIERS GENERAUX

OFFICIERS SUPERIEURS

OFFICIERS SUBALTERNES

OFFICIERS MARINIERS

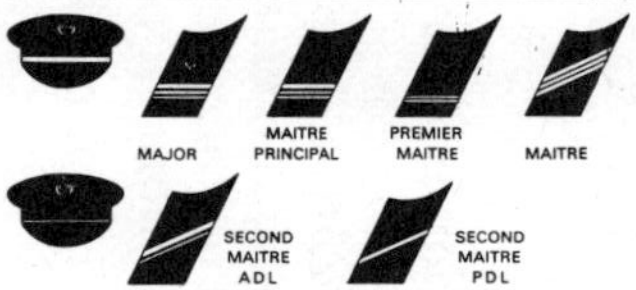

QUARTIERS-MAITRES ET MARINS

ARMEE DE L'AIR

Les insignes de grade apparaissent sur la casquette et sur les manches
Ce sont :

des broderies d'or
des étoiles d'argent
des galons de métal or ou argent
des galons de laine orange

OFFICIERS GENERAUX

OFFICIERS SUPERIEURS

OFFICIERS SUBALTERNES

SOUS-OFFICIERS

MILITAIRES DU RANG

GENDARMERIE NATIONALE

Les insignes de grades apparaissent :

- pour les officiers, majors, adjudants-chefs et adjudants : sur le képi et sur les manches
- pour les maréchaux des logis-chefs et gendarmes sur les manches seulement
- pour les gendarmes auxiliaires : sur les épaulettes

OFFICIERS GENERAUX

OFFICIERS SUPERIEURS

OFFICIERS SUBALTERNES

SOUS-OFFICIERS

GENDARMES AUXILIAIRES

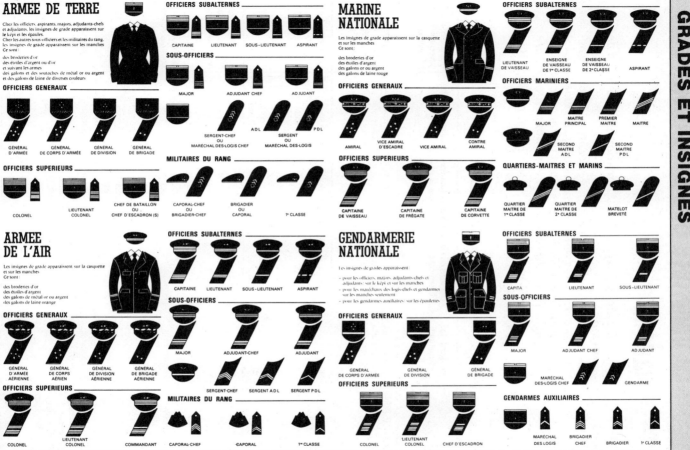

Le ministère de l'Éducation nationale

Le rôle du ministère de l'Éducation nationale est le suivant :
— mettre en place la politique éducative du gouvernement, définir les objectifs pédagogiques, élaborer les programmes et les diplômes afin d'uniformiser l'enseignement et les diplômes sur l'ensemble du territoire
— assurer le recrutement, la formation et la gestion des personnels.

■ L'organisation des différents établissements

	Qui décide la construction ? Qui finance ?	**Qui dirige l'établissement ?**	**Quelles sont les instances de gestion et de concertation ?**	**Les enseignants**	**Qui décide des ouvertures ? Des fermetures ?**
UNIVERSITÉ 74 universités	Ministère : Ex. de financement : 75 % Etat, 25 % collectivités locales	Président d'Université élu par le Conseil de l'Université	Conseils d'Université	• Professeurs d'Université • Maîtres de conférence	Pour diplôme national : ministère; diplôme d'université : conseil d'université
Institut universitaire de Technologie (I.U.T.) 68 I.U.T.	Ministère	Directeur élu par le Conseil d'administration	Conseil d'administration	• Professeurs d'enseignement supérieur • agrégés, • certifiés, • professionnels (vacataires)	Diplôme national : ministère
LYCÉES 2 439 établissements 1 630 000 élèves	Région	Proviseur nommé par le ministre	Conseil d'administration comprenant — le personnel de direction et des personnalités — élus des personnels, des parents d'élèves et des élèves • organe délibératif et consultatif	Professeurs • agrégés, • certifiés, • d'enseignement technique	La Région détermine les besoins de formation en établissant un schéma prévisionnel des formations des collèges et des lycées
COLLÈGES 4 783 établissements 2 643 000 élèves	Département	Principal nommé par le ministre		Professeurs • agrégés, • certifiés, • d'enseignement général (PEGC)	
ÉCOLES maternelles et élémentaires 59 500 écoles 5 774 000 élèves	Commune après avis de l'Inspecteur d'Académie	Directeur nommé par l'Inspecteur d'Académie	Conseil d'école comprenant les enseignants, les représentants de la commune et des parents • organe consultatif	Instituteurs	Commune

LA HIÉRARCHIE DANS L'ÉDUCATION NATIONALE

▲ Niveau national : le Ministre

• Nommé : par le Président de la République.

• Responsable : de la mise en œuvre de la politique nationale en matière d'éducation.

• Il a sous son autorité directe : les Inspecteurs généraux de l'Éducation nationale. Ils assument une mission d'évaluation et d'animation du système éducation.

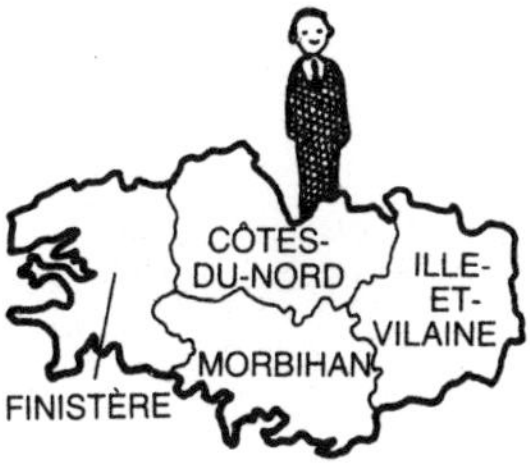

▲ Niveau académique : le Recteur

• Nommé : par décret pris en conseil des ministres.

• Responsable : de l'exécution des décisions du ministre.

• Il est assisté de conseillers techniques : les Inspecteurs pédagogiques régionaux (IPR) et les Inspecteurs de l'enseignement technique (IET) qui exercent des missions d'évaluation et d'animation dans les lycées (il y a 26 académies en métropole + 2 outre-mer [Antilles, La Réunion]).

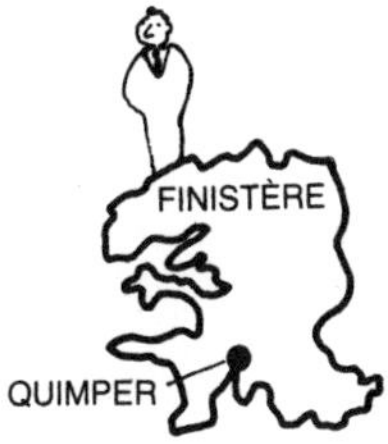

▲ Niveau départemental : l'Inspecteur d'Académie

• Nommé : par le Président de la République.

• Responsable : des services départementaux de l'Éducation nationale.

• Il a sous ses ordres : les Inspecteurs départementaux de l'Éducation nationale (IDEN) chargés de l'évaluation et de l'animation dans les écoles et l'Inspecteur de l'information et de l'orientation.

▲ Niveau local : le Chef d'Établissement

(proviseur, principal, directeur)

• Nommé : par le ministre après inscription sur une liste d'aptitude.

• Responsable de l'organisation et du fonctionnement de l'établissement.

• Il a sous ses ordres : un proviseur-adjoint (principal-adjoint en collège), des conseillers d'éducation, des enseignants.

Le Médiateur

Le Médiateur s'efforce de régler les situations individuelles nées du fonctionnement défectueux d'un service public. L'institution du Médiateur a été créée par la loi du 3/1/1973 et modifiée par la loi du 24/11/1976.

■ Qui est le Médiateur ?

— Il est à la tête d'une administration qui comprend des rédacteurs, des assistants, des conseillers techniques et des correspondants dans les départements qui informent le public (ils tiennent leur permanence à la préfecture).

— Le Médiateur est nommé pour 6 ans par décret pris en conseil des ministres*. Il ne peut être mis fin à ses fonctions avant l'expiration de ce délai qu'en cas d'empêchement constaté. p. 40

■ Quel est son rôle ?

— Son rôle consiste à démêler des affaires administratives compliquées, des litiges entre un particulier et une administration de l'État, une collectivité territoriale, un établissement public. L'organisme mis en cause doit être français.

— Des exemples d'intervention des services du Médiateur :

Excès de zèle d'un commissaire de police qui exigeait 3 photos pour établir une carte d'identité alors que la loi n'en prévoit que 2 : une pour la carte d'identité et une pour la sous-préfecture ou la préfecture. Avec la 3e photo, il constituait un fichier détaillé sur les habitants du quartier.

Courrier non réexpédié au destinataire, mais retourné à l'expéditeur alors que l'ordre de réexpédition avait été normalement enregistré aux PTT.

Intervention d'huissier, par erreur : à la suite d'une confusion d'identité entre 2 sœurs, un huissier se trompe d'appartement et fait saisir le mobilier.

Litige opposant un particulier avec les Services de la redevance audiovisuelle à propos d'un téléviseur portable imposé deux fois.

■ Comment faire appel au Médiateur ?

— Tout particulier peut introduire une demande s'il s'estime lésé par un service public mais sa requête doit obligatoirement être transmise au Médiateur par l'intermédiaire d'un député ou d'un sénateur*. Le recours est gratuit. p. 42 et 44

— Un parlementaire peut, de sa propre initiative, saisir le Médiateur d'une question de sa compétence qui lui paraît mériter son intervention.

— Sur la demande d'une des six commissions permanentes* de son assemblée, le président de l'Assemblée nationale ou du Sénat peut également transmettre au Médiateur toute pétition dont son assemblée a été saisie. p. 46

■ De quel pouvoir dispose-t-il ?

— Le pouvoir de recommandation : lorsqu'une réclamation lui paraît justifiée, le Médiateur fait, à l'administration* concernée, toutes les recommandations qui lui paraissent de nature à régler les difficultés et toutes les propositions tendant à améliorer son fonctionnement. La publication des recommandations au Journal Officiel reste le moyen de persuasion ultime. p. 64

— Le pouvoir d'injonction : en cas d'inexécution d'une décision de justice*, le Médiateur peut enjoindre (c'est-à-dire inviter) l'organisme mis en cause à s'y conformer dans un délai qu'il fixe. Si cette injonction n'est pas suivie d'effet, elle fera l'objet d'un rapport spécial qui sera publié au Journal Officiel. Cette « menace » de publication suffit le plus souvent à débloquer certaines situations complexes. p. 108

On peut rattacher la fonction de Médiateur à celle des « ombudmen » (d'origine suédoise) à l'étranger.

■ Le bilan d'une action

Les services du Médiateur examinent chaque année plus de 3 000 dossiers.

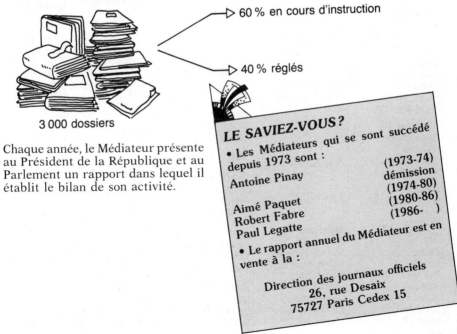

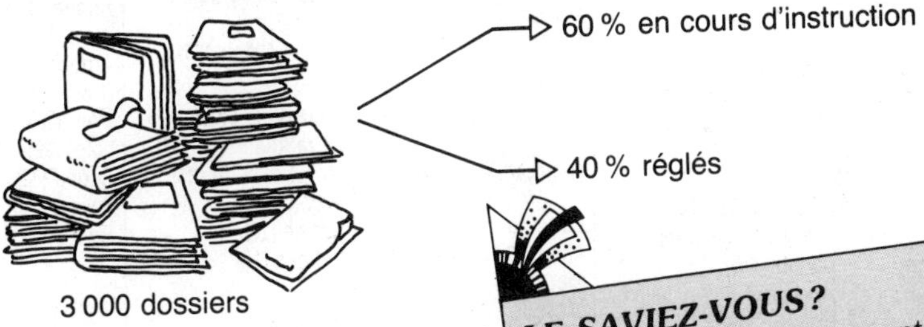

Chaque année, le Médiateur présente au Président de la République et au Parlement un rapport dans lequel il établit le bilan de son activité.

LE SAVIEZ-VOUS ?

• Les Médiateurs qui se sont succédé depuis 1973 sont :

Antoine Pinay	(1973-74) démission
Aimé Paquet	(1974-80)
Robert Fabre	(1980-86)
Paul Legatte	(1986-)

• Le rapport annuel du Médiateur est en vente à la :

Direction des journaux officiels
26, rue Desaix
75727 Paris Cedex 15

La région

La loi de décentralisation du 2 mars 1982 prévoit la création d'une nouvelle collectivité locale : la RÉGION. Cette réforme importante renforce son rôle en lui donnant de nouvelles compétences qui étaient jusqu'à présent exercées par l'État.

■ La région : une collectivité territoriale

La région est une collectivité territoriale, constituée par un ensemble de départements* regroupés en fonction de leur appartenance à des intérêts économiques et culturels. p. 86

Les 96 départements français sont regroupés en 22 régions. Les régions d'outre-mer sont au nombre de 4 : la Guadeloupe, Guyane, Martinique et Réunion.

■ Les 26 régions françaises et leurs conseillers régionaux

Alsace
Bas-Rhin (27)
Haut-Rhin (20)

Aquitaine
Dordogne (12)
Gironde (34)
Landes (10)
Lot-et-Garonne (10)
Pyrénées-Atlant. (17)

Auvergne
Allier (13)
Cantal (6)
Haute-Loire (8)
Puy-de-Dôme (20)

Bourgogne
Côte-d'Or (16)
Nièvre (9)
Saône-et-Loire (19)
Yonne (11)

Bretagne
Côtes-du-Nord (16)
Finistère (25)
Ille-et-Vilaine (22)
Morbihan (18)

Centre
Cher (11)
Eure-et-Loir (12)
Indre (8)
Indre-et-Loire (17)
Loir-et-Cher (10)
Loiret (17)

Champ. Ardennes
Ardennes (11)
Aube (10)
Marne (18)
Haute-Marne (8)

Corse
Corse-du-Sud (28)
Haute-Corse (33)

Franche-Comté
Territ. de Belf. (6)
Doubs (18)
Jura (10)
Haute-Saône (9)

Guadeloupe (41)

Guyane (31)

Ile-de-France
Essonne (20)
Hauts-de-Seine (27)
Ville de Paris (42)
Seine-et-Marne (18)
Seine-St-Denis (26)
Val-de-Marne (23)
Val-d'Oise (18)
Yvelines (23)

Languedoc-Roussillon
Aude (10)
Gard (18)
Hérault (23)
Lozère (3)
Pyrénées-Orient. (11)

Limousin
Corrèze (14)
Creuse (8)
Haute-Vienne (19)

Lorraine
Meurthe-et Mos. (22)
Meuse (7)
Moselle (31)
Vosges (13)

Martinique (41)

Midi-Pyrénées
Ariège (6)
Aveyron (10)
Haute-Garonne (29)
Gers (7)
Lot (6)
Hautes-Pyrénées (9)
Tarn (13)
Tarn-et-Garonne (7)

Basse-Normandie
Calvados (19)
Manche (16)
Orne (10)

Haute-Normandie
Eure (15)
Seine-Maritime (38)

Nord-Pas-de-Calais
Nord (72)
Pas-de-Calais (41)

Pays de la Loire
Loire-Atlantique (31)
Maine-et-Loire (21)
Mayenne (9)
Sarthe (16)
Vendée (16)

Picardie
Aisne (17)
Oise (21)
Somme (17)

Poitou-Charentes
Charente (12)
Charente-Marit. (17)
Deux-Sèvres (12)
Vienne (12)

Provence-Alpes-Côte-d'Azur
Alpes-de-Haute Provence (4)
Hautes-Alpes (4)
Alpes-Maritimes (26)
Bouche-du-Rh. (49)
Var (21)
Vaucluse (13)

Réunion (45)

Rhône-Alpes
Ain (13)
Ardèche (9)
Drôme (12)
Isère (28)
Loire (22)
Rhône (42)
Savoie (10)
Haute-Savoie (15)

DIVISION DE LA FRANCE MÉTROPOLITAINE EN RÉGIONS

ÉTAT
VIE POLITIQUE
ADMINISTRATION
COLLECTIVITÉS LOCALES
JUSTICE
INTERNATIONAL

L'organisation d'un Conseil régional

Le Conseil régional administre la région. Il « règle par ses délibérations les affaires de la région ». A sa tête, le président dirige les débats du Conseil régional, il est aussi l'exécutif de la région.

■ Une collectivité territoriale

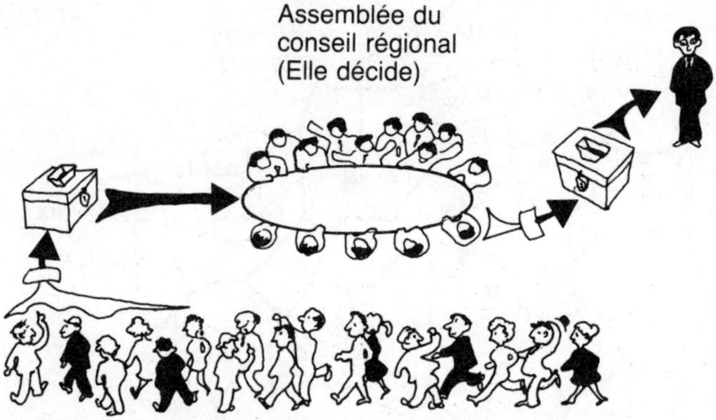

■ Le Conseil régional

— Les conseillers régionaux sont élus dans chaque département pour six ans, au suffrage universel direct*. L'effectif des conseils régionaux et la répartition des sièges sont fixés par la loi. p. 20

— Le Conseil régional a son siège au chef-lieu de la région, à l'Hôtel de Région.

• Il vote le budget* de la région. p. 85
• Il délibère sur les affaires régionales qui lui sont soumises.
• Il approuve le Plan régional, et concourt à l'élaboration du Plan national.

■ Le président du Conseil régional

Il est élu par le Conseil régional.

• Il préside les réunions du Conseil régional.
• Il est chargé de l'exécution des décisions et des délibérations du Conseil.
• Il dirige les services administratifs de la région.
• Il saisit le Comité économique et social de tous les problèmes qui sont de sa compétence (budget, plan et orientations générales).

■ Le Comité économique et social : assemblée consultative

Ses membres sont désignés par les différentes organisations professionnelles, économiques, scientifiques et culturelles de la Région.

CONSEIL, COMMISSIONS ET SERVICES

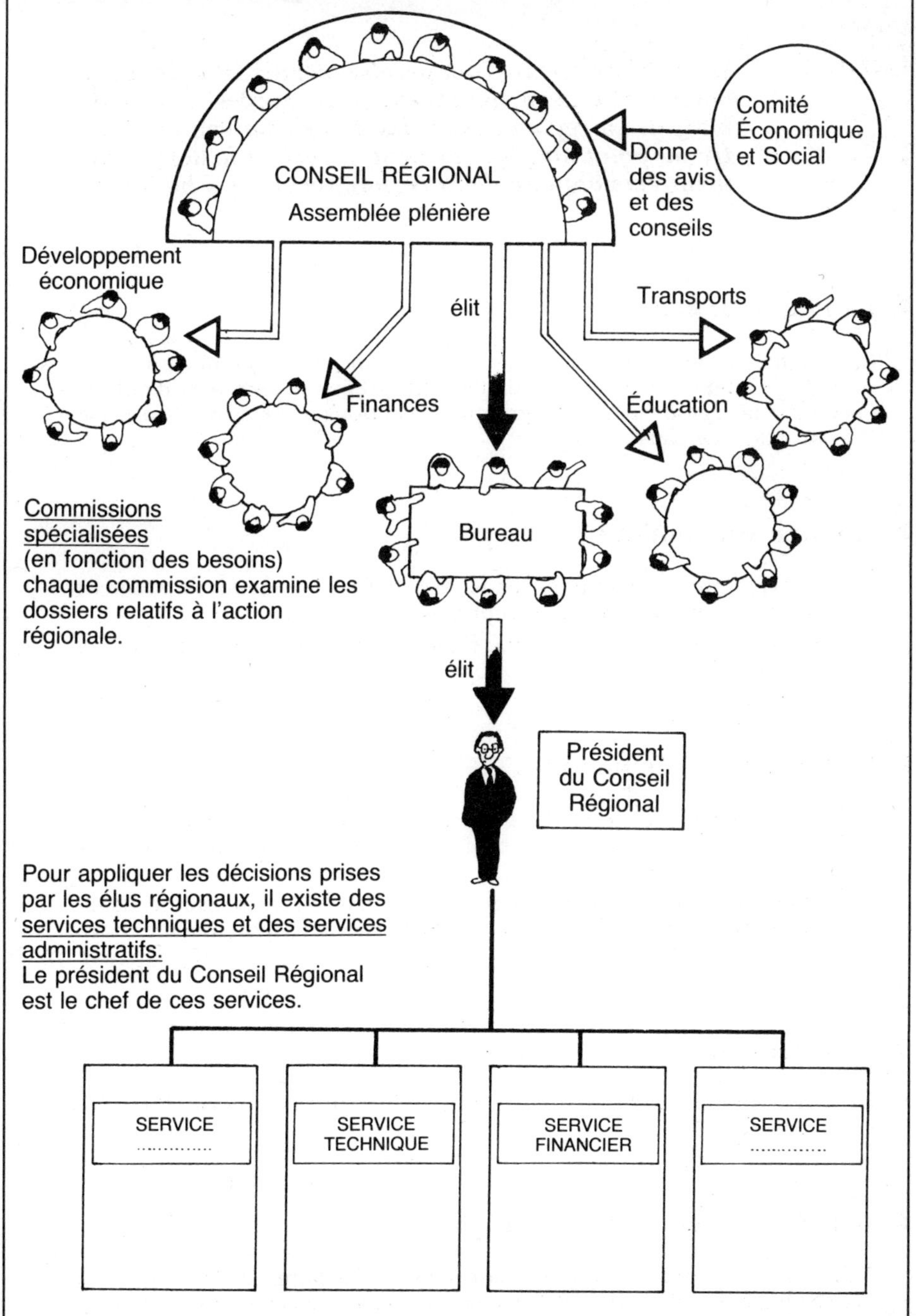
CONSEIL RÉGIONAL
Assemblée plénière
Comité Économique et Social
Donne des avis et des conseils
Développement économique
Finances
élit
Transports
Éducation
Bureau
Commissions spécialisées
(en fonction des besoins)
chaque commission examine les dossiers relatifs à l'action régionale.
élit
Président du Conseil Régional
Pour appliquer les décisions prises par les élus régionaux, il existe des services techniques et des services administratifs.
Le président du Conseil Régional est le chef de ces services.
SERVICE ....
SERVICE TECHNIQUE
SERVICE FINANCIER
SERVICE ....

Le rôle du Conseil régional

De nombreux textes ont précisé, depuis 1982, les compétences de la région qu'elle peut exercer grâce à un budget. La région assure les actions suivantes : mettre au point un plan régional, favoriser le développement économique de la région, former les hommes.

■ Le Plan régional

La région détermine les objectifs du développement économique pour une période de cinq ans. Un contrat de Plan État-région fixe la part de l'État et celle de la région sur des programmes d'actions prioritaires et précise les moyens financiers.

■ L'action économique

Les interventions économiques tendent soit à favoriser le développement économique, soit à aider les entreprises en difficulté.

Exemples : versement d'une prime régionale à la création d'entreprise, prime régionale à l'emploi.

■ La formation des hommes

— La formation professionnelle continue et l'apprentissage : la région met au point un plan de formation professionnelle en fonction des besoins et de l'avenir régional.

— L'enseignement du second degré : la région est responsable de la construction, de l'équipement et des dépenses de fonctionnement des lycées*. p. 76

■ Le logement

La région définit des priorités en matière d'habitat et apporte des aides complémentaires.

■ Autres compétences de la région

La région a la possibilité d'intervenir dans les domaines de la culture, de l'environnement, de la recherche, des transports, des communications et du tourisme.

RECETTES ET DÉPENSES DU BUDGET RÉGIONAL

▲ Où va l'argent ? Les dépenses

Transports et infrastructures

Aménagement de routes, ports maritimes, de gares, sécurité routière, météorologie...

Formation des hommes

Initiation à l'informatique, constructions scolaires, actions de formation permanente...

Action économique

Maîtrise de l'énergie, productions agricoles, diversification de l'économie régionale...

Habitat

Réhabilitation des quartiers urbains, amélioration des logements sociaux...

Aménagement régional

Restructuration des agglomérations, assainissement...

Culture et sports

Musique, aménagement de lieux de spectacles, musées, salles sportives.

Frais de personnel

Charges de fonctionnement des assemblées et des services

Remboursement des emprunts

▲ D'où vient l'argent ?

Participation de l'État

• Diverses dotations globales destinées à aider le fonctionnement et l'équipement des régions.

• Les participations diverses de l'État. Exemple : financement au titre du contrat de Plan.

Recettes d'emprunt

Moyen normal de financement du budget d'une collectivité locale. Financement effectué soit à partir du réseau public (Caisse des Dépôts et Consignations, Caisse d'Épargne...), soit sur le marché financier par le lancement d'un emprunt public régional.

Recettes fiscales

— La taxe régionale.
Elle s'ajoute aux quatre taxes locales (taxe foncière sur les propriétés bâties, taxe foncière sur les propriétés non bâties, taxe d'habitation, taxe professionnelle).

— La taxe sur les droits de mutation.
Cette taxe est perçue sur chaque transaction immobilière (vente, achat...).

— La taxe sur les permis de conduire.

— La taxe sur les cartes grises.

Le département

Créé par la Révolution, le département a été conçu dans le cadre d'un découpage géographique destiné à rationaliser l'organisation administrative du territoire.

Napoléon donna un rôle prépondérant au représentant de l'État, le préfet, détenteur de l'exécutif.

La division du territoire français en départements

— La France est divisée en 96 départements métropolitains et 5 départements d'outre-mer.

— Chaque département est divisé en cantons dont le nombre varie de 14 (Territoire de Belfort) à 76 (département du Nord).

— Le canton est une division intermédiaire entre l'arrondissement et la commune. Il constitue une circonscription électorale pour l'élection des conseillers généraux.

Les différents départements et leurs chefs-lieux

Ain	Bg-en-Bresse
Aisne	Laon
Allier	Moulins
Alpes-de-Hte-P.	Digne
Alpes (Hautes-)	Gap
Alpes-Maritimes	Nice
Ardèche	Privas
Ardennes	Mézières
Ariège	Foix
Aube	Troyes
Aude	Carcassonne
Aveyron	Rodez
Bouches-du-Rh.	Marseille
Calvados	Caen
Cantal	Aurillac
Charente	Angoulême
Charente-Mar.	La Rochelle
Cher	Bourges
Corrèze	Tulle
Corse du Nord	Bastia
Corse du Sud	Ajaccio
Côte-d'Or	Dijon
Côtes-du-Nord	St-Brieuc
Creuse	Guéret
Dordogne	Périgueux
Doubs	Besançon
Drôme	Valence
Eure	Evreux
Eure-et-Loir	Chartres
Finistère	Quimper
Gard	Nîmes
Garonne (Hte-)	Toulouse
Gers	Auch
Gironde	Bordeaux
Hérault	Montpellier
Ille-et-Vilaine	Rennes
Indre	Châteauroux
Indre-et-Loire	Tours
Isère	Grenoble
Jura	Lons-le-Saunier
Landes	Mt-de-Marsan
Loir-et-Cher	Blois
Loire	St-Etienne
Loire (Haute-)	Le Puy
Loire-Atlant.	Nantes
Loiret	Orléans
Lot	Cahors
Lot-et-Garonne	Agen
Lozère	Mende
Maine-et-Loire	Angers
Manche	Saint-Lô
Marne	Reims
Marne (Haute-)	Chaumont
Mayenne	Laval
Meurthe-et-Mos.	Nancy
Meuse	Bar-le-Duc
Morbihan	Vannes
Moselle	Metz
Nièvre	Nevers
Nord	Lille
Oise	Pontoise
Orne	Alençon
Pas-de-Calais	Arras
Puy-de-Dôme	Ct-Ferrand
Pyrénées-Atlan.	Pau
Pyrénées (Htes-)	Tarbes
Pyrénées-Orien.	Perpignan
Rhin (Bas-)	Strasbourg
Rhin (Haut-)	Mulhouse
Rhône	Lyon
Saône (Hte-)	Vesoul
Saône-et-Loire	Mâcon
Sarthe	Le Mans
Savoie	Chambéry
Savoie (Hte-)	Annecy
Seine-Maritime	Rouen
Sèvres (Deux-)	Niort
Somme	Amiens
Tarn	Albi
Tarn-et-Gar.	Montauban
Var	Toulon
Vaucluse	Avignon
Vendée	La Roche/Yon
Vienne	Poitiers
Vienne (Haute-)	Limoges
Vosges	Épinal
Yonne	Auxerre
Belfort (Ter. de)	Belfort

RÉGION PARISIENNE

Essonne	Evry
Hauts-de-Seine	Nanterre
Paris (Ville de)	
Seine-et-Marne	Melun
Seine-St-Denis	Bobigny
Val-de-Marne	Créteil
Val-d'Oise	Pontoise
Yvelines	Versailles

OUTRE-MER

Guadeloupe	Basse-Terre
Guyane	Cayenne
Martinique	Fort-de-France
Réunion	St-Denis
St-Pierre-et-M.	St-Pierre

DIVISION DE LA FRANCE EN DÉPARTEMENTS

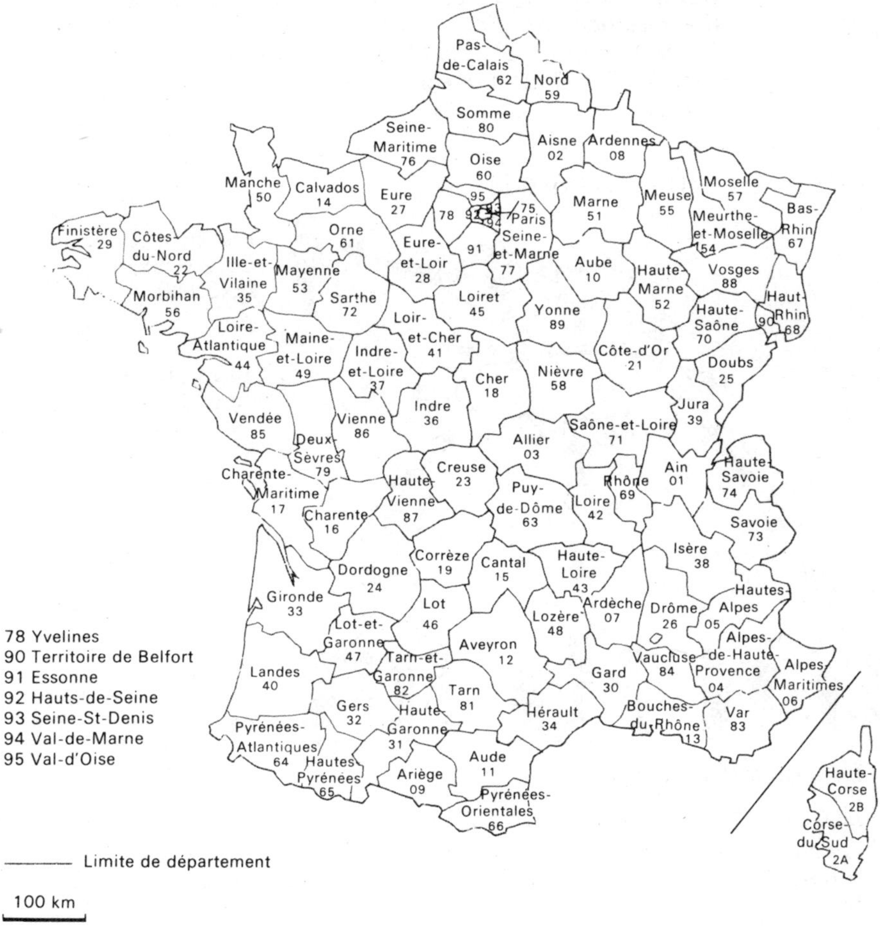

L'organisation d'un Conseil général du département

Depuis la loi de décentralisation du 2 mars 1982, le département est devenu une collectivité locale dans laquelle un élu, le président du Conseil général, exécute les décisions d'une assemblée élue au suffrage universel.

■ Une collectivité territoriale

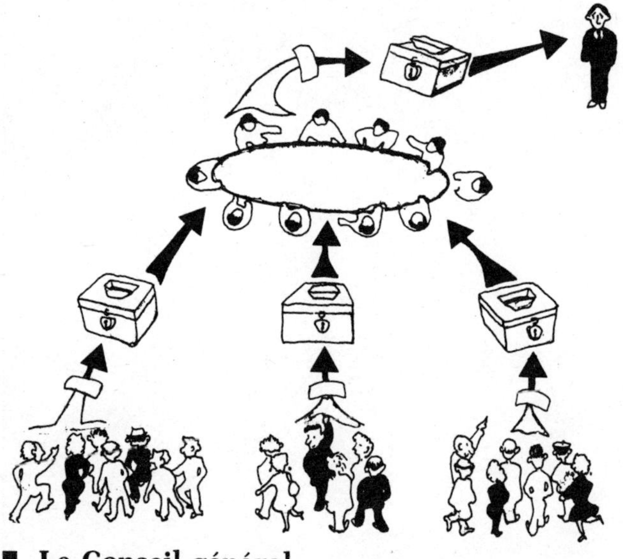

■ Le Conseil général

Le Conseil général* a son siège à l'Hôtel du département. p. 90

Les conseillers généraux sont élus dans chaque canton, pour 6 ans, au suffrage universel direct. Le Conseil général est renouvelable par moitié tous les 3 ans. p. 20

Le Conseil général règle par ses délibérations « les affaires du département ». Il vote le budget* départemental. p. 91

■ Le président du Conseil général

— Il est élu pour 3 ans par les conseillers généraux.

— Il est chargé de préparer et d'exécuter les délibérations du Conseil général. Il est l'ordonnateur des dépenses du département et le chef des services du Conseil général.

Le président du Conseil général est assisté d'un bureau composé de vice-présidents et éventuellement d'autres membres.

CONSEIL, COMMISSIONS ET SERVICES

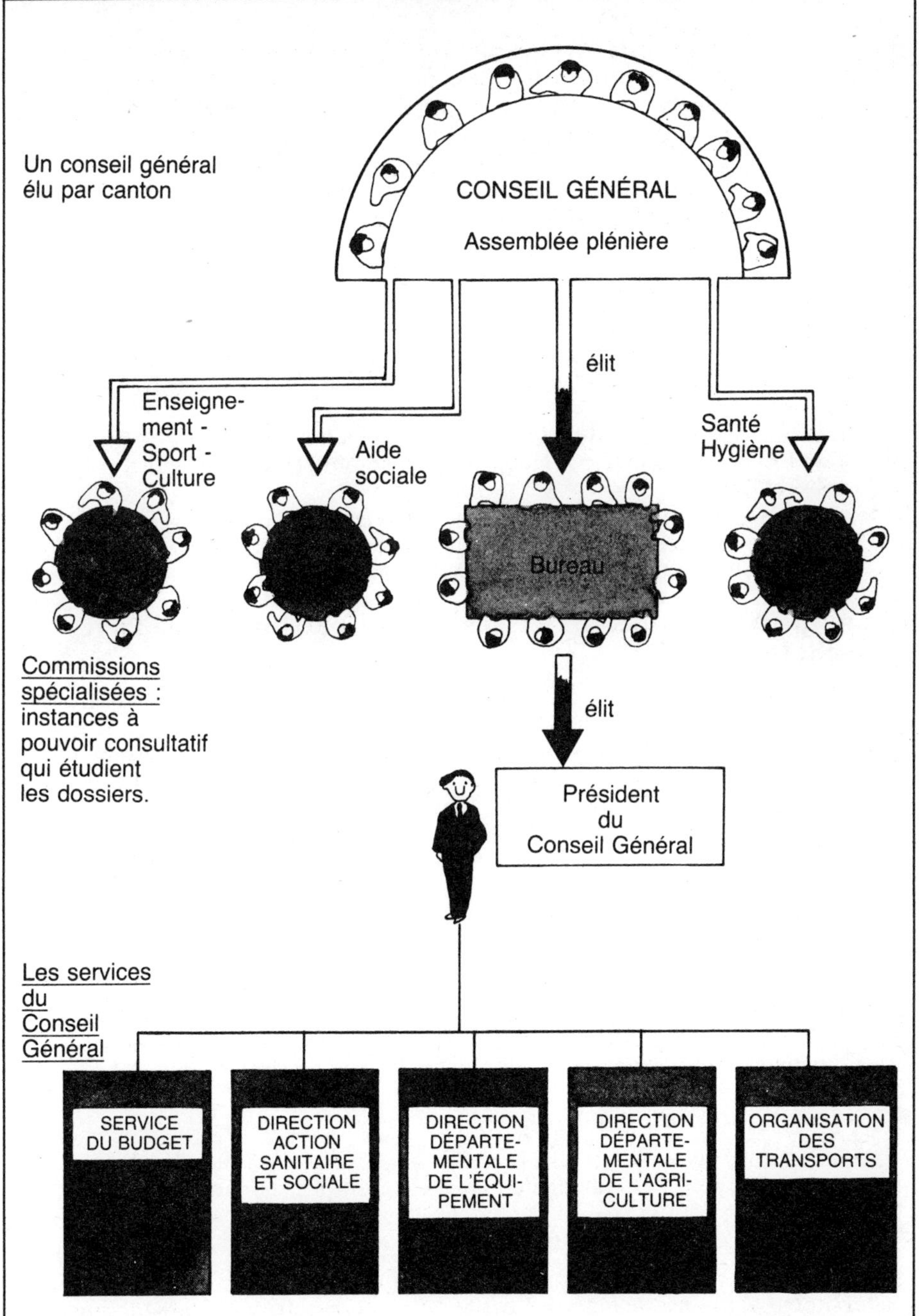

Un conseil général élu par canton
CONSEIL GÉNÉRAL
Assemblée plénière
élit
Enseignement - Sport - Culture
Aide sociale
Santé Hygiène
Bureau
élit
Commissions spécialisées : instances à pouvoir consultatif qui étudient les dossiers.
Président du Conseil Général
Les services du Conseil Général
SERVICE DU BUDGET
DIRECTION ACTION SANITAIRE ET SOCIALE
DIRECTION DÉPARTEMENTALE DE L'ÉQUIPEMENT
DIRECTION DÉPARTEMENTALE DE L'AGRICULTURE
ORGANISATION DES TRANSPORTS

Le rôle du Conseil général

Les présidents des assemblées départementales jouent un rôle important dans la vie locale. Les élus départementaux sont responsables, à part entière, de la gestion d'un budget départemental.
Le Conseil général intervient dans les domaines suivants : aide sociale et santé, équipements collectifs, éducation, aide aux communes.

■ Aide sociale et santé

Le Conseil général est responsable :

— des prestations d'aide sociale : aide médicale, aide sociale à l'enfance, aide sociale aux familles, aide aux personnes handicapées, aide aux personnes âgées ;

— de la prévention sanitaire : vaccination, protection maternelle et infantile, lutte contre certains fléaux sociaux comme la lèpre, le cancer, la tuberculose ;

— des services sociaux qui assurent, au plan local, la mise en œuvre des politiques d'aide sociale et des actions médico-sociales (service d'action sociale, service départemental de vaccination...).

■ Équipements collectifs et gestion du patrimoine départemental

— Entretien et réparation de la voirie routière : 350 000 km de route sont classés dans la voirie départementale,

— Aménagement du territoire rural : ex. : mise en place d'un programme d'aide à l'équipement rural, financement du remembrement rural,

— Construction et amélioration des bâtiments administratifs à caractère social, culturel, sportif, éducatif (bibliothèques, musées) ou de protection des personnes et des biens (subvention au service départemental de protection contre l'incendie, construction de gendarmeries).

■ Éducation

Le Conseil général est responsable :

— de la construction, de l'équipement et de l'entretien des Collèges* : p. 76

— de la politique des transports scolaires non urbains. Les départements peuvent définir les services, et choisir le mode d'exploitation.

■ Aide aux communes

Aider les communes* les moins favorisées : subventions à titre des dépenses engagées pour les classes de neige, les cantines scolaires. p. 92

■ Intervention économique

Le Conseil général peut favoriser le développement économique de son territoire, et assurer le maintien des services nécessaires à la satisfaction des besoins de la population en milieu rural.

RECETTES ET DÉPENSES DU BUDGET DÉPARTEMENTAL

▲ Où va l'argent ? Les dépenses

Aide sociale et santé

C'est la part la plus importante.

Voies de communication et infrastructures

Routes départementales, liaisons diverses. Patrimoine départemental.

Urbanisme et logement

Éducation

— Sports
— Culture
— Transports

Interventions économiques en faveur de l'environnement

Équipements téléphoniques, plantations.

Frais de personnel

Charges de fonctionnement des services administratifs

Remboursement des emprunts

▲ D'où vient l'argent ? Les recettes

Participation de l'État

L'État effectue plusieurs dotations pour aider chaque département à s'équiper.

Recettes fiscales

— Taxe différentielle sur les véhicules à moteur (la vignette).

- Droits d'enregistrement.
- Taxes espaces verts, etc.

Recettes fiscales des impôts directs

Ce sont des cotisations prélevées sur les impôts locaux au profit du département.

Produits des emprunts

La commune

La commune est la plus petite division administrative française.

C'est une collectivité territoriale qui est gérée par des représentants élus : le Conseil municipal et le maire.

■ Une collectivité territoriale

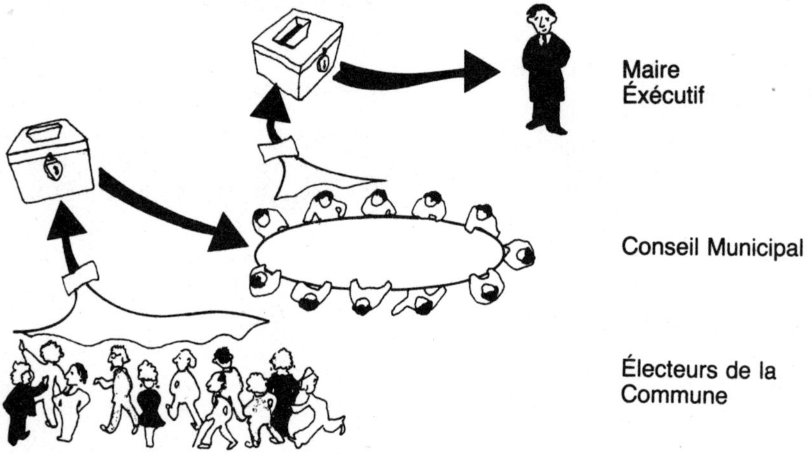

■ Quels services pouvez-vous attendre de votre mairie ?

— Élections :

• inscription sur les listes électorales. La liste des électeurs est valable pour toutes les élections* politiques (municipales, cantonales, régionales, législatives, européennes, présidentielles); p. 20

— Les services de l'état civil :

• déclaration de naissance, de décès, de reconnaissance d'enfant naturel;

— Les services sociaux dans chaque commune : le Bureau d'aide sociale gère l'ensemble de toutes les formes d'actions sociales mises en place par la commune, en accord avec les organismes institutionnels (DDASS, CAF et CPA maladie). L'aide sociale peut prendre diverses formes : aide sociale à l'enfance, aux personnes âgées, aide médicale, aide en nature...

— Les services de l'urbanisme et du logement :

• consulter le Plan d'Occupation des Sols (P.O.S.). Élaboré sous la responsabilité de la commune, le P.O.S. fixe les règles de constructibilité du territoire communal;

• demander un certificat d'urbanisme qui précise les règles particulières de construction applicables à une parcelle de terrain;

• obtenir un permis de construire.

L'ORGANISATION D'UNE COMMUNE

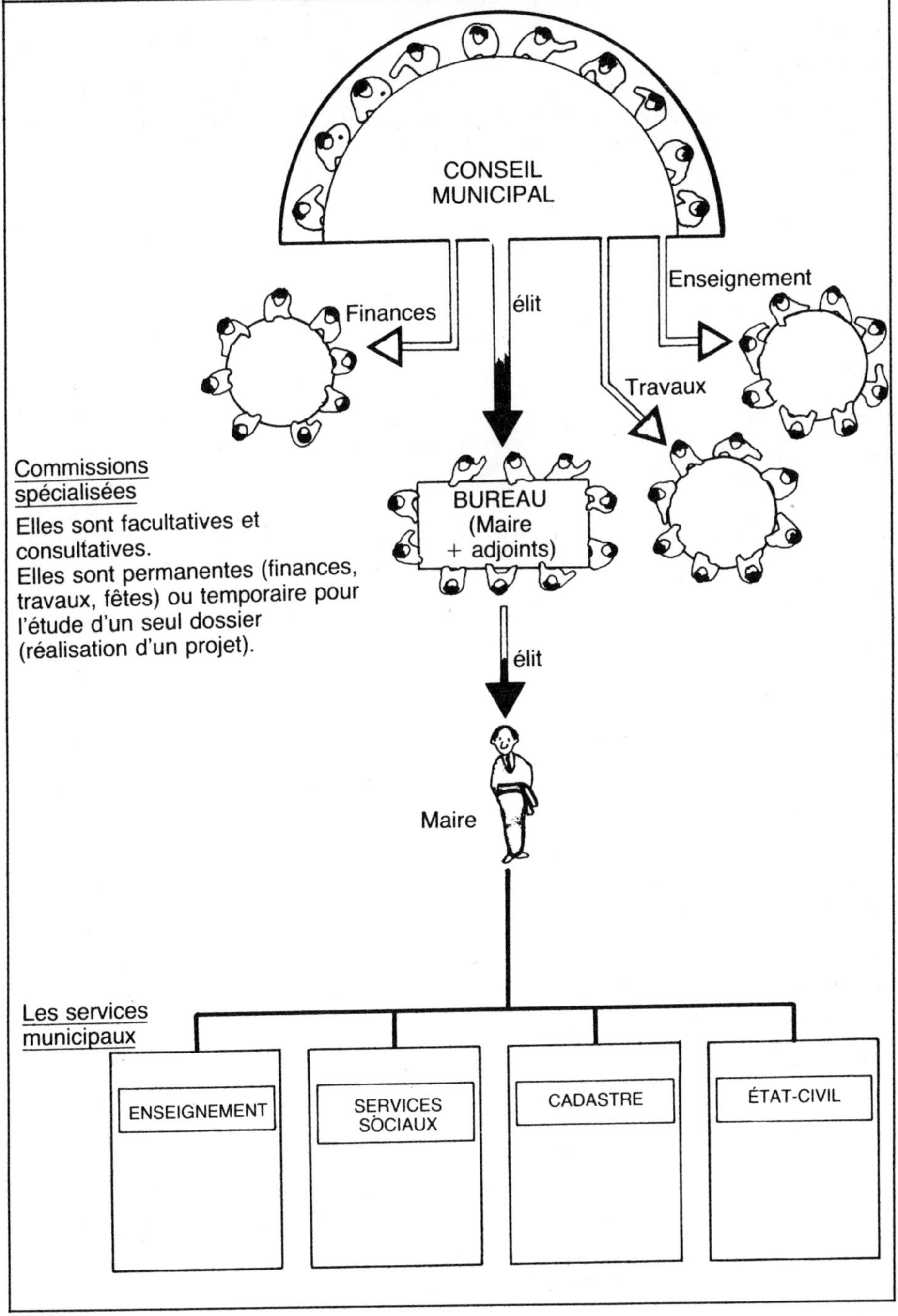
CONSEIL MUNICIPAL
Finances
élit
Enseignement
Travaux
Commissions spécialisées
Elles sont facultatives et consultatives.
Elles sont permanentes (finances, travaux, fêtes) ou temporaire pour l'étude d'un seul dossier (réalisation d'un projet).
BUREAU (Maire + adjoints)
élit
Maire
Les services municipaux
ENSEIGNEMENT
SERVICES SOCIAUX
CADASTRE
ÉTAT-CIVIL

Les élections municipales

Elles ont lieu tous les 6 ans au suffrage universel direct, au scrutin de liste selon un mode mixte. Le nombre de conseillers municipaux varie en fonction de l'importance de la commune.

■ L'élection des conseillers municipaux

Pour les communes de moins de 3 500 habitants, l'élection des conseillers municipaux se fait au scrutin majoritaire* à 2 tours. p. 24

Les conseillers municipaux des communes de 3 500 habitants et plus sont élus au scrutin de liste à 2 tours selon un mode mixte* (mélange de scrutin majoritaire et proportionnel). p. 28

■ Qui peut être conseiller municipal ?

Pour être éligible, le candidat doit avoir au moins 18 ans,
être français ou naturalisé depuis plus de 10 ans,
jouir de ses droits civils et politiques,
être inscrit sur les listes électorales.

Il faut avoir 21 ans pour être maire.

Remarque :

Dans les communes de plus de 500 habitants, deux époux peuvent siéger dans un même Conseil municipal.

■ La durée du mandat

Un conseiller municipal est élu pour 6 ans. Les élections municipales ont donc lieu tous les 6 ans.

Si un siège de conseiller devient vacant, pour quelque cause que ce soit, le candidat, venant sur la liste immédiatement après le dernier élu, prend la place.

COMBIEN DE CONSEILLERS MUNICIPAUX ?

Le nombre des conseillers municipaux varie en fonction de l'importance de la population de la commune.

Il existe 36 400 communes et 35 400 ont moins de 10 000 habitants.

Les communes de moins de 10 000 habitants représentent 98 % des communes et 48 % de la population française.

COMMUNES	Nombre des membres du conseil municipal
De moins de 100 habitants	9
De 100 à 499 habitants	11
De 500 à 1 499 habitants	15
De 1 500 à 2 499 habitants	19
De 2 500 à 3 499 habitants	23
De 3 500 à 4 999 habitants	27
De 5 000 à 9 999 habitants	29
De 10 000 à 19 999 habitants	33
De 20 000 à 29 999 habitants	35
De 30 000 à 39 999 habitants	39
De 40 000 à 49 999 habitants	43
De 50 000 à 59 999 habitants	45
De 60 000 à 79 999 habitants	49
De 80 000 à 99 999 habitants	53
De 100 000 à 149 999 habitants	55
De 150 000 à 199 999 habitants	59
De 200 000 à 249 999 habitants	61
De 250 000 à 299 999 habitants	65
De 300 000 habitants et au-dessus	69

PARIS : 163
MARSEILLE : 101
LYON : 73

LE SAVIEZ-VOUS ?

Vous habitez une commune de plus de 3 500 habitants, votre bulletin est nul dans les cas suivants :

a) listes « panachées » dans lesquelles le nom d'un ou plusieurs candidats a été remplacé par celui ou ceux d'un ou plusieurs candidats d'une autre liste, ou celui de toute autre personne ;

b) listes dans lesquelles l'ordre de présentation aura été modifié ;

c) listes incomplètes, c'est-à-dire comportant moins de noms que de sièges à pourvoir ;

d) listes comportant plus de noms que de conseillers à élire ;

e) bulletins établis au nom de listes non régulièrement enregistrées.

Le maire et son Conseil municipal

Les communes sont administrées par des conseils élus. Les Conseils municipaux peuvent intervenir à l'égard de toutes les affaires communales dans le cadre de la législation existante. Le pouvoir de décision est matérialisé par l'adoption de délibérations qui s'imposent à tous, et en particulier aux administrés.

■ Le maire

— Le maire est élu, au scrutin secret, parmi les membres du Conseil municipal.

— Il est à la fois l'agent exécutif de la commune, chargé de mettre en application les décisions du Conseil municipal, mais il est, aussi, le représentant de l'État.

— Il est aidé par des adjoints au maire qui peuvent le remplacer en cas d'empêchement, ou exercer, par délégation, certaines fonctions.

Le nombre des adjoints au maire ne peut excéder 30 % de l'effectif du Conseil municipal.

■ Le maire : un agent exécutif du Conseil municipal

— Il convoque le Conseil municipal, dont il est le président.

— Il prépare et exécute les décisions du Conseil municipal.

— Il est chargé de l'exécution du budget* : paiement des dépenses engagées et encaissement des recettes. p. 99

— Il représente la commune, par délégation du Conseil municipal. Par exemple, pour la signature des contrats.

— Il recrute le personnel communal et il est responsable de l'organisation des services municipaux.

— Il assure la police municipale et la police rurale pour garantir le bon ordre, la sécurité et la salubrité publique. Par exemple, il prend des arrêtés municipaux pour réglementer la circulation ou le stationnement sur les voies publiques.

■ Le maire : un représentant de l'État

Il est chargé :

— d'assurer la publication des lois et règlements* de la République; p. 50

— de participer à certaines opérations administratives : révision des listes électorales, recensement de la population, établissement des listes de conscription, organisation des élections;

— d'exercer les fonctions d'officier d'état civil (tenue des registres d'état civil et célébration des mariages);

— d'exercer les fonctions d'officier de police judiciaire. Il constate les contraventions en dressant un procès-verbal.

LE RÔLE D'UN CONSEIL MUNICIPAL

— Le Conseil municipal règle par ses délibérations les affaires de la commune.

— Il se réunit au moins quatre fois par an à la mairie. Les séances sont publiques.

— Les domaines d'intervention des élus municipaux sont très variés.

Par exemple :

— la construction et l'entretien des équipements collectifs : voirie communale, école maternelle et primaire, stade, piscine, centre de loisirs, crèches...

— l'organisation des services de distribution d'eau, de ramassage des ordures ménagères, traitement des eaux usées...

▲ Voter le budget de la commune

Le budget doit prévoir toutes les dépenses et toutes les recettes de la commune.

▲ Organiser le fonctionnement quotidien des services municipaux

Chaque commune possède une organisation administrative, variable d'une commune à l'autre, en fonction des moyens dont elle dispose et des objectifs définis par le maire.

▲ Aménager le domaine public et assurer certains services collectifs

Les communes jouent un rôle de plus en plus important pour satisfaire les besoins collectifs des habitants.

▲ Désigner

Les représentants du Conseil municipal ou du maire dans les différents organismes extérieurs (syndicat intercommunal, district par exemple).

▲ Intervenir

pour favoriser le développement économique ou pour protéger les intérêts économiques et sociaux de la commune, par l'octroi d'aides diverses en complément de celles de la région.

▲ Favoriser les manifestations culturelles et sportives et développer la vie associative

Exemple : foire, exposition, concert, festival...

Budget et impôts locaux

Le budget d'une commune est la traduction financière de la politique poursuivie par le Conseil municipal. Les dépenses doivent être globalement couvertes par les recettes. Il en résulte que cet équilibre est souvent réalisé par une augmentation des impôts locaux.

■ Les différentes étapes de l'année budgétaire

Le budget de la commune est voté en plusieurs fois :

— Le budget primitif

Voté en début d'année, il donne les principales orientations de l'action du Conseil municipal pour l'année. Il fixe le taux des impôts locaux qui seront perçus pour financer les dépenses.

— Le compte administratif

C'est le compte rendu de la gestion budgétaire de l'année précédente. On s'aperçoit parfois que cette gestion est équilibrée, ou qu'elle a pu dégager des économies.

— Le budget supplémentaire

Il est voté en cours d'année pour réajuster les prévisions initiales. Toute décision prise par le Conseil municipal* qui engage une dépense doit p. 96 figurer dans le budget.

■ Impôts locaux. Qui est imposable ?

— La taxe foncière sur les propriétés bâties : impôt versé par le propriétaire d'un immeuble.

— La taxe foncière sur les propriétés non bâties : impôt versé par le propriétaire de terres et terrains de toute nature.

— La taxe d'habitation : impôt payé par le propriétaire ou le locataire d'une habitation meublée.

— La taxe professionnelle : impôt payé par les personnes physiques ou morales exerçant une activité professionnelle non salariée (commerçants, industriels, artisans...).

En payant les impôts directs locaux, on paye en réalité quatre impôts : à la commune, à la communauté urbaine* (ou au district), au département, p. 100 à la région.

Les taux d'imposition sont variables d'une commune à une autre et peuvent changer chaque année.

RECETTES ET DÉPENSES DU BUDGET COMMUNAL

▲ Où va l'argent ? Les dépenses

Frais de personnel

— Traitements
— Indemnités
— Charges sociales

Participations et subventions

— Charges obligatoires relatives au fonctionnement des services intercommunaux
(ex. : districts, communauté urbaine...).
— Subventions versées aux associations

— Comité des fêtes
— Groupe sportif
— etc.

Intérêts versés pour les emprunts effectués

Autres dépenses

Denrées, fournitures, services extérieurs.

Remboursement des emprunts

Dépenses d'équipement

— Achats de biens meubles et immeubles
— Travaux divers
— etc.

▲ D'où vient l'argent ? Les recettes

Produits d'exploitation et domaniaux relatifs aux services rendus aux usagers

— Crèches
— Piscines
— Cantines
— Colonies
— etc.

Dotation globale de fonctionnement versée par l'État

Recettes fiscales

— Quatre impôts directs locaux
— Diverses taxes : taxe d'enlèvement des ordures ménagères, taxe de balayage, taxe de séjour, etc.

Subventions reçues

Autres recettes

Ventes de biens communaux par exemple.

Emprunts

Les communes ont très souvent recours aux emprunts pour financer leurs investissements (Caisse des dépôts, Caisse d'Épargne, Caisse d'aide à l'équipement des collectivités locales, etc.)

Syndicats de communes - Districts - Communautés urbaines

La coopération intercommunale permet aux communes de réunir des moyens financiers pour satisfaire des besoins collectifs. Les communes peuvent choisir de se réunir dans un syndicat communal, dans un syndicat mixte, dans un district ou dans une communauté urbaine.

■ Qu'est-ce qu'un syndicat de communes ?

— Le syndicat de communes possède un statut d'établissement public et une personnalité distincte de chacune des communes concernées.

— Il est créé à l'initiative des Conseils municipaux*. p. 96

— Il dispose d'un budget propre.

— On distingue :

- des syndicats intercommunaux à vocation unique (S.I.V.U.) chargés de la gestion d'un seul service. Dans ce cas, les communes doivent créer autant de syndicats que d'activités communes. Exemples : — électrification, adduction d'eau, voirie, assainissement, transports scolaires... — « Syndicat intercommunal d'études et de programmation » (chargé par les communes d'élaborer un schéma directeur en matière d'urbanisme) ;
- des syndicats intercommunaux à vocation multiple (S.I.V.O.M.) chargés de la réalisation de plusieurs services. Exemple : adduction d'eau, assainissement et voirie.

■ Qu'est-ce qu'un syndicat mixte ?

Un syndicat mixte peut réunir des communes, départements*, établissements publics pour réaliser un équipement important. p. 86

Exemple : aménagement touristique d'une vallée qui s'étend sur 100 km, traverse deux départements et quarante communes.

■ Qu'est-ce qu'un district ?

Le district est une institution de regroupement applicable à toutes les communes, y compris les communes rurales.

C'est un établissement public à caractère administratif. Il assure, à la place des communes, différents services et fait face au problème d'équipement dans une agglomération ou dans une zone rurale.

Exemple de services assurés par un district : services d'incendie et de secours, collecte et incinérations des ordures ménagères, récupération du verre, transports urbains.

■ Qu'est-ce qu'une communauté urbaine ?

— Établissement public constitué par le regroupement des communes* dans des agglomérations de plus de 50 000 habitants. p. 92

— La communauté urbaine a la charge des services et équipements intéressant toute l'agglomération. Elle est une véritable administration de l'agglomération qui se superpose à celles des communes. Elle permet de mieux maîtriser le phénomène urbain et favorise l'utilisation cohérente des moyens dans les domaines suivants :

• Développement et aménagement, schémas directeurs, plans d'occupation des sols, programmes locaux de l'habitat, constitution de réserves foncières intéressant la communauté...

• Création et équipement des zones d'habitation, des zones de rénovation urbaine, des zones de réhabilitation, des zones industrielles, des zones artisanales et des zones portuaires.

• Services de secours et de lutte contre l'incendie.
Transports urbains de voyageurs.
Eau, assainissement, création de cimetières, abattoirs, marchés, marchés d'intérêt national, voirie et signalisation, parcs de stationnement.

■ Caractéristiques de toutes ces formes de coopération

— Chaque organisme a un statut d'établissement public et une personnalité distincte de chacune des communes concernées.

— Le principe de création d'un syndicat est le volontariat.

— Chaque établissement public possède son propre budget, alimenté soit par les fonds des communes associées, soit par les impôts directs locaux pour les districts et les communautés urbaines.

— La gestion est assurée par les représentants des conseils municipaux* de chaque commune. p. 96

L'organisation administrative de Paris

Paris est la capitale d'un État fortement centralisé où se trouvent le pouvoir politique et le pouvoir économique du pays. Au dernier recensement, la population totale de Paris était de 2 176 243 habitants, celle de la région Ile-de-France 10 073 000 habitants.

■ Le statut de Paris : une commune et un département

La loi du 31 décembre 1975 a fait de Paris une commune*, dont l'organisation est régie pour l'essentiel par le Code des Communes. p. 92

■ Le maire

— La commune de Paris est administrée par un maire et un Conseil municipal* — dénommé conseil de Paris — composé de 163 élus, conseillers de Paris. L'élection des conseillers de Paris se déroule dans le cadre du secteur électoral, chaque secteur représentant un arrondissement. Il y a 20 arrondissements à Paris. p. 96

— Le maire est élu par les conseillers de Paris pour 6 ans.

Il ne peut pas être président du Conseil régional d'Ile-de-France, mais il peut être membre du gouvernement.

Il n'est pas responsable de la police municipale qui revient au préfet de police, haut fonctionnaire nommé par l'État.

■ Le Conseil de Paris

— Le territoire de Paris recouvre deux collectivités territoriales : la commune de Paris et le département de Paris.

— Une même assemblée « le Conseil de Paris » siège :

• soit en formation de Conseil municipal*, présidée par le maire de Paris ; p. 96

• soit en formation de Conseil général*, dont le Maire de Paris est président. p. 88

■ Les Conseils d'arrondissement

— La loi du 31 décembre 1982 a institué pour les communes de Paris, Marseille et Lyon de nouvelles structures élues à l'échelon local : les Conseils d'arrondissement et le maire d'arrondissement.

— Les élus de Paris sont au nombre de 517 : 163 conseillers de Paris, 354 conseillers d'arrondissement.

— Le Conseil d'arrondissement est présidé par un maire d'arrondissement, élu parmi les membres du Conseil municipal.

PARIS

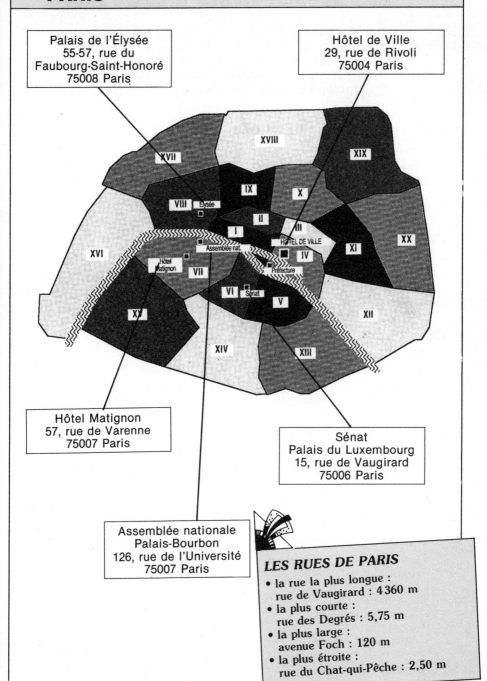

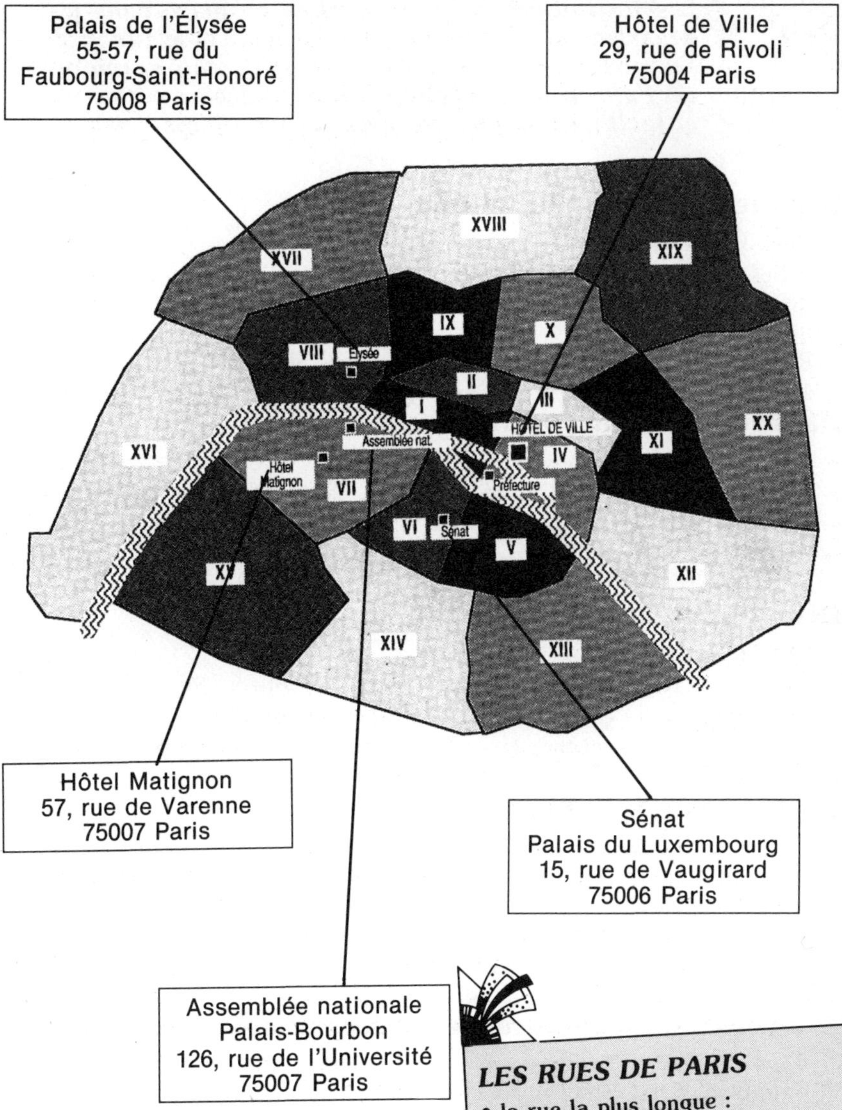

LES RUES DE PARIS

- la rue la plus longue :
  rue de Vaugirard : 4 360 m
- la plus courte :
  rue des Degrés : 5,75 m
- la plus large :
  avenue Foch : 120 m
- la plus étroite :
  rue du Chat-qui-Pêche : 2,50 m

Les départements d'outre-mer

Les institutions publiques mises en place dans les départements d'outre-mer ont plusieurs objectifs : préserver les particularités locales, maintenir et renforcer l'attachement à la République française, permettre et faciliter les relations avec les territoires voisins.

■ Département de la Guadeloupe

— Chef-lieu : Basse-Terre.

— Villes principales : Pointe-à-Pitre, Saint-Martin, Saint-Barthélemy.

— Situation : archipel des Antilles, formé de neuf îles principales dans la mer des Caraïbes.

— Ressources : sucre, banane, rhum, tourisme, élevage.

■ Département de la Martinique

— Chef-lieu : Fort-de-France.

— Villes principales : La Trinité, Le Marin, Sainte-Marie, Le Lamentin.

— Situation : dans la mer des Caraïbes, l'île a 80 km de long sur 30 de large.

— Ressources : sucre, banane, ananas, rhum, avocat, tourisme.

■ Département de la Guyane

— Chef-lieu : Cayenne.

— Villes principales : Saint-Laurent-du-Maroni, Kourou, Sinnamary.

— Situation : sur la côte Nord-Est de l'Amérique du Sud.

— Ressources : bois, pêche, agriculture, centre spatial de Kourou.

■ Département de la Réunion

— Chef-lieu : Saint-Denis.

— Villes principales : Saint-Pierre, Saint-Paul, Saint-Benoît, Le Tampon, Saint-Joseph, Saint-André, Saint-Louis, Le Port.

— Situation : dans l'océan Indien, à 800 km à l'Est de Madagascar.

— Ressources : sucre, rhum, essences végétales, élevage, pêche.

■ L'organisation administrative des départements d'outre-mer

— Dans l'ensemble, la législation et la réglementation métropolitaines s'appliquent aux départements d'outre-mer. L'organisation administrative des services de l'État et le rôle des services départementaux sont les mêmes qu'en métropole.

— Chaque département possède, en plus, un Conseil régional* élu au suffrage universel direct, doté de larges compétences et assisté chacun d'un Comité économique et social et d'un Comité de la culture, de l'éducation et de l'environnement. p. 82

— Depuis la création de la C.E.E., les départements d'outre-mer s'intègrent progressivement dans l'espace communautaire.

ORGANISATION CIVILE ET MILITAIRE D'OUTRE-MER

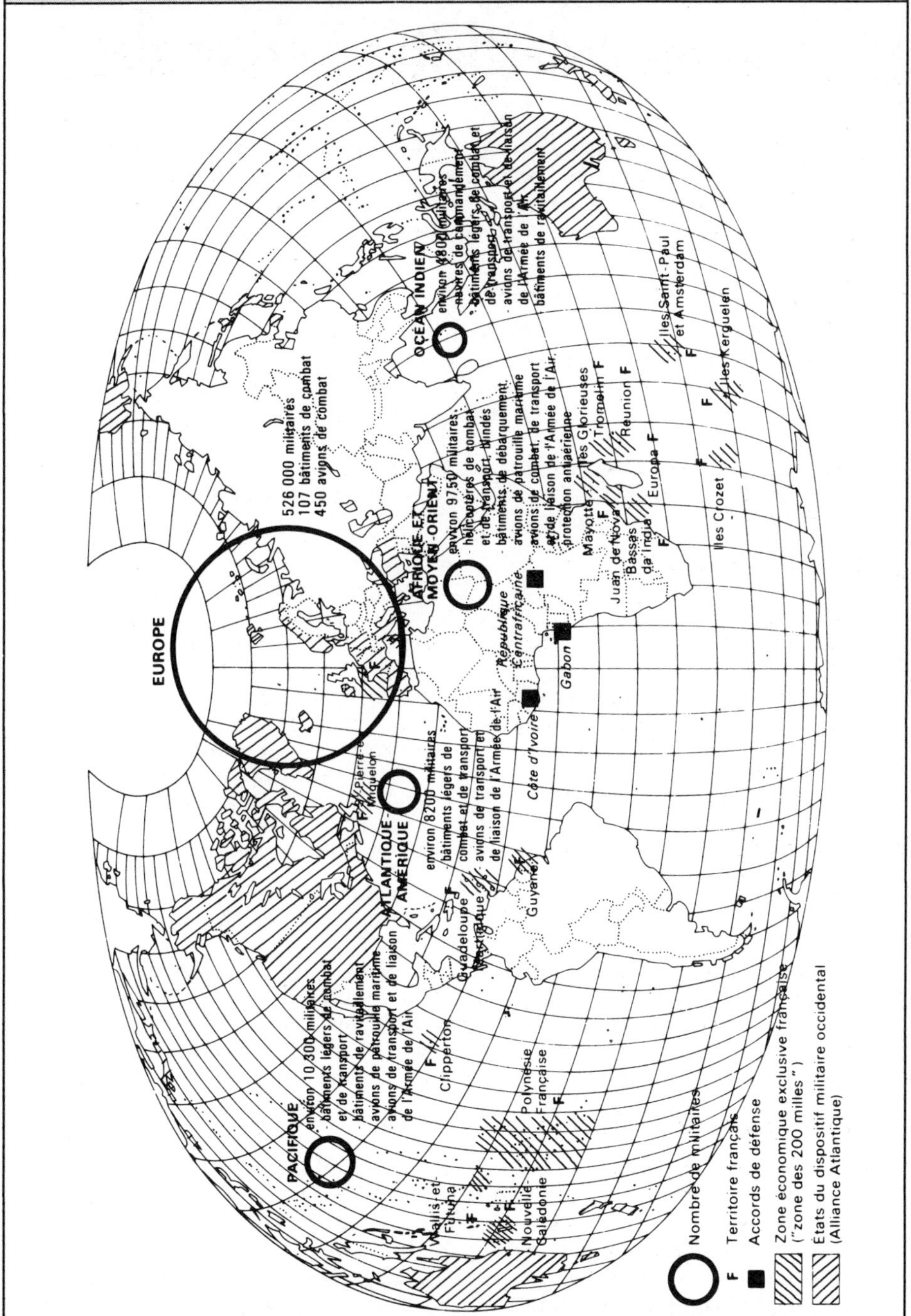

EUROPE
526 000 militaires
107 bâtiments de combat
450 avions de combat
OCÉAN INDIEN
environ 4800 militaires
navires de commandement
bâtiments légers de combat et de transport
avions de transport et de liaison de l'Armée de l'Air
bâtiments de ravitaillement
AFRIQUE ET MOYEN-ORIENT
environ 9750 militaires
hélicoptères de combat et de transport, blindés
bâtiments de débarquement
avions de patrouille maritime
avions de combat, de transport et de liaison de l'Armée de l'Air
protection antiaérienne
ATLANTIQUE-AMÉRIQUE
environ 8200 militaires
bâtiments légers de combat et de transport
avions de transport et de liaison de l'Armée de l'Air
PACIFIQUE
environ 10 300 militaires
bâtiments légers de combat et de transport
bâtiments de ravitaillement
avions de patrouille maritime
avions de transport et de liaison de l'Armée de l'Air
Saint-Pierre-et-Miquelon
Guadeloupe
Martinique
Guyane
Côte d'Ivoire
Gabon
République Centrafricaine
Mayotte
Juan de Nova
Bassas da India
Europa
Îles Glorieuses
Tromelin
Réunion
Îles Crozet
Îles Kerguelen
Îles Saint-Paul et Amsterdam
Clipperton
Polynésie Française
Nouvelle-Calédonie
Wallis et Futuna
Nombre de militaires
F Territoire français
Accords de défense
Zone économique exclusive française ("zone des 200 milles")
États du dispositif militaire occidental (Alliance Atlantique)

Les territoires d'outre-mer et les collectivités territoriales

Les territoires d'outre-mer font partie de la République française. Ils ne font pas partie du Marché Commun. Ils sont représentés à l'Assemblée nationale, au Sénat et au Conseil économique et social.

■ Nouvelle-Calédonie et Polynésie

— Nouvelle-Calédonie : île de la Nouvelle-Calédonie, île des Pins, îles Loyauté, îles du Nord, situées dans l'océan Pacifique.

— Polynésie française : 150 îles dans la partie orientale du Pacifique. Iles de la Société, l'archipel des Tuamotu-Gambier, l'archipel des Marquises, les îles Australes.

— La Nouvelle-Calédonie et la Polynésie française disposent d'une large autonomie (loi du 6/9/84). Ces statuts reconnaissent l'identité propre du territoire (emblème, hymne, langue).

■ Wallis et Futuna

— Deux archipels situés à 230 km l'un de l'autre au nord d'une ligne allant des îles Fidji aux Samoa, à 200 km de la Nouvelle-Calédonie et à 300 km de Tahiti.

— Territoires d'outre-mer, Wallis et Futuna disposent d'un statut d'autonomie (loi du 19/7/61) : un administrateur supérieur représente le gouvernement de la République, une Assemblée territoriale, un Conseil de territoire de 6 membres dont 3 sont membres de droit (les 3 chefs traditionnels ou « rois » de Wallis et Futuna).

■ Les Terres Australes et Antarctiques françaises (T.A.A.F.)

— Elle sont divisées en quatre districts très éloignés les uns des autres : îles Saint-Paul et Amsterdam, îles des Crozet, îles des Kerguelen, Terre Adélie.

— Territoires d'outre-mer, les Terres Australes et Antarctiques (leur siège est à Paris) sont placées sous l'autorité d'un Administrateur supérieur qui relève directement du Secrétariat d'État* aux DOM-TOM. Un conseil p. 40
consultatif de sept membres est chargé d'assister le chef du territoire. Les T.A.A.F. n'ont pas de représentants parlementaires.

■ Saint-Pierre et Miquelon et Mayotte

— Saint-Pierre et Miquelon : situé dans l'océan Atlantique, à l'entrée du golfe du Saint-Laurent, à moins de 25 km des côtes de Terre-Neuve.

— Mayotte : île qui fait partie de l'archipel des Comores, à l'entrée nord du canal du Mozambique, dans l'océan Indien.

— Collectivités territoriales de la République, Saint-Pierre et Miquelon ainsi que Mayotte sont administrés par un Conseil général, un préfet, p. 90
commissaire de la République, représente le gouvernement.

DOM-TOM - COLLECTIVITÉS TERRITORIALES ?

	Superficie (en km²)	Nombre d'habitants	Distance de Paris (en km)
Départements d'outre-mer (1)			
— Guadeloupe	1 780	328 400	6 792
— Martinique	1 100	326 536	6 858
— Guyane	90 000	73 022	7 072
— Réunion	2 510	515 808	9 342
TOTAL	95 390	1 243 766	
Territoires d'outre-mer (2)			
— Nouvelle-Calédonie	19 103	145 368	16 743
— Polynésie française	4 200	166 753	15 713
— Wallis et Futuna	274	12 408	16 065
— T.A.A.F.	439 603	200	
TOTAL	463 180	324 729	
Collectivités territoriales			
— Mayotte	375	54 600	7 953
— Saint-Pierre et Miquelon	242	6 041	4 279
TOTAL	617	60 641	
TOTAL GÉNÉRAL	559 187	1 629 136	

(1) Résultats du recensement de 1982
(2) Résultats du recensement de 1983

UNE POPULATION MOBILE

- **En près de 30 ans, de 1954 à 1982, le nombre de personnes nées dans les DOM-TOM installées en métropole a été multiplié par plus de 11.**
- **Plus d'une personne sur cinq née aux Antilles vit en métropole.**
- **Sur 10 personnes nées dans les DOM-TOM recensées en métropole en mars 1982, 6 sont installées en région Ile-de-France.**
- **Dans les TOM, la monnaie utilisée est le franc du Pacifique (100 CFP = 5,50 FF).**

Les différents tribunaux

Les tribunaux veillent à l'application des règles de droit; placés sous la responsabilité de l'État, ils rendent la justice « Au nom du peuple français ».

■ Le Tribunal des Conflits

Une affaire complexe dépend-elle des juridictions administratives ou des juridictions judiciaires ? C'est le Tribunal des Conflits qui décide quelle est la juridiction compétente.

■ Les juridictions administratives

Le Conseil d'État et les Tribunaux administratifs sont compétents pour régler les conflits entre les individus et l'administration. Selon l'importance de l'affaire c'est le Conseil d'État ou le tribunal administratif qui examine les recours après les élections ou les différends entre les individus et les collectivités locales.

■ Les juridictions judiciaires pénales

La Cour d'Assise, le Tribunal Correctionnel, le Tribunal de Police* répriment et sanctionnent les atteintes à la loi. La gravité de l'infraction détermine le tribunal qui juge. p. 124, 122 et 120

■ Les juridictions judiciaires civiles

Le Tribunal d'Instance et le Tribunal de Grande Instance* règlent les problèmes nés des relations entre individus (dettes, contrats, divorces, etc.). p. 116 et 118

■ Les tribunaux d'exception

Ils sont compétents au cours de l'activité professionnelle.

Le Conseil de Prud'hommes.

Le tribunal de Commerce.

Le tribunal des Baux ruraux.

La commission de la Sécurité sociale.

■ Les juridictions judiciaires de recours

La Cour d'Appel* rejuge lorsqu'une des parties n'est pas satisfaite du jugement. p. 132

La Cour de Cassation* juge la forme du jugement et assure une certaine uniformité dans l'interprétation des lois. p. 134

ORGANISATION SIMPLIFIÉE DES TRIBUNAUX

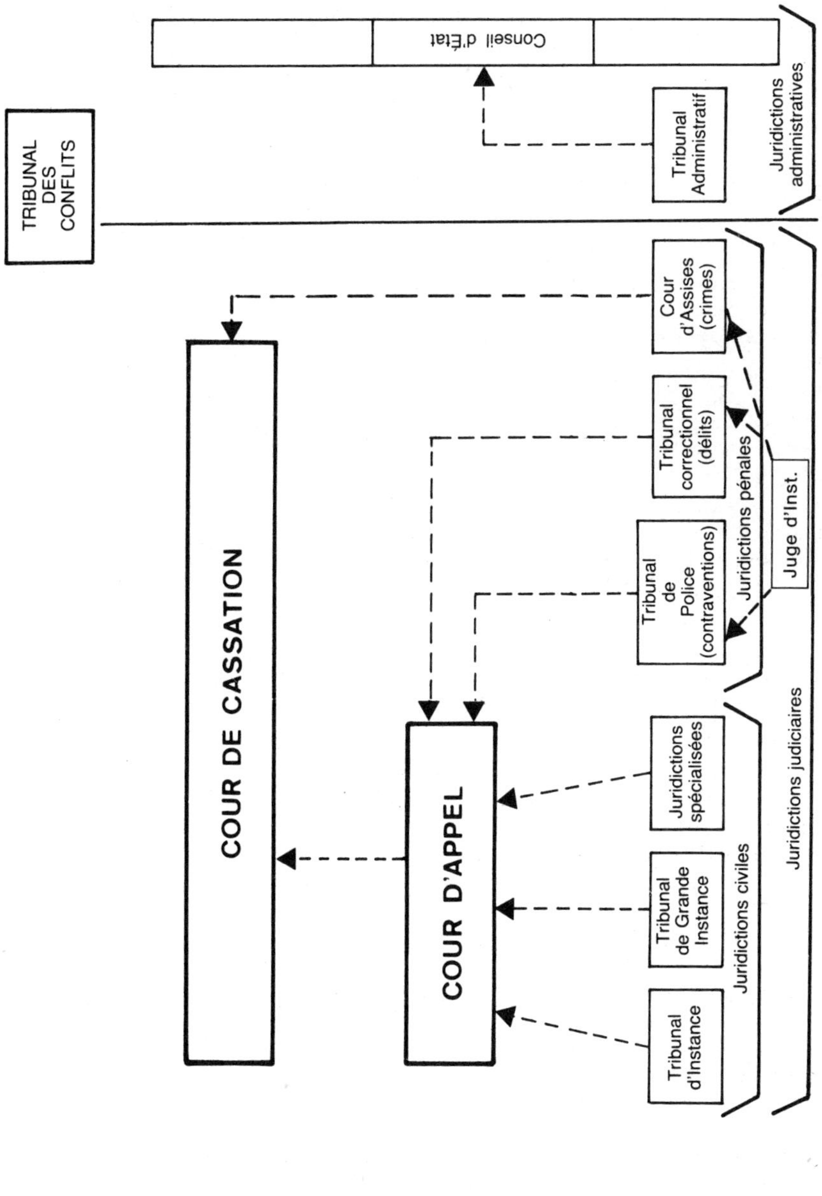

* Tribunal de Commerce, Conseil de Prud'hommes, Juge des loyers commerciaux, Commission du Contentieux de la Sécurité sociale, etc.

Le personnel de la justice

Il existe deux grandes catégories de personnel. L'une chargée de rendre la justice ou de requérir : ce sont les magistrats. L'autre est chargée d'aider les justiciables : ce sont les avocats. Ils sont aidés par les auxiliaires de justice.

■ Les magistrats du siège : les juges

— Les juges instruisent les affaires et tranchent les conflits en rendant des jugements ou des ordonnances. On les appelle les magistrats du siège car ils rendent la justice assis. Nommés par le gouvernement*, ils sont inamovibles, c'est-à-dire qu'on ne peut les déplacer sans leur accord, ils répondent de leurs actes devant le Conseil supérieur de la Magistrature. p. 40

— Le Conseil supérieur de la Magistrature comprend 9 membres désignés par le Président de la République* : 3 membres de la Cour de Cassation, 3 magistrats du siège, 1 Conseiller d'État et 2 personnalités n'appartenant pas à la magistrature. p. 36

Son président est le Président de la République, son vice-président le Garde des Sceaux. Quand il est réuni en Conseil de Discipline, il est présidé par le Premier Président de la Cour de Cassation*. p. 134

Le C.S.M. est garant de l'indépendance des magistrats (art. 65 de la Constitution).

— Certains juges ont des fonctions particulières :

• Le Juge d'Instruction, c'est un magistrat du siège qui est saisi des affaires pénales. Il rassemble les éléments du dossier et renvoie l'affaire devant le tribunal compétent. Il décide de la détention provisoire.

La réforme du code de procédure pénale prévoit que dans les affaires graves ou délicates il ne soit plus seul. L'instruction est suivie par trois juges.

• Le Juge de l'application des peines intervient après le jugement pendant l'exécution de la peine et même après la sortie de prison.

■ Les magistrats du Parquet ou ministère public

— Ce sont les procureurs et les substituts. Ils réclament l'application de la loi devant les tribunaux, ils sont chargés de défendre la société. On les appelle magistrats du parquet, ils requièrent debout.

— Les procureurs dirigent la police judiciaire* (police et gendarmerie), ils reçoivent les plaintes et veillent à l'exécution des décisions du tribunal. Nommés par le gouvernement, c'est un corps hiérarchisé soumis à l'autorité du Garde des Sceaux (ministre de la Justice). p. 70

Les avocats

Ils servent d'intermédiaire entre le plaideur et le juge. Spécialistes du Droit ils conseillent soit en renseignant, soit en aidant à rédiger un acte, soit en cherchant un règlement amiable. Ils assistent le justiciable dans ses contacts avec les juridictions. Ils prennent la parole devant le tribunal et rédigent les actes qui exposent les points de vue du plaideur. Ils représentent le demandeur ou le défendeur et accomplissent les actes en leur nom.

Les greffiers

Ce sont des fonctionnaires chargés de l'administration des juridictions. Ils conservent les scellés, l'argent consigné lors d'un procès et les archives. Ils assistent aux audiences et gardent les traces de leur déroulement. Ils consignent les interrogatoires menés par les Juges d'Instruction. Ils tiennent les registres du tribunal et délivrent les copies des jugements.

Les avoués

— Les avoués exercent devant la Cour d'Appel* et rédigent les actes de la procédure, en particulier les déclarations d'appel, mais ils ne plaident pas devant la Cour. p. 132

Les conseils juridiques

— Les conseils juridiques donnent des conseils et rédigent les actes, en particulier auprès du Tribunal de Commerce et des Administrations.

Les huissiers

— Les huissiers portent à domicile les décisions de justice ou les assignations, ils font des constats à la demande des particuliers ou des magistrats. Ils pratiquent les saisies.

Le Tribunal administratif

Il juge les litiges entre l'Administration et les particuliers. Le particulier peut demander l'annulation d'une décision, c'est le recours en excès de pouvoir, ou demander réparation, c'est le recours en pleine juridiction.

■ Qui juge ?

— Ce ne sont pas des magistrats, ce sont d'anciens élèves de l'École nationale d'Administration (ENA). Fonctionnaires nommés par décret, ils dépendent du ministre de l'Intérieur. p. 70

— Ils sont indépendants mais ne sont pas inamovibles. Ils sont à la fois conseillers administratifs auprès des commissaires de la République du département et juges administratifs. p. 68

■ Quelles affaires le Tribunal administratif juge-t-il ?

— Il juge : tout ce qui concerne une décision de l'Administration, la plupart des dommages entraînés par l'activité de l'Administration, tous les contrats passés par l'Administration, les litiges relatifs aux impôts directs et à la TVA. p. 64

— Exceptions : les accidents de la circulation (même si un véhicule de l'Administration est en cause), les impôts indirects, les litiges concernant les services publics industriels (SNCF, EDF...) pour lesquels les juridictions judiciaires restent compétentes.

■ Quand recourir au Tribunal administratif ?

— Soit après, soit en l'absence d'une décision de l'Administration

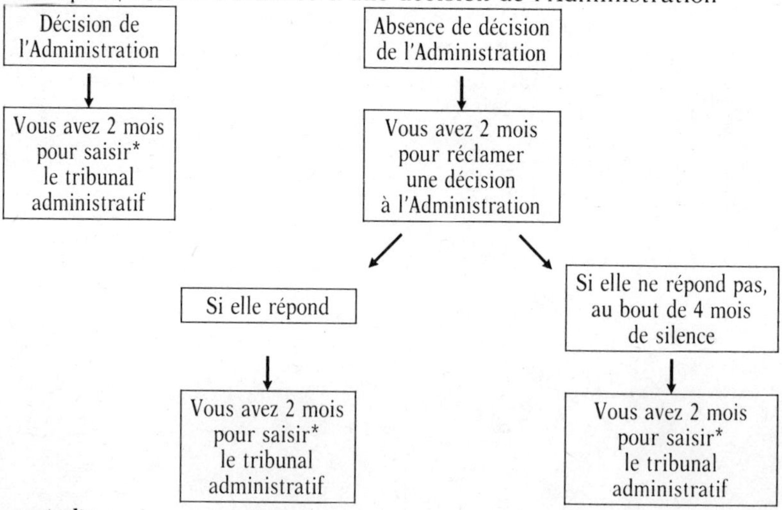
Décision de l'Administration
Vous avez 2 mois pour saisir* le tribunal administratif
Absence de décision de l'Administration
Vous avez 2 mois pour réclamer une décision à l'Administration
Si elle répond
Vous avez 2 mois pour saisir* le tribunal administratif
Si elle ne répond pas, au bout de 4 mois de silence
Vous avez 2 mois pour saisir* le tribunal administratif

Cas particuliers :

Élections municipales ou cantonales, vous n'avez que 15 jours pour en contester* les résultats.

— Avant d'agir devant le Tribunal administratif, deux solutions existent :

Le recours gracieux en s'adressant à l'Administration avec laquelle existe le litige.

Le recours hiérarchique en s'adressant à l'autorité supérieure, par exemple au commissaire de la République pour la décision prise par le maire.

■ La procédure

Le tribunal compétent est celui du lieu du contentieux, par exemple le lieu du dommage ou le lieu où est situé un immeuble dans le cas d'un problème d'urbanisme. Dans les autres cas il faut saisir le Tribunal administratif dont dépend l'administration qui a pris la décision contestée.

— Le tribunal est saisi par l'envoi d'une lettre recommandée dans laquelle on expose ses griefs et ses prétentions, c'est la requête.

— Toute la procédure est écrite, au moment de l'audience un juge (le commissaire du gouvernement) expose les faits et les arguments de chacun. Il s'appuie sur le dossier et présente ses conclusions au tribunal.

Il n'est pas chargé de défendre l'Administration, il doit éclairer le tribunal, et peut conclure par une condamnation de l'État.

— Les juges, 3 en général, se réunissent pour prendre une décision, et rendent leur jugement à une date qu'ils précisent à la fin de l'audience. Cette action qui consiste à rendre un jugement non à l'issue de l'audience, mais plus tard, s'appelle la mise en délibéré.

— Le jugement est notifié aux intéressés par lettre recommandée.

■ Quelles peuvent être les décisions du Tribunal ?

Le Tribunal administratif peut annuler la décision de l'Administration si la loi n'a pas été respectée. Il peut aussi attribuer une indemnité pour réparer le dommage causé à quelqu'un par l'Administration.

■ Y a-t-il des voies de recours ?

L'appel est possible devant le Conseil d'État*. L'assistance d'un avocat au p. 114
Conseil d'État est alors obligatoire.

■ Les privilèges de l'Administration

Le privilège du préalable, c'est-à-dire qu'elle peut faire valoir ce qu'elle pense être son droit sans intervention du juge ; le privilège de l'exécution d'office, c'est-à-dire qu'elle peut recourir à la contrainte pour faire exécuter une décision ; agissant ainsi elle oblige l'individu à se placer en position de demandeur alors qu'elle-même se trouve dans la position plus confortable de défendeur.

Le Conseil d'État

Le Conseil d'État participe ou aide par ses conseils à rédiger des projets de loi et de décrets. Le Conseil d'État est ensuite chargé de juger les litiges dans lesquels l'administration est mise en cause. Il devient ainsi la juridiction suprême en matière administrative.

■ Qui est membre du Conseil d'État ?

— Les membres du Conseil d'État sont des fonctionnaires* et non des magistrats, ils ne sont pas inamovibles. Il y a quatre grades parmi le personnel du Conseil d'État : p. 65

• Les Auditeurs de seconde classe issus de l'École nationale d'Administration (ENA) et les Auditeurs de première classe choisis parmi les précédents.
• Les Maîtres des requêtes, 3/4 sont pris parmi les Auditeurs, 1/4 vient de l'Administration.
• Les Conseillers d'État, recrutés 2/3 parmi les Maîtres des requêtes et 1/3 dans l'Administration.
• Il existe aussi des Conseillers d'État en service extraordinaire, ils sont nommés pour une durée limitée par le gouvernement en raison de leurs compétences.

— Le Premier ministre* est le président du Conseil d'État, son suppléant est le ministre de la Justice. Ils assurent très rarement cette fonction qui est exercée par le vice-président du Conseil d'État. p. 38

— Les Auditeurs et les Maîtres des requêtes préparent les dossiers qui seront ensuite examinés par les différentes formations du Conseil d'État.

— Les Conseillers d'État délibèrent et décident sur les affaires qui leur sont soumises.

■ Quel est le rôle du Conseil d'État ?

Il a un double rôle, celui de conseil et celui de juge.

— Un rôle de conseil pour les textes élaborés par le gouvernement* (qui peut ne pas en tenir compte) un rôle consultatif sur l'interprétation d'un texte administratif. Il donne son avis sur des décisions d'intérêt public : association, naturalisation, changement de nom par exemple. p. 40

— Le rôle juridictionnel est triple :

1. Il juge directement certaines affaires importantes, de portée nationale, annulation de décrets*, nomination de hauts fonctionnaires, décision d'un ordre professionnel : médecins, architectes, par exemple. p. 50
2. Il juge en appel les décisions des Tribunaux administratifs*. p. 112
3. Il est juge de Cassation des juridictions administratives spéciales : Commissions des pensions de guerre, des rapatriés, des conseils de l'ordre... et Cour des Comptes.

ORGANISATION ET PROCÉDURE

▲Organisation du Conseil d'État

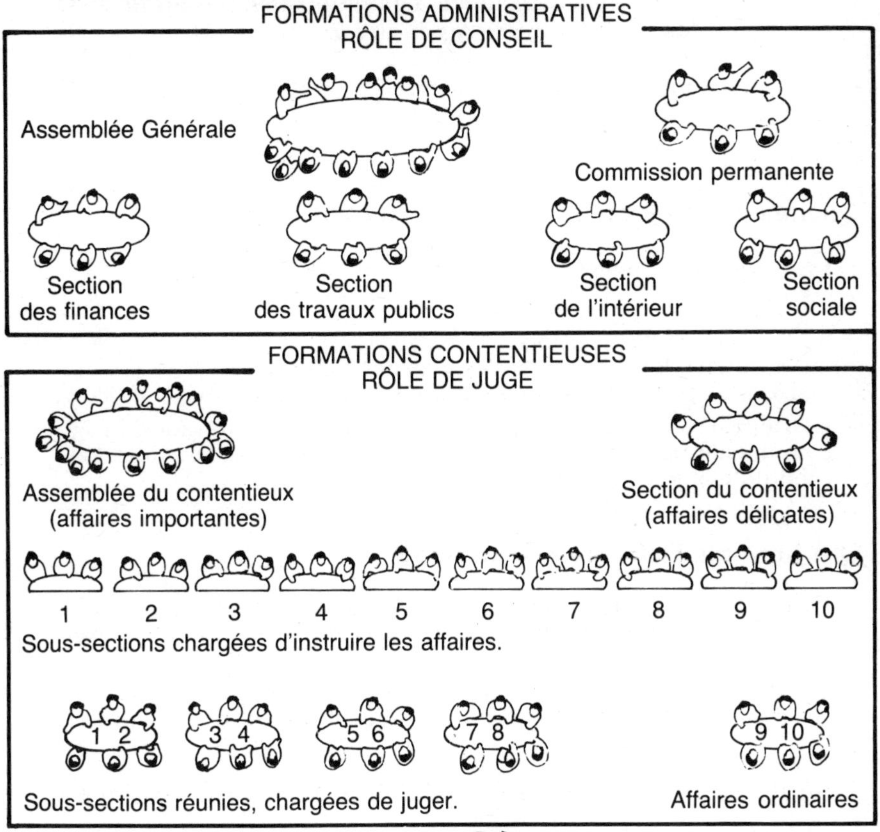

▲Quelle est la procédure ?

Si un jugement est contesté, le délai pour l'appel est de deux mois. La procédure est identique à celle du tribunal administratif, cependant l'assistance d'un avocat au Conseil d'État est obligatoire et toutes les observations sont faites par écrit.

LA COUR DES COMPTES

La Cour des Comptes contrôle les comptes de l'administration. Elle vérifie la bonne utilisation de l'argent de l'État.

En cas d'irrégularité elle forme une Cour de discipline budgétaire et financière qui instruit les affaires et peut condamner à des amendes.

La Cour des Comptes rédige un rapport annuel, dans lequel elle donne le résultat de ses vérifications et elle présente des suggestions pour améliorer les résultats des comptes publics.

Le Tribunal d'Instance

Le Tribunal d'Instance juge rapidement les affaires les plus simples entre les individus.

■ Quelles affaires du Tribunal d'Instance juge-t-il ?

— Le Tribunal d'Instance est compétent pour les litiges relatifs :
aux loyers
à la saisie des meubles
à l'exécution des pensions alimentaires
à la tutelle des mineurs et des majeurs handicapés
aux affaires qui mettent en jeu des sommes inférieures à 30000 F.

— Le tribunal compétent est celui du domicile du défendeur sauf s'il s'agit d'un mineur ou d'un majeur incompétent, dans ce cas le tribunal est celui du domicile de la personne à protéger.

■ Qui juge au Tribunal d'Instance ?

— Un juge unique, car les affaires sont simples et nécessitent une décision rapide. Souvent le juge cherchera une conciliation entre les adversaires.

— Les attributions du juge d'instance sont gracieuses lorsqu'il tente une conciliation, elles sont contentieuses lorsqu'il tranche dans un procès.

■ Y a-t-il des recours contre la décision du juge d'instance ?

Il y en a quatre :

1. L'opposition du défendeur absent et non représenté au procès.
2. La tierce opposition faite par une personne étrangère au procès mais qui peut être concernée par la décision.
3. L'appel*, si une des parties n'est pas satisfaite et que l'affaire porte sur une réclamation supérieure à 13000 F. Le délai est d'un mois. p. 132
4. Le pourvoi en cassation si l'une des parties estime que la procédure n'a pas été régulière, et s'il n'est pas possible de faire appel en raison du montant du litige. p. 134

PROCÉDURES

Au tribunal d'instance, comment une affaire se déroule-t-elle ?

On peut soit se défendre seul, soit se faire représenter (la présence d'un avocat n'est pas obligatoire). Trois possibilités peuvent se présenter.

▲ Possibilité 1 : la conciliation

Le demandeur s'adresse au tribunal pour faire comparaître son adversaire. Le juge tente une conciliation.

▲ Possibilité 2 : le jugement

Si la conciliation échoue, le juge délivre la citation à comparaître devant le tribunal.

A l'audience, le tribunal est informé de la nature du litige et des réclamations. Après avoir entendu les parties le juge décide.

▲ Possibilité 3 : l'injonction de payer

Dans le cas d'une dette non payée, le créancier présente sa requête au juge. Si le juge estime la créance justifiée il autorise l'injonction de payer (on demande au débiteur de payer sa dette). L'injonction de payer est signifiée par exploit d'huissier ou par lettre recommandée du greffier.

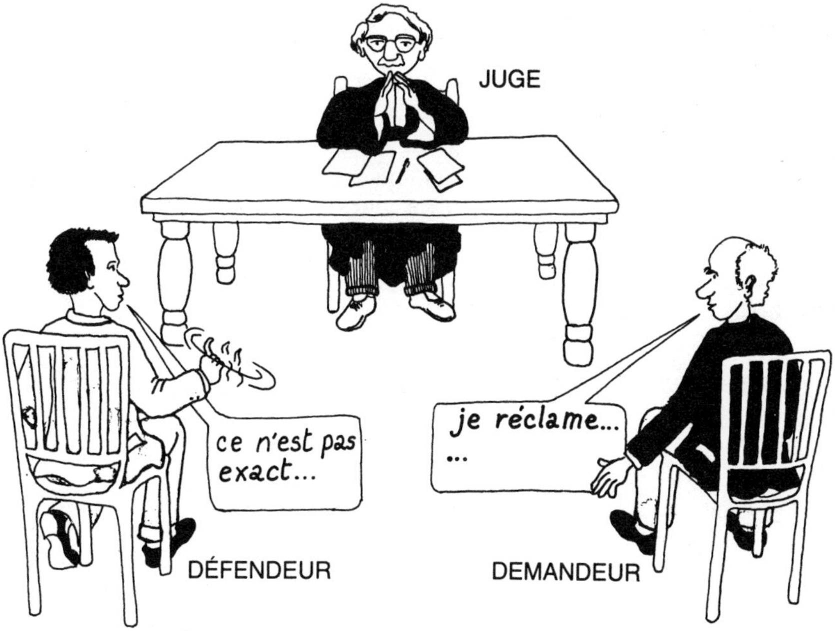

Le Tribunal de Grande Instance

Le Tribunal de Grande Instance (T.G.I.) juge les affaires complexes sur le plan des personnes et sur celui des biens. Les audiences sont publiques, sauf dans le cas d'affaires familiales (divorce par exemple) où le procès a lieu en Chambre du Conseil. La présence d'un avocat est obligatoire.

■ Quelles affaires le Tribunal de Grande Instance juge-t-il ?

— Le Tribunal de Grande Instance est compétent pour les affaires relatives aux personnes : divorce, filiation, adoption, successions, nationalités, rectification d'état civil.

— Il est également compétent pour certaines affaires relatives aux biens : droit de propriété, brevet d'invention, saisie d'immeubles, expropriation, affaires qui mettent en jeu des sommes supérieures à 30 000 F.

— Le tribunal compétent territorialement est toujours celui du défendeur sauf s'il s'agit : d'un immeuble, d'une succession, d'un contrat : le tribunal est celui du lieu où ils sont situés ou exécutés.
Ou s'il s'agit d'une pension alimentaire, le tribunal est alors celui du demandeur.

■ Qui juge au Tribunal de Grande Instance ?

— Trois juges, c'est une juridiction collégiale.

— Le Président peut statuer sur le fond du litige en cas d'urgence, par une ordonnance de référé. Il est juge des référés.

— Le Président peut satisfaire la requête d'une des parties, protéger les biens réclamés (par exemple). Il est alors juge des requêtes.

■ Y a-t-il des recours contre la décision du Tribunal de Grande Instance ?

Les voies de recours sont les mêmes que pour le Tribunal d'Instance*, l'opposition, la tierce opposition, l'appel, le pourvoi en cassation. p. 116

LE DÉROULEMENT D'UNE AFFAIRE

Au Tribunal de Grande Instance, comment une affaire se déroule-t-elle ?

1. Introduction de l'instance

   L'assignation : le défendeur est mis au courant du contenu exact du litige et des réclamations faites par le demandeur; cet acte rédigé par un huissier est appelé exploit d'huissier.

2. Instruction de l'affaire

   La reproduction de l'acte d'assignation est remise au greffe.

   Le greffier inscrit l'affaire au rôle et lui donne un numéro.

   Le défendeur charge un avocat de le défendre, les parties échangent leurs prétentions et leurs conclusions.

3. Jugement

A l'audience les avocats font connaître oralement leurs conclusions.

Le juge décide.

Le greffier rédige l'original du jugement. Le jugement contient les noms des parties et le motif de la demande, les motifs ou « attendus » qui ont permis au juge de prendre sa décision, ainsi que les modalités d'exécution de la décision.

La première copie du jugement est envoyée aux avocats.

En cas de condamnation elle est signifiée par huissier à la personne condamnée.

Le Tribunal de Police

Le Tribunal de Police juge les infractions appelées contraventions : cueillir des fruits chez son voisin, stationner illégalement, laisser divaguer des animaux par exemple.
Les peines encourues vont jusqu'à 2 mois de prison et 6000 francs d'amende.

■ Qui juge au Tribunal de Police ?

— C'est le juge d'Instance, assité d'un greffier*, qui décide seul en matière pénale. p. 110

— Le ministère public est représenté par le procureur de la République* ou un substitut. Dans les cas les moins graves c'est le commissaire de police* qui fait office de ministère public. p. 110 p. 71

■ Comment fonctionne le Tribunal de Police ?

— Il y a trois types d'actions.

— La procédure normale : celui qui a commis une contravention est convoqué devant le Tribunal pour répondre aux accusations portées contre lui par le ministère public. Le contrevenant peut se faire représenter par un avocat.

— Une procédure simplifiée : l'ordonnance pénale. Le juge décide à partir du dossier. Lorsque la décision du juge a été communiquée au contrevenant, celui-ci a 30 jours pour payer l'amende ou pour faire opposition, dans cette dernière hypothèse le juge revient à la procédure normale.

— L'amende forfaitaire : elle concerne les contraventions les moins graves et les plus fréquentes. Le contrevenant peut payer au moment où l'agent verbalise, ou régler par un timbre amende. Si on conteste la contravention on revient à une procédure normale.

■ Y a-t-il un recours contre la décision du Tribunal de Police ?

Il est possible de faire appel* si la peine est supérieure à 5 jours de prison ou à 160 francs d'amende. p. 132

Sinon le pourvoi en cassation* est possible. p. 134

L'ENQUÊTE ET L'INSTRUCTION

On est poursuivi par la justice pénale après une enquête et une instruction.

L'enquête recherche qui a commis l'infraction.

L'instruction tente à la fois d'éclairer les circonstances de l'infraction et la personnalité du responsable.

▲ L'enquête

L'enquête est menée par la police judiciaire (police ou gendarmerie) placée sous l'autorité du procureur. Cette enquête est déclenchée soit après une plainte de la victime, soit après la constatation de l'infraction.

▲ L'instruction par le juge d'instruction

L'instruction est facultative pour les contraventions, elle est obligatoire pour les crimes.

Le juge d'instruction rassemble les renseignements sur la personnalité de l'inculpé et recherche des preuves. Il peut désigner des experts et nommer des commissions rogatoires (faire procéder à des perquisitions ou à des saisies). Il délivre les mandats d'arrêt et décide de la détention provisoire. Lorsque l'instruction est terminée, il renvoie l'affaire devant la juridiction compétente.

▲ L'instruction par la Chambre des mises en accusation

— En cas de renvoi devant la Cour d'Assises, il y a vérification d'instruction, devant la Chambre des mises en accusation. Elle confirme la juridiction qui doit juger. Si les preuves sont insuffisantes, la Chambre des mises en accusation peut délivrer un non-lieu, au contraire si les preuves sont concordantes elle délivre un arrêt de mise en accusation : l'inculpé devient accusé.

— La Chambre des mises en accusation est l'organisme d'appel des décisions du juge d'instruction.

▲ La justice pénale : caractéristiques

Elle juge tous les actes qui sont des infractions à la loi. Le Code Pénal contient un inventaire des infractions et des peines qui leur sont applicables.

Il y a une double action : l'action publique qui doit punir et l'action civile qui doit réparer.

Le ministère public réclame une punition au nom de la société, c'est l'action publique.

La partie civile réclame pour la victime ou sa famille la réparation du dommage, c'est l'action civile.

Le Tribunal Correctionnel

Le Tribunal Correctionnel juge les infractions appelées délits : le vol, l'escroquerie, l'abandon de famille par exemple.
La peine encourue au Tribunal Correctionnel peut aller jusqu'à 20 ans d'emprisonnement.

■ Comment le Tribunal Correctionnel est-il saisi ?

— Par le juge d'instruction* après l'enquête et l'instruction. p. 110

— Par le procureur après une plainte ou un flagrant délit.

— Par la victime si les preuves sont suffisantes pour que l'affaire ne réclame pas d'instruction.

■ Quel est le Tribunal Correctionnel qui va juger ?

Le Tribunal Correctionnel sur le territoire duquel le délit a été commis. Cependant d'autres tribunaux correctionnels peuvent être saisis : celui dont dépend le domicile du prévenu, celui du lieu de l'arrestation, celui du lieu de l'emprisonnement de l'inculpé.

■ Qui juge au Tribunal Correctionnel ?

Trois juges, c'est une juridiction collégiale.

Le ministère public est représenté par le procureur* ou un substitut. p. 110

Si le président le décide, le juge peut être unique, pour les chèques sans provision, pour les blessures par imprudence par exemple.

■ Quelle est la procédure au Tribunal Correctionnel ?

1. Le prévenu est interrogé sur son identité et sur les circonstances dans lesquelles l'acte a été commis.
2. Le ministère public présente les preuves, ensuite le président écoute et interroge les témoins.
3. On écoute ensuite la plaidoirie de la partie civile (si elle existe), puis intervient le procureur (ou le substitut); il réclame une peine ou tout simplement l'application de la loi, c'est-à-dire la peine inscrite au Code Pénal pour le délit en cause. Enfin l'avocat de la défense tente d'expliquer et d'excuser le prévenu.
4. Les trois juges se retirent pour délibérer ou même se concertent à voix basse avant de rendre le jugement.
5. La sentence est prononcée par le président, elle est motivée et rendue publiquement.

Les procès du Tribunal Correctionnel sont publics.

DU DÉLIT A LA CONDAMNATION

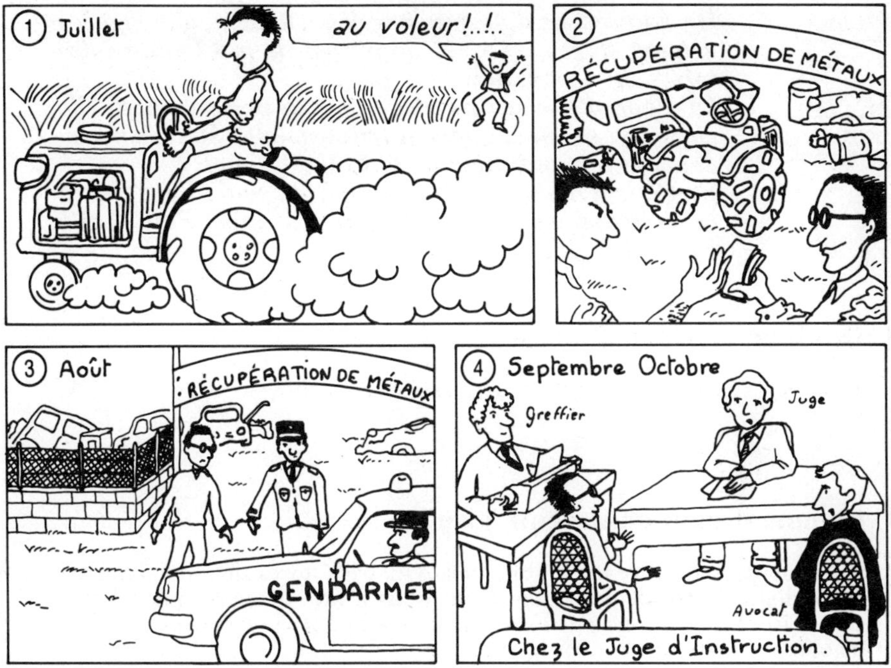

LE CASIER JUDICIAIRE

Toutes les condamnations sont inscrites sur un fichier national, le casier judiciaire. Il existe trois types d'extraits :

- le bulletin n° 1 contient toutes les condamnations ; il est destiné aux autorités judiciaires ;
- le bulletin n° 2 ne comporte que certaines condamnations; il est destiné à l'administration ;
- le bulletin n° 3 comporte les condamnations à plus de 2 ans d'emprisonnement et certaines interdictions, c'est celui qui vous est envoyé.

Pour obtenir un extrait de votre casier judiciaire, il faut le demander au Casier judiciaire national 10, rue Lancheau, 44079 Nantes, en joignant une fiche d'état civil.

La Cour d'Assises

Il y a une Cour d'Assises par département, elle juge les crimes, après un arrêt de renvoi de la Chambre des mises en accusation.
La Cour d'Assises ne siège pas en permanence, elle siège par session, souvent trimestrielle, sous la présidence d'un conseiller de la Cour d'Appel.
En Cour d'Assises, la condamnation peut aller jusqu'à la réclusion perpétuelle. La peine de mort a été abolie en 1981.

■ Qui juge en Cour d'Assises ?

Trois juges professionnels (la cour), assistés de 9 citoyens tirés au sort (le jury).

■ Comment peut-on devenir juré ?

Une liste préparatoire est établie par le maire*, après un tirage au sort sur la liste électorale de la commune. Mais il faut avoir plus de 23 ans, savoir lire et écrire, ne pas avoir été condamné, ni exercer une activité incompatible (policier, député, etc.). p. 96

A partir des listes préparatoires, une commission établit une liste annuelle. Sur cette liste, le président du TGI de la ville où siège la Cour d'Assises tire au sort le jury d'Assises composé de 35 jurés titulaires et de 10 suppléants, 30 jours avant le début de la session. Ces jurés sont convoqués pour le début de la session. Le juré, ainsi désigné, doit se rendre à la convocation sous peine d'amende. (Des dispenses sont accordées dans certains cas : âge, maladie, voyage, si l'on a déjà été juré.)

■ Comment se déroule un procès aux Assises ?

La gravité des infractions jugées aux Assises, et le fait que les décisions ne pourront être remises en cause en appel, rendent la procédure complexe.

1. Avant l'audience :

   Le président rend visite à l'accusé. Il le prévient des charges retenues contre lui. Il l'interroge et s'assure qu'il bénéficie d'un avocat.

2. Au début de l'audience :

   Le président tire au sort les 9 jurés et leur fait prêter serment. Il fait l'appel des témoins qui se retirent pour ne paraître que lorsqu'ils seront appelés.

3. L'audience :

   Le greffier* lit l'arrêt de renvoi c'est-à-dire l'acte d'accusation. p. 110

   Le président interroge l'accusé sur son identité, son passé.

Le président entend ensuite les témoins et les experts qui jurent de « dire la vérité ».

L'avocat* de la partie civile plaide. p. 110

Le ministère public (avocat général) requiert et demande une peine.

L'avocat de l'accusé plaide pour tenter de diminuer ou d'excuser la faute.

Le président lit la liste des questions auxquelles la cour et le jury devront répondre, ceux-ci se retirent pour délibérer.

COUR D'ASSISES

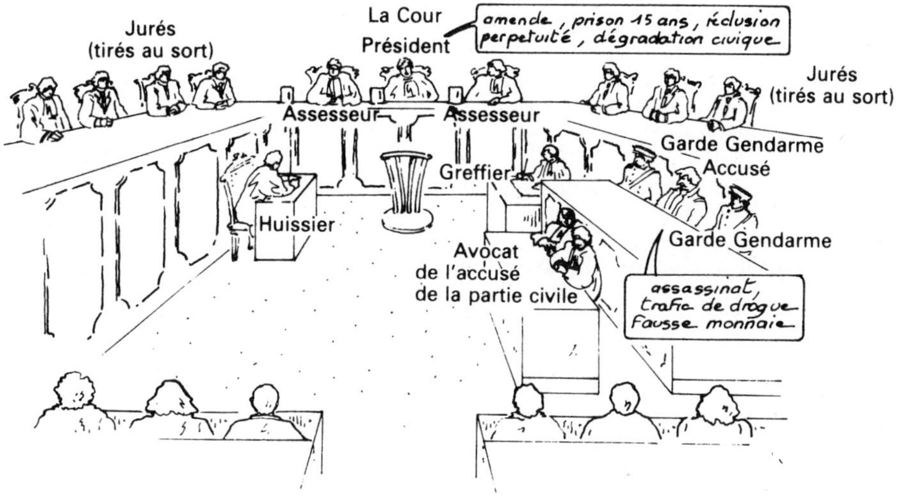

4. Les délibérations :

La cour et le jury se retirent pour décider si l'accusé est coupable et s'il a des circonstances atténuantes.

Les délibérations ont lieu à huis clos, elles doivent rester secrètes même après le procès.

5. La sentence :

Après les délibérations, le président lit ce qui a été décidé :
- La culpabilité (8 voix contre 4 sont nécessaires).
- La peine (décidée à la majorité simple).
- Les dommages et intérêts accordés à la victime (décidés uniquement par la cour).

Le Tribunal pour enfants

La justice des mineurs s'intéresse à l'enfant et à l'adolescent.
Elle a un double aspect :
• au plan pénal, elle sanctionne et réinsère les mineurs délinquants ;
• au plan civil, elle protège des mineurs en danger physique ou moral.

■ Qui participe à la justice des mineurs ?

— Le Juge des enfants est désigné par décret pour 3 ans au sein de chaque Tribunal de Grande Instance*. Il est choisi parce qu'il s'intéresse aux jeunes. p. 118

— En cas de délit ou de crime, le procureur désigne un juge d'instruction* qui est en général spécialiste des problèmes des jeunes. p. 110

■ Quel est le déroulement d'une affaire ?

— S'il s'agit d'un délit, le Juge des enfants est assisté de deux assesseurs non professionnels.

Les assesseurs sont choisis pour 4 ans par le ministre de la Justice parmi des personnes qui s'intéressent à l'enfance.

— S'il s'agit d'un crime, la Cour d'Assises* des mineurs juge les mineurs, de plus de 16 ans, ayant commis un crime. p. 124

La démarche de la cour vise à répondre à deux interrogations : faut-il protéger ou condamner ? Faut-il, en fonction de l'âge, adoucir la peine ?

— Dans les deux cas, les débats ne sont pas publics, tout compte rendu de presse est interdit. La présence d'un avocat est obligatoire.

■ Quelles sont les mesures qui peuvent être prises ?

— Les enfants sont rarement mis en détention, ils sont placés dans un foyer d'accueil ou restent dans leur milieu familial sous le contrôle d'un éducateur. La mesure éducative est recherchée avant tout, la condamnation pénale doit rester une exception.

— L'éducateur doit apporter son aide et son soutien au jeune qui lui est confié et informer le magistrat de l'évolution de la situation.

FONCTIONNEMENT DE LA JUSTICE PÉNALE DES MINEURS

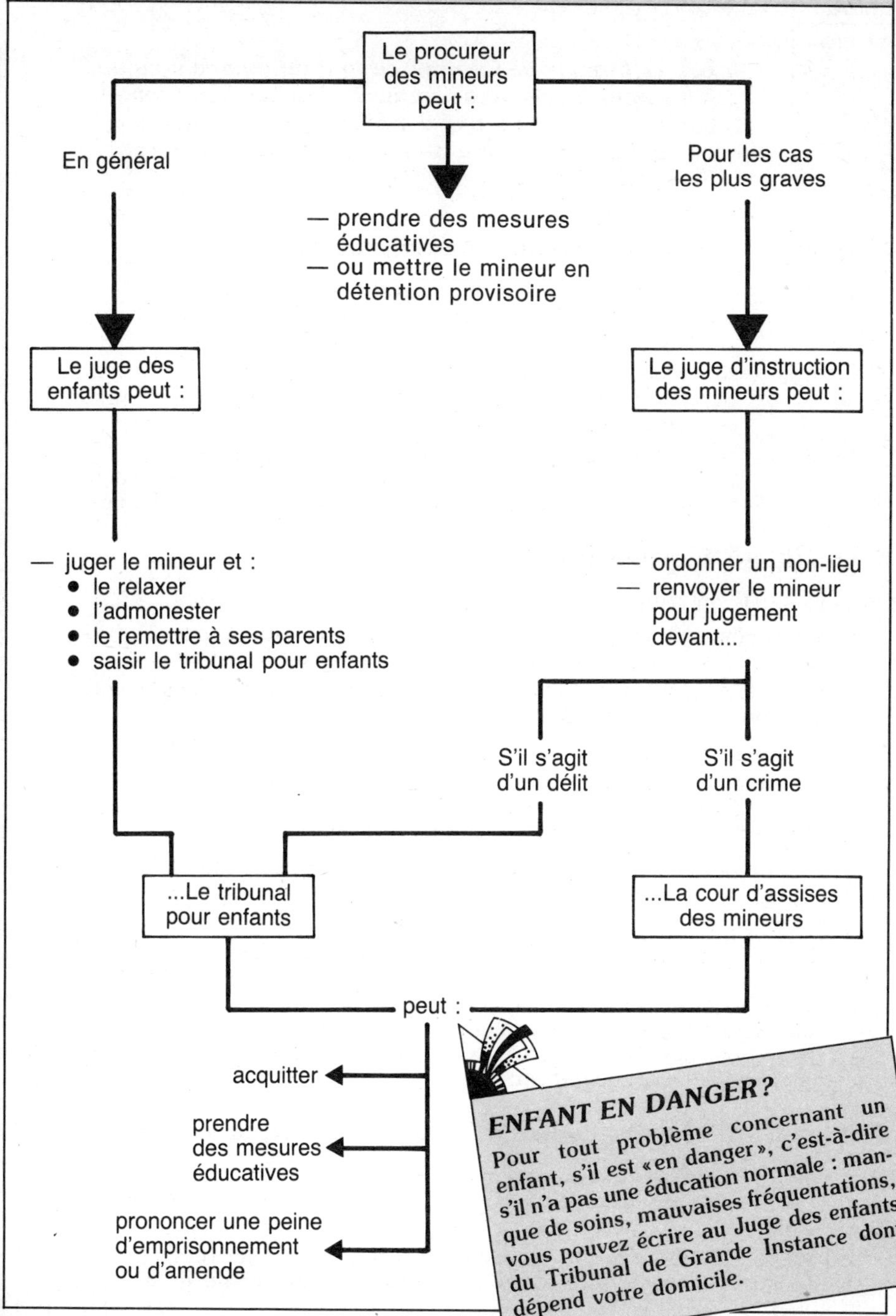

Le procureur des mineurs peut :
En général
Pour les cas les plus graves
— prendre des mesures éducatives
— ou mettre le mineur en détention provisoire
Le juge des enfants peut :
Le juge d'instruction des mineurs peut :
— juger le mineur et :
• le relaxer
• l'admonester
• le remettre à ses parents
• saisir le tribunal pour enfants
— ordonner un non-lieu
— renvoyer le mineur pour jugement devant...
S'il s'agit d'un délit
S'il s'agit d'un crime
...Le tribunal pour enfants
...La cour d'assises des mineurs
peut :
acquitter
prendre des mesures éducatives
prononcer une peine d'emprisonnement ou d'amende

ENFANT EN DANGER?

Pour tout problème concernant un enfant, s'il est « en danger », c'est-à-dire s'il n'a pas une éducation normale : manque de soins, mauvaises fréquentations, vous pouvez écrire au Juge des enfants du Tribunal de Grande Instance dont dépend votre domicile.

Le Tribunal de Commerce

Les Tribunaux de Commerce sont uniquement compétents pour les affaires commerciales. Les juges sont des commerçants élus par d'autres commerçants.
La justice est rendue plus rapidement que devant le Tribunal d'Instance.

■ Quelles affaires le Tribunal de Commerce juge-t-il ?

Les litiges entre commerçants dans l'exercice de leur commerce, contestation sur la conformité d'une marchandise, sur son prix, sur le délai de livraison, par exemple;

les litiges concernant les actes de commerce par nature, contestations sur la signature d'un effet de commerce : lettre de change, billet à ordre, par exemple;

les litiges concernant les actes de commerce par accessoire, contestations sur une transaction de nature civile, vente, location-gérance, engagée pour un commerce par exemple;

■ Quelle est la procédure suivie ?

— La saisie du tribunal

- Le demandeur dépose au greffe une assignation qui informe l'adversaire qu'il va y avoir une action contre lui devant le tribunal.
- Les adversaires déposent au greffe une requête conjointe dans laquelle ils exposent leurs désaccords.

— Le procès

- Si le dossier est complet, c'est-à-dire si les juges consulaires ont en mains tous les éléments pour leur permettre d'apprécier le litige, l'affaire est jugée à l'audience la plus proche.
- Si le dossier est insuffisant, un juge rapporteur est désigné pour mettre l'affaire en état, c'est-à-dire compléter le dossier.
- Le procès commercial ressemble à un procès civil.

Il y a assignation du défendeur, puis comparution devant le tribunal, soit en étant présent, soit en se faisant représenter par une personne de son choix ou un avocat*. La procédure est orale, le demandeur fait p. 110 connaître ses prétentions contenues dans l'assignation, le défendeur répond par des arguments oraux ou par écrit. Après avoir écouté les juges rendent leur jugement.

■ Y a-t-il un recours contre la décision du tribunal ?

Jusqu'à 13000 francs, le jugement est rendu en dernier ressort, c'est-à-dire qu'il n'est pas susceptible d'appel, seul le pourvoi en cassation est possible.

Au-delà de 13000 francs, le jugement est rendu en premier ressort, c'est-à-dire que l'on peut faire appel devant la Chambre civile de la Cour d'Appel*. p. 132

LES JUGES DU TRIBUNAL DE COMMERCE

▲ Les juges, appelés juges consulaires, sont élus pour deux ans par un collège électoral élu chaque année par les commerçants.

Pour être électeur : il faut être inscrit au registre du commerce.

Pour être éligible : il faut avoir plus de 30 ans, être inscrit au registre du commerce depuis plus de 5 ans.

▲ Le président du Tribunal de Commerce est élu pour trois ans.

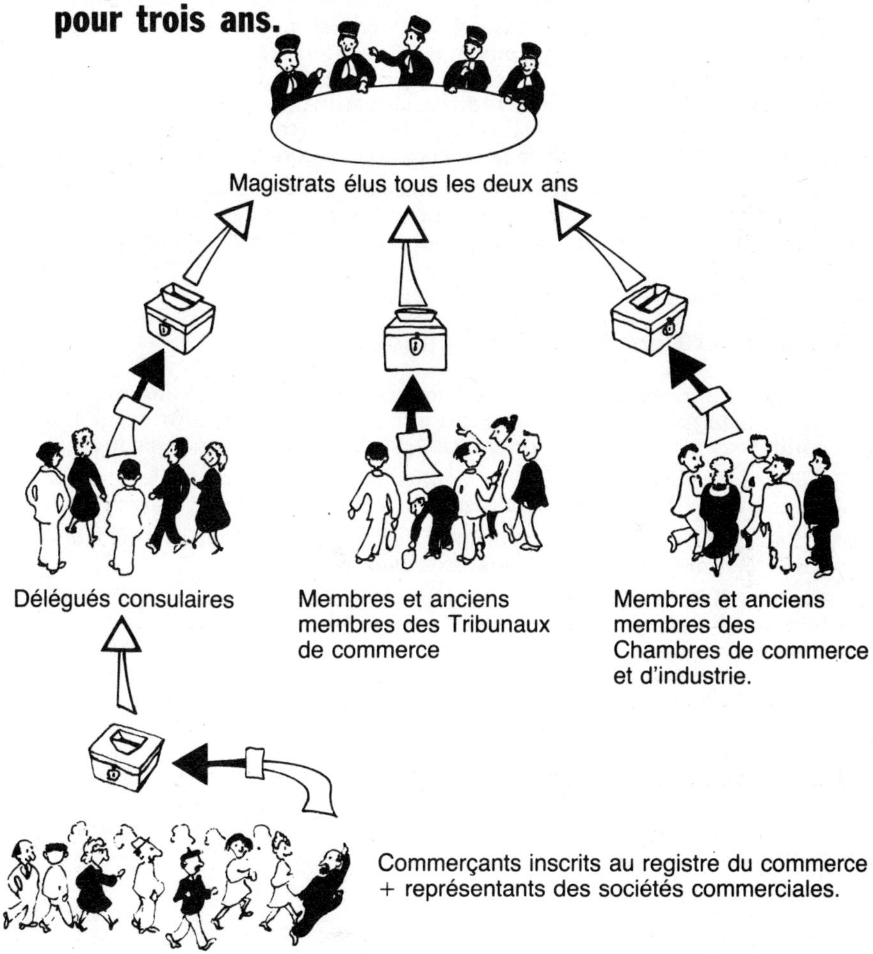

▲ Les juges consulaires sont assistés d'un greffe, mais le greffier exerce une profession libérale, ce n'est pas un fonctionnaire, mais un officier public (comme un huissier).

Le Conseil de Prud'hommes

Le Conseil de Prud'hommes est un tribunal spécialisé chargé de résoudre les conflits individuels, issus du contrat de travail.

■ Quelle est la compétence du Conseil de Prud'hommes ?

— Elle dépend du contenu. Le Conseil de Prud'hommes juge les litiges nés du contrat de travail : le paiement des indemnités après la rupture du contrat, le licenciement abusif, les problèmes de délai congé, de congés payés, d'heures supplémentaires, la restitution des documents permettant de s'inscrire à l'ANPE et de bénéficier des ASSEDIC. Il juge aussi les différends nés de la non-exécution du contrat d'apprentissage.

— Elle dépend du territoire. Le Prud'homme est celui du lieu de travail. La section (industrie, commerce, agriculture, activités diverses, encadrement) est celle qui correspond à l'activité professionnelle du demandeur.

■ Qui juge au Conseil de Prud'hommes ?

— Les juges, appelés conseillers prud'hommes sont élus pour 5 ans au scrutin de liste proportionnel*, les uns par les salariés, les autres par les employeurs. Ils siègent en nombre égal : c'est un tribunal paritaire. p. 26

• Pour être électeur il faut : avoir plus de 16 ans, exercer une activité professionnelle (avoir un contrat de travail ou d'apprentissage).

• Pour être éligible il faut : avoir plus de 21 ans, être de nationalité française, être inscrit sur les listes prud'homales.

— Le Conseil de Prud'hommes est composé de cinq sections avec chacune huit conseillers (4 employeurs et 4 salariés). En assemblée générale le Conseil élit pour un an le président et le vice-président général. Les présidents et vice-présidents de section sont également élus pour un an, alternativement employeur et salarié.

■ Quelles sont les voies de recours ?

Les mêmes que pour les tribunaux civils, le délai d'appel est indiqué sur la notification du jugement.

ORGANISATION ET PROCÉDURE

▲ Organisation d'un Conseil de Prud'hommes

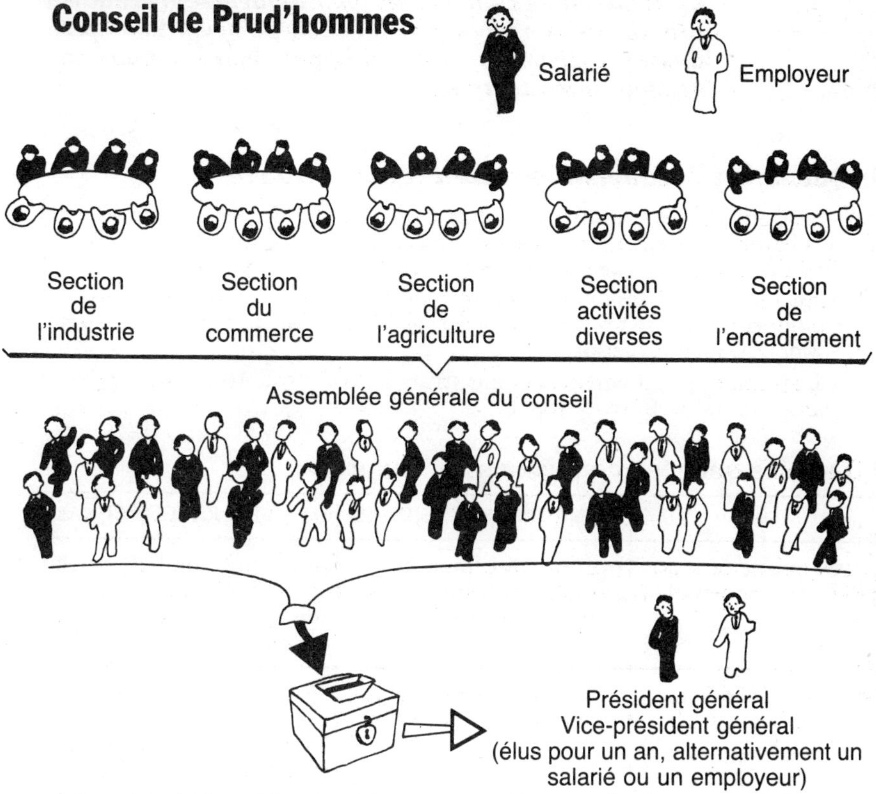

▲ La procédure

— En cas d'urgence, le conseil décide sous 8 jours. C'est le référé prud'homal qui permet par exemple d'obtenir le paiement de salaire, les documents permettant de s'inscrire à l'ANPE et de toucher les indemnités de chômage.

— Après une demande auprès du greffe du Conseil, les parties sont convoquées pour une conciliation qui se déroule devant un conseiller prud'homme salarié et un conseiller prud'homme employeur. En cas d'échec, l'affaire est renvoyée devant le bureau de jugement.

— L'audience de jugement a lieu devant deux conseillers salariés et deux employeurs. Les parties doivent être présentes ou se faire représenter, par un avocat, un délégué syndical, ou un tiers. S'il y a partage des voix, on fait appel au juge d'Instance pour trancher : il est le juge départiteur.

La Cour d'Appel

La partie qui s'estime lésée, par le jugement rendu en premier ressort, peut porter le litige devant une juridiction supérieure, la Cour d'Appel, pour obtenir une décision plus favorable.

■ Quelle est l'organisation d'une Cour d'Appel ?

— La Cour d'Appel se divise en chambre civile, chambre correctionnelle et chambre sociale (appel pour les juridictions spécialisées). La Chambre des mises en accusation est une chambre de la Cour d'Appel.

— En audience ordinaire la chambre est formée par 3 magistrats, elle en comporte 5 pour les affaires civiles renvoyées devant la Cour d'Appel par la Cour de Cassation.

— Le premier président et les magistrats de la Cour d'Appel sont appelés conseillers de Cour d'Appel.

■ Quelles sont les conditions de l'appel ?

	DANS UN PROCÈS CIVIL	DANS UN PROCÈS PÉNAL
Après quelle décision peut-on faire appel ?	Après un jugement rendu en premier ressort (litige supérieur à 13000 francs).	Après une condamnation à plus de 5 jours de prison, ou plus de 160 francs d'amende.
Dans quel délai ?	1 mois après le jugement. 15 jours pour le référé.	10 jours après la condamnation. 2 mois si l'appel vient du procureur.
Par qui ?	Celui qui s'estime lésé.	Accusé ou victime ou ministère public.
Quels sont les effets de l'appel ?	L'exécution du jugement est suspendue.	
L'appel est-il toujours possible ?	Non si le montant des réclamations est inférieur à 13000 francs.	Non après un arrêt de la Cour d'Assises.

■ Quelle est la procédure ?

— Le déroulement du procès est identique à celui suivi devant le Tribunal de Grande Instance*. p. 118

— En civil il faut un avoué qui rédige les actes et un avocat qui plaide et qui conseille.

— On reprend toute l'affaire. Aucune des parties ne peut introduire de nouvelles demandes.

■ Quelle peut-être la décision ?

— La décision s'appelle un arrêt d'appel. Elle peut, soit confirmer le jugement précédent, soit aggraver ou diminuer la responsabilité, la peine ou l'amende.

— Le jugement est rendu en dernier ressort, seul le pourvoi en cassation* est possible. p. 134

■ Les régions judiciaires

Il y a 30 Cours d'Appel en France, elles regroupent plusieurs départements, mais le découpage est différent de celui des régions, ce sont les régions judiciaires.

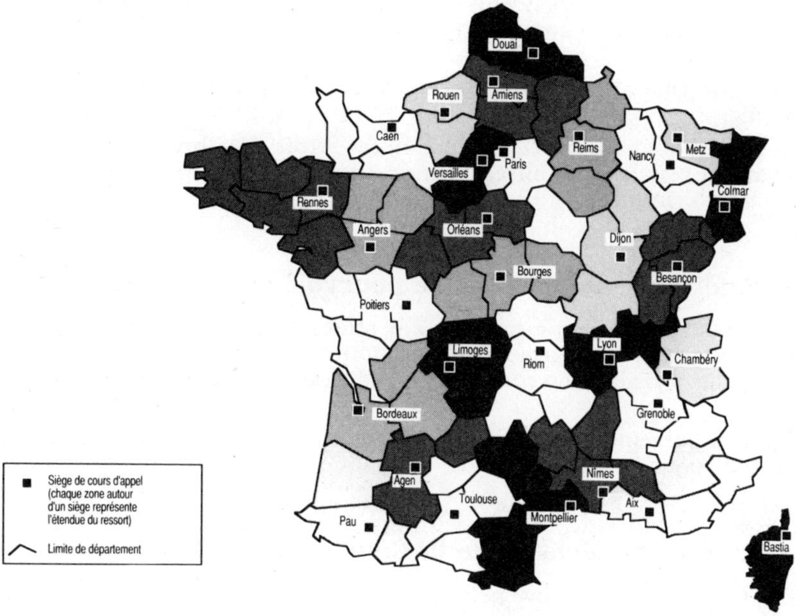

■ Y a-t-il d'autres recours que l'appel ?

— La tierce opposition : c'est un recours peu fréquent fait par une personne qui n'était ni demandeur ni défendeur mais qui peut être concernée par la décision du juge. On recommence le procès.

— L'opposition : la partie absente ou non représentée demande au tribunal qui a rendu un jugement que l'affaire soit à nouveau jugée. Il faut que l'absent ait une excuse valable et qu'il ne soit pas possible de faire appel.

Le délai pour présenter l'opposition est de 1 mois pour les juridictions civiles, de 10 jours pour les juridictions pénales (il n'est pas possible de faire opposition à un arrêt de Cour d'Assises).

Lorsque l'opposition est acceptée par le tribunal, on reprend complètement le procès.

La Cour de Cassation

Elle ne juge pas le fond, c'est-à-dire les arguments développés, elle juge la forme c'est-à-dire le jugement et les arrêts d'une affaire.

La Cour de Cassation casse les décisions d'un tribunal et renvoie l'affaire devant un tribunal identique.

■ Quelle est l'organisation de la Cour de Cassation ?

— Un premier président, 6 présidents de Chambre et 77 conseillers participent aux jugements. Ils sont assistés de conseillers référendaires qui préparent les dossiers.

— Un procureur général*, assisté d'avocats généraux représente le ministère public. p. 110

— Les conseillers sont répartis en six chambres : trois chambres civiles, deux chambres civiles spécialisées (l'une commerciale, l'autre sociale), une chambre criminelle.

■ Quelles conditions réunir pour se pourvoir en cassation ?

— La Cour de Cassation peut être saisie par toutes les parties d'un procès, même par le procureur général de la Cour de Cassation quand il estime qu'une décision, non contestée, est contraire à la loi ou à l'intérêt général.

— Lc délai pour présenter un pourvoi est de 5 jours pour la justice pénale et de 2 mois pour la justice civile.

■ Quelle peut-être la décision de la Cour de Cassation ?

— Si la Cour de Cassation trouve qu'il n'y a rien d'anormal dans la décision, elle rend un arrêt de rejet du pourvoi.

— Si elle trouve la réclamation justifiée, elle rend un arrêt qui annule le jugement et renvoie l'affaire devant une juridiction de même nature.

■ Le procès en révision

— Si toutes les possibilités de recours sont épuisées, on peut dans des circonstances exceptionnelles demander qu'une décision soit annulée et que l'affaire soit rejugée.

— La révision est possible si l'on découvre de nouveaux éléments de preuve ou une fraude.

Le délai est de deux mois après la découverte de l'élément nouveau. La Cour de Cassation examine si la demande est fondée pour un nouveau jugement.

LA PROCEDURE

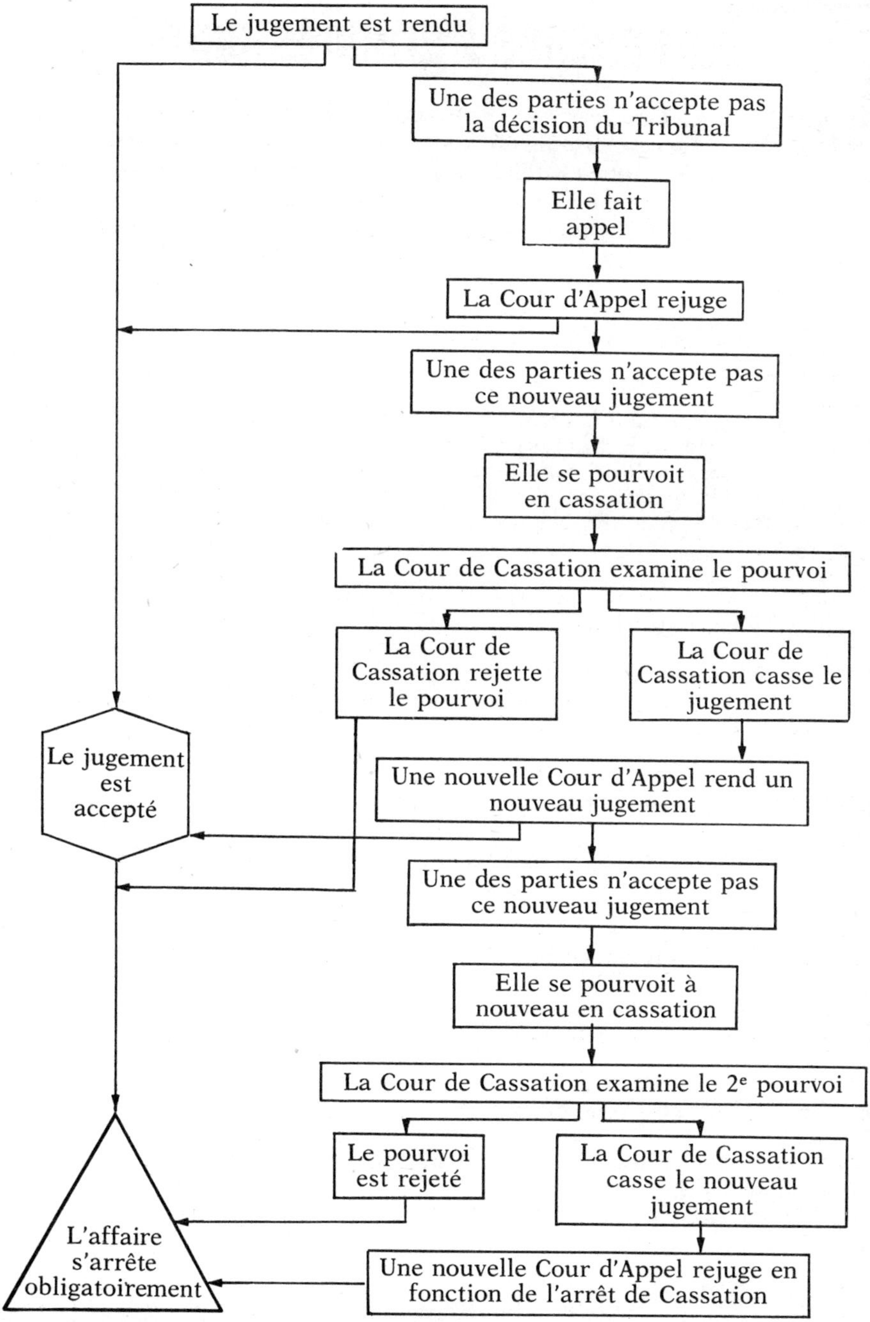
Le jugement est rendu
Une des parties n'accepte pas la décision du Tribunal
Elle fait appel
La Cour d'Appel rejuge
Une des parties n'accepte pas ce nouveau jugement
Elle se pourvoit en cassation
La Cour de Cassation examine le pourvoi
La Cour de Cassation rejette le pourvoi
La Cour de Cassation casse le jugement
Le jugement est accepté
Une nouvelle Cour d'Appel rend un nouveau jugement
Une des parties n'accepte pas ce nouveau jugement
Elle se pourvoit à nouveau en cassation
La Cour de Cassation examine le 2e pourvoi
Le pourvoi est rejeté
La Cour de Cassation casse le nouveau jugement
L'affaire s'arrête obligatoirement
Une nouvelle Cour d'Appel rejuge en fonction de l'arrêt de Cassation

La Communauté Economique Européenne : grandes dates

La Communauté Economique Européenne (CEE), que l'on appelle aussi Marché Commun, a été créée dans les années difficiles de la guerre froide. Il s'agissait alors de relancer l'Europe sur des bases solides et de rendre tout conflit entre pays européens impossible.

■ 1951 : La CECA ou Communauté Européenne du Charbon et de l'Acier

Le 9 mai 1950, le ministre français des affaires étrangères, Robert Schuman, définit les objectifs du plan qui porte son nom.
Le traité de Paris du 18 avril 1951 donne naissance à la CECA. La Belgique, la République fédérale d'Allemagne, l'Italie, le Luxembourg, la France et les Pays-Bas mettent en commun les ressources de base : le charbon et l'acier.

■ 1957 : l'Europe des six

Le traité de Rome du 27 mars 1957 institue la CEE et la Communauté européenne de l'énergie atomique (Euratom). L'Europe des six est créée : elle groupe les pays de la CECA.

■ 1973 : l'Europe des neuf

En 1973, aux six pays fondateurs, se joignent le Danemark, l'Irlande et le Royaume-Uni.

■ 1981 : l'Europe des dix

En janvier 1981, la Communauté s'élargit encore et l'adhésion de la Grèce porte à dix le nombre des Etats membres.

■ 1985 : l'Europe des douze

Le 12 juin 1985, l'Espagne et le Portugal signent l'acte d'adhésion qui entre en vigueur le 1er janvier 1986.
L'Europe se trouve élargie en direction de la Méditerranée.

L'EUROPE DES DOUZE

	Capitale	Superficie (en millions de km²)	Habitants (en millions)	Densité (hab./km²)
Belgique	Bruxelles	30	9,8	322
Danemark	Copenhague	43	5,1	118
Espagne	Madrid	505	38,6	76
France	Paris	551	55,5	100
Grèce	Athènes	132	10	75
Italie	Rome	301	57,1	190
Irlande	Dublin	70	3,5	50,8
Luxembourg	Luxembourg	3	0,36	139
Portugal	Lisbonne	92	10,2	111
Pays-Bas	Amsterdam	37	14,4	92,5
R.F.A.	Bonn	249	61	245
Royaume-Uni	Londres	245	56,6	91,7

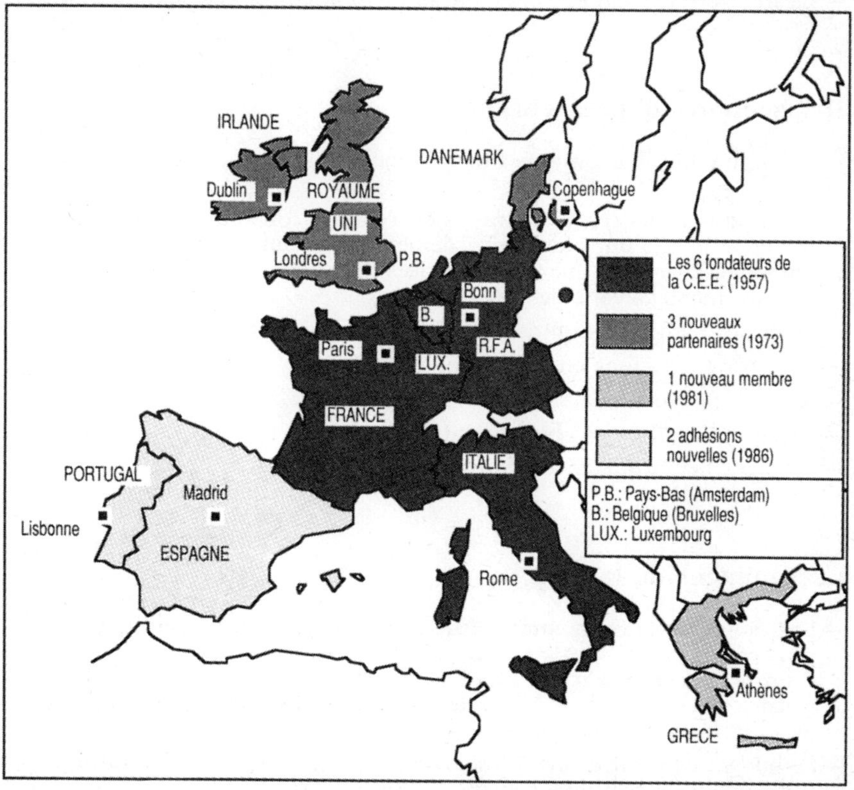

ÉTAT
VIE POLITIQUE
ADMINISTRATION
COLLECTIVITÉS LOCALES
JUSTICE
INTERNATIONAL

Les interventions de la Communauté Economique Européenne

L'idée principale du traité de Rome, signé en 1957, est d'associer les économies des Etats de la CEE dans un vaste marché commun.

Le Marché Commun cherche à constituer un ensemble économique européen capable de se mesurer avec les ensembles économiques américain et soviétique.

■ Les principales dispositions du traité de Rome

— L'élimination, entre les Etats membres, des droits de douane. Ce fut chose faite en 1977.

— L'établissement d'un tarif douanier commun entre chaque pays de la CEE et les Etats qui ne font pas partie de la CEE.

— La libre circulation des personnes, des services et des capitaux.

■ Des secteurs d'intervention

La Communauté Economique Européenne à mis en place des politiques visant à :

— garantir la concurrence entre les entreprises. Une entreprise ne doit pas bénéficier d'une aide gouvernementale qui lui permettrait de vendre moins cher alors que les entreprises concurrentes ne bénéficieraient pas des mêmes avantages;

— favoriser l'amélioration des conditions de vie et d'emploi;

— soutenir les régions en difficulté;

— unifier les droits sociaux dans les différents Etats;

— garantir l'égalité des chances entre hommes et femmes;

— protéger l'environnement.

■ Les finances de la CEE

— La Communauté Economique Européenne dispose de ressources financières :

• un pourcentage sur les TVA* nationales; p. 63

• les droits de douane et les prélèvements sur les marchandises importées des pays non membres de la CEE.

— Le budget de la CEE sert à financer la politique agricole, la politique régionale et la politique sociale.

Le système monétaire européen

Créé en mars 1979, le système monétaire européen ou SME possède une unité monétaire : l'écu. L'écu a été adopté afin d'éviter toute fluctuation incontrôlée des taux de change.

L'Europe verte

— C'est en janvier 1962 que naît une politique agricole commune. Les principes de cette « Europe agricole » sont :
  • l'unité de marché, c'est-à-dire la libre circulation des produits agricoles et alimentaires et l'harmonisation des normes de qualité;
  • la préférence communautaire qui protège les producteurs européens contre les importations à bas prix provenant du reste du monde;
  • le système des prix communs : les prix communs des produits agricoles sont fixés en écus mais, pour compenser l'effet des variations de change des monnaies nationales sur les prix communs, des « montants compensatoires monétaires » (les MCM) ont été établis.

— La solidarité financière existe avec le Fonds Européen d'Orientation et de Garantie Agricole (FEOGA) qui assure le financement de la politique agricole commune.

L'Europe bleue

Une politique commune de pêche existe depuis le 25 janvier 1983.
Dans la zone des 200 milles (soit 370 km) autour des côtes des pays membres de la CEE, un règlement unique s'applique à tous les pêcheurs. Il prévoit la juste répartition des quotas de pêche entre Etats et la liberté d'accès aux eaux communautaires de tous les pêcheurs européens.

Vers une « Europe politique » ?

Lors de l'accord signé en décembre 1985, les Etats de la CEE ont affirmé leur volonté de « formuler et mettre en œuvre, en commun, une politique étrangère européenne. »

1992

Ouverture des frontières avec libre circulation des personnes, des services et des capitaux.

ÉTAT
VIE POLITIQUE
ADMINISTRATION
OLLECTIVITÉS LOCALES
JUSTICE
INTERNATIONAL

Les institutions de la CEE. Comment fonctionne la Communauté ?

Les 12 Etats de la Communauté Economique Européenne sont indépendants politiquement ; pourtant ils prennent, au niveau européen, un certain nombre de décisions applicables dans chaque Etat membre. Pour mettre en place cette législation, la CEE a été dotée d'institutions propres.

■ Le conseil des ministres

— Le conseil est composé de 12 ministres (un par gouvernement) mais sa composition varie selon le sujet traité. Suivant les cas il réunit les ministres des finances, les ministres de l'agriculture...

— Il se réunit à Bruxelles.

— Il prend des décisions et adopte les lois communautaires.

— Les impulsions majeures du conseil des ministres sont données par la réunion périodique des chefs d'Etat et de gouvernement désignée sous le nom de Conseil européen.

■ La commission européenne

— Elle comprend 17 membres, au moins 1 par Etat, nommés pour 4 ans, d'un commun accord, par tous les Etats membres. Ils doivent agir en toute indépendance.

— La commission européenne siège à Bruxelles.

— Elle propose les « lois communautaires », veille au respect des traités.

— Elle cherche à concilier les points de vue des Etats membres et joue un rôle important dans les négociations.

— Elle est aussi l'exécutif de la communauté. Elle est responsable devant le Parlement.

■ Le Parlement européen

— Avec l'entrée de l'Espagne et du Portugal, le nombre des parlementaires européens est porté à 518 députés. Ils sont élus, depuis 1979, tous les 5 ans, au suffrage universel*, par les citoyens de la communauté. p. 20

— Il siège à Strasbourg.

— Il contrôle l'action de la commission et veille à l'intérêt communautaire. Il donne son avis sur les propositions de la commission avant que le Conseil des ministres ne prenne sa décision.
C'est lui qui, en dernier ressort, arrête le budget de la CEE adopté par le conseil.

■ La Cour de Justice

— Elle comprend 13 juges et 6 avocats généraux.

— Elle siège à Luxembourg.

— Elle assure le respect du droit dans l'exécution des traités et tranche les conflits qui pourraient naître à l'occasion de ce droit.

■ Le Comité Economique et Social

— Il est formé de représentants des différentes catégories intéressées, de la vie économique et sociale. (syndicats, patronat, consommateurs...)

— Il siège à Bruxelles.

— Il est consulté avant l'adoption de nombreuses décisions.

■ La Cour des Comptes

— Elle est formée de représentants de chaque Etat.

— Elle siège à Luxembourg.

— Elle contrôle la gestion des finances communautaires.

POUR EN SAVOIR PLUS :

Bureau d'information de la commission des Communautés Européennes :

61, rue des Belles Feuilles
75782 Paris Cedex 16

L'ONU : origine et principes

L'Organisation des Nations Unies, désignée plus souvent sous le sigle de ONU, est née en 1945. Elle a succédé à la Société des Nations ou SDN créée après la Première Guerre mondiale, en 1919, sur la proposition du président américain Wilson. A sa création, elle comptait 51 membres, elle en compte 159 en 1986. Ces 159 Etats membres groupent 98 % de la population mondiale.

■ L'origine de l'ONU

— L'expression « Nations Unies » est du président Franklin-D. Roosevelt. Dès août 1941, Winston Churchill et Franklin Roosevelt, dans la « Charte de l'Atlantique », annoncent au monde leur volonté de créer à la fin de la guerre une organisation capable de préserver la paix.

— En janvier 1942, les représentants des gouvernements de 26 nations signent « La Déclaration des Nations Unies » dans laquelle ils s'engagent à poursuivre ensemble la guerre contre les puissances de l'Axe.

— Les conférences de Moscou (novembre 1943), Téhéran (janvier 1944), Dumbarton Oaks (août-octobre 1944) et Yalta (février 1945) étudient les principes d'une vaste organisation internationale destinée à maintenir la paix et la sécurité.

— La Charte des Nations Unies a été signée le 26 juin 1945, à San Francisco, par les représentants de 50 nations. (La Pologne, qui n'avait pas été représentée à la Conférence, a signé la Charte plus tard mais est néanmoins considérée comme l'un des 51 membres originaires.)

— L'Organisation des Nations Unies a officiellement commencé d'exister le 24 octobre 1945, la Charte ayant été ratifiée par la Chine, les Etats-Unis, la France, le Royaume-Uni et l'URSS et par la majorité des autres pays signataires.

■ Le rôle et les principes de l'ONU

— Les buts de l'ONU sont les suivants :
MAINTENIR la paix et la sécurité internationales.
DEVELOPPER entre les nations des relations amicales.
REALISER la coopération internationale en résolvant les problèmes internationaux d'ordre économique, social, culturel ou humanitaire et en développant le respect des droits de l'homme* et des libertés fondamentales. p. 8
ETRE UN CENTRE où s'harmonisent les efforts des nations vers ces fins communes.

— L'Organisation des Nations Unies est fondée sur le principe de l'égalité de ses membres. Les Etats-membres doivent régler leurs différends de manière pacifique.
L'ONU ne peut intervenir dans les affaires intérieures d'un Etat.

■ Le fonctionnement de l'ONU

— Les Etats qui désirent devenir membres de l'ONU doivent accepter les principes de la Charte. Ils sont admis par décision de l'Assemblée générale sur recommandation du Conseil de Sécurité de l'ONU. De la même manière, des membres peuvent être suspendus ou exclus par l'Assemblée générale sur recommandation du Conseil de Sécurité.

— Les langues officielles de l'Organisation des Nations Unies sont : l'anglais, l'arabe, le chinois, l'espagnol, le français et le russe.

Les institutions de l'ONU

Depuis l'adoption de la Charte des Nations Unies à San Francisco en 1945, le monde a connu des mutations profondes : armement atomique, processus de décolonisation. Au centre de cette mutation, du jeu des tendances contradictoires, se trouve l'Organisation des Nations Unies, porteuse d'espoirs, de réalisations et de dialogue.

■ L'Assemblée Générale

— Elle est composée des représentants de tous les pays membres de l'ONU. A sa première réunion à Londres en 1946, l'Assemblée Générale comptait 51 membres, elle en compte actuellement 159. Grand ou petit, riche ou pauvre, un pays dispose d'une seule voix.

— Elle siège à New York.

— L'Assemblée Générale, qui tient une session ordinaire annuelle, est la seule instance mondiale où sont examinés les grands problèmes internationaux (course aux armements, croissance démographique, environnement, développement économique, condition des enfants, des femmes...).
Elle élit, sur proposition du Conseil de Sécurité, le Secrétaire Général de l'ONU, les membres non permanents des différents organes, les juges de la Cour Internationale, vote l'admission des nouveaux membres et arrête le budget de l'Organisation.

■ Le Conseil de Sécurité

— Le conseil se compose de 15 membres. Cinq d'entre eux sont membres permaments : la Chine, les Etats-Unis, la France, le Royaume-Uni, l'URSS. Les 10 autres membres sont élus par l'Assemblée Générale pour 2 ans.

— Le Conseil de Sécurité est chargé du maintien de la paix et de la sécurité internationales. Tandis que les autres organes de l'ONU adressent aux gouvernements des recommandations, le Conseil est le seul à pouvoir prendre des décisions ayant force obligatoire et à les faire appliquer par des voies allant de la négociation aux sanctions économiques et à la force armée d'observation (« les casques bleus »). Mais les décisions doivent être prises sur un vote affirmatif de 9 membres dans lequel doivent figurer les votes affirmatifs des 5 membres permanents. C'est la règle de l'unanimité des grandes puissances que l'on appelle le « veto ». L'utilisation par l'un des 5 membres permanents de son droit de veto (vote négatif) bloque les débats et empêche la décision.

■ Le Conseil Economique et Social

— Composé de 54 membres, il se réunit deux fois l'an à Genève et à New York.

— Il reçoit mandat de l'Assemblée Générale pour coordonner les activités de l'ONU dans le domaine économique et social auquel vont plus de 80 % des ressources de l'ONU. De nombreuses institutions spécialisées lui sont rattachées (UNESCO, FAO, OMS, OIT...)

■ Le Conseil de Tutelle

— Il est composé des 5 membres permanents du Conseil de Sécurité.

— Chargé de superviser l'administration des territoires sous tutelle, il a de moins en moins de questions à examiner car il ne reste qu'un territoire sous tutelle : la Micronésie, administrée par les USA.

■ La Cour Internationale de Justice

— La Cour internationale de justice, dont le siège est à la Haye, est composée de 15 juges élus conjointement par l'Assemblée Générale et le Conseil de Sécurité.

— Elle juge les différends que peuvent lui soumettre les Etats. Elle rend des arrêts clarifiant des questions juridiques internationales.

■ Le Secrétariat Général

Doté d'un personnel recruté dans le monde entier, le Secrétariat est dirigé par un Secrétaire général qui applique les directives des autres organes de l'ONU et sert de porte-parole à l'organisation. Il est élu pour 5 ans par l'Assemblée générale, sur recommandation du conseil de sécurité, il est rééligible.

ONU : institutions spécialisées

L'ONU intervient pour aider les pays en voie de développement. Son aide revêt différents aspects : enseignement, encadrement, aide financière, programme alimentaire... Ces réalisations sont l'œuvre des institutions spécialisées rattachées au conseil économique et social de l'ONU.

■ L'OMS ou organisation mondiale de la santé

— Son siège est à Genève.

— Son but est d'amener tous les peuples du monde au niveau de santé le plus élevé.

■ La FAO ou organisation des Nations Unies pour l'alimentation et l'agriculture

— Son siège est à Rome.

— Son but est d'améliorer le développement agricole des pays en voie de développement en leur apportant une aide technique.

■ L'UNESCO ou organisation des Nations Unies pour l'éducation, la science et la culture

— Son siège est à Paris.

— Son but est de contribuer à la paix en développant la collaboration des Nations dans les domaines de l'alphabétisation, de la protection du patrimoine culturel, des droits de l'homme.

■ L'OIT ou organisation internationale du travail

— Son siège est à Genève.

— Son but est l'élaboration d'un droit international du travail et d'un programme d'amélioration des conditions de travail.

■ Le FMI ou fonds monétaire international

— Son siège est à Washington.

— Son rôle est de faciliter le bon fonctionnement des mécanismes monétaires entre les pays pour éviter une crise monétaire internationale.

■ La BIRD ou banque internationale pour la reconstruction et le développement

— Son siège est à Washington.

— Son but est de financer, dans les pays les moins favorisés, des projets de développement par des prêts.

LE SYSTÈME DES NATIONS UNIES

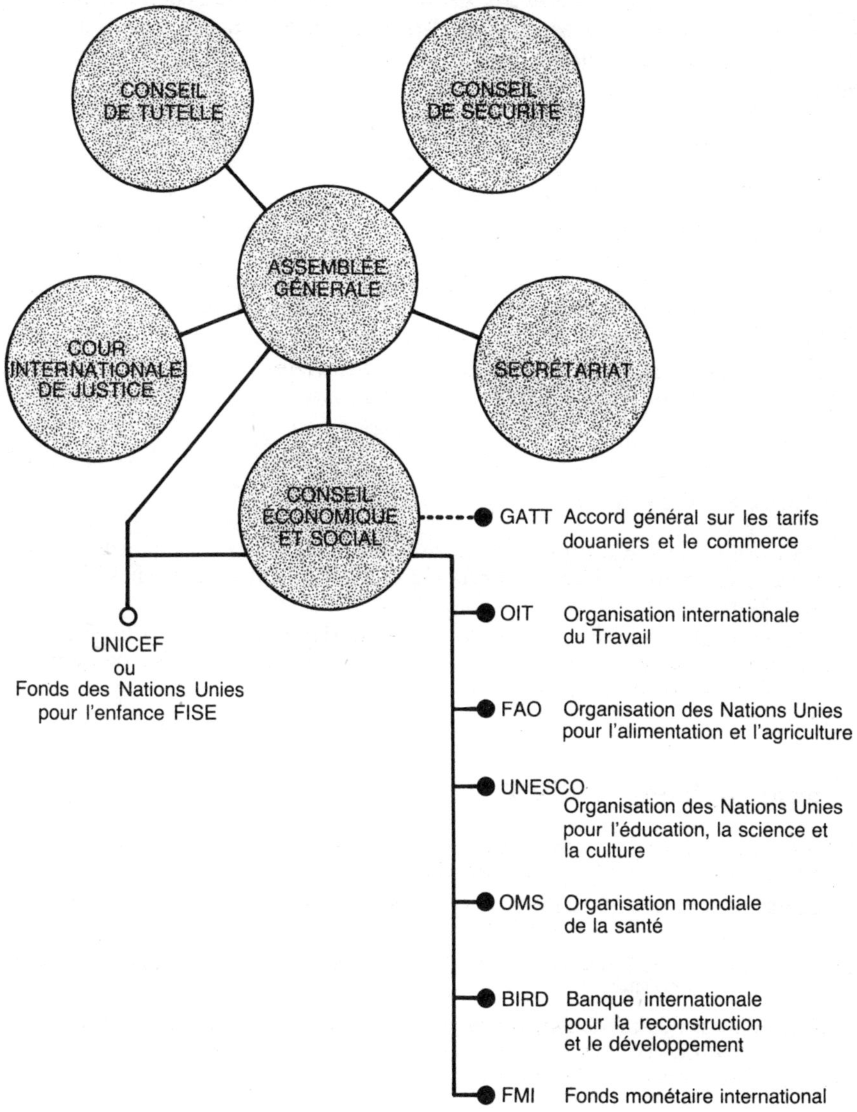
CONSEIL DE TUTELLE
CONSEIL DE SÉCURITÉ
ASSEMBLÉE GÉNÉRALE
COUR INTERNATIONALE DE JUSTICE
SECRÉTARIAT
CONSEIL ÉCONOMIQUE ET SOCIAL
UNICEF
ou
Fonds des Nations Unies
pour l'enfance FISE
GATT Accord général sur les tarifs douaniers et le commerce
OIT Organisation internationale du Travail
FAO Organisation des Nations Unies pour l'alimentation et l'agriculture
UNESCO Organisation des Nations Unies pour l'éducation, la science et la culture
OMS Organisation mondiale de la santé
BIRD Banque internationale pour la reconstruction et le développement
FMI Fonds monétaire international

L'OTAN

L'Organisation du Traité de l'Atlantique Nord est née après la Deuxième Guerre mondiale et crée une alliance militaire entre 16 États.

■ La création de l'OTAN

Le traité de l'Atlantique Nord ou « pacte atlantique » fut signé le 4 avril 1949 à Washington entre la Belgique, le Canada, le Danemark, les Etats-Unis, la France, l'Islande, l'Italie, le Luxembourg, la Norvège, les Pays-Bas, le Portugal et le Royaume-Uni. La Grèce et la Turquie adhèrent en 1952, l'Allemagne fédérale en 1955 et l'Espagne en 1982.

La France reste membre de l'alliance politique mais ne participe plus au système de défense depuis 1966.

■ Le but de l'OTAN

Le traité de l'Atlantique Nord est un traité d'alliance contre toute attaque armée du territoire de l'un des Etats signataires en Europe ou en Amérique du Nord.

Cette organisation est née de la volonté des Américains de contenir la poussée du communisme en Europe et de la crainte des Européens de ne pouvoir seuls résister à cette pression.

■ L'organisation de l'OTAN

Le conseil de l'Atlantique Nord est composé des représentants des 16 gouvernements. Il se réunit 2 fois par an.

Il reçoit les avis du comité militaire composé des représentants des états-majors.

Les programmes de l'OTAN visent à rétablir l'équilibre des forces stratégiques face à l'URSS.

L'OTAN dispose de forces de moyenne portée ayant un rôle de dissuasion et des forces nucléaires tactiques destinées à détruire des forces militaires sur les champs de bataille.

■ Les bases militaires de l'OTAN

Grande-Bretagne (Ecosse) - Grèce - Groenland (Thulé, base alerte-radar) - Islande (qui n'a pas d'armée nationale, 3300 américains assurent sa défense) - Italie (cinq bases) - Turquie - Chypre - Espagne - Maroc.

FORCES DE L'OTAN

▲ Armes nucléaires tactiques en Europe

Total : 7000 têtes nucléaires
(sans la France)

- Avions porteurs.
- Chasseurs bombardiers (F-4C (Phantom); F-104G (Starfighter)).
- Missiles (types Pershing, Sergeant, Honest John, Lance).
- Artillerie avec munitions nucléaires.
- Missiles sol-air avec ogives nucléaires (type Nike).

▲ Forces terrestres

Total : 15742 chars avec 1767000 hommes (y compris la France)

- 16 divisions blindées.
- 24 divisions mécanisées.
- 10 divisions d'infanterie et parachutées.
- 84 stations de surveillance radar.
  18 boeing 707 équipés du système de contrôle et d'alerte aéroporté AWACS qui permet de détecter les appareils volant à basse altitude et multiplie par 20 le volume de surveillance des radars.

▲ Forces aériennes

Total : 3447 avions de combat tactique.

- 376 avions de reconnaissance.
- 2332 chasseurs et avions d'attaque au sol.
- 711 intercepteurs.
- 28 bombardiers légers.

▲ Rampes de lancements de missiles sol-air

- 1662 rampes de lancement (dont plus de 1000 en Allemagne fédérale).

▲ Forces navales

(Forces françaises exclues)

- 14 porte-avions d'attaque.
- 14 croiseurs.
- 121 destroyers.
- 460 frégates, escorteurs.
- 188 sous-marins (d'attaque).

Forces françaises : 2 porte-avions, 1 frégate lance-missiles, 36 bâtiments de combat, 23 sous-marins (dont 6 nucléaires), 1 porte-hélicoptère.

Vie pratique

Quelques démarches de la vie courante

DÉMARCHES	OÙ EN FAIRE LA DEMANDE ? COÛT	DURÉE DE VALIDITÉ	DÉLAI / OBSERVATIONS
Carte d'identité	Commissariat de Police Timbre fiscal	10 ans	1 à 20 jours. Si vous êtes mineur, autorisation des parents.
Passeport	Commissariat ou Mairie Timbre fiscal	5 ans	10 jours à 3 semaines. A retirer soi-même.
Permis de conduire	Par l'intermédiaire d'une auto-école ou en candidat libre à la Préfecture du domicile Taxes	—	15 à 20 jours après la réussite. En cas de changement matrimonial (mariage, divorce) l'obtention d'un nouveau formulaire est gratuite.
Carte grise	Préfecture du domicile (à Paris, annexes des mairies) Taxe régionale	—	Tout de suite à 48 h. Elle ne peut être établie qu'à un seul nom soit monsieur, soit madame.
Extrait d'un acte de l'état-civil : naissance - mariage	A la Mairie où l'acte a été fait Gratuit	3 mois	48 h à 8 jours. Pensez à joindre une enveloppe timbrée pour l'envoi.
Copie d'un acte de décès	A la Mairie où l'acte a été fait Gratuit	3 mois	48 h à 8 jours. Il est impossible d'obtenir un extrait.
Fiche d'état civil : Fiche individuelle Fiche familiale	 Mairie Mairie Gratuit	3 mois	Immédiat. Sur présentation de la carte d'identité, du livret de famille.
Attestation de domicile	par une déclaration sur l'honneur	—	Mais il est souvent exigé la présentation d'une quittance (loyer, EDF).

DÉMARCHES	OÙ EN FAIRE LA DEMANDE ? COÛT	DURÉE DE VALIDITÉ	DÉLAI / OBSERVATIONS
Extrait de casier judiciaire	Casier Judiciaire National 107, rue Randreau 44079 Nantes Cedex Gratuit	3 mois	1 à 3 semaines. Si vous êtes né en France métropolitaine ou à l'étranger.
	Greffe du Tribunal de Grande Instance de votre lieu de naissance Gratuit	3 mois	1 à 3 semaines. Si vous êtes né dans un territoire ou département d'Outre-Mer.
Carte d'électeur	En général à la mairie du domicile Gratuit	—	S'inscrire avant le 31 décembre précédant les élections. Pour être électeur : — être de nationalité française; — avoir 18 ans; — jouir de ses droits civils et politiques.
Copie ou photocopie conforme	Mairie ou Commissariat ou Gendarmerie Gratuit	—	Tout de suite ou 24 h. Présenter l'original signé.
Permis de chasser	Mairie ou Préfecture Payant	—	Chaque année, le permis doit être visé et validé.
Permis de pêche	Association de pêche (le plus souvent chez un marchand d'articles de pêche) Payant	1 an	Aucun. La taxe varie en fonction de la catégorie des rivières.

Quels papiers conserver ?

QUELS PAPIERS ?	COMBIEN DE TEMPS ?	A QUOI SERVENT-ILS ?
• Votre état civil Le livret de famille	toute la vie	Remis aux époux le jour du mariage, il permet dans n'importe quelle mairie la délivrance immédiate des fiches d'état-civil.
• Vos études Les diplômes	toute la vie	Ils attestent de votre qualification professionnelle, de votre niveau d'études. Ne jamais donner l'original !
• Votre travail Bulletins de paie	toute la vie	Ils permettent de faire valoir vos droits à la retraite et de calculer le montant de votre pension.
Certificats de travail	toute la vie	Ils vous permettent d'attester de votre qualification professionnelle et des fonctions que vous avez occupées.
• Votre santé Dossiers médicaux importants	toute la vie	Ils permettent de connaître l'état des maladies infectieuses ou chroniques, les opérations chirurgicales déjà subies.
Avis d'arrêt de travail ; certificat de grossesse	30 ans	La sécurité sociale dispose de ce délai pour vous réclamer des sommes injustement versées.
• Votre logement Bail et quittances de loyer	5 ans	Le propriétaire dispose de ce délai pour réclamer des sommes soi-disant dues : charges locatives...
État des lieux	durant le temps de location	Il est nécessaire pour vous faire rembourser votre caution.
Factures d'eau, de gaz, d'électricité, de téléphone	2 ans	Cela vous permet de contester une facture anormalement élevée en montrant quelle est votre consommation habituelle.
Les devis de réparation et de travaux	jusqu'au paiement de la facture	Ils garantissent le prix à payer. L'entrepreneur doit respecter le devis qu'il a établi.

QUELS PAPIERS ?	COMBIEN DE TEMPS ?	A QUOI SERVENT-ILS ?
• Votre automobile La facture d'achat	jusqu'à la revente et au moins 2 ans	Article du code civil.
Le carnet d'entretien	jusqu'à la revente	Cela vous permettra en cas de vice caché de prouver que votre voiture a été entretenue conformément aux indications du constructeur.
Les factures de réparation	jusqu'à la revente	Vous pourrez justifier auprès de l'acheteur des soins avec lesquels vous avez entretenu votre voiture.
• Vos assurances Les bons de garantie	durant le temps de la garantie	C'est le bon daté, remis par le distributeur, qui vous permet de faire jouer la garantie.
Le contrat d'assurance	jusqu'à sa résiliation	Il vous permet de connaître avec précision les risques pour lesquels vous êtes couverts et vos obligations envers votre assureur.
Les quittances des primes	2 ans	Article L 114-1 du code des assurances.
L'avis de rembourse-ment d'un sinistre	30 ans	C'est le temps que vous avez pour engager une action contre le responsable de ce sinis-tre ou son assureur.
• Votre compte bancaire ou CCP Talons et relevés ban-caires	30 ans	Ils serviront de preuve en cas de litige sur un paiement. Les banques ne gardent les relevés de compte que 10 ans.
Bordereaux de verse-ment, ordres de virement	jusqu'à ce que vous en trouviez trace sur un relevé	Jusqu'au relevé, ils sont la seule preuve des opérations bancaires que vous avez effectuées.
Chèque bancaire chèque postal	moins de 3 ans moins d'un an	Passé ce délai, vous ne pourrez plus les encaisser.
• Vos impôts et taxes La taxe TV	3 ans	Décret du 17.03.1968.
Déclarations de reve-nus et justificatifs, avis d'imposition	4 ans	Article 1966 du code des impôts. Le fisc peut vous demander des arriérés d'impôt sur cette période s'il s'aperçoit d'une erreur ou d'une fraude.

Passer un contrat

	VOUS PASSEZ UN CONTRAT...	QUI ENTRAÎNE DROIT ET OBLIGATIONS
Vous vous mariez	CONTRAT DE MARIAGE, signé par les époux devant un notaire avant le mariage civil	Gestion des biens et propriétés de chacun des époux, répartition en cas de dissolution du mariage.
Vous louez un logement	CONTRAT DE BAIL, signé par le propriétaire et le locataire	Le propriétaire offre la jouissance du logement. Le locataire paye un loyer et entretient le logement.
Vous vous assurez	POLICE D'ASSURANCE entre l'assureur et l'assuré	La compagnie d'assurances assure un dédommagement en cas de sinistre. L'assuré paye une prime (ou cotisation en matière sociale).
Vous faites ouvrir les compteurs. **Vous demandez le téléphone**	CONTRAT entre EDF-GDF et l'usager CONTRAT entre les P et T et l'abonné	EDF-GDF fournissent l'électricité ou le gaz. L'usager paye les consommations et l'abonnement.
Vous faites l'achat d'une marchandise	Par ACCORD ORAL sur la marchandise et sur le prix ou par un bon de commande	Le vendeur fournit la marchandise, assure la garantie et éventuellement la livraison à domicile. Le client paye.
Vous demandez un crédit	CONTRAT de CRÉDIT passé entre vous, le vendeur et la société de crédit	Le vendeur fournit la marchandise. La société de crédit paye le vendeur. Le client rembourse le prix de la marchandise et les intérêts.
Vous faites réparer, entretenir	CONTRAT de GARANTIE avec le vendeur, ou CONTRAT d'ENTRETIEN avec une société	Le vendeur, l'artisan, la société d'entretien exécutent certains travaux. Le client paye.
Vous voyagez	CONTRAT avec la SNCF ou une compagnie de transports, matérialisé par le TITRE de TRANSPORT	La SNCF assure le transport des voyageurs avec obligation de sécurité. Le voyageur doit être muni d'un billet composté.
Vous vous faites soigner	CONTRAT entre le MÉDECIN, le DENTISTE, l'ÉTABLISSEMENT HOSPITALIER et le malade	Le médecin, l'hôpital, assurent le diagnostic et s'engagent à mettre en œuvre les moyens de la guérison. Le malade ou les assurances payent.

Impôts

Dans quelle situation devez-vous faire une déclaration de revenus aux impôts?

Vous êtes célibataire, sans personne à charge	Vous avez moins de 18 ans, deux possibilités	■ Vos parents ajoutent vos revenus aux leurs, et vous ne faites pas de déclaration. ■ Vos parents demandent l'imposition séparée : vous faites une déclaration.
	Vous avez 18 ans dans l'année, trois possibilités	■ Vos parents ajoutent à leurs revenus ceux dont vous avez disposé jusqu'à la date anniversaire de vos 18 ans. Vous déclarez les revenus dont vous avez disposé à partir de cette date. ■ Vos parents demandent une imposition séparée pour les revenus dont vous avez disposé jusqu'à vos 18 ans. ■ Vous demandez le rattachement au foyer fiscal de vos parents pour toute l'année.
	Vous avez plus de 18 ans	■ **Vous faites votre déclaration.** Toutefois, vous pouvez demander le rattachement au foyer fiscal de vos parents si vous entrez dans l'un des cas suivants : • vous avez moins de 21 ans; • vous avez moins de 25 ans et vous êtes étudiant; • vous effectuez votre service national.
Vous êtes célibataire, vous avez un enfant à charge	■ **Vous constituez un foyer fiscal distinct de vos parents.** Toutefois vous pouvez demander le rattachement au foyer fiscal de vos parents si vous entrez dans l'un des cas suivants : • vous avez moins de 21 ans; • vous avez moins de 25 ans et vous êtes étudiant; • vous effectuez votre service national; • vous êtes infirme	
Vous êtes marié avec ou sans enfants à charge	■ **Vous constituez un foyer fiscal à part.** Toutefois vous demandez le rattachement au foyer fiscal de vos parents ou des parents de votre conjoint(e) si vous ou votre conjoint(e) entrez dans l'une des situations suivantes : • moins de 21 ans; • étudiant(e) de moins de 25 ans; • service national; • personne infirme.	

Être locataire

Démarches	Avant la location	Pendant la location	En fin de location
	Vous arrivez dans l'appartement	**Vous habitez**	**Vous quittez l'appartement**
Contrat de location	— Vous devez exiger au moment de signer : • la copie de la dernière quittance de loyer; • le montant réel des charges de l'année précédente; • la copie de l'état des lieux au départ du précédent locataire; — Demandez-les à votre propriétaire ou à l'agent immobilier (mandataire du propriétaire).	Vous relisez chaque année votre contrat qui contient les conditions d'augmentations du loyer.	— Vous prévenez votre propriétaire 3 mois avant de quitter les lieux, par lettre recommandée avec accusé de réception. — Relisez votre contrat : chapitre résiliation.
État des lieux	Vous notez par écrit l'état de l'appartement, pièce par pièce, en présence du propriétaire, ou à défaut vous faites constater par un huissier. Dans ce cas, les honoraires sont à partager avec le propriétaire.	Vous devez demander à votre propriétaire l'autorisation de faire des travaux.	Vous faites un nouvel état des lieux qui sera à comparer au 1er. En cas de dégradation importante, le propriétaire peut vous demander des dédommagements.
EDF - GDF	Vous demandez l'ouverture des compteurs (délai à prévoir 4 à 5 jours). Téléphonez à l'agence locale EDF (adresse dans l'annuaire) pour prendre rendez-vous.	Vérifiez les relevés; en cas de facture erronée, prenez contact avec l'agence locale.	Prévenez votre agence locale pour le transfert d'abonnement (au plus tard 3 jours avant le départ). Vous téléphonez à l'agence locale pour prendre rendez-vous afin de faire fermer les compteurs.
Eau chaude	Vous avez un compteur individuel : demandez le relevé de celui-ci au syndic. Son adresse vous sera donnée par votre propriétaire.	Facilitez l'accès aux compteurs pour le relevé environ 2 fois par an.	Demandez un relevé du compteur au syndic.

Démarches	Avant la location	Pendant la location	En fin de location
	Vous arrivez dans l'appartement	**Vous habitez**	**Vous quittez l'appartement**
Téléphone	Vous demandez le branchement payant ou le rétablissement de la ligne. Téléphonez à l'agence commerciale en faisant le 14. L'appel est gratuit.		Vous demandez la suspension de la ligne ou son transfert payant. Téléphonez au moins 8 jours avant et signalez votre nouvelle adresse.
Assurances	— Vous devez vous assurer obligatoirement contre « l'explosion, l'incendie, les dégâts des eaux ». — Vous pouvez vous assurer contre le vol. Consultez différentes compagnies d'assurances et choisissez.	Vous avez fait des achats importants (chaîne hi-fi, magnétoscope...) : faites augmenter le capital assuré.	— Vous faites transférer vos assurances sur le nouveau logement en donnant sa description ou — Vous résiliez le contrat en respectant le délai de préavis : relisez votre contrat dans les deux cas.
Allocation de logement ou Aide personnalisée au logement	Vous effectuez une demande auprès de la Caisse d'Allocations familiales de votre domicile pour connaître la possibilité d'aides. Adressez-vous à la mairie pour avoir l'adresse.	Vous bénéficiez d'une aide : faites remplir l'attestation envoyée par la Caisse concernant le montant de votre loyer (1 fois par an).	Vous signalez à la Caisse le changement d'adresse, le nouveau loyer. Vous demandez si la prime de déménagement peut vous être versée.
Taxe d'habitation	Vous étiez locataire précédemment : vous payez pour le logement précédent. Vous devez signaler votre nouvelle adresse au Centre des Impôts.		Vous aurez à payer la taxe d'habitation pour l'année en cours : signalez votre changement au Centre des Impôts.

Sources des illustrations

p. 37 : Dessin d'Alain Letoct ; p. 39 : Service photographique - Premier ministre ; p. 43 : M. Gounot ; p. 45 : Archives Nathan ; p. 71 : Service de l'information et des relations publiques du ministère de l'Intérieur ; p. 143 : photo Pix.

Iconographie : M.T. Mathivon
Illustrations : J.P. Magnier

Imprimerie TARDY QUERCY S.A. BOURGES
N° d'Éditeur : T 50505-I (D.o.VII) CP - *Imprimé en France* - Juillet 1988 - N° 14627